NEW NAME FOR LOVE

She was no longer Mariah. She had a new name to go with her new life among the people who had saved that life.

No-din. At first it seemed so strange—yet from Echohawk's lips it did not seem strange at all.

"*No-din,*" he said. "Woman of the wind. Such a beautiful name." He reached a hand to her face. "You are as beautiful as your name. Your features are delicate. Your lips are as soft as a rose petal."

His sudden, burning kiss caught her offguard, stealing her breath away. But then sweet, unbearable desire twined her arms around his neck as she returned the kiss with a passion that she had never known was locked inside her . . . waiting to be released by love's magic key. . . .

WILD ECSTASY

by

Cassie Edwards

AN ONYX BOOK

ONYX
Published by the Penguin Group
Penguin Books USA Inc., 375 Hudson Street,
New York, New York 10014, U.S.A.
Penguin Books Ltd, 27 Wrights Lane,
London W8 5TZ, England
Penguin Books Australia Ltd, Ringwood,
Victoria, Australia
Penguin Books Canada Ltd, 10 Alcorn Avenue,
Toronto, Ontario, Canada M4V 3B2
Penguin Books (N.Z.) Ltd, 182–190 Wairau Road,
Auckland 10, New Zealand

Penguin Books Ltd, Registered Offices:
Harmondsworth, Middlesex, England

First published by Onyx,
an imprint of New American Library,
a division of Penguin Books USA Inc.

First Printing, May, 1992
10 9 8 7 6 5 4 3

Copyright © Cassie Edward, 1992
All rights reserved

 REGISTERED TRADEMARK—MARCA REGISTRADA

Printed in the United States of America

For Audrey LaFehr,
a special editor . . .
a joy to work with.

Author's Note

For the most part, the Chippewa have been neglected by historians, perhaps because they fought no bloody battles against the western-driving pioneers who overwhelmed them in the nineteenth century.

Yet historically the Chippewa were one of the most important Indian nations north of Mexico. Their expansive northern woods of Minnesota contained valuable resources, which caused them to play an important role in regional enterprises. The Chippewa remain on their native lands today, still a proud people, and continue to make their living from fishing, farming, lumbering, and mining as they have done for centuries.

I found my study of the Chippewa a most rewarding and heartwarming experience. It is a pleasure to write about them.

My face in thine eyes, thine in mine appears,
And true plain hearts do in the faces rest,
Where can we find two better hemispheres
Without sharp north, without declining west?
Whatever dies, was not mix'd equally;
If our two loves be one, or thou and I
Love so alike that none can slacken,
  none can die.

—JOHN DONNE

1

The day is done, and the darkness
Falls from the wings of night,
As a feather is wafted downward
From an eagle in his flight.

—LONGFELLOW

The Minnesota Wilderness August 1824

The evening shadows were long. The sky was awash
with a crimson blush as the sun faded on the horizon,
a mellow sighing of turtle doves breaking the cool,
deep silence.

Riding in a canter ahead of a slow procession of
many travois being dragged behind horses and dogs,
Echohawk saw a frightened buck on the run, the white
rosette of its rump seeming to hang for the smallest
fraction of time at the top of each frantic bound, like
a succession of sunbursts against the darkening forest.

Then Echohawk gazed down at the river at his one
side, admiring the reflection of the green foliage of the
maple, birch, and aspen trees that lined the riverbank,
disturbed only by silver-scaled fish that now and then
came to the surface with a sudden flip that started
circles of ripples.

A deep, throaty cough, one that was filled with
pain, drew Echohawk from his silent reverie. Echohawk jerked his head around, and rage filled his dark,
fathomless eyes as he gazed down at his father, Chief
Gray Elk, who lay on a travois behind Blaze, Echohawk's prized rust-colored stallion. Echohawk's father's pride had been stripped from him, as well as
his health, by a vile white man the whites of whose
eyes were *o-zah-wah*, yellow, the color of a coward's.

Echohawk's gaze moved beyond his father to the many other travois. Some transported bundles of blankets, parfleches of dried meat, and those who were too elderly to ride or walk.

Others carried the wounded from a recent raid on their village, a village they had chosen to leave behind—a place of sadness and many deaths.

Even to let himself conjure up memories of the man he now called Yellow Eyes sent spirals of hate throughout Echohawk. Because of him and his Sioux friends, led by the renegade White Wolf, many proud Chippewa had died, Echohawk's wife and unborn child among them, his father among the wounded. Because of Yellow Eyes and White Wolf, the Chippewa had been uprooted and a new place of peace and prosperity was now being sought.

Echohawk's eyes narrowed when he recalled another raid on his father's people twelve winters ago, when Echohawk had been a young brave of eighteen winters. His people had suffered many losses at the hand of those vile white men that day. And then, as now, the conflict had caused his band of people to move elsewhere, never wanting to stay where there had been so many deaths . . . so much blood spilled.

But Echohawk was proud to know that his chieftain father had wounded the white leader *that* day. Surely the man even now hobbled around on only one leg!

Echohawk tightened his reins and brought his horse to a halt. He turned to his people and thrust a fist into the air. "*Ee-shqueen*! Stay!" he shouted, the responsibilities of his father's people his own until his father was able to perform in the capacity of chief again. "We shall rest for a while, then resume our journey!"

Echohawk sat for a moment longer in his saddle, observing his people. He could see relief in their eyes over being allowed to rest, and realized only now how hard he had been driving them to get them to their planned destination.

But the fate of his people lay in *his* hands, and he realized the importance of getting them settled in a village soon, and into a daily routine. When the snows began coloring the ground and trees in cloaks of white, many deaths would come to those who were not prepared.

Dismounting, his brief breechclout lifting in the breeze, his moccasined feet making scarcely a sound on the crushed leaves beneath them, Echohawk went to his father and knelt down beside him, resting himself on his haunches. "How are you, *gee-bah-bah*, Father?" he asked, gently rearranging the bear pelts around his father's slight form. His heart ached with knowing how it used to be before the vicious raid. His father had been muscled and strong. Vital. All of this had been robbed from him at the hands of Yellow Eyes and White Wolf, and someday, somehow, the evil man would pay. . . .

"*Nay-mi-no-mun-gi*, I am fine," Chief Gray Elk said, his voice weak. With squinting eyes he looked past Echohawk at the loveliness of the surroundings, feeling serenity deep in the core of his being.

He turned his gaze back to Echohawk, a smile fluttering on his thin bluish lips. "Soon we shall be there, my son," he said, wheezing with each word. "Do you not see it? Do you not feel it? This is a place of peace. A place of plenty. Surely we are near Chief Silver Wing's village. Surely we are also near Colonel Snelling's great fort, where Indians come and go in peace. Ah, my son, they say there is much good trading at Fort Snelling. We have been wrong not to move our people closer before now." He coughed and paled. "It is best that we are here, my son. It is best."

"*Ay-uh*, yes, and we will soon be making camp," Echohawk said, nodding. "Our scouts have brought us to the Rum River. It is the same river that flows past Chief Silver Wing's village. It is this same river that flows into the great Mississippi River that flows past Fort Snelling." He nodded again. "*Ay-uh*, soon we will be there, *gee-bah-bah*."

Gray Elk slipped a hand from beneath the pelts and clasped onto one of Echohawk's, in his eyes a gleam of hope. "My son, Chief Silver Wing and I have been friends since our youth, when, side by side, we fought the Sioux for territorial rights," he said, sucking in a wild gulp of air, then continuing to speak. "It will be good to see him again."

Gray Elk's grip tightened on Echohawk's hand. "When Chief Silver Wing last came to me and we shared in a smoke and talk, he spoke of the abundance of wild rice plants that bend heavy with rice in the countless lakes and marshes near his village, and skies that are alive with waterfowl," he continued softly. "Soon we share all of this with Chief Silver Wing and his people. Soon you will participate in the hunt again while our women gather the rice. Once more our people will be happy, Echohawk."

"We shall ride together on the hunt, *gee-bah-bah*," Echohawk encouraged, wanting so badly for this to be so. If his father died, his heart would be empty. He had lost his mother during an intensely cold winter fifteen winters ago, and his wife and unborn child only recently. Surely the Great Spirit would not take his father from him also!

"You will get well," Echohawk quickly added. "You *will* ride your horse again."

But Echohawk doubted his own words. His father was a leader who had ruled his people with kindly wisdom, and was struggling to stay alive long enough to see that his people could begin a life anew close to two old friends, one Indian and one white. They planned to make camp within a half-day's ride from Chief Silver Wing, also Chippewa, and a half-day's ride from Fort Snelling, where Colonel Josiah Snelling was in charge—a friend to all Indians.

Echohawk, a wise and learned man at his age of thirty winters, knew that his father had another reason for having chosen to make camp close to Chief Silver Wing's village. Gray Elk hoped that perhaps Echohawk might find a wife among Chief Silver Wing's people to replace the one that he was mourning.

But Echohawk did not see how anyone, ever, could take his wife's place in his heart, nor the child that Fawn had been carrying within her womb at the time of her death. Because of her death, Echohawk had thought strongly of taking his own life, his grief was so intense, but had known that his father and his people needed him too much for such a cowardly act—and also because a suicide had no chance to enter into paradise.

"It *is* wise, my son, to move more closely to people that can be relied upon," Gray Elk said, as though sensing his son's doubts. "And trading will be profitable with the white people who frequent Fort Snelling. Echohawk, you can trade in beaver. As you have seen on our journey here, buffalo and deer abound in this region, and Silver Wing spoke of muskrat and marten that were as plentiful as mice."

"*Ay-uh*, it will be good hunting and trading, Father," Echohawk said, remembrances of his last hunt flooding him. Had it only been thirty sunsets ago when he had brought home a fat venison for his wife to cook? Had it only been thirty sunsets ago when he had watched her lovingly as she had sat across from him eating and laughing softly at his tales of the hunt? His gut ached with loneliness and despair, even now hearing the ring of her laughter and seeing the peace and love in her dark, beautiful eyes.

Gray Elk slipped his hand from Echohawk's and patted his cheek gently. "Echohawk, it is soon the smoky time, when leaves put on their war paint and the war drums of the wind become louder," he said, a quavering smile touching his lips. "It is time to place sadnesses from your heart and choose a woman to warm your bed. And must I remind you, my son, that you are the only son of your father and must sire a son yourself. My grandson, your son, will be the future defender of our people, whose lives will depend upon his courage and skills. If the child is a girl, she will be the future mother of a noble race."

Gray Elk patted Echohawk's cheek again, then lowered his trembling hand and slipped it beneath the warmth of the bear pelts. "For our people, place sadnesses of your loss from your mind and heart," he softly encouraged. "That is the way it should be. It is for you to ensure the future of our band of Chippewa. Only you, my son. My time is soon over."

Weary from the lengthy dialogue, Gray Elk exhaled a heavy sigh, then closed his eyes. "*Gee-kee-bing-gwah-shee*," he said, barely audible. "My son, I am getting sleepy. I . . . must . . . sleep."

Guilt spread through Echohawk like wildfire. His father, a man of fifty-seven winters, was recovering much too slowly from a bullet wound in his chest. It had been hard to listen to his father pour his heart and soul out to him without being torn with anger and guilt, Echohawk having failed at defending his people the day of the raid. The raiders had come too suddenly upon his people while so many of them were away from the village, burning off the pine needles from the ground to ensure against forest fires later. Echohawk had been among those setting and controlling the fires. By the time word had reached him of the massacre, the raiders had had a head start on him and his braves, and during the chase had slipped away like ghosts in the night.

Echohawk had returned to his injured wife just as she had spoken her last words to him. She had revealed to Echohawk that a white man with the eyes of a coward and the renegade Sioux White Wolf had led the attack. It was the man with the eyes of a coward that had fired the bullets that had felled both Fawn and Chief Gray Elk.

Echohawk brushed a kiss across his father's brow, then rose to his full height, tears streaming down his cheeks. He doubled his hands to his sides in tight fists and looked up at the darkening heavens, vowing revenge.

But first he had his father's wishes to fulfill. *Then* he would find the man with the eyes and heart of a coward. Also, one day he would come face-to-face with White Wolf. The renegade Sioux would *not* die an easy death.

"Vengeance will be mine!" he said beneath his breath, then turned his gaze back to his father when he awakened long enough to speak a few more words.

Dutiful son that he was, Echohawk knelt down again beside his father. He leaned his ear close to his father's lips, for his words were now no more than a whisper.

"May the Great Spirit watch over you, my son," Gray Elk said, very aware of the despair and hurtful anger in the depths of his son's dark eyes. "He will guide you in which way is best for our people once I am gone. Remember this, Echohawk. Hungering for vengeance is like a festering sore inside one's heart. It will never heal.

"Peace, on the other hand, can give you comfort. Even as I lie here, a victim of hate and greed, I am at peace, for it was not I who initiated the raid which ended in many deaths and sorrows. Those that did are condemned forever to walk paths of darkness, their souls never to find peace. Practice restraint as taught to you as a child, and live in peace, my son. It is best for the future of our people."

Echohawk flinched when his father again grasped his hand. "Echohawk, if you should die before you father a son, the future chief of our people, what then of our people?" he said, his voice filled with desperation. "Find a woman who will be the 'flower of your wigwam.' Have a son soon. At a very early age see that he assumes the task of preserving and transmitting the legends of his ancestors and his race."

Echohawk was at a loss for words, not knowing how to cope with his father's soft, tormented pleadings for a grandson. Echohawk did not see how he could ever desire another woman. His very soul even now cried out for Fawn, his beloved. He could still feel her softness within his arms. He could still hear how she so sweetly spoke his name. None other could be as sweet! As wonderful! How could he make such a promise that he felt he could not keep?

Yet he knew that what his father had said was true. The future of their people did depend on a succession of sons, and to have sons, one must have a wife.

But one's heart must be ready for a wife! Echohawk despaired to himself.

"Go to *nee-ban*, sleep, Father," Echohawk urged as he once again slipped his father's hand beneath the warmth of the pelts. "*Wah-bungh* tomorrow. We shall discuss wives and grandsons tomorrow."

Gray Elk gazed up at Echohawk, the slowly rising moon casting enough light on his son to enable him to see him and his handsomeness, and be assured that here was a man who would not go wifeless for long. How could any woman resist such a tall and vigorous, good-looking man with sparkling dark eyes? How could any woman not notice Echohawk's hair that was as thick and long, and as black as the raven's wing, and his hard and proud mouth? And how could any woman not want to bear Echohawk a son, knowing that his offspring would have the same muscular strength, the same easy grace, and the same power of endurance as his father?

Echohawk arched an eyebrow when he saw a

strange sort of peace pass over his father's face as he closed his eyes, his features smoothing out as if he had just entered into a pleasant fantasy. As troubled as Echohawk was, he wished that he could join his father in the same sort of magical place, where all sadnesses are left behind.

But he realized all too well that many responsibilities awaited him.

Rising to his full height, he did not turn to look at his people. He quickly mounted his horse and began riding away in a slow canter, his father's travois dragging behind him, knowing that soon everyone would follow.

Ay-uh, so much depended on him.

His people's very existence.

2

One morning, very early, before the sun was up,
I rose and found the shining dew on every
buttercup. . . .

—STEVENSON

One Year Later,—August 1825

The bedroom was flooded with sunlight, revealing a
room of inexpensive tastes, and a father and daughter
in conflict. Mariah Temple stood defiantly before her
father, her jaw tight with anger. She clenched and
unclenched her hands at her sides, finding it hard to
continue obeying a father who, since Mariah's mother's death twelve long years ago, had become unrea-
sonable in his demands.

"Papa, you can't force me to cut my hair," Mariah
said, her voice flat with determination. "You can't
expect me to go that far to please you." She glanced
down at the way she was dressed and shuddered, then
gazed angrily up at her father again. "I've worn these
damnable shapeless breeches and scratchy shirts because I had no choice after you burned all of my
dresses. You even burned Mother's so I couldn't
sneak into one of them." Her lips curved into a sullen
pout. "Papa, I can hardly even recall how it felt to
wear a dress."

Her fingers went protectively to her hair. She drew
its long red tresses back from her shoulders and
cupped as much of it as possible within her hands. "I
shan't *ever* forget how it feels to have long hair, because I won't ever agree to cutting it," she snapped,
taking a step back from her father as he moved toward
her, dragging his lame leg behind her.

"Are you finished?" Victor Temple said in an impatient growl. "My, but you do go on sometimes, just like your mother used to. Not only do you have her looks, but also her temperament."

His gaze swept over Mariah. Each time, it was a new shock to him to see a daughter so startlingly pretty, with eyes so dark and velvet brown on a flawless face, and abundant hair that gleamed and rippled with such life it seemed more vivid than the brightest red. Her short straight nose was that of an appealing and mischievous young woman. Her lips were rosy and soft, and there was nothing weak about her pretty chin.

She is so small and vulnerable, Victor thought to himself with a quick rush of tenderness. And so proud and bullheadedly stubborn!

"If I am like my mother, so be it," Mariah said, lifting her chin proudly. She had been six when her mother had died, the mystery of it always troubling her. Her father had not let Mariah see her mother on her deathbed, nor had he explained how or why her mother had died at such a young age.

But it was the remembrances of her mother the six years that she had shared with her that still filled Mariah's heart with such love whenever she let herself get caught up in missing her. No mother could have been as sweet—as understanding.

She peered intensely up at her father, recalling how he had been before his wife's death. In appearance he had changed, now weathered with age at fifty-five. He was a round-shouldered man with a leathery face and brush of chin whiskers, and with a lame leg that made his movements jerky and sometimes uncontrolled.

Those many years ago, before his leg affliction, he had been handsomely neat, always clean-shaven, and had always stood proudly tall and square-shouldered. Although Mariah had thought him to be a decent sort of man at that time, it was the years since that had colored her image of him.

And it had not only been the death of his wife that seemed to have changed him, she mulled to herself. The change had happened shortly after the burial, when he had left to have council with some of the Indian chiefs in the area, having brought his wife and daughter to the Minnesota wilderness to establish a trading post long before Fort Snelling had been a part of the setting.

At that time, as now, it was not unusual for her short-tempered father to get into conflicts with the neighboring Indians to establish his territorial rights if they would not meet with him and speak peacefully of sharing the abundance of wildlife in the area.

This one time in particular, when her father had been gone for several days, he had returned from a skirmish with some Indians, wounded. He had almost lost his leg as a result of that battle, hardening his heart into someone Mariah did not even enjoy calling "father." He had become a bitter, unpleasant man, one whom most called sinister. Mariah herself was very aware of the crooked dealings and raids that her father participated in with the devious, evil Tanner McCloud.

Just the thought of Tanner McCloud made shivers run up and down Mariah's spine. He was a man of no scruples, who surely did not know the meaning of honesty. And with the whites of his eyes yellowed by some strange, unknown disease, he was also a man who was anything but pleasant to look at. When he gazed at Mariah with those yellow eyes, she always felt as though he was undressing her. For sure, Mariah wearing men's attire had not fooled him. He knew what lay beneath the bulky oversize jackets worn over her cotton shirts, and breeches twice the size of what she should be wearing, held up by a rope tied at her waist—a girl having developed into a woman at her ripe age of eighteen.

"And so you want to be like your mother, eh?" Victor said, brandishing the scissors in the air as he talked, as though they were a weapon. "Do you want to be dead at age twenty-three?" He slipped the scissors into his rear pants pocket and grabbed Mariah by the arm. "Daughter, that ain't going to happen if I have anything to say about it. I've protected you just fine these past years. I don't intend to stop now."

Mariah paled. "Papa, please don't," she begged, trying to jerk free of his grasp. "My hair is all that is left that is pretty about me. At least at night, when I remove my dreadful mannish clothes, I can look in the mirror and see that I *am* a woman. Papa, do you want me to forget? Do you? Don't you ever want to see me married to a fine gentleman? Don't you even want grandchildren?"

"And where do you expect to find what you call a 'fine gentleman' way out here in this wilderness?" he scoffed, grasping her arm more tightly. "Those I have met are anything but what I would want for a son-in-law. Most are filthy, with only one thing on their minds when they see the flash of a woman's skirt. Their one concern is getting that skirt lifted and pokin' her until they get their hunger for sex filled for that moment."

Mariah gasped and her face became flushed with embarrassment, her father having never before spoken of sex in her presence.

But even this did not stop her argument. "While gathering supplies at Fort Snelling, I saw many men who were surely gentlemen," she said, daring him with a haughty gaze. "The soldiers are all so very polite. And . . . some are *quite* handsome."

She cast her eyes downward. "But of course, none have ever approached me," she murmured. "They

think they are walking past a young lad when they
pass by me in the courtyard of the fort.''

She looked back up at him with an anxiousness in
her eyes. "Papa, I've always fooled them before by
wearing my hair coiled beneath my hat," she said in
a rush of words. "Please? Please let me continue hiding my hair instead of cutting it.''

"That only works if the hat stays in place," Victor
said, going to the window, peering down below at the
pack mules being unloaded. He could see many prime
pelts among those being carried into his trading post,
and did not want to take much more time with this
chore at hand. He wanted to make sure those who
assisted him at his post did not cheat him while his
back was turned.

He wheeled around and faced Mariah again. "The
day you tripped over a bale of hay at the fort? Your
hair came rushing out from beneath your hat like
streamers of sunshine. And who had to be there, to
be witness to the truth of your identity? That damned
Colonel Snelling and his wife, Abigail. Since then they
haven't let me alone, chiding me for forcing you to
wear breeches and shirts. Why, Abigail even forced
one of her dresses on me one day and flat told me to
let you wear it. Of course I burned it as soon as I got
it home.''

Again he turned and stared out the window, anger
filling him at the thought of Josiah Snelling and of
their relationship long before they had met again while
Fort Snelling was being built. Victor had assumed that
Josiah Snelling was in his past when he brought his
family to the Minnesota wilderness.

But after all those years they were forced to endure
one another's company again, for Victor was not
about to move his successful trading post to rid himself
of the colonel again. He had even had to place all
thoughts of vengeance against Colonel Snelling from
his mind, finding the supplies at Fort Snelling too

valuable not to go to the fort and buy them when necessary.

Mariah often accompanied him, only because he had seen her worth in assisting him choose the proper kitchen supplies.

Otherwise she would have been kept at the trading post, away from the wondering eyes of Colonel Snelling. Should the colonel have ever looked close enough, he might have seen too much that was familiar about her.

Victor turned abruptly and went back to Mariah. He grabbed her by the wrist and turned her so that her back was to him. He yanked the scissors from his pocket and lifted them to her hair. "Now, let's not hear any more argument about this haircut," he snarled. "It'll be done in a flash."

Tears began streaming from Mariah's eyes when she felt the first yank on her head as the scissors began to slice through her thick hair. "Oh, Papa, why? Why?" she demanded, sobbing. "I'll never understand! Never!"

"First, Mariah, there's that damnable Tanner McCloud. I've got to put his ideas of wantin' you from his mind once and for all. I've got to make you as unpleasant to look at as possible. Cuttin' your hair seems to be the only way. That damn Tanner. He's been askin' me every day for permission to marry you. *Now* he won't bother me with such nonsense."

"You don't have to cut off my hair because of him," Mariah wailed, feeling ill at her stomach when she saw her first lock of hair fall at her feet. "You know that I'd never let that man get near me. Papa, I have a mind and will of my own. And I can shoot a firearm same as you. You taught me well enough. If that man came near me, I'd not hesitate shooting him."

"It's not only him," Victor said, continuing to snip away at her hair. "Your mother's prettiness got her

in trouble with men more than once. I'm here to make
sure that don't happen to you."

A sob lodged in Mariah's throat when another thick
hunk of hair fell at her feet. She closed her eyes,
knowing that she would end up being the ugliest
woman in the world!

"What do you mean by that?" she finally said,
slowly opening her eyes again, forcing them away
from the hair piling up on the floor. "What sort of
trouble did my mother get into with men?"

Victor momentarily drew his scissors away from Mariah's hair. He stepped around in front of her. He
looked down at her with narrowing gray eyes. "You
forget I ever said that," he flatly ordered. "That was
a slip of the tongue. Just remember that when you're
as pretty as a picture, men are drawn to you like bees
to honey." He stepped behind her again and resumed
his cutting. "That's what I meant about your mother.
She had men fallin' at her heels from all walks of life.
It'd be the same with you, if I'd allow it. But I ain't.
So don't give me no more mouth about it."

Mariah stood numbly quiet until her father was finished with the dreaded chore. When she heard him
place the scissors on her nightstand beside her bed,
she stared blankly down at the hair on the floor, and
became choked up all over again with the need to cry.

But there were no more tears. What seemed to have
taken their place was a building resentment toward
her father, which she feared was nearing hate.

Kneeling, she began to scoop up her precious
strands of hair, its softness like the down of bird feathers against the flesh of her hands. She stiffened inside
when her father's shadow fell over her.

"There is something else I have to say to you,"
Victor said, drawing Mariah's eyes quickly up. He
placed a hand at her elbow and helped her up to stand
before him.

"Oh, no, Papa," she cried. "Whatever more could you want with me? Haven't you already done enough?"

"What I have done, for the most part in your behalf, is to guarantee your survival here in the Minnesota wilderness in case something happens to me," Victor said, gripping Mariah's shoulders with his hands. "I have taught you enough of the Sioux and Chippewa tongues for common purposes, and taught you the trick of the Indian trade to perfection. I have taught you how to shoot all firearms, and how to ride a horse better than most men. Today . . . today . . ."

Clutching her loose strands of hair to her bosom, Mariah looked fearlessly up at her father, yet wary of what else he had planned for her. Even he seemed hesitant to tell her.

"Today? What about today?" she asked, almost afraid to hear the answer.

"I plan to teach you further ways of survival," Victor said, dropping his hands away from her. He went to the window and stared into the shadowy depths of the forest that stretched out far beyond the land that had been cleared for his trading post.

An instant dread grabbed Mariah at the pit of her stomach. "What do you mean?" she said in a low gasp.

Victor turned on a heel and stared at her. He reached a hand to his pants leg and ran his fingers over his leg, feeling nothing, only numbness. "An Injun took too many important things from my life. Because of him, I am half-crippled and . . ."

He stopped in mid-sentence, then went and stood over Mariah. "A year ago, Chief Gray Elk settled within only a half-day's ride from Fort Snelling. His village is only an hour's ride from our trading post. And by damn, that's way too close for my liking."

He paused, then added, "You've questioned me many times this past year about why I've not gone to Fort Snelling as often for supplies, and why I've forbidden you to go at all. I've avoided your questions before, because I had not yet decided what to do about Gray Elk. But now that I've made my plans, there's no reason not to tell you. It's because Echohawk, Gray Elk's son, is at Fort Snelling so often. Even the Injuns do most of their trading at the riverbank, instead of inside the walls of the fort, which, for the most part, is reserved only for civilized people. I did not want to chance coming face-to-face with Echohawk. I thought he just might recognize me. He saw everything the day I was wounded. I'm sure he hates me no less now." He paused and an evil glint rose in his gray eyes. "It seems that Echohawk is in my way now as much as his chieftain father ever was. He's got to die also, Mariah. And anyone else at the village who gets in the way of the gunfire!"

He cupped her chin in his hand. "And you're going to ride with me," he said flatly. "If nothing else, that'll make a man outta you."

Mariah was rendered almost speechless by what her father was saying. And that he had chosen to make her a part of such a vicious plan made her heart grow cold. "You can't be serious," she finally said, inching away from him. "Papa, what you are planning to do is wrong. It's out-and-out murder. And never would I be a part of such an act. I hold no grudges against the Indians. In fact, I admire them. They are an innocent, proud people. How can you want to just go and kill them? Nothing any one Indian has done to you can warrant you going and slaughtering a whole village of Indians."

She slipped the hair from her arms, onto her bed, then placed her hands on her hips in defiance. "And were the truth known, I imagine you were the one who shot off that first gunfire against Gray Elk and his people all those years ago. You deserved what you got. It could have been worse, you know. Your scalp could be hanging in Chief Gray Elk's wigwam even now."

Victor took a quick, clumsy step forward, his face red with rage. He raised his hand and brought its backside against Mariah's face, causing her head to go sideways in a jerk. "I will have no more of your insolence," he shouted. "You are going with me. That's final."

Her cheek stinging from the blow, her eyes filled with tears of anger, Mariah placed the coolness of her palm against her face. "Never," she hissed.

"Then I will have no choice but to lock you in the storm cellar for several days for punishment," Victor said, bending to speak into her face.

Paling, Mariah wavered. "You wouldn't do that to me," she gasped. "You . . . just . . . wouldn't."

"I have no choice," Victor said, picking up his cane from Mariah's bed. He leaned his weight against it as he walked toward the door. "Come on, now. We may as well get the punishment on its way."

Mariah stood her ground. "No," she murmured, fearing the rats that frequented the cellar, which were sometimes as big as cats. "That won't be necessary. I'll do as you say."

But she vowed to herself that this was the last time he would force anything on her. At her first opportunity she was going to escape his wrath. Tonight, after they returned from the venture she dreaded with all of her heart and soul, she would flee from her father's trading post and go to the protective custody of Colonel Snelling at the fort. From there she would chart her future.

"How will you explain your attack on Chief Gray Elk and his people to Colonel Snelling?" she blurted. "Don't you know how hard he is trying to keep peace among the Indians and settlers?"

"He ain't trying hard enough," Victor said, smiling crookedly. "All I'll have to tell him is that some of

Gray Elk's murderin' redskins came to my trading post and stole from me and came close to killing you in the process. I'll just say I was defendin' you from such an assault.''

"And you expect him to believe that?" Mariah said, her voice rising in pitch, daring another face slap. But her father had not even heard her. He was staring intensely out the window. Mariah was hearing the arrival of many horses outside, and went to look out the window also. When she saw the lead rider, she froze inside and turned quick eyes to her father.

"And so the cheating, vile Tanner McCloud is going to assist you in this raid?" she accused. "That's why he's come with so many men?"

"Dammit, no," Victor said, kneading his brow. "We've enough men of our own workin' for me here at the post without bein' bothered by anyone else." His face became flushed again with anger. "That sonofabitch. He's come again to speak in your behalf. He told me the last time he was here that he was goin' to bring a great bride price." He wheeled angrily around and began working his way toward the door, his cane, as it came in contact with the wooden floor, sounding ominous. "You see? He's lived in the wilderness so long he thinks he's bargaining for an Injun squaw! Well, I'm goin' to set him straight once and for all. In fact, I'll tell him that I don't want to see his lousy yellow eyes around here again. He's pestered me one time too many."

Mariah didn't have time to say anything else. With the aid of the cane, her father moved quickly, and was soon gone from the room, slamming the door behind him.

Mariah stifled a sob behind a hand as she gazed with a deep longing down at her hair on the bed.

Then she went to a drawer in her nightstand and pulled out a mirror. Her fingers trembled as she lifted it. When she saw her reflection, and how her hair now lay flat and lifeless against her head, only just past her ears, she turned her eyes away and threw the mirror across the room.

As it shattered into dozens of pieces, it was not enough to silence the loud shouting going on below her in the main store of her father's trading post. Never had she heard her father so mad.

Never had Tanner McCloud cursed so loudly, so violently.

And then it was all quiet. She went to the window again and watched Tanner and his men ride away in a cloud of dust, her father standing outside with his rifle aimed at Tanner's back. She wished she could go back to bed and then get up again to find that everything was as it had been those many years ago when she had had a mother to confide in.

Never had she felt as alone as now.

3

We should often be ashamed of our very best actions, if the world only saw the motives which caused them.

—LA ROCHEFOUCAULD

A vicious storm had delayed the attack on the Chippewa, leaving the rivers and creeks rumbling with swollen, rushing water, their banks being eaten away with the churnings.

But it had not delayed the ambush indefinitely. Soon the sun had replaced the dark clouds in the sky. And as though living a nightmare, Mariah rode her mouse-gray mustang into the Indian village beside her father, her face smeared with ash, the same as the others under her father's command—a disguise against possible recognition.

She witnessed the carnage as her father and his men swarmed through the Indian village in a senseless frenzy, spraying the Chippewa with volleys of gunfire and tossing torches, which soon had the bark dwellings wrapped in sheets of flames, the smoke and fire belching out with a sound like thunder.

The crash of Indian pottery split the air like a shriek. Pistols flamed and bullets spattered, the reports from the guns deafening. Horses reared and plunged, trampling fallen Indian women who tried to flee from their outdoor cooking fires, into the protection of the forest.

A few of the aged were saved at the expense of the younger women who so very bravely interposed their slim bodies between the elderly and the firing weapons. Old men and young boys alike were running around, frantically snatching up whatever weapons they could find, but too soon falling among the bloodied figures strewn across the ground.

The village was a chaos of screaming confusion and the pall of smoke. The air was thick with the acrid stench of black powder, of burning hides, and of blood.

"Be sure not to leave anything of value!" Victor shouted to his men. "And get some of that corn yonder for roasting!"

Mariah, having not fired a shot, thanked God she had at least been spared that. She hung back and looked pityingly at the women and wailing children who huddled in the center of a circle of braves. The men fought valiantly, keeping the foe off by firing into the attackers.

Then her heart sank as several of her father's men began charging and firing point-blank into those braves. The Indians soon became a ring of bodies, those surviving reaching for the attackers to pull them from their horses. The horses reared, hooves flailing, trying to get away.

Outraged by the horror of it, Mariah had a strong urge to switch sides and fight alongside those Indians, who were dying like wolves, fighting to the last gasp without noise or complaint.

Instead she pulled at her horse's reins and swung her around, desperate to get away from the massacre. She didn't get far. Too soon she found herself face-to-face with an Indian brave standing in her horse's way, who if he had chosen to, could have killed her instantly.

But she was still dressed in the clothes of a boy, the jacket loose over her shirt, her breeches large and slouchy, hiding beneath them the curves that she could now boast at the age of eighteen.

And the ploy seemed to have worked well. The Indian must have taken her for an innocent lad forced into battle, for the handsome brave did not raise his firearm against her, nor did he grab for his knife, which was so handy in a sheath at his waist.

For what seemed an eternity, but was in truth only a few moments, Mariah and Echohawk stared at each other, long enough for Mariah to be struck by his extraordinary presence. A young man of obvious physical power, he wore no shirt, his copper body reflecting the sun like fire. His legs were sheathed in fringed leggings that were so tight she could see their muscled contours. He was tall, with raven-black hair framing his noble shoulders. His eyes were the darkest of all midnights, large and flashing. He had high cheekbones and a mouth that was hard and proud.

As quickly as he had appeared, the brave was gone, leaving Mariah shaken by how intensely he had affected her. Shivers ran up and down her spine as she realized that soon he could lie dead among the already fallen braves.

Desperately she looked around for her father, wanting to go to him and beg him to give up this senseless assault.

When she finally caught sight of him on his horse, still wreaking havoc in the village, she grew weak all over, gasping when she saw a brave take aim at her father with his rifle.

"No!" she screamed, knowing that her father was not aware of being targeted. It didn't take much thought to know what she must do. In an instant she had her rifle removed from its gun boot at the side of her horse. She aimed, pulled the trigger, and winced when she saw the bullet graze the Indian's shoulder, causing him to drop his weapon.

Feeling eyes on her as she thrust the rifle back inside its boot, she turned and found the handsome brave staring at her again, apparently having witnessed her action. She knew that he must be regretting having let her pass when he had had the perfect opportunity to kill her.

Her insides grew cold and a scream froze on her lips when her father was suddenly there behind the brave, the butt of his rifle cracking across his skull. She watched, horrified, as the handsome brave stumbled forward, dropped his rifle, fell to his knees, then crumpled to the ground, unconscious. She felt the prick of tears as she gazed at the blood seeping from his head wound, knowing that it could soon snuff the life from him.

Victor eased his horse up next to Mariah's. "It looks as though Echohawk won't be causing me any more problems," he said, staring triumphantly at the fallen brave.

Mariah looked over at her father, then down at the handsome brave, her face ashen. "That's . . . Echohawk?" she said, her voice quaking. Then her jaw tightened and she glared at her father. "And what of his father? Did you also brutalize him?"

"More than that," Victor bragged. "He's now entering what the Injuns call the Land of the Hereafter. And none too soon, I'd say. He lived way longer than what was civil for the likes of him."

Mariah stared disbelievingly at her father a moment longer, hardly able to bear this cold, heartless side of him that made her not want to admit that he was any kin to her at all, much less her father.

She gazed with contempt around her, seeing the men under her father's command heavy-laden with plunder. She wheeled her horse around and rode away, wanting to distance herself from it all. As soon as she could, she would slip away from her father and go to Fort Snelling, and not only for her own welfare. She would plead with Colonel Snelling to come to the aid of the Chippewa. If there were survivors when this was over, they were going to need someone with compassion to help them through the winter.

That man with compassion had to be Colonel Snelling! He was there to help everyone, both red- and white-skinned. And no matter what harm befell her father when she revealed his role in the massacre, she knew that she must.

As she saw it, it was time that her father was stopped. His ruthlessness must not be allowed to go on.

For now, she had no choice but to return to her father's trading post, along with the others. But when night came, she would flee the life that she had grown to abhor.

She flinched when her father rode up beside her, his men following on their sweating steeds. Even though some of them were wounded, and some were tied across their horses, dead, loud laughter and shouts of victory filled the air, the Indian village having been left in a heap of smoking ruins.

She would never forget the sight of the fallen braves being wept over by women and children. And how could she forget that among those fallen Chippewa was the tall and handsome brave with the sparkling dark eyes? In that brief moment of eye contact, there had been something about him that had stirred strange longings within Mariah—longings that she did not even recognize or understand.

Thinking of the valiant brave lying there, even now possibly dying, sent her heart into a tailspin of regret. Should he die, she would never forgive herself for this damnable raid—a raid that she had participated in, for she *had* shot one of the braves herself. She gave silent thanks to the heavens that she had inflicted only a flesh wound.

Still, guilt soared through her, making the journey back to her father's trading post even more unbearable. And once there, she was forced to sit with the

men, outside by a roaring fire, part of a victory celebration. As she sat stiffly on a blanket, watching the
sky darkening overhead, she bided her time while
wine and whiskey flowed like fountains on into the
night.

When she saw that her father was perhaps too
drunk to notice, she slipped away from the celebration
and went to the barn, readying her horse for travel.
Watching over her shoulder, she led her mouse-gray
mustang away from the barn by foot and onto the
open prairie.

Feeling safe enough, she quickly mounted her steed
and rode away into the shadows of night, in search of
the beaten paths that would lead her through the forest to Fort Snelling.

Echohawk awakened to wails of mourning on all
sides of him, the women of the dead braves clawing
at their own faces and arms with their fingernails, pro-
ducing deep, bleeding gashes. Dazed by the blow to
his head, he slowly pushed himself up from the
ground. When he was standing, he swayed from a
light-headedness that nearly felled him again.

But he had to go to the aid of his people, their
cries reaching into his heart with a tearing sadness. He
staggered ahead, events blurring in his mind.

He blinked, trying to focus on things around him.
But no matter how hard he tried to see, all that was
there was a strange sort of dark haze.

The throbbing pain of his head led his hand to the
lump, and he soon felt the break in the skin and the
blood that had caked dry.

"A head injury," he whispered to himself, fear cutting through his confusion. Now he recalled the very
instant that the white man had cracked the butt of his
rifle over his head—recalled, even, that had he not
been engrossed in looking at the young lad who had

wounded one of his braves, the older white man would never have been able to sneak up on him.

Now both the lad and the white man were the target of his hate, as both were responsible for so much.

He blinked and rubbed his eyes again, his heart sinking when realization came that the white man had not succeeded in killing him, but instead had taken his vision from him! All that he could make out was shadow and light!

Knowing what was expected of him at this time of sorrow for his band of Chippewa, no matter his condition, he collected himself.

His father.

His people.

They needed him!

As hands began clutching at him, and voices reached him with utter despair, begging him to help, Echohawk felt his way through the ravaged village, soon discovering the true depths of the massacre. Everywhere there were bodies to be stepped over and around.

For a moment his brain burned, the world seeming to have been annihilated. So many innocent women, children, and braves were dead and now entering the Land of the Hereafter.

But he was relieved that many of his people's most valued braves had not been at the village to be slain or maimed. These braves were far away, on a hunting expedition. Upon their return, they would find much sorrow, and then they would aid Echohawk in his thirst for vengeance.

"Father," he whispered to himself, having not yet found his way to his father's large dwelling that sat back from the others on a slight rise. He welcomed strong hands on his arms as two braves came and steadied him between them after seeing his legs begin buckling beneath him, his weakness worsening with each step.

The braves identified themselves when they realized that Echohawk could not actually see them.

"It is I, Yellow Wolf," one of them said. "Of the St. Croix band of Chippewa."

"And it is I, Helping Bear, also of the St. Croix band," the other said. "We were passing by in a canoe, on our way to Fort Snelling, when we saw smoke. We followed it to the scene of this massacre. We have come to offer assistance. We will continue on our own journey later."

"I know you both well. It is good of you to come to my people's aid," Echohawk said thickly. "My eyesight. It has been robbed from me."

"If you wish, we will be your eyes," Yellow Wolf said solemnly.

"For now, *ay-uh*, yes," Echohawk said, nodding. "But only for the moment. It is important that I learn to fend for myself."

He paused, then said, "*Gee-bah-bah*. Take me to my father." His heart was anxious to see his chieftain father, yet wary that he might not have survived the attack. The white man who had led the attack had seemed determined to wipe out this band of Chippewa, and surely that included their chief.

Helping Bear and Yellow Wolf exchanged troubled glances, then looked solemnly at Echohawk. "Chief Gray Elk . . ." Helping Bear said, his voice drawn. "He is dead, Echohawk."

Knowing that his worst fear had proved true, a sudden, stabbing despair filled Echohawk. It fully engulfed him when Helping Bear and Yellow Wolf helped him down beside his father and he was able to touch the coldness of his flesh.

Drawing on the restraint that his father had taught him from the moment he could understand right from wrong, Echohawk stilled the cries of remorse that so badly wanted to escape from deep within him.

Kneeling beside his father, he embraced him. Ah,

how blessed he had felt when his father's health had returned after having established their new village along the Rum River, only a half-day's ride from his father's longtime friend Silver Wing.

But, Echohawk despaired to himself, he had not been blessed a second time. Gray Elk had not been given another chance.

His palate parched from rage, Echohawk felt as though he was suffocating. In a husky low voice he vowed to his father that he would be the kind of chief Gray Elk would expect him to be. He vowed that he would be a strong and loyal leader of his people.

But to himself, alone, Echohawk was wondering how he could follow the road of peace that his father had always taught him. His blood was boiling with anger and humiliation; he could feel it flowing in his veins like molten lava.

Vengeance!

His heart—his very soul—cried out for vengeance.

Echohawk clung to his father and mourned silently for a moment longer, then found himself surrounded by more survivors of the massacre, who had fled into the darker depths of the forest during the attack.

Yellow Wolf and Helping Bear helped Echohawk to his feet. Although he could not see his people, he turned to them and faced them, to give them the confidence they needed in their new leader. They looked to him now for their future. For leadership. For survival. He was their chief, and he knew that for now he must place them and their welfare even before his desire to have revenge.

Helping Bear leaned closer to Echohawk and whispered, "Echohawk, perhaps it is best that you cannot see. Some who stand before you are wounded. Some are carrying their dead children. It is a sight that is most unbearable."

Echohawk's heart ached, and he could not help but feel the helplessness of this situation, especially now that he could not see well enough to be the leader that his people needed at this time. So much depended on him.

"One by one, come to me, my people," Echohawk said, reaching his hands out toward them. "Let me embrace each of you. Then I shall tell you what we must do to survive."

Although his knees were growing weaker by the minute, and his head was throbbing incessantly, Echohawk began embracing his people, himself drawing much comfort from them.

When this was done, he stood before them all, tall and unbending like a tree, his eyes unfocused yet bold and fathomless as he spoke to them. "My people, for the moment my eyesight has been weakened by the blow to the head that I received during the white man's attack," he said, forcing his voice to sound strong, and most important of all, calm. "But do not fret. We shall endure! We will go to Chief Silver Wing's village and ask for assistance until the wounds of your hearts and flesh are healed, and until my vision clears, to ensure you a chief that can work at full capacity."

He held his chin high and squared his back. "Busy yourselves at making many travois," he instructed. "Go and find the dogs and horses that were scattered during the raid. The dead and most seriously injured will travel by travois."

Soon this was done and the slow journey began to Chief Silver Wing's village. To prove his worth to his people, Echohawk had chosen to travel on foot, only occasionally accepting Yellow Wolf's and Helping Bear's assistance as they walked beside him.

As Echohawk took each step, his weakness worsening, his hate for the raiders deepened inside his heart. Hate was etched inside his heart for all mankind, it seemed. How could he forget that white man who, those many winters ago, raided, killed, and maimed so many of his father's people? How could he forget the cowardly "Yellow Eyes," who had recently taken so much from Echohawk and his people?

And now there was another white man whose heart was as evil and black, and whose face troubled Echohawk. Although smeared with ash, he had seen something familiar in his features, yet he could not put his finger on just what.

His thoughts went to a white man that stood out from all of the rest, a man who was everyone's friend. If not for the kindness of Colonel Snelling, and of the honest traders that Echohawk had become acquainted with at Fort Snelling, he would believe that all people with the white skin were bad.

But he knew that this was not so. It was just a few that he vowed to kill. In time vengeance *would* be his. One by one the evil men would die. Even if Echohawk had to learn how to fight without his eyesight!

Echohawk's troubled thoughts went to the youngest of the raiders today. There had been something different about the young lad. Strange, how through the smeared ash he had seen such feminine features.

And there had been some hidden mystery in those dark eyes.

An intense bitterness seized Echohawk, and he vowed that this lad, also, must die. No one involved in the raids on his people would be spared his vengeance.

No one!

The sound of the horses' hooves behind him made another cause for sadness enter Echohawk's heart. His beloved horse, Blaze, had been among the missing horses today, and he felt that a man without a horse was only half a man.

This, also, gave him reason to hate—to plan a terrible vengeance.

4

Think that the day lost whose low descending
sun views from thy hand no noble action done.
                                        —BOBART

As Mariah drove her mustang endlessly onward, feeling as wild as the breeze that blew, she tilted her face
toward the flaming glory of the sunrise. She inhaled
a quavering breath, so glad that she was finally free
of her tyrant father.

Wearily she lowered her eyes, momentarily closing
them. Oh, how they burned from lack of sleep! Her
head would nod, and then just as quickly she would
become alert again as to why she had not taken the
time to sleep in her flight from her father. She must
get to Fort Snelling. The colonel would send assistance
to the Chippewa as soon as he was aware of their
needs.

Oh, God, she lamented to herself, she felt as responsible as her father for the Indians' desolation, yet
she reminded herself that she had been forced to ride
with him and his men.

Knowing that, however, did not lessen her guilt.
Perhaps it would lessen once she was able to get assistance for the Indians.

"But is it too late for Echohawk?" she despaired
aloud. The instant his chieftain father had died, he
had become chief of his people. His people needed
him, for if he died, they would have lost two chiefs in
one attack.

To think of that possibility, and to know that she

had been a part of it, though an unwilling participant, made Mariah thrust her heels into her horse's flanks, urging him faster, into a harder gallop across the land.

Then her spine stiffened as she became aware of the stench that was troubling her nostrils, and soon she caught sight of a black pall of smoke that lay heavily in the air through the break in the trees a short distance away. Clearly she was not far from the ravaged Indian village.

She yanked her reins, causing the mustang to come to a sudden shuddering halt. She studied the low-hanging clouds of smoke, seeing in her mind's eye what was hiding behind it, the scene of the Indian village having been etched onto her consciousness like a leaf fossilized in stone. She knew that she should make a wide swing around it, to avoid the survivors seeing her and possibly killing her.

But some unseen force made her snap her reins and nudge her steed with her knees, sending her mustang into a slow trot, until she was through the smoke and near enough to the village to see that it was deserted.

Her mustang slowly loped into the village, and she was torn by what to do. Even if she did arrive at Fort Snelling as planned, how could the colonel help the Indians if he didn't know where they were?

"He'll know where to look for them," she whispered to herself.

She urged her horse into a hard gallop away from the burned-out village, knowing that she must get to the fort in haste. The Indians must be found quickly and offered assistance in their time of need and sorrow! And she was anxious to see if Echohawk was among the survivors.

She gazed heavenward. "Oh, God, please let him be alive," she prayed softly. "Please. . . ."

She rode hard across straight stretches of meadows, then was forced to wind her way through forest land, still fighting the urge to sleep, hunger now joining her miseries, gnawing at the pit of her stomach.

She came to a creek that had to be crossed before going onward. She dismounted and studied the rushing waters, a rude reminder of the storm that had delayed the attack of the Chippewa village. The water in the creek had not yet receded, even now tearing savagely at the banks, leaving them torn and furrowed in its wake.

Mariah caught sight of a black snake as it glittered and slid into a rift in a cottonwood tree near her, reminding her that water moccasins were prominent in this area, should she try to cross the creek, and fail.

Casting fear aside, she looked farther upstream, seeing that it wandered willfully to the right and left, with many a turn.

Then she spied an irregular line of large stepping-stones that the water was rushing across. That seemed to be her only hope of crossing the creek today, or perhaps even tomorrow, unless she traveled farther upstream to see if it was shallower somewhere else.

"I don't have time for that," she murmured to herself. "The *Indians* don't have that much time for me to waste. . . ."

Wary of her decision, yet knowing that she didn't have much choice, Mariah rode onward until she reached the stones. Gripping hard to the horse's reins, placing her knees solidly against the sides of her mustang, she urged her horse onto the rocks, its hooves unsteady as the rush of the water slapped against them.

Wide-eyed, scarcely breathing, Mariah watched as her horse seemed to brave the savagery of the water well enough, sighing when the opposite shore was almost reached.

But just as she was urging her mustang to solid ground, its hooves slipped. Mariah was thrown forward to the ground as the horse toppled back into the creek, swiftly carried away in the current. When Mariah landed on the ground, her head hit with a thud, momentarily stunning her.

When she regained her full faculties, her eyes became wild as she looked desperately around her. Her heart sank when she recalled her mustang being taken downstream. She hoped it would climb ashore where the current slowed.

But now she would have to travel the rest of the way to Fort Snelling on foot!

"How can I?" she sighed woefully, placing her hand to the small of her back. It seemed that every bone in her body ached from the damnable fall.

A more terrifying thought seized her. "My rifle!" she gasped aloud. "It was on my horse!"

Weaponless, and without a horse, she knew that she was at the mercy of anything and anyone that happened along. She had no choice but to get to her feet and start her long journey to Fort Snelling. Delaying even a moment longer could cost her her life!

"But I'm so tired," she whispered lethargically. "I'm . . . so . . . hungry."

She stretched out on the ground, hugging herself to ward off the chill. "I'll sleep for just a little while, *then* go on my way. . . ."

Her eyes closed. Sleep came to her quickly . . . a *deep* sleep.

Exhausted from the journey, and weak from his injury, Echohawk staggered toward Chief Silver Wing's circle village of skin lodges that were fitted among birch trees, the leaves of the white birch trembling in the breeze. A few children at play on a slight rising of ground were the first to perceive Echohawk and his people. A cry of "Strangers arriving!" sounded the alarm, and mounted braves soon rode out of the village and stopped close to Echohawk, recognizing him.

Yellow Wolf held Echohawk alert as Wise Owl, one

of Chief Silver Wing's most valued braves, dismounted beside him.

"Echohawk, what has happened to you and your people?" Wise Owl said, recalling the last time he had been with Echohawk. They had shared in the hunt. They had later shared cooked venison over an outdoor fire before going their separate ways to their own villages. Theirs had become a special friendship.

Echohawk recognized the voice of his friend. "Wise Owl," he breathed out, his voice barely audible. "My father, Gray Elk, lies dead on a travois behind me. Our people were attacked by white men. Our village . . . It was . . . destroyed."

With a weak and limp hand Echohawk gestured toward his people, who stood devotedly behind him. "These are but a few of the survivors," he said sadly. "Others are on the hunt and will soon discover the carnage left at our village."

He paused, inhaling a quavering breath, then resumed speaking. "We have come to ask Chief Silver Wing for assistance. He was a valued friend of my father's." He swallowed hard. "And since I have bcome acquainted with him this past year, he is also a trusted friend of mine."

"It is with much sorrow that I hear of your misfortunes," Wise Owl said, taking Echohawk by the arm. "Come. You will ride with me. I will take you to Chief Silver Wing. He will be saddened also by the news you are bringing him. He held Chief Gray Elk in the highest regard."

Echohawk shrugged himself away from Wise Owl's gentle grip. "I enter your village on foot with my people," he said, lifting his chin proudly, even though sieges of light-headedness were throwing him off balance. He was not sure how much longer he could stay alert, much less continue walking.

But he must, he thought stubbornly.

For his people, he must!

"As you wish," Wise Owl said, giving Helping Bear a troubled glance as Echohawk grabbed for Helping Bear to keep himself from tumbling to the ground.

After Wise Owl saw that Echohawk was going to be all right, with Yellow Wolf moving quickly to his other side to offer assistance, he mounted his horse again and rode ahead, escorting Echohawk and his people on toward the village.

As Echohawk entered the village, he felt the presence of many on all sides of him. He did not have to see to know that these were Chief Silver Wing's people coming to gaze and to ask questions about those who were arriving so downtrodden.

But if he *could* see, he knew that he would recognize many of these faces, having joined them in feasting and celebrating on various occasions this past year, his father so proudly sitting at Chief Silver Wing's right side.

But that was in the past, those good times of camaraderie with his beloved father. Now all that he had were memories—wondrous, precious memories.

It was hard for him to accept what his education had taught him—that death is but a change for the better, and that it is more than anything unworthy and womanish to shun it.

Oh, but if only his father had been able to shun death this time, as he had in the past.

When Chief Silver Wing's large domed conical lodge of bark and reed mats was reached, Helping Bear and Yellow Wolf stepped away from Echohawk. "We will return now to our journey to Fort Snelling," Helping Bear said, placing a friendly hand on Echohawk's shoulder. "*Nee-gee*, friend, let hope fill your heart, not despair."

Yellow Wolf took Helping Bear's place before Echohawk as Helping Bear stepped aside. He embraced Echohawk, then stepped back from him. "May the Great Spirit bless you with sight again soon, my brother," he said, his voice choked with emotion.

"In time I *will* see again," Echohawk said firmly. "Pity then those who have gone against my people."

There were more fond embraces and words of thanks, and then Wise Owl escorted Echohawk, alone, inside Chief Silver Wing's dwelling.

Chief Silver Wing was sitting at the fire in the center of the room, carving a pipe stem. On Echohawk's entrance, he looked up, startled. "*Nee-gee*, friend, what has happened?" he said, stunned to see Echohawk's wound, and also his eyes, which seemed to be blank.

Wise Owl guided Echohawk over to Chief Silver Wing. Echohawk looked down at the chief, seeing only shadows of what he knew was a man of fifty-seven winters, a man of dignity and reserve, with graying hair and lined face.

"It was the *chee-mo-ko-man*, white men," he said between gritted teeth. "They came and burned and killed. My father. He was one of those who is now entering the Land of the Hereafter."

Chief Silver Wing shook his head with grave sorrow, then waved his wife over to Echohawk.

Nee-kah knew what he asked of her even though he had not voiced it aloud. She cast a glance of recognition on Echohawk and spread a robe for him to sit on. Wise Owl led him down onto the robe, and Nee-kah then removed Echohawk's moccasins and gave him another pair for present use.

She then went and stood obediently behind her husband, feeling Echohawk's pain as she gazed sadly down at him. He was a man much younger than her husband, and had she not already been wedded to Chief Silver Wing, she would have offered herself to Echohawk to be his wife. She had never seen such a handsome Chippewa as he.

As for her husband, she had been chosen by him,

a much younger person than he, to bear him children that his other wives had failed to. She placed a hand on her abdomen, smiling, knowing that even now that child he wanted was growing within her womb.

She prayed that it would be a son. That would please her husband twofold!

"It is with a sorrowful heart that I have heard of the misfortune of your people and of your father's passing," Chief Silver Wing said. "My village is now your village. Your people will live as one with my people until you see fit to leave."

"That is kind," Echohawk said, nodding. Then he spoke with more anguish. "Chief Silver Wing, my father is dead! My eyes are dry and I want something to make the tears come in them!"

"In time, my son, tears will come to you," Chief Silver Wing said solemnly. "Then all of your sadness will be washed from your heart." He leaned closer, studying Echohawk's eyes. He waved a hand before them, seeing only a slight sense of reflex on Echohawk's part. "You do not see. Why is that?"

"That is something I am living with," Echohawk said in a grumble. "When I was wounded, my eyesight was impaired."

Chief Silver Wing gazed at the head wound, then turned and looked up at his wife. "*Mah-szhon*, go. Take Echohawk to the wigwam that was yours before our marriage," he said softly. "You will see to his comforts. Tend to his wound. Give him food. Until he is better, my wife, he is yours. Do you understand?"

Nee-kah's dark eyes widened as she glanced over at Echohawk, then down at her husband. "*Ay-uh*, I understand," she murmured. "I will do this for you, my husband."

Chief Silver Wing turned his attention back to Echohawk. "I lend you my wife for a while," he said, smiling. "She is my fourth wife, but can cook better than all other three put together." He took Nee-kah's hand and urged her to a kneeling position beside him. "And, Echohawk, finally I have a wife who is capable of bearing me a child. She is four months pregnant. She makes me proud. So very proud."

Such talk of wives and children catapulted Echohawk's thoughts back to the time when he was so proud to boast of his wife being with child. It tore at his heart, this absence of a wife—and of a child that would never be.

"That is good," he said, rising slowly to his feet. "And may the Great Spirit bless you more than once with children." He recalled Nee-kah in his mind's eye, and her innocent loveliness, and smiled as he felt her presence at his side as she stepped up next to him. "And your beautiful wife will bear you beautiful children.'"

Nee-kah cast her eyes downward, her face burning with a blush.

And then she took Echohawk's hand. "*Mah-bee-szhon*, come. I will now take you to your dwelling," she said, her voice lilting. "You must mend quickly, for your people need you. I will help in that mending."

Wise Owl stepped aside as Nee-kah led Echohawk outside and slowly to his assigned wigwam.

Once inside, she helped him down onto a sleeping platform and covered him with a bear pelt and blankets, and soon had a roaring fire blazing in the firepit in the center of the dwelling.

"I must leave now to go and get supplies for your stay here," Nee-kah said, looking tenderly down at Echohawk. "I shall return soon."

Echohawk nodded, then closed his eyes, sighing deeply.

He opened his eyes again in a flash as he felt another presence in the room. He bolted to a sitting position, trying to see who was there. He damned the white man who had taken his sight from him when he could not make out anything but the shadow of a man kneeling beside him.

"It is I," Silver Wing said, kneeling down close to Echohawk's sleeping platform. "I have brought you many things." He placed a rifle in Echohawk's hand. "This is for you. Keep it with you at all times. If white men destroyed your village, ours might be next."

"*Mee-gway-chee-wahn-dum*, thank you," Echohawk said, lifting the rifle, liking the feel of it in his hands.

"Also I have brought you a bow and arrows, should you prefer that weapon over the firearm," Silver Wing said, placing the bow and arrows at Echohawk's side on the sleeping platform.

"You are more than kind," Echohawk said, laying the rifle aside. He reached out for Silver Wing, searching, then clasping his hand on his shoulder. "My father was right to want to rekindle your friendship and live close to you. You are a special man, a man of heart."

"You would be as generous had it been I who came to you sightless and fatherless," Chief Silver Wing said solemnly. He paused, then added, "I also offer you land for burial of your people's loved ones."

Echohawk almost choked on a sob, so moved was he by Chief Silver Wing's continuing generosities. "My people," he said. "Those who have survived. Are they all being seen to? I do not want to be favored over them. I am now their chief. My oath as chief binds my life first to the lives of my people."

"Each has been taken in by a separate family," Chief Silver Wing assured. "None will want for anything. And this will be so until you choose to leave our village."

Echohawk reached out and hugged Chief Silver Wing tightly, for a moment feeling as though he was in his father's presence.

Then, embarrassed, he drew away.

A kind, firm hand on his shoulder made Echohawk

warm clear through. "My heart is grateful," he said. Then he scowled as he once again remembered the massacre. "I will avenge my people. I will begin hard practicing with weapons soon, to perfect what sight that I have left. They who are responsible for my people's misfortunes will die!"

Chief Silver Wing gazed down at Echohawk, saddened by and wary of the bitterness in his voice and heart. He knew that no good could come from it. The white people had become the law in these parts. If Echohawk killed for revenge, then so would more Chippewa be slain because of it.

It was Silver Wing's sincere desire to help curb Echohawk's anger and to find a more peaceful solution to what had happened again to the red men of the forest. For their survival, that was the only way. Too quickly the white people were outnumbering the red man in the Minnesota wilderness.

"I have brought you something else," Silver Wing said, placing a pipe and otter-skin tobacco pouch on Echohawk's lap. "When you smoke from this pipe, think peaceful thoughts."

Echohawk's mind was no longer on what Silver Wing was saying or was offering. He was feeling hot, and then cold. Yet he did not complain out loud, although he knew that he was being weakened even more now by a fever.

"I shall return later to see how you are faring," Silver Wing said, rising. "Nee-kah will be here shortly. She will bathe your wound. She will feed you broth. Tomorrow will be a brighter day for you, Echohawk. You will see that I am right."

After Chief Silver Wing left the wigwam, Echohawk laid the pipe and tobacco pouch aside and eased back down onto the thick layer of pelts. His thoughts were becoming fuzzy. His scalp seemed on fire.

"*Gee-bah-bah*, Father," he whispered, reaching a hand out toward the fire, thinking that he saw his father's image in the dancing flames. "Father, do you hear me? Do you see me? Your *nin-gwis*, son, oh, how he misses you!"

He moved to his side and closed his eyes, his body racked with hard chills as his temperature began to rise.

He found himself drifting somewhere between midnight thoughts and the flaming glory of a Chippewa sunrise. . . .

Fully clothed, reeking of dried perspiration and alcohol, Victor Temple tossed fitfully in his bed, his drunken slumber broken by dreams of horror. In the nightmare, he and Mariah were nude and chained together, forced to stand upon a scaffold, while Indians looked at them with hate in their eyes, ready to shoot arrows into their flesh.

Victor awakened with a start, a cold, clammy sweat on his brow, his hands drenched with perspiration, and his eyes fixed.

Shaking himself out of the dream, he jumped from the bed and poured himself a glass of whiskey, drinking it in fast gulps.

Then, recalling Mariah's part in the dream and in the Indian massacre that he had commanded, he rushed to her room to see if she was all right. When he discovered that she was not there, alarm filled him.

"She's been abducted!" he cried aloud. "While I slept, my daughter was abducted!"

His thoughts became scrambled as he wondered who could have done it. "Tanner?" he whispered, then shook his head, thinking that Tanner wouldn't be that foolish.

"Injuns?" he said, panic rising inside him.

He ran down the steps to the lower floor, then from the house, frantically waving his hands. "My daughter's gone!" he shouted, drawing men from their bunks. "Saddle up! We've got to find her!"

5

More firm and sure the hand of courage strikes,
When it obeys the watchful eye of caution.
                                        —THOMSON

Autumn's warming rays filtering down through the
stands of hemlock and spruce were welcome as Mariah
awakened from a night of bone-chilling temperatures.
She wiped her eyes with the back of her hand as she
slowly rose to a sitting position beside the creek, trying to organize, think logically, slowly recalling what
had happened. She had braved the raging waters of
the swollen creek, but had lost the battle, it seemed.
She had been thrown from her horse, her beloved
mustang having then been carried away in the current.
She had been momentarily stunned, and then had discovered that she had been too tired to travel onward
by foot. She had not meant to, but she had slept all
night!

Her parched lips drew her eyes to the creek, its
waters having receded. Crawling to the embankment,
she cupped her hands and lowered them into the water
for a drink, then winced when she caught her reflection in the shine of the water. She hardly recognized
herself! Her face was covered with mud, also her hair
was tangled with its muck and mire.

She glanced down at her clothes, seeing that they
were no better off. They were stiff with dried mud.

The crunching of leaves behind Mariah made her
turn her head in a jerk to see what had made the

sound, again feeling her helplessness since she had no rifle for protection.

But she was soon relieved and rose slowly to her feet when she found only an Indian maiden standing there gazing down at her, instead of a fierce brave. And wasn't the Indian maiden lovely with her eyes of a deep, deep brown, her braided waist-length hair even darker than her eyes?

Mariah's gaze traveled over the maiden, seeing that she was attired in a long-sleeved buckskin dress, tightly drawn over her stomach, revealing that she might be with child. She also wore a lovely blue tunic beaded in a leaf-and-flower design, and knee-high moccasins.

Mariah did not even feel threatened when she realized that the maiden's one hand was on a sheathed knife at her waist, her other hand clutching a basket filled with what appeared to be an assortment of wild herbs, apparently picked from the forest bed. There was too much kindness in the gentle features of the maiden's face for her to use the knife against Mariah—a person quite visibly without weapons.

"I am *nee-gee*, a friend," Mariah said softly, so glad that her father had taught her enough of the Chippewa language to get by.

She then tried to reach the beautiful maiden in her own tongue, knowing that most Indians in this region knew the English language well enough, since they traded with the white people at Fort Snelling. "I am a friend in need of help. Can you offer me assistance? I no longer have a way to travel to Fort Snelling, my destination. My horse lost its footing and threw me, then was swept away in the swift current."

Still the maiden did not speak, seeming to be taking her time to come to a decision about Mariah, about whether she spoke the truth or lied.

Then Mariah became wary herself. "Are you Chippewa or Sioux?" she asked, her voice revealing her

wariness. She feared the Sioux. They had not made
peace with the white people as readily as had the
Chippewa.

To Mariah's relief, the maiden finally spoke.

"Nee-kah is Chippewa." Her eyes roved over Mariah, then locked eyes with her. "Your name?"

Mariah stiffened, afraid to reveal her name to Nee-
kah, unsure of whether or not the news had spread of
her father's attack on Echohawk's village, and her part
in it.

Nee-kah's eyebrows lifted, finding it strange that
this white lad who had been so talkative before now
chose to be quiet.

But she could not delay returning to her village any
longer by playing word games with the lad. She had
left only long enough to find the herbs necessary for
Echohawk's healing. He had become fevered and now
awaited her return.

Through the night she had become concerned about
this temperature that had risen so quickly, seeming to
rob him of his senses. She was frightened over this,
for the white man's attack had not only taken away
most of his eyesight but also could perhaps eventually
cost him his life.

"*Mah-bee-szhon*, come," Nee-kah said. "White
boy, you will go with me to my village. Chief Silver
Wing will decide what then will become of you."

Mariah fell into step beside Nee-kah, through
woods mixed with meadow, the pine forest crowding
up to the shore of the land. She was relieved that the
maiden had not demanded a name, yet feared being
taken to a powerful Chippewa chief, especially since
she had been part of a Chippewa massacre only
yesterday.

And she did not know if she should correct Nee-
kah's mistaking her for a boy and tell her that she was
a young woman, like herself.

She quickly decided that revealing too many truths at this time could be dangerous.

Especially claiming the name "Temple" in these parts now could possibly be her death decree.

She set her jaw angrily when she thought of her father. He had not taken into consideration the outcome of his decision to slay many Chippewa yesterday, when there were other villages of Chippewa in the area who could avenge their fallen comrades!

Her father had not considered the danger in which he had placed his daughter, which proved to her that his caring for her came second to his lusty need of vengeance against a Chippewa that had rendered him a half-cripple all of those years ago.

Dizzy from hunger and the trauma of the fall, and fearing the outcome of her appearance in the Chippewa village, Mariah stumbled and fell.

Nee-kah stopped quickly and set her basket on the ground. She knelt down beside Mariah. "*Ah-neen-ay-szhee-way-bee-zee-en?*" she said, gently touching Mariah's arm.

Then, assuming that the white person who looked at her with a keen puzzlement in her eyes surely did not understand her Chippewa language all that well, she decided to speak in the English tongue that she had learned quickly enough from her chieftain husband.

"What is wrong with you?" Nee-kah asked. "Are you ill?"

Mariah blinked nervously at Nee-kah and smiled weakly. "I'm fine," she murmured. "Or I will be, once I get some food in me."

"You will be given food after you have council with my husband," Nee-kah said, placing a hand to Mariah's elbow, helping her up from the ground. She smiled at Mariah. "And do not despair. My husband, Chief Silver Wing, is a fair, kind man. He will not treat you harshly. You are but a mere lad. And you carry no weapon with which to harm my people. *Ay-uh*, yes, you will be treated kindly by my chieftain husband."

"You are Chief Silver Wing's wife?" Mariah said, her eyes widening in surprise. "I know of him. He is much . . ."

"Much older?" Nee-kah said, laughing softly as she gave Mariah another sweet smile. "*Ay-uh*, yes, my husband is older. I was chosen because of my youth to be his wife so that I might bear him a child." She placed her hand on her abdomen. "This I do for him gladly. I have not had a blood course for four moons! I am with child."

Mariah was stunned, even embarrassed by Nee-kah's innocent openness. She had always imagined the Indian women to be bashful and quiet, living only in the shadow of, and for, their husbands.

But Nee-kah seemed filled with a love of life led by a free spirit. Mariah liked her instantly.

"How nice," Mariah finally said, yet offered no further conversation. Her attention was drawn to the village that was now within sight through a break in the trees a short distance away. The birchbark wigwams were ranged in a great horseshoe shape in a wide bend of a tree-fringed creek, the dwellings all facing the east, offering the traditional welcome to the spirit of the rising sun. The first thin smoke of the morning cook fires rose in the cool air, drifting to the southeast.

Mariah was now aware that all along, while asleep on the ground beside the creek, she had not been very far from the Indian village. From the very beginning she had taken wrong paths on her journey to Fort Snelling!

But of course she should have expected no more from herself. Always before when she had traveled to Fort Snelling, she had been with her father, and not especially attentive to which particular paths he was taking to get there.

"We are there," Nee-kah said, her chin held high as she led Mariah into the village. She smiled at the women who were moving to and fro, some carrying firewood, others water. And she understood why they stared questioningly at the stranger at her side. The young lad was in desperate need of a bath. Though he was covered with mud, it was quite clear that the lad with her was white, and at this moment in time any white people were cause for alarm in their village.

Yet surely they saw this young lad as she did— harmless, and as someone who would perhaps be frightened of *them*.

The smoke from the fires outside the wigwams and the food cooking over them gave a pleasant scent to the morning air, making Mariah's stomach growl unmercifully from hunger. She gaped openly at the great sheets of buffalo backs roasting over the fires, dripping their fat into the blaze, the dripping, burning grease sputtering.

It had been too long between meals. At the time of her escape from her father, food had been the last thing on her mind. Though a part of survival, food had taken second place to getting away from the evil clutches of her father and seeking help at Fort Snelling.

Mariah walked as close to Nee-kah as possible, aware of the many eyes on her as she was taken through the village of wigwams. She tried not to look at the Chippewa women and children soon clustering around her. She kept her focus straight ahead, on a wigwam that was larger than the others, most surely Chief Silver Wing's. While shopping at Fort Snelling, she had heard much talk about Chief Silver Wing, and most prominent of this gossip was that he was a kind Chippewa leader. She had even gotten glimpses of him at times throughout the years. He had been a muscled, tall, and noble-visaged man with kind eyes.

But if he was aware of the attack on his Chippewa neighbor, she wondered warily to herself, what then of his kindness toward people with white skin now, no matter that she was only one person, taken as a defenseless lad, at that?

A scowling brave stepped suddenly in Mariah and Nee-kah's path, his eyes two points of fire, his arms folded tightly across his bare copper chest.

Fear grabbed Mariah at the pit of her stomach when the brave glared down at her, his jaw tight.

Then she sighed with relief when he gave Nee-kah the same sour look, making Mariah realize that not all of his anger was directed at herself—but instead, obviously, at Nee-kah.

"And so you succeeded at eluding me again, did you, Nee-kah?" Wise Owl said, his voice a low grumble.

"Nee-kah is not a frail thing who cannot fend for herself," Nee-kah said stubbornly.

"You again defy your husband, your chief, by going into the forest without me, your appointed guard?" Wise Owl said, his eyes shifting to Mariah. "And should this white lad have been an adult, with adult weapons. What then, Nee-kah?"

"Nee-kah knows not to approach large white men who sport weapons," she snapped. "This boy? I saw that he was no threat. I offered him assistance." She firmed her chin and looked defiantly up at Wise Owl. "Perhaps I should have killed him, Wise Owl, with my knife? And left him as food for bears?"

"You may wish you had," Wise Owl said, his eyes roving over Mariah. "This lad has family. His father could be near with firearms. Perhaps you have opened ways for an attack on our people." He grabbed Mariah by a wrist. "Come. You will tell my chief why you are close to our village."

Mariah paled as Nee-kah grabbed her wrist away from Wise Owl.

"He is mine," Nee-kah hissed. "I will take him to my husband. Not you!"

"One day you will trust white people too much," Wise Owl said, then turned and strode away.

"Come with me," Nee-kah said, leading Mariah on to the larger wigwam. "And do not let Wise Owl's harsh words frighten you. His heart is in the right place. He is one of my husband's most devoted braves."

Stepping up to the larger wigwam, Mariah glanced over at Nee-kah, trying to get reassurances again from her that she would be treated fairly, but Nee-kah was no longer paying heed to her fears. She was raising the moose-skin entrance flap, and soon stepped aside for Mariah to enter.

Swallowing back her fear, Mariah went inside the conical dwelling, immediately seeing Chief Silver Wing. He was sitting beside the firepit, attaching colorful feathers on the bowl of his pipe. She was quickly in awe of this man, as she had been before. He wore only a breechclout, revealing to her a man of over six feet, surely packing two hundred pounds of brawn on his massive frame. The only things about him that came close to revealing his age were the wrinkles grooved into his wise face and some threads of gray woven through his shoulder-length raven-black hair. A bear-claw armlet on his right arm proved him to be a man of distinction.

"My husband?" Nee-kah said, setting her basket of herbs aside. She went and sank onto her knees beside Chief Silver Wing. "I have brough you a young lad whose horse threw him and left him stranded not far from our village. I have offered him assistance. Was I wrong to?"

Chief Silver Wing gazed up at Mariah, his keen and piercing eyes roving slowly over her. "And why were you so close to my village?" he finally asked, his kind face solemn.

"I was on my way to Fort Snelling," Mariah said, fearing having to tell him more than she wanted to.

"You, alone, were going to Fort Snelling?" Chief Silver Wing asked, his jaw tightening. "It is not a normal thing for a boy your age to be riding alone." He set his pipe aside and folded his arms across his chest. "Where are those who were riding with you? Are they also near my village? Do they come to do us harm?"

"I was riding alone," Mariah said, fear gripping her insides when she realized that he saw her as an enemy. "There was no one riding with me when my horse threw me."

Chief Silver Wing looked over at Nee-kah. "My wife, why is it that you brought the white lad to me, instead of Wise Owl?" he asked, his eyes accusing. "Did you again turn your back on my orders? Did you go into the forest alone?"

"I do not like to search for medicinal herbs with a brave always there, spoiling my concentration," Nee-kah said softly. "And I did not travel that far, my husband."

"What am I to do with you, my young wife?" Chief Silver Wing said, a gentle smile tugging at his lips.

Then he became solemn again. "This time your escapade caused you no mishap. But what of the next?"

The scolding sent Nee-kah's gaze to the floor, humbled by her husband's words and by his sincere love for her.

Then she looked quickly up as Chief Silver Wing rose to his feet, clapping his hands. Two braves soon came into the wigwam and took their places on each side of Mariah.

"Take him away!" Chief Silver Wing said in a snarl. "He will be our prisoner until we see if what he says is true. If we discover that he was riding alone, then we will release him, lend him a horse, and let him go on his way. If we find others close by, then we will know that he has lied, and he will suffer for such a lie!"

"I am not lying," Mariah cried, wincing when the braves grabbed her wrists painfully and began dragging her away. "Please listen to me! Please!"

She looked frantically at Nee-kah. "Nee-kah!" she begged. "Tell your husband that I am not your enemy! Tell him again, Nee-kah, that I do not even carry a weapon!"

"Young lad with the shrill voice of a woman, your words are wasted on my wife," Chief Silver Wing said, drawing Nee-kah next to him possessively. "She, too, knows the dangers of the white people's words, which are so often said with forked tongues!"

Forcing herself not to cry, wanting to look brave in the eyes of this stubborn Indian chief, Mariah quit struggling and was allowed to walk peacefully between the two braves to a small wigwam set back from the others.

When she was taken inside and shoved to the floor, she expected to be tied and gagged, and was relieved when they did neither. They soon left her alone in the small cold dwelling, the fire in the firepit having burned down to only smoldering ashes.

She wanted to busy herself, to try to bide time until the chief decided to believe her, now wishing that she had been brave enough to tell him the full truth. That might have been better for her, if she could have convinced him that she had had only the Chippewa people's welfare at heart all along.

Moving to her knees, crawling to the firepit, she gathered up some loose twigs scattered on the floor beside the firepit and laid them on the glowing embers. Leaning low over them, she began to blow on them, sighing with relief when her efforts stirred up some sparks that soon turned into flames burning along the twigs.

And when a pleasant fire was burning, she looked more closely at the wigwam. It was neat and clean. Cedar boughs were spread on the floor, with mats spread over them for comfort. On a sleeping platform at one end of the dwelling were more mats and coverings, rolled up into bundles. Toboggans and snowshoes hung on the walls.

She crawled across the soft mat floor and took one of the bundles from the platform. Unrolling the furs, she spread them on the floor beside the fire, then sat down close to the warmth and tried to see something positive in that the chief had not ordered his men to kill her or to tie and gag her. She could not tell whether or not he had heard of the massacre in the neighboring village, or if he was cautious every time any strangers came near, without reason.

"Whatever," she whispered to herself, "I am an Indian captive!"

Just as she was trying to think of a way to escape, a noise at the entrance flap made a quick fear grab at her heart. She sighed and smiled when Nee-kah came into the wigwam, all sweetness and smiles.

"I have brought you nourishment," Nee-kah said, handing Mariah a makuk, a dish made of thick bark, filled with rabbit stew. She then filled another makuk with a cold drink made of raspberries and water, and placed this on a mat before Mariah.

"Did your husband give you permission?" Mariah asked, eyeing the stew hungrily, its rich smell causing her stomach to growl.

"I do not have to ask his permission for every move I make," Nee-kah said, shrugging. She sat down beside Mariah. "And I did promise you food, did I not? *Wee-si-nin.* Eat."

Mariah's eyes lit up, most definitely seeing a friend in this beautiful mother-to-be. She had been given no spoon or fork, so she began to eat ravenously with her fingers, realizing that Nee-kah was studying her even more closely in the light of the fire.

"Beneath that mud I believe I would find a face that is too pretty to be a boy's," Nee-kah said, moving a hand to flick some of the dried mud from Mariah's chin.

Mariah almost choked on her food. If Nee-kah did discover that she was a woman, then Nee-kah would wonder why Mariah had not been truthful about this, and perhaps see that Mariah could have lied about other things as well.

"Nee-kah!"

A voice outside the wigwam was Mariah's reprieve, for Nee-kah scrambled quickly to her feet, just in time for Chief Silver Wing to come into the wigwam and find her there.

"You are here instead of seeing to our most valued guest?" Chief Silver Wing said, his voice sharp.

"I went to him," Nee-kah quietly explained. "He was asleep. Nee-kah did not want to disturb his sleep. Rest is valuable also. When he awakens, then I shall force more medicinal liquid between his lips."

"And so, while waiting, you spend time with the white lad?" Chief Silver Wing said, his brows meeting together as he frowned. He gestured with a hand for Nee-kah to go to him. "My wife, you trust too easily. Come. We leave the boy to the food you were so generous to bring to him."

Nee-kah smiled weakly over her shoulder at Mariah as her husband led her to the entrance flap, then left with him, leaving Mariah alone, fearing that the new friendship she had thought to have found had just ended.

"I must find a way to escape," she whispered, her heart pounding at the thought of trying. She gazed at the closed entrance flap, having seen a guard standing just outside as Nee-kah and her husband had left. "If

I could slip past the guard and steal a horse and resume my journey to Fort Snelling, then later I could
explain everything to Nee-kah and let her know that
her trust had not been misplaced."

Yes, that was what she would do. Later tonight,
when the villagers were asleep, hopefully the guard
would also drift off long enough for her to flee past
him.

She began stuffing the most solid pieces of the stew
into her mouth, not wanting to get stranded again
somewhere without a full stomach.

Nee-kah slipped back inside Echohawk's wigwam
and took her place at his side.

Echohawk stirred awake momentarily. He gazed
through his blind haze up at Nee-kah, his limbs too
weak to rise from his sleeping platform.

"Lie still," Nee-kah said, running a cool, gentle
hand across his fevered brow. "Nee-kah will make you
feel better."

Her thoughts returned to the young lad in the wigwam not far from this one in which Echohawk lay so
ill. She looked questioningly down at Echohawk, then
shrugged, having decided it was best not to reveal to
him, at least yet, that a white boy was in the village,
fearing it would upset him.

Yet, would he even be aware of what she was saying? she wondered. He had become mindless with the
fever.

She moved away from Echohawk and stood in the
shadows as a Mide priest entered and began performing his healing rituals over Echohawk.

6

All's to be fear'd, where all is to be lost.
— BYRON

Mariah placed another log on the fire, then peered up at the smoke hole. A full night had passed. The sky was just beginning to lighten, which meant that escape would be virtually impossible should she wait much longer. Soon the sun would rise, and with it the Chippewa people, bustling around, doing their morning chores.

Having slept erratically through the night, checking on the guard outside her door each time she had awakened, she was still bone-tired.

She glanced toward the entrance flap, frustrated over having not once found the guard asleep through the night.

Her chance to escape had become an impossible task!

Yawning, stretching her arms over her head, Mariah decided that she would try just one more time. If the guard was still awake, then she would have another full day to wait.

The mud on her face even tighter this morning, since she had not been given a basin of water to wash herself, Mariah rose quietly to her knees and crawled to the entrance flap. With trembling fingers and an anxious heart she lifted the flap, and her heart frolicked within her chest when she discovered that, finally, the guard had fallen asleep!

And not only had he fallen asleep. While he was

asleep, his fingers had loosened around the rifle and he had dropped his weapon!

Her pulse racing, her eyes searching wildly around for any signs of anyone stirring in the village, she was filled with exhilaration.

Finally!

She would be able to leave this horrid place!

She would steal a horse and hurry on to Fort Snelling. The colonel would be a godsend to those Chippewa who had lost not only a good number of their people but also their means of survival—their village!

Mariah wondered just how far Echohawk and his people had traveled by now, and if Colonel Snelling would ever be able to find them, to offer assistance.

Determination firming her jaw, Mariah crawled stealthily from the wigwam, her eyes never leaving the sleeping brave. She smiled to herself when his snores reverberating into the air gave proof that it was safe not only to slip past the brave but also to take his rifle for good measure.

Her heart pounded as she inched her hand toward the rifle. When her fingers were securely around its barrel, she brought it slowly toward her.

Then, clutching it hard, she crawled on around to the back of the wigwam and out of the viewing range of the brave, should he awaken.

Mariah moved slowly to her feet and leaned her back against the wigwam, taking time to get her breath, trying to get her heartbeats slowed. She was afraid that if she got caught escaping, she would be shot on the spot, without further questions.

Especially now that she had a firearm in her possession.

Getting her bearings before going any farther, Mariah scanned the land for a good route of escape. Her eyes stopped when she found the Indians' horses at the edge of the forest, grazing inside a fence. She studied them closely and chose which one would be the easiest to steal. Several of them were still saddled, apparently ready for riding should an emergency strike the village.

Again she looked slowly around her. When she still saw no one, she took a deep quavering breath, then sprang away from the building and began running toward the horses. Once there, she scooted beneath the fence.

Going to her chosen steed, a palomino pony, she ran her hand down its withers in an effort to make an instant friend. When it turned to her and nuzzled her hand with its snout, its eyes dark and warm as it gazed up at her, she knew that she had won her first victory today.

Smiling, she took the pony's reins and led it to the gate. After getting it outside, she felt that it was best to lead it away from the village on foot. That would make less noise.

After peering back at the village again to see if anyone had come out of a dwelling since she had started out for the horses, and seeing that she was still safe, she hurried the pony onward until she found the river. She had decided to follow it to its outlet at the Mississippi River, which then would take her on to Fort Snelling.

Just as she reached the sand beach at the river mouth and felt that it was safe to mount the palomino pony and ride away, she stiffened inside. Up ahead, through the thickness of the trees, she could hear voices and soft laughter.

"Who could that be?" she whispered to herself, an eyebrow forking. It was early. She had thought that everyone was still asleep in the village.

She tethered the pony to a low-hanging limb, and with her rifle poised for firing, tiptoed on through the forest and stopped suddenly. She stared disbelievingly at two young Indian lovers on a blanket beside the river, nude. Her face turned crimson at having caught the young brave and maiden in the midst of a passionate tryst, their bodies tangling while making love, their mouths hungrily kissing.

Embarrassed, feeling quite the intruder on such a private moment, Mariah started to turn and leave, realizing that these two lovers were so intense in their lovemaking they wouldn't be aware of a horse riding through the forest close to their love nest.

But then something else caught her eye, stopping her further escape. Her heart began to pound as she watched a water moccasin slithering across the water in a determined fashion, heading straight for the embankment where the two were making love. One of these young people would soon be the target of this snake! It was obvious that it had spied them and was going straight for them!

"What do I do?" Mariah worried to herself, knowing that should she intervene and kill the snake, her escape to Fort Snelling would be stopped. One blast from the rifle and the whole Indian village would be drawn from their sleep. Her escape would soon be discovered, for they would follow the sound of the gunfire and find her.

Beads of nervous perspiration pearled up on her brow as she watched the snake getting closer and closer to the shore, the young lovers still too involved in their passion to know that something evil was moving their way.

"I must!" Mariah whispered agonizingly to herself. Having learned well the art of shooting a firearm from her father, who had taught her most of the skills of young men, she lifted the rifle, aimed, and just as the snake began slithering from the water, pulled the trigger. A perfect aim, she hit the snake broadside, spattering its body back into the water in scaly pools of blood.

Mariah gazed at the young couple, who had bolted to their feet. They were watching the snake as its severed body floated away, then looked over to Mariah, their eyes wide with wonder.

The young maiden was the first to realize the dilemma that she was in as she glanced down at her nudity, then up at her lover.

In a rush, the young woman had pulled on her dress, the young brave his breechclout, as their eyes never left Mariah.

Mariah started to leave without explaining, explanations not necessary since they had seen the slain snake, but she was stopped when suddenly Wise Owl and several braves were there, in her path.

In what seemed a flash of lightning, Wise Owl had taken the rifle from Mariah, while another brave had her wrists twisted behind her.

"*Gah-wen*, no! Do not harm him," the young brave said, stepping forth. "He killed a water moccasin that was only moments away from biting me or Wild Flower."

Mariah bit her lower lip to keep herself from crying out as the brave's hand did not lessen its grip on her wrist. It seemed that Wise Owl and his companions had not heard what the young brave said. They apparently did not think that her having saved the two young lovers was a redeeming act at all. And because of their stubbornness, she was going to lose all of her freedoms again, and perhaps her life.

Yet Mariah could not feel that she had made a wrong decision. She was proud of her act of selflessness, and would do it again if given the choice between her own freedom and the lives of these two beautiful young people.

Wild Flower stepped to the young brave's side, her eyes downcast as he slipped an arm possessively around her waist. The blush to her cheeks was proof of her embarrassment.

"Wild Flower, you leave your bed before your mother and father and come and meet Brown Bear by the river? You were so caught up in each other you did not see the snake approaching you? What were you doing, daughter? Better it not be that you went further than holding hands!" Wise Owl grumbled, stepping up to his daughter, lifting her chin with a forefinger, so that her eyes were forced to meet the anger in his. "My daughter, you shame yourself by such actions. Go. Return to our dwelling. Do not leave again until you have my permission!"

Sobbing, Wild Flower turned with a jerk away from her father, and without casting her lover a glance, ran toward the village.

Wise Owl stepped up to Brown Bear. "It would be simple to banish you from our tribe for what you have done this morning," he said blandly. "But you have proved more than once that you are a young brave with much promise. And so shall you also be a good husband. You will marry my daughter. Soon."

"This I do with much pride," Brown Bear said, lifting his chin boldly. Then he glanced over at Mariah. "And what of the young lad? In my eyes, he is a hero, and should be treated as such."

Wise Owl went to Mariah and stood over her, glaring down. "Release your hold on this lad," he ordered his brave. Then he stood there a moment longer, as though contemplating her fate.

Mariah went almost limp with relief when he suddenly smiled at her and clasped a friendly, gentle hand on her shoulder.

"I will forget that you did this act of bravery in the midst of escaping from our village of Chippewa," Wise Owl said. "It would have been easy for you to have gone on your way, with only selfish thoughts of self. Instead, your thoughts and deeds were for someone else. My daughter and her future husband! And because of this I shall encourage Chief Silver Wing to give you your freedom." He nodded. "But you will not leave our village before I offer you clean clothes, a bath, and much food."

Mariah's heart thrilled at the thought of having become an instant friend of this powerful Chippewa brave. It seemed that he had much influence with Chief Silver Wing.

Yes, she would soon be free. Then she would ride with haste to Fort Snelling.

She regretted with all of her heart that she had been sidetracked so long. The wounded, ailing Indians from Echohawk's village had needed assistance immediately. Some had perhaps even died because of her inability to get help sooner than this.

But she knew that she could not act too hastily in wanting to leave these Indians. Again they might get suspicious of her. And she was not free to confide in them about why she was so desperately eager to get to Fort Snelling. They must never know her part in the massacre. Too soon their trust of her would be cast into the wind.

"Brown Bear, take the white boy back to the wigwam that he escaped from," Wise Owl said. "I will talk to Chief Silver Wing. He will also see the lad as someone who is a friend, not a foe." Wise Owl moved to Mariah and gazed down at her. "Soon you will be free to go wherever you choose to go. If you need an escort, even that will be arranged."

"Thank you for everything," Mariah said, her voice low, trying to sound boyish. "I appreciate everything that you are doing for me." Seeing so much kindness in these Indians made her guilt twofold for having been forced to be a part of the raid against others of their same race. Oh, but if they should ever discover this truth, how quickly their attitude about her would change! As quickly as she had become their friend, she would again be their enemy.

"Come," Brown Bear said, nodding to Mariah. "I am indebted to you. How can I ever repay you?"

"It's not necessary," Mariah said, falling into step next to him. "That I am being looked to as a friend is all that is important to me." She smiled at him. "And I was glad to be able to save you and your beautiful friend from that horrid snake. Water moccasins are deadly. Your death would have been instant."

"*Ay-uh*, yes, instant," Brown Bear said, his smile fading. Then he looked quickly over at Mariah, his eyes dancing. "I shall give you my most prized bow. My grandfather made it for me. While you carry it into the hunt, my grandfather's spirit will be with you, always."

Mariah smiled weakly over at him. "Truly, you don't need to give me anything," she murmured. "Especially not something that has so much meaning to you. All I want is to be able to go on my way. Soon."

"As Wise Owl said, first you must accept clean clothes, a bath, and food," Brown Bear said, guiding her on into the village and toward the wigwam in which she had been imprisoned. "This is expected of you, white boy. You must accept our gifts graciously, or look to my people as though you see our ways as beneath you."

Mariah swallowed hard, not wanting to do anything to upset the Indians now that she had gained a foothold with them. "I appreciate all of your people's kindnesses," she said, glad to see Nee-kah waiting for her at the doorway of the small wigwam.

"I heard of your heroism," Nee-kah said, rushing toward Mariah. She took Mariah's hand and led her into the small dwelling. "I have been assigned many duties these past several days," she giggled. "You are now one of them."

Mariah looked down at a basin of water, then over at a clean fringed outfit of breeches and shirt, and then at the food awaiting her beside the fire. It was a feast. There were fish, broth, rice with maple sugar, and dried berries.

"First I bathe you," Nee-kah said, her hands eager on Mariah's heavy jacket, already removing it.

Mariah panicked, knowing that if she did not stop Nee-kah, her secret would soon be revealed. And she did not see that as wise. She now had the Indians' trust. Should they see her deceit, then what?

"I can undress and bathe myself," Mariah said, gently easing Nee-kah away from her. "You can go on to your other duties. Your husband seemed angry at you last night for having neglected someone who was in need of your care. Perhaps that is where you should be, even now. We don't want your husband getting mad at you again."

"My husband sent me here," Nee-kah said, shrugging. "And as for Echohawk, I have seen to his head wound and fever already today. I have even bathed him with herb water to help get his temperature down. And even after all of this, all he does is sleep." She slipped Mariah's shirt over her shoulders. "Now, just stand still. I think it is time that mud is washed off your face so that I can see the true features of my friend."

Mariah was in a stunned state from having heard Nee-kah mention Echohawk's name, and that he was here, only a few dwellings away.

Of course, she thought, her pulse racing. Why hadn't she thought of it earlier? Echohawk *would* bring his ailing people to a neighboring tribe of Chippewa, for assistance.

"This Echohawk you mentioned," Mariah dared to say, trying to hold on to her shirttail so that Nee-kah couldn't lift it over her head. "Is he . . . going to die?"

"Echohawk is a courageous fighter," Nee-kah said, jerking and yanking on Mariah's shirt, trying to get its tail end away from her. "He will live. But it will take time. His body is racked with fever." She stopped and sighed heavily as she placed her hands on her hips, staring frustratedly at Mariah. "Will you quit fighting against my undressing you? I have seen boys without clothes before. Seeing you will be no different."

Mariah laughed softly, seeing a trace of humor in the moment, yet fearing the end result. She panicked again when Nee-kah forgot the struggle with the shirt, yanking Mariah's breeches down, to rest around her ankles. The only thing left to hide the fact that she wasn't a boy were her bland cotton undergarments. And Nee-kah had already placed her hands at the waistband, beginning slowly to lower them.

Mariah backed away from Nee-kah. "You don't want to do that," she said shrilly.

"I have never before in my life seen such a bashful boy," Nee-kah fussed, again placing her hands on her hips.

"Then Echohawk is going to be all right?" Mariah said, changing the subject in an effort to postpone her having to undress, besides wanting to know more about Echohawk.

"Not entirely," Nee-kah said, taking a slow step toward Mariah. "He was partially blinded by a man's rifle that was used to knock him unconscious. But in time I think Echohawk will be victorious over even that. He will see again. The Great Spirit will make it so."

Mariah paled, in her mind's eye recalling Echohawk's beautiful large eyes. "Blind?" she gasped. She placed a hand to her mouth, stifling a sob behind it. "I'm so sorry. So very sorry."

"As we all are," Nee-kah said solemnly. "But he will see again. I do not doubt that for a moment. He is a fighter. He will win this battle. For his people, he must."

"Why is he here instead of his own village?" Mariah asked, still inching away from Nee-kah, and knowing too well the answer to her own question. She just needed more time to figure out how she could refuse to undress any further.

"People with skin of your coloring came and ravaged Echohawk's village," Nee-kah said, taking a firm grip on Mariah's shirttail. "He brought his people to my husband's village. They are all being seen to."

In a flash Nee-kah had Mariah's shirt over her head, and what Nee-kah discovered beneath it sent her head reeling with surprise.

"A boy with breasts of a woman?" she gasped, then fled from the wigwam screaming.

Mariah grabbed up her clothes and held them against her to hide behind, knowing that she didn't have enough time to get back into them.

And she was right.

Too soon Nee-kah had returned, Chief Silver Wing at her side.

7

All our actions take their hues from the complexion of the heart,
As landscapes their variety from light.

—BACON

Mariah could not help but tremble as Chief Silver Wing stood before her, for a moment a quiet question in his eyes.

Then she paled and her heart lurched when he grabbed her clothes from her arms, his gaze settling on her well-formed breasts.

Finally he spoke. "Nee-kah came to me with a tale that the young lad who is being celebrated a hero in our village has the body of a woman," he said, his eyes showing the puzzlement he felt as he looked slowly up at Mariah. "What she said is true, yet I, the wise chief that I am, know that cannot be so."

He stepped closer and ran his fingers through Mariah's hair. "Yet, still, your hair, the color of the sun's flames, is short, the same as a boy's," he puzzled further. "It is very strange that you, a woman, should choose to dress and behave as a boy. The Chippewa women would be shamed should their hair be clipped, unless, of course, it is done while mourning the loss of a loved one. And they would not wear men's breeches and shirts to hide the wonders of their bodies. Why would you? Tell me. I am here to listen. Tell me, even if your deceit is for the Chippewa only!"

Feeling cornered, Mariah realized that she had no choice but to answer him.

Yet for now she would tell him only half-truths.

"It is not of my doing that my hair is cut and that I am wearing the clothes of a boy," she blurted out, her pulse racing. "I am a woman forced by an evil father to dress and behave like a boy! I have fled my father's wrath. I was on my way to Fort Snelling, to seek help there, and to live my life as a woman."

Without taking his eyes off Mariah, Chief Silver Wing spoke to Nee-kah. "Go. Get one of your dresses and a pair of moccasins," he said softly. "Bring them here. *Wee-weeb*, quickly, my wife. Quickly. This woman has suffered enough humiliations because of an evil father."

Nee-kah rushed away. Mariah breathed much more easily. Then she stiffened again when he resumed questioning her.

"Am I wrong to believe you?" he said, thrusting her clothes back into her arms for her to hide behind. "Or is that innocence I see in your eyes enough, to know that what you say is true?"

"I am telling the truth," Mariah said, fearing that, as astute as he was, he would see beyond that which she had already said, and would demand to know more.

"Why did you not reveal this to us sooner?" Chief Silver Wing asked calmly. "And how did you know the skills of a rifle so well that you killed the water moccasin with one gunfire?"

"Not only did my father force me to dress as a boy, he also forced me to behave like one," Mariah said, glad to see Nee-kah there again, hoping that she would somehow draw the conversation away from the direction it was taking. "I was taught well the art of firearms. Also, the art of speaking some of your Chippewa language. My father told me that all of this was for my survival."

"In part, he was right," Chief Silver Wing said, taking the buckskin dress and moccasins as Nee-kah handed them to him. He leaned toward Mariah. "Take these. Wear them. You are now a woman. And you are a pretty woman, except for your hair. It looks like it is just growing out from a scalping."

"My father even forced this disgrace of cutting my hair upon me," she said, taking the garments, relishing their softness against her flesh.

"This father you speak of with anger," Chief Silver Wing said, kneading his chin thoughtfully. "Would I know him? Is he among those who trade often at Fort Snelling?"

A sudden fear gripped Mariah's insides. "My father has been to Fort Snelling," she murmured. "But not often. It has been a while now since he has been there. Others go for our supplies."

"Then I would not know him," Chief Silver Wing said, shrugging. His eyebrows forked. "You have yet to tell us your name."

"Mariah," Mariah said, yet not offering her last name. There was a chance that Echohawk had recognized her father and had known his name. Never could she breathe the name "Temple" across her lips while in the presence of the Chippewa.

"Mariah," Chief Silver Wing said, his eyes smiling down at her. "That name—it has to do with the wind, does it not?"

"Yes, Mariah is the wind," she said, smiling back at him, relieved that he did not ask her last name.

"No-din," Nee-kah offered softly as she stepped to Mariah's side. *"No-din* means 'wind' in the Chippewa language. Would you mind if we called you No-din?"

"Please do," Mariah said, sighing. "That is so lovely."

"After you eat and rest, you will be accompanied by many braves safely to Fort Snelling," Chief Silver Wing said, placing a hand to her bare shoulder. "You will always be remembered by my people. You saved two of our most prized possessions. Our youth is our future."

Mariah was not hearing everything that he was saying. What had stuck in her mind was that she would soon be escorted to Fort Snelling. Earlier, that was what she would have wanted. But now that she knew that Echohawk was in this village recovering from his head wound, she did not want to leave.

Somehow she wanted to be able to see him. If she could, she even wanted to find a way to make everything up to him.

"Does it matter how long I stay in your village?" Mariah asked guardedly, not wanting to arouse their suspicions about her reason for asking.

Echohawk!

"But you were trying to escape our village only a short while ago," Chief Silver Wing said, his eyes narrowing. "And you now wish to stay? Be a part of us?"

"I only now realize how weak I am from my recent adventures," Mariah quickly explained, the white lie slipping easily across her lips. "It could take me days to get my strength back. Would you mind if I stayed until . . . until . . . I have?"

She paused, then smiled up at him. "And until only a short while ago I wasn't welcomed in your village as a friend," she murmured. "You considered me an . . . enemy. I saw no choice but to try to escape."

Chief Silver Wing's eyes lit up and he nodded. "*Ay-uh*, yes, that is so," he said. Then he touched Mariah's mud-caked cheek. "*Nee-gee*, friend, it is time for my wife to make you pretty."

With that, he turned and left, leaving Mariah and Nee-kah alone, quiet in their exchanged admiring glances.

And then Nee-kah giggled and rushed to Mariah, taking the buckskin dress and her other clothes from her arms. "First you must be bathed," she said, tossing the clothes aside. "And then your hair will be washed and combed, your cheeks will be reddened with the juice of bloodroot, and then you will eat heartily! Your weakness will soon be gone. You will be shown everything of my village. My people see you as someone very special." She stifled another giggle behind her hand. "They are going to be very surprised to see your transformation from a mere boy to a beautiful lady."

"You don't know how anxious I am myself to be able to wear a dress," Mariah said, gazing down at the buckskin garment, beautifully decorated with colorful beads.

She gazed also at the moccasins. They were puckered around the front, Chippewa-style, intricately designed with beads and dyed porcupine quills.

Mariah fell to her knees beside the basin of water, bent over it, and splashed some onto her face. When Nee-kah offered her a cloth and a scented bar of soap, Mariah looked up at her questioningly. "The soap," she said. "It is perfumed." She looked then at a comb that Nee-kah had removed from a birchbark case. "And you even have a comb. I would have never guessed that you would have such luxuries as these."

Nee-kah knelt beside Mariah, proudly clasping the comb. "*Ay-uh*, Nee-kah has both perfumed soap and a comb," she said, her eyes dancing. "My chieftain husband acquired these for me at Fort Snelling after he heard that I was carrying his child." She glanced down at her comb, then back at Mariah. "I consider both things my most cherished possessions."

"And you are sharing them with me?" Mariah said, touched by Nee-kah's continued generosity and show of friendship.

"Friends share many things," Nee-kah said, laying aside her comb. "Now let this friend scrub the rest of the mud from your face and wash your hair." She frowned as she gazed at Mariah's short-cropped hair. "You father should be ashamed for forcing you to wear your hair in such a fashion. It would please Nee-kah so much to be able to braid your hair and wrap it in long rolls of otter fur, to make you even prettier for my people to see."

"It will take many months for my hair to grow long enough for braiding," Mariah sighed, then bent lower over the basin as Nee-kah busied her fingers smoothing the soap across Mariah's hair, then washing it vigorously. "I know that I will grow impatient while waiting, for I was so proud of my long hair. While Father was cutting it, it was as though a part of my heart was being torn away."

"If you wish, I will help you pass the time required for your hair to grow," Nee-kah said anxiously. "It is wonderful that you proved to be a woman! We can do so much together!" She paused and leaned her face down close to Mariah's. "And we can talk about so many things. I love to talk. Do you? How many words do you know in the Chippewa language? I can teach you so many more!"

Mariah laughed softly, finding Nee-kah so refreshing, and such a joy to be around. Mariah had been denied any female relationships since her mother's death. Her father had been determined to turn her totally into a man.

"I know some Chippewa words," Mariah said, wrapping a towel around her hair, rubbing it briskly. "It would be so nice to be taught more." Her eyes wavered as she wondered just how long she could delay leaving.

She placed the towel aside and quickly washed the rest of herself, then was glad to finally be able to put on the dress. She ran her hands down the full length of the buckskin garment, having never felt anything as soft, as comforting, to a body that had become so used to coarse fabrics.

Nee-kah stepped away from Mariah and gazed with parted lips at her. "You are most *mee-kah-wah-diz-*

ee, which means 'beautiful,' " she said, sighing. "The mud had hidden your better qualities beneath it. But not so much that I was unable to know that you were too pretty to be a boy."

Mariah smiled at Nee-kah, enjoying feeling feminine again. She had ached to wear a dress for so long, and to have someone compliment her, instead of having those sidelong glances from men who were surely thinking that she was one of those "strange" boys that preferred boys over girls.

Nee-kah went to Mariah with a buckskin pouch. "Hold this," she said, thrusting the pouch into Mariah's hand. "It contains a mixture of herbs and bark that I will rub into your hair. It will give your hair luster, strength, and life. Hopefully, it will even encourage it to grow much faster." She began rubbing the mixture into Mariah's hair. "The Chippewa wear their hair long not only because it is more beautiful that way but also because we believe our strength is in our hair. So shall it be for you one day, once your hair has grown to its desired length."

Mariah was half-hearing what Nee-kah was saying, her thoughts having strayed back to Echohawk. She had to see him. And she wanted to spend some time with him. It was her plan to get permission to assist Echohawk however she could, to make up for his misfortunes caused by her father, and even herself.

And because he was partially blind, not able to see her and make out her true identity, she would be able to get away with her scheme.

"Nee-kah," Mariah began, ready to test Nee-kah's true strength of friendship, "you have spoken of Echohawk. You said that he was not well. And you also said that you have been assigned to look after him."

"*Ay-uh*, yes, that is so," Nee-kah said, stepping away from Mariah, nodding approvingly when she saw the shine of her hair. She then took the pouch from Mariah and handed her another one, then proceeded with dipping her fingers into this mixture, soon reddening Mariah's cheeks with the juice of a bloodroot plant.

"I know of Echohawk," Mariah dared to say. "I have heard of his courage. Of his bravery. It would please me so to be able to do something to help him in this time of his sorrow." She gazed into Nee-kah's eyes as Nee-kah stepped back and smiled, again pleased at how she had made Mariah even more beautiful than before.

"Nee-kah, you know that you can trust me, don't you?" Mariah continued, her voice sounding more guarded than what she would have preferred.

"*Ay-uh*, you have proved that you are a trustworthy person. My people look to you as a hero—or should I now say heroine?" Nee-kah said, taking the pouch from Mariah, setting it aside. "And why do you ask?"

"Let me relieve you of some of your duties to Echohawk. Let me go to him and offer him *my* services," Mariah said in a rush of words, watching for Nee-kah's reaction. "This is something I could do to repay your people's kindnesses to me while I am regaining my strength before leaving for Fort Snelling."

Nee-kah was quiet for a moment as she gazed studiously into Mariah's eyes. "You need not do anything else for my people," she murmured. "You have already done enough. Because of your bravery and concern for human life, did you not save two of our beloved young ones?"

"But I want to do this, Nee-kah," Mariah said, taking Nee-kah's hands, squeezing them affectionately. "Please allow it. You could show me which herbs to use in doctoring Echohawk's fever. And while I am with him, you could rest awhile, you and your unborn child. Please, Nee-kah? It would make me feel important to be able to assist you in such a way."

Nee-kah pondered over the decision a moment longer, then smiled at Mariah. "All right," she murmured. "I see no harm in it. You are a most sincerely sweet and caring person for wanting to do this. You are not what I would have thought white people would be like. You are filled with much love and compassion."

Mariah's heart began thudding wildly. "Then you are saying that I can go to Echohawk?" she said, trying to hide the anxiousness in her voice. "That I can sit with him and offer him assistance?"

"When he discovers it is you offering this assistance, he will be honored," Nee-kah said, discounting for the moment the hate that he was feeling for the white people who had recently caused him so much heartache. Mariah was different. He would soon see that also, once his fever was cured and his senses were returned to normal.

Nee-kah placed a blanket around Mariah's shoulders, its background like new-laid snow, interwoven with symbols in the scarlet and russet and gold of autumn leaves, and the blue of summer skies. "No-din, wear this, a gift from Nee-kah, to keep you warm on these cooler nights of autumn," she said softly.

Mariah thrilled inside at the thought of having found such a friend, and also loving the way Nee-kah had called her No-din, her newly appointed Chippewa name. She stroked the blanket, feeling its utter softness, then eased into Nee-kah's embrace. "Thank you," she murmured. "I love it. Oh, how I love it."

Nee-kah walked Mariah through the village until they came to the small dwelling that once had been hers before she married Chief Silver Wing. In it now lay an ailing chief—the beloved Echohawk.

Mariah stiffened when she heard some sort of chanting coming from inside the wigwam. She looked quickly over to Nee-kah, questioning her with her eyes.

"That is a Mide priest, one of our people's shamans of the grand medicine society, the Mide-wi-win, that you are hearing," Nee-kah said matter-of-factly. "He comes now and then to work his cures over Echohawk. Come. Let us go inside. You can watch."

Mariah's knees were weak at the thought of seeing Echohawk again, having never forgotten their eye contact during the surprise ambush. Should he recognize her, so much would be lost to her.

Shakily she followed Nee-kah into the wigwam.

8

In what distant deeps or skies
Burnt the fire of thine eyes?

—BLAKE

Upon entering Echohawk's wigwam, Mariah scarcely breathed. The room was dim, the fire's glow and the faint light drifting down from the smoke hole in the ceiling giving off only enough light for her to see a man standing over Echohawk, who lay on a sleeping platform in the deep shadows along one wall, furs spread over him, up to his chin.

From this distance Mariah could not see Echohawk's face, but seeing how still he lay proved that her father had inflicted upon him a terrible injury.

Guilt spread through her like wildfire when she thought of that very instant she had seen her father bring the butt of his rifle across Echohawk's skull. She ached inside to know how this injury had affected him.

He was partially blind—and he just might die!

Oh, but she wished from the bottom of her heart that she would be given a chance to make things up to him.

To see him full of life again.

To see the sparkle of his fathomless dark eyes. . . .

"Come," Nee-kah whispered, drawing Mariah from her troubled thoughts. Nee-kah tugged on her hand. "Let us sit down. We do not want to disturb the Mide priest's healing ritual."

Mariah smiled weakly and nodded. She followed

Nee-kah's lead and sat down on a soft mat in the far
shadows, away from the Mide priest. She straightened
her back and folded her legs beneath her as she leaned
forward, wanting to see Echohawk's face, yet still faint
to her because of the damnable darkness of the
wigwam.

She could not relax. The Mide priest's appearance
was frightening. Two dark lines were painted upward
from his eyes, signifying he could foretell the future.
The lines from his ears meant that he knew what was
happening far away. He wore a white buckskin
auzeum, breechclout, embroidered with porcupine
quills and decorated with silver and copper ornaments.
His arms and hands had two lines painted on them,
to show that his touch was lethal. The *megis* at his
throat, the white seashell from the ocean, indicated
great power.

Folding her hands on her lap, Mariah watched attentively as the priest sat down beside Echohawk's
platform. When he picked up his drum and began to
sing a high-pitched chant, his rawhide-covered drum
thumping out the beat as he sang, the thump-thump
of the drum unnerved Mariah even more.

To her, it seemed to carry with it the sound of
doom.

As though Nee-kah had read Mariah's thoughts, she
leaned over and whispered into Mariah's ear. "The
deep throb of the water drum the Mide priest is playing represents the heartbeat of the creator, the Great
Spirit," she explained. She lifted her nose into the air
and sniffed. "And, No-din, do you smell the sweetness? Cedar boughs are burning in the lodge to purify
the air."

Again Mariah smiled weakly, too soon realizing the
complexities of the Chippewa's beliefs. She wondered
if it was wise at all to try to fit into the culture, even
if only for a while, in an attempt to make up to Echo-

hawk and his people the wrongs she and her father had done them. Her efforts might be looked on as too foreign—as trivial, and wrong.

Yet she must not let anything dissuade her. She must do it for Echohawk.

Nee-kah leaned even more closely to Mariah. "Do you see the eagle feather in the Mide priest's beaver hat?" she whispered. "This is worn as a badge of his profession. Do you see the pouch at his belt? In the pouch are sacred items used in his magic practices . . . the claw of a bear, the rattle of a snake, a bird's wing, the tooth of an elk, and bits of tobacco. Now, watch further the exhibition of his Mide magic."

The priest bent over Echohawk and placed a sacred white shell on the furs which covered him, and began to shake his medicine rattle over him, and sang:

> You will recover,
> You will walk and see again.
> It is I who say it;
> My powers are great.
> Through our white shell
> I will enable you to
> Walk and see again.

The Mide priest droned song upon song. Mariah swallowed hard as she continued to watch, becoming fearful that perhaps what she saw as witchcraft hocus-pocus might do Echohawk more harm than good. What Echohawk needed was real medicine, not strange songs sung over him and strange shells placed atop him.

She wanted to get up and speak her piece about how she felt, yet she knew to do so would be to condemn herself in the eyes of not only her friend, Nee-kah, but also the whole village. She was here because of their tolerance. She did not have the right to interfere in their beliefs, no matter how strange they seemed to her.

She stretched her neck to see what the priest was now about to do. He had gotten a cloth bundle from behind him and was unwrapping it. Her eyes widened as he took out a tail feather from an eagle, yet she saw that something still remained covered in the cloth.

Exhaling a nervous breath, she made herself relax as she continued to observe the curing ritual.

The Mide priest took the feather in his right hand and smoothed out its edges with his left. Settling himself on his haunches beside Echohawk, he leaned forward and wedged the feather in an upright position in the furs that were spread over Echohawk. After placing the feather there, he picked up his drum again and began another song.

Mariah got caught up in the melancholia of this song, finding it beautiful—even mystical. She closed her eyes and let herself get carried away, as though on soft downy clouds above the earth. She experienced many things while in this semitrance state. She could hear so many things—the sighing of the wind as it blows through the tall pines; the soothing sound of waves lapping against the stones on the beach; and the fading noise of an animal crashing its way through the brush.

The song suddenly rose to a high vibrato, wrenching Mariah out of her reverie. Her eyes blinked nervously and her heart pounded, wondering about this moment of strangeness that she had just experienced. It made her fear the priest even more. He did seem to have powers that she had only moments ago scoffed at.

She flinched with alarm when the last drumbeat sounded and the feather jumped from atop Echohawk and fluttered to the floor as though it had a life of its own.

Confessing to herself that she was spellbound by the priest's performance, Mariah watched almost anxiously as he unwrapped the remainder of the cloth bundle.

Now he held two wooden figures in his hand. One apparently represented a male, the other a female. They were carved out of white ash and had movable heads and arms, and were attached to the bodies in a manner not discernible to her.

The medicine man then smoothed out a square of white cloth on the mat-covered floor and laid the figures on their backs on one half of the cloth, and carefully folded the other half over them so that they were completely covered.

Once again taking up his drum, he sang another song. It consisted of many repetitions of the sound "ho-ho" in a rather deep and guttural tone. As he sang, he closed his eyes and seemed unaware of anything around him. Sweat formed on his brow.

Craning her neck to take a better look, Mariah was startled to see movement under the cloth. The heads seemed to be turning back and forth, and the arms were moving up and down. She did not know if they were actually moving or if she was the victim of some sort of illusion.

Nee-kah leaned over and took her hand. "Do not fear this that you see," she reassured softly. "The spirits have given the Mide the powers to do these feats of magic. But he is exhausted now. He will go to his medicine lodge and rest."

Mariah watched almost breathlessly as he picked up his paraphernalia and was gone, leaving the wigwam strangely quiet.

"Let us now go to Echohawk," Nee-kah said, yanking on Mariah's hand.

Mariah needed no further encouragement. She was anxious to see how Echohawk had fared during the performance that had mystified, even frightened her. Never had she seen anything like it, and deep within her heart she hoped never to see it again. It seemed to defy all teachings of the Bible that she had absorbed on those long winter nights before her mother had died. She could even now hear the soft, sweet voice of her mother as she had read the verses, explaining the meaning of those that seemed too difficult for a child of four and five.

Her heart thumping wildy, Mariah went with Nee-kah to Echohawk's side. She had expected him to be asleep, for he had lain so quietly while the medicine man performed over him.

But his eyes were open. His gaze seemed to be burning into her flesh as she knelt beside him, Nee-kah no longer there, instead at the far shadows, picking up some buckskin pouches from the floor.

Mariah breathed anxiously, afraid that at any moment Echohawk would speak accusing, angry words at her. For it did seem as though he was looking not only at her face but also deep into her soul, where her secrets were hidden—secrets that would condemn her in his eyes.

"Nee-kah?" Echohawk said, his voice revealing his weakness. "You have come again to sit at my side? Did you witness, also, the beauty in the Mide's performance today?"

Realizing that Echohawk did not know her, Mariah sighed with relief, and her heart jumped with a sudden joy, knowing that her plan would be easily carried out under these conditions.

Yet again she was plagued by remorse, seeing first-hand how her father's blow to Echohawk's head had affected him. She wondered if he would ever see again.

And his face was so pale. He was so ravaged by fever.

She reached a hand to Echohawk's brow and

touched it soothingly. "No, I am not Nee-kah," she said softly, seeing a quick, wary puzzlement cross his face.

"It is No-din," Nee-kah quickly interjected as she came to kneel beside Mariah. "She has come to assist me. She will sit at your side and look after you while I give myself and my unborn child much-needed rest."

Echohawk squinted his eyes, so badly wanting to see this sweet-voiced woman at Nee-kah's side, yet still unable to make out anything but movement and shadow.

He again cursed the white man for having impaired his sight.

"I do not know a No-din," Echohawk said, finding it hard to stay awake, the fever having sapped all of his energy. But at least for the moment he had regained a portion of his senses and could talk as someone not crazed. He had surely worried Nee-kah as he had rambled on in his delerium, saying what, he did not even know himself!

Mariah stiffened and drew her hand from his brow, looking cautiously over at Nee-kah, wondering how she would explain to Echohawk just how she happened to be there, offering her services, when, in truth, she was not of Chippewa descent at all.

"She is not of our band of Chippewa, or yours," Nee-kah explained softly, sinking a cloth into a basin of water, handing it to Mariah. She nodded silently toward Echohawk, Mariah soon catching the meaning. She took the cloth and smoothed it gently across Echohawk's hot brow.

"Then from which band is she?" Echohawk said, sighing as he enjoyed the cool cloth on his brow. "Why is she giving of herself to make me more comfortable?"

"She is not Chippewa at all," Nee-kah said, her

voice thin, unsure of his reaction when he discovered that Mariah was white.

But he seemed to be drifting off even as he had spoken, so that even if she took the time to tell him the full truth of Mariah, and how she happened to be there, he would not recall it the next time he awakened.

"Do not worry yourself over who she is," Nee-kah murmured, leaning close to Echohawk's ear as his eyes fluttered closed. "Just accept her kindness, Echohawk. She is special, Echohawk. And soon, when you are better, you will see for yourself just how special she is."

Mariah bit her lower lip, wishing that Nee-kah wouldn't make over her so much, when, if the truth were known to this sweet Chippewa maiden, Mariah would be hated.

Perhaps even put to death!

"He is asleep again," Nee-kah whispered. "He no longer feels the cool softness of the cloth. Let me take this time while he sleeps to show you the medicines used to make him better."

Mariah sat down beside Nee-kah and listened, yet her heart was elsewhere. This close to Echohawk, so that she had been witness again to his handsome face, many things had stirred within Mariah that had felt deliciously strange.

As before, it had been an instant attraction, one that unnerved her.

And it was futile, this attraction to a man who would one day loathe the sight of her. Once he regained his sight and could see who this No-din really was . . . Oh, but how *would* he react?

Chills rode Mariah's spine as she envisioned that moment of eye contact, when truths were revealed. She could almost feel his powerful hands on her throat, squeezing the life from inside her!

"No-din?" Nee-kah said, looking questioningly at

Mariah. She placed a hand to her brow. "Your brow is cold with perspiration. Do you regret being here? Would you rather leave? Although I do not wish to, I would tell my husband that you would prefer going on to Fort Snelling. Would that make you more comfortable, No-din?"

A quick panic seized Mariah. She couldn't leave Echohawk now, no matter what the outcome would be in the end.

Hopefully, after he saw her devotion to him, he might be able to forget the ugly past—including her part in the ambush.

"No, I do not wish to go on to Fort Snelling," she said in a rush of words. "But please be patient with me, Nee-kah. All of this is new to me. I've never been in an Indian village before, much less participated in its daily functions. I will be all right. I promise you." She glanced over her shoulder at Echohawk, a warmth swirling through her so wonderful when her gaze rested on his face, she knew that she would chance anything to be with him.

"Then so be it," Nee-kah said, nodding. "Now, let me continue teaching you our ways of doctoring our ill, other than that which is done by our medicine men." She gestured with a hand over an assortment of herbs and roots that she had spread on the floor for Mariah to see. "These are collected from the forest. There are black root, bur-vine root, wild cherry, and dogwood, all dried and ready to use. And also you can make some boneset tea. You boil down walnut bark till it is pitchy. . . ."

Mariah listened eagerly, intrigued anew by the Chippewa beliefs.

Victor Temple drew his reins tight, urging his black stallion to stop. Groaning, he rubbed his lame leg. "Where is that damn Tanner McCloud?" he growled, looking over at his men, who had followed his lead and stopped. "He seems to have dropped off the face of the earth!"

"I'd begin lookin' for Mariah elsewhere," Bart, one of his most devoted trappers, said. "Dammit, Victor, we've been everywhere lookin' for Tanner, when you're not even sure he's the one who abducted her."

Another trapper edged close to Temple. "Did you ever think that it's just possible that she left on her own?" he said, nervously twisting and untwisting the end of his thick mustache. "That was a foolish thing to do, Victor—makin' her become a part of the Injun ambush. She cain't be havin' much respect for any of us after that, especially you, her pa."

Victor raised a hand and slapped the trapper across the face, causing an instant hush throughout the cluster of men. "I didn't ask for your opinion," he shouted. "So don't give it to me!"

"Victor, what say we go to Fort Snelling?" Bart suggested, having ignored Victor's angry outburst against the other trapper. "Let's just take a look-see. She might be there."

Victor turned glaring eyes to Bart. "Are you sayin' you also think she ran away on her own?" he said, his teeth clenched.

"I ain't sayin' nothin' 'cept we can't rule out anything," Bart said, his dark eyes daring Victor to lash out at him, ready to fight back. "If you want your daughter back, I'd say we'd best think of every angle. Wouldn't you agree, Victor?"

Victor's gaze dropped to the ground. He shook his head wearily, then nodded. "Yup, I guess so," he said, looking back up at Bart. Then he doubled a fist into the air. "Let's ride, boys! And if she ain't there, we'll be goin' from Indian village to Indian village to find her."

Another hush accompanied this order, everyone fearing even the sight of Indians now, after having wreaked havoc on one of their villages—leaving one

Indian chief dead, the other one wounded, perhaps dead by now.

Victor flicked his reins and nudged the sides of his horse with his knees, sending it into a hard gallop across the straight stretch of meadow, his insides an upheaval of dread and fear.

9

Act well at the moment, and you have performed a good action to all eternity.

—LOVATER

Several Days Later

Fresh from a bath and a hair washing, Mariah felt
lovely today. She was attired in a buckskin dress stud-
ded with beads resplendent in colors significant of the
green earth and the blue sky, and a tunic with the
most costly adornments of the milk teeth of the elk
fastened in a row on front.

She had a spring in her step as she hurried toward
Echohawk's wigwam. Nee-kah had just told her that
when she last saw Echohawk, he had been more
alert—had even attempted standing.

This change surprised Mariah. For days now she
had sat with him while he slept most of the time. And
when he was awake, they had not shared in conversation. Seemingly troubled, he had stayed aloof, staring
blankly into the flames of the fire, yet occasionally
accepting her gentle hand on his brow, as though her
being there had been enough.

He hardly said a word to her, which she thought
was fortunate for herself, since she was not ready to
share in conversation with him. She knew that in time
she would be faced with his questions, fearing that he
would immediately discover who she was. She wanted
this special time with him to develop a bond between
them that he might find hard to break, no matter the
color of her skin or her identity.

He had questioned her only that first time about

who she was, after the Mide priest's performance. But it seemed that his memory of that moment had deserted him. It was as though he still thought that Nee-kah was with him most times.

Casting aside fears that today might be the day of discovery, Mariah lifted the entrance flap to his wigwam partway. But just before entering, she stopped and inhaled a nervous breath.

Courage.

She needed much courage to get past what could be awkward moments with Echohawk. His health had apparently improved.

Then what of his eyesight?

Wanting to get the wonder behind her, she stepped inside, stopped instantly, her heart lurching when she found herself looking into the barrel of a rifle.

Her eyes remained locked on the rifle, her knees feeling rubbery, thinking that she had not only been discovered, but was perhaps breathing her last breaths of life.

Surely Echohawk was not going to shoot her!

"Nee-kah?" Echohawk said, lowering the rifle to his side, swaying in his weakness as he settled back down onto his fur-covered platform. "I did not mean to frighten you with the rifle. When I discovered that my legs would hold me, I wanted to test the strength of my hands by holding a rifle. Soon I will be using the firearm in daily practice. I do not want to forget how!"

Her pulse racing, Mariah went weak with relief that he had meant no harm, and still did not realize who she was. She stepped further into the wigwam and moved to her knees beside Echohawk's platform.

"No, it is not Nee-kah," she murmured, gazing into his dark eyes, realizing that they were still partially sightless, for as his eyes locked on her, she could tell that he was not truly seeing her. There was the same blank stare, the frustration evident in his slight frown.

"Then who is there?" Echohawk said, resting his rifle on his lap. "I have felt your presence before. Your name. What is your name?"

"Her name is No-din," Nee-kah said, suddenly entering the wigwam. She came and knelt beside Mariah. "Echohawk, do you not recall the one other time I spoke her name to you? Are you not aware that she, too, sat at your bedside and bathed your feverish brow? She fed you and gave you herbal medicines?"

"I now recall another time, but until this moment it faded from my consciousness when my fever worsened," Echohawk said glumly. "From then on, time and everything else have been a blur. Nee-kah, only *your* name came to mind when I felt a presence at my side."

He reached a hand out to Mariah and began roaming his fingers slowly over her face, causing a melting sensation to spread at the pit of her stomach. "Until only moments ago I did not realize that her presence was different from yours," he said. "There is something unusual about her, yet I do not know what."

"Her skin coloring, her language, and her way of speaking are different," Nee-kah said guardedly.

Echohawk drew his hand away, recoiling now at the thought of having touched a woman whose skin matched that of those he hated so much. "She is white?" he growled, circling a hand around his rifle again, clutching hard to it. "Why is she here? Who is she?"

The moment of warmth that had filled Mariah at the mere touch of his hand on her face changed to something cold and fearful knotting inside her abdomen. She eyed the rifle warily, then looked slowly up at Echohawk again, recoiling when she saw the intense hate in his eyes and the set of his jaw.

"She is a friend," Nee-kah said, herself eyeing the rifle. "A special friend."

"I have only one true friend whose skin is white,"

Echohawk grumbled. "That is Colonel Josiah Snelling. Others I do not trust. I have reason for this mistrust. I am here today, partially blinded, because of evil people with white skins and black hearts! Now that my mind is cleared of its feverish haze and I can think clearly, I live for the time when I can torture and murder the man with the limp and the young boy who rode at his side!"

Mariah shivered and paled at his words, having never thought that his hate for her and her father could be this strong. Her first instincts were to flee, but deep down inside, where her desires were formed, she knew that she felt too much for Echohawk to leave him. Now she must work twice as hard to make him trust—even love—her before he realized that she was in truth the lad he sought to kill!

She would volunteer her services to him in all manner of endeavor.

She would be his eyes!

"Echohawk," Nee-kah said, placing a gentle hand to his cheek. "Do not upset yourself so with such talk of vengeance. Your father was a man of peace. My father shares in such efforts. Please try to forget those who have wronged you. Live for the future. Your people's future. They have suffered too much already. Regain your strength, Echohawk. Use your wisdom and strength to better your people, not cause them more suffering by going into warring against the whites."

"Not all whites," Echohawk said, his voice a sneer. "Only those who have caused this heartache for my people. I soon will begin practicing with my weapons, to learn to fire accurately, even with my affliction. I will soon avenge my people!"

"A few white people's lives are not worth what it could bring your people," Nee-kah warned. "Please, Echohawk, forget your need to avenge your people, when all they want now is to rebuild their village and begin their lives anew."

Mariah had sat stiffly quiet, listening to the debate between Nee-kah and Echohawk, fearing offering her own thoughts on the subject, then finally spoke up. "Echohawk, I am sorry for any wrong that has been brought to your people because of people of my skin coloring," she said, reaching her hand to touch one of his, recalling so blissfully those few times that she had held on to his hand while he had slept. Even then she had known that she loved him.

Yes, she marveled to herself:

She loved him!

With all of her heart and soul!

Echohawk jerked his hand away from hers as though it were a hot coal. Again he clutched onto his rifle, glaring at Mariah, still seeing her as only shadows and light. "You have not said why you are here," he said flatly. His gaze went to Nee-kah. "And why did you allow it, Nee-kah? She does not belong! Why would you think that she did?"

"She belongs in our village now, as much as you or I," Nee-kah defended. "She is a woman of much courage. She, alone, saved Wild Flower and Brown Bear. In the eyes of our people she is a heroine. It was I who brought her to our village. I found her alone, weakened after being thrown from her horse. And she has asked to stay until she is stronger, and also has offered to help care for you. I saw no harm in it. And she has been dutifully at your side since."

Echohawk's mind was swirling with questions, finding it unacceptable that Nee-kah, or even her husband, would have so carelessly allowed a white woman into his wigwam, no matter if she was being called some sort of heroine.

Yet he was recalling the sweetness of Mariah's voice and the gentleness of her hands, all the while thinking they were Nee-kah's. He had not wanted to feel anything at the time, knowing that Nee-kah was married to Chief Silver Wing, but a bond had been formed, and now he knew that it was the white woman that he had begun to have special feelings for.

He turned his head away, distraught over this discovery.

"Echohawk," Mariah said softly, "I want to do more for you now that you are stronger. Please allow it. I feel so ashamed of how your people have been treated by my people. I want to compensate, in some little way, for the harm that has befallen you. I would even like to stay at your side at all times and become your eyes until you can see. I could accompany you when you start practicing with your weapons. I could be your eyes, telling you when your aim was right or wrong. I could help you hone your skills by doing this."

Deep down inside herself, Mariah was torn with loyalties. If she did help Echohawk hone his skills with his weapons, she had to expect that he would use those skills against her father.

Yet she understood why Echohawk wanted to kill him—was *driven* to.

And she felt that she owed Echohawk so much. He had lost almost everything because of her father.

Echohawk turned his eyes quickly back to her, squinting, so badly wanting to see her. When he had touched her face, he had felt its fine, delicate features, knowing that she was surely even more beautiful than Nee-kah.

"Echohawk needs no more of your assistance," he said, his voice drawn. "Especially when I practice firing my weapons. That is a man's work. Not a woman's. Especially not a *white* woman's! Leave. That is what would make me happy. Go. Return to your home."

He squared his shoulders and leaned closer to Mariah. "Your home," he said, arching an eyebrow. "Where do you make your home?"

Mariah's insides tightened, fear grabbing at her heart. "I have no home," she said quickly, in a sense telling the truth.

"Why is that?" Echohawk asked, again reaching a hand to her face, roaming his fingers over it. Then his hand went to her hair, gasping when he discovered its length. "Your hair! What has happened to your hair? Did you cut it while in mourning for a loved one?"

Mariah's heart was pounding, feeling trapped. If he would put two and two together, recalling the length of the hair of the lad that had partaken in the ambush, then he could conclude that the lad, in truth, was she!

Yet she had no choice but to tell him as much of the truth as she dared to.

"If you must know, I fled an evil father who forced many unfortunate things upon me," she said. "He even cut my beautiful hair. That is why I have no home. I was fleeing his wrath. I was on my way to Fort Snelling to seek help. But I was stopped when my horse lost its footing in the creek and threw me. I was then at the mercy of whoever found me." She smiled over at Nee-kah. "I was fortunate that it was Nee-kah, the sweet, kind person that she is."

Echohawk peered sightlessly over at Nee-kah. "At a time when our people had just suffered so much at the hands of white people, you dared bring one into your village?" he said, his voice sharp. "And your chieftain husband? Did he approve?"

"*Gah-ween*, no, not entirely," Nee-kah said weakly. "No-din was taken prisoner. She escaped. And while escaping, she discovered Brown Bear and Wild Flower at the river. They . . . they did not notice a water moccasin ready to bite. No-din, knowing that she would be forfeiting her escape by killing the snake, shot it. This is why all of our people see her as trustworthy. This is why she is being celebrated as a heroine. So must you, Echohawk, accept this as true. Mariah is very much a part of our village now."

"Mariah?" Echohawk said, frowning over at Mariah, yet still not seeing her. "Your name is Mariah? You have called yourself No-din."

"That is my Chippewa name," Mariah said, gulping hard when she saw an instant look of horror on Echohawk's face.

"You have even been given a Chippewa name?" he gasped. His jaw tightened and he shook his head back and forth. "This I do not understand. Never shall I understand."

"Echohawk, I wish you no harm," Mariah pleaded. "I only wish to help right some of the wrongs done you. Please allow it."

"*Gah-ween-wee-kah*, never," he hissed. He gestured with a wave of a hand toward the entrance flap. "*Nah-quszly*, leave. *Ah-szhee-gawh*, now! I am soon to be taken to the resting place of my father and those of my people who are buried with him. I do not wish to have a white woman accompany me where she is not wanted."

Stifling a sob behind her hand, Mariah rose and ran to the entrance flap, rushing outside. Blinded with tears, she went to her wigwam and threw herself on a pallet of furs close beside her firepit.

The fire was warm on her flesh, but her heart was cold and aching. She saw no chance at all of getting close to Echohawk, yet she was not going to give up this easily! She would stay at the village indefinitely. She would find a way to make him realize that she was a friend—even more than that. She had felt a bonding between them, that which could develop into something more, now especially since he had admitted to having felt a difference in hers and Nee-kah's presences when they had taken turns sitting with him.

"I know he doesn't hate me," she cried to herself.

"He just wants to so badly, he won't allow himself to give me a chance!"

When she heard hoofbeats passing by just outside of her wigwam, Mariah went listlessly to the entrance flap, lifted it, and peered out. She wiped tears from her eyes as she watched Echohawk riding by, flanked on each side by two braves, who were keeping a close eye on him, lest he should start to fall from the horse in his weakness.

A deep sadness engulfed her as she went back to the fire and sat down beside it. She felt helpless— totally helpless.

Drained of all energy and hope, she stretched out beside the fire and fell into a restless sleep, then was drawn quickly awake when she heard a voice that was familiar to her speaking close by outside. She paled and her insides tightened when she realized who was there, in the very same village as she! And thank God Echohawk had gone to his father's burial grounds! For the man he hated with all his might was there, bold as an eagle, mixing with the Chippewa, after having just slain so many!

She went to the entrance flap and scooted it aside only slightly, spying her father still on his stallion, yet most of his identity hidden in the shadows of a large-brimmed hat pulled low over his brow. He wore a large buckskin cape, hiding his lame leg beneath it.

Yes, Mariah thought bitterly, he was very well disguised.

She watched breathlessly as Chief Silver Wing went to her father and stared coldly up at him.

"I do not know you," the chief said, his voice far from friendly. "Why do you come to my village?" He looked cautiously from side to side, at Victor's two companions, realizing that there were others hidden in the forest, for his braves had come with such a warning. The three white men had entered the village only because Chief Silver Wing allowed it, his braves' weapons drawn on them at all times.

"I come in peace. I am searching for my daughter," Victor said, keeping his voice low and unthreatening. "She disappeared several days ago. Is there a chance that you might have seen her?"

Mariah's heart raced, praying that the chief would recall why she had fled her father. And she prayed that the chief would recall how she had been welcomed into the village, almost as one of them, since her act of bravery.

"This daughter," Chief Silver Wing said, his voice steady. "What is her name?"

"Mariah," Victor said softly. "She goes by the name Mariah."

Chief Silver Wing's jaw tightened as he recalled how No-din had spoke so unfavorably of such a father, and how she had fled his wrath. "*Gah-ween*, no, I do not know of such a person named Mariah," he said, the lie coming easy across his lips. "Now leave, white man. You have no cause to be here."

Victor glared down at the chief for a moment, then wheeled his horse around and rode briskly away.

Mariah went limp with relief. When Nee-kah came into the wigwam and lunged into Mariah's arms, she clung to her friend, feeling blessed for having found someone so compassionate, when in truth, it could have been so different. These Chippewa could have burned her on a stake, or could have gladly handed her over to her father, to rid themselves of her.

Instead, they were protecting her as though she were truly one of them.

She clung to Nee-kah, hoping that Echohawk would eventually feel the same about her.

10

An able man shows his spirit by gentle words
and resolute actions; he is neither hot nor timid.
—CHESTERFIELD

Several Days Later

The day was pleasantly warm, even though the trees
had changed to marvelous shades of gold, russet, and
crimson. To bide time until she could find out where
Echohawk had gone for target practice, Mariah was
with Nee-kah and several other Indian women on a
root-digging expedition, helping to collect roots to dry
for the upcoming winter's use.

As she trod through the forest, Nee-kah at her side,
Mariah became lost in thought. She had decided never
to give up on her promise that she would find a way
to make wrongs right for Echohawk. Sitting vigil at
his side while he had been recovering had not been
enough, it seemed. Once he had recovered enough to
be alone, to do things as he liked, and at his own
pace, he did not allow her near him.

Yet Mariah did not take that too personally. He
had not allowed anyone to be with him in his time of
awkwardness while trying to learn again how to survive in everyday ritual and to aim accurately at a target with impaired eyes. True, he had refused to let
her become his eyes, but he had also refused trusted
braves who had offered their services.

"No-din, we Chippewa are constantly aware of the
need of conservation," Nee-kah said, quickly wrenching
Mariah from her thoughts. "When we gather roots,
some plants are left for seed. Earth is mother, who

furnishes the food, and we Chippewa are considerate not to leave her scarred." She paused and brushed away a string of cobweb as it floated just in front of her face, one of the aggravations of autumn. "A few berries are always left on bushes for birds and squirrels and other animals," she further explained. "We never forget that the animals are the future food for our people."

"That is such a lovely way of explaining it," Mariah said, shifting her basket from one hand to the other. "I am discovering that the Chippewa are quite artistic, not only in designs I have seen on their clothes and dwellings but also in expressing their thoughts."

Nee-kah's lips parted to talk some more, but she giggled when one of the young boys accompanying their mothers on the outing sneaked up behind her and hit the underside of the basket she was carrying, dumping the roots she had gathered, then went to Mariah and did the same.

"Why, he's a little scalawag, isn't he?" Mariah said, giggling as she looked down at her spilled roots, then at the lad as he scampered away, soon spilling another woman's basket.

Nee-kah turned to Mariah, eyeing her questioningly. "Scalawag?" she said, an eyebrow forked. "I know many words of your language, but never have I heard that strange-sounding word before."

Mariah knelt to the ground and began scooping up roots, placing them back in her basket. "It has the same meaning as 'rascal,' which suggests mischievousness. I would say that little brave is one of the most mischievous boys I have ever seen." She glanced over at the boy, whose mother had just caught up with him, scolding him. "A scalawag," she murmured, laughing softly. "But cute."

She helped Nee-kah gather her spilled roots, then her smile faded and she rose slowly back to her feet, stunned to see how the small brave was being reprimanded. His mother had placed him in a basket cradle, tied him into it, then stuck the point of the frame into the ground.

"The poor child," Mariah gasped, paling.

"He will not dump any more baskets," Nee-kah said, shrugging. "We can now finish gathering our roots beneath the trees without further annoyances from the . . ." She gazed over at Mariah, screwing her face up into a curious look. "What was the word, No-din, that you used to describe his behavior?"

Mariah gazed a moment longer at the child, who was crying fitfully, then over to Nee-kah, knowing that this was just another custom that she would learn to accept. "Scalawag," she said, pronouncing the word slowly.

Nee-kah placed her hand on her abdomen. "I must be sure that my son or daughter is not a scalawag," she said, giggling.

"I'm sure mine will be," Mariah said, laughing softly. "I would play with and torment a child with my own mischievous ways. The poor child would not be able ever to have a solemn moment."

Mariah's laughter faded, her thoughts catapulted back to Echohawk. Loving him so much, and missing him terribly, she allowed herself to wonder how it might be to have his children, should she ever be given the chance. His handsomeness would surely transfer into any child borne of him.

A son.

Ah, a son with a copper skin and eyes of midnight would be such a wonder, such a joy, to experience!

And a daughter. How beautiful a daughter by him would be!

She glanced over at Nee-kah, seeing her utter loveliness. It would be wonderful to have a daughter that looked exactly like her and had the same generous, sweet personality. . . .

She was brought back to reality when out of nowhere a lone buffalo wandered into the area, way too close to the child. The boy's eyes caught sight of it, elevating his crying to something piercing, fright evident in the child's huge dark eyes.

"*Gah-ween*, no!" the mother screamed, dropping her basket to the ground, rushing toward her son as the buffalo began wandering even closer to the screaming child.

Mariah watched with horror, stifling a scream when the buffalo bent low over the boy, eye to eye, nose to nose.

The boy's mother kept running, waving her arms and screaming at the bull. Then she stopped and gasped, horrified as the bull suddenly thrust out its massive tongue and licked the boy's face.

Mariah leapt up and ran toward the boy, then stopped, dismayed when the buffalo sauntered away, soon out of sight.

Her shoulders relaxed and she inhaled a nervous breath when the mother released the child from his prison, holding him in her arms, hugging him tightly.

"Nee-kah has never seen such a sight," Nee-kah said, stepping up to Mariah's side. "I thought the boy would be killed. The Great Spirit must have touched the buffalo's heart, making him love the Chippewa, instead of hate. The Great Spirit will now also look over the buffalo and allow no arrows or bullets to pierce its flesh."

The sound of gunfire carrying on the wind made Mariah's heart skip a beat. She glanced quickly in the direction of the sound, hearing another gunshot, and realized that, unaware, she had found the place where Echohawk had chosen to do his target practicing.

"*Mah-szhon*, go to him," Nee-kah said, placing a gentle hand on Mariah's arm. "I know that it has been hard not to."

"Would you really mind?" Mariah said anxiously, looking down at her basket of roots, then back up at

Nee-kah. "Have I gathered enough roots? I want to play a beneficial role in your village. I do not want to just take, and not give."

"You have given of yourself in many ways," Nee-kah said, smiling softly at Mariah. "It is my people who still owe you so much."

Mariah's eyes wavered and she looked away from Nee-kah, guilt awash throughout her again as she recalled the bloody massacre and her part in it. She feared the day that Nee-kah and her people would discover the truth. They would then regret all of the praise they had bestowed upon her.

But this was now. Echohawk was near. And even though he had forbidden her to accompany him, she could not stay away now that she was so close.

Nee-kah took Mariah's basket. "Go," she said, nodding toward the repeated gunfire. "If you do not feel comfortable letting him realize you are there, at least watch Echohawk and see how he fares today with his practicing." She frowned, sadness heavy in her eyes. "I so fear for him if he cannot find any accuracy with his weapons. He has always been a proud man. And he has the need to regain that pride."

"If only he would allow me to help him," Mariah said, frustrated. "I would so enjoy being the one who helped him regain some of his confidence, even if he can't see clearly enough to shoot as well as he did before . . . before . . . the attack."

"He would not even allow any braves to accompany him today," Nee-kah said, sighing heavily. "This, too, is a part of that pride. He wants to prove that he can fend for himself, totally."

"Then I shall just go and watch," Mariah said, although she wanted far more than that. She hungered to hear him ask her to stand at his side—be his eyes. It would be a fair exchange, she thought to herself, for he had her heart!

"Go with care," Nee-kah said, leaning a kiss to Mariah's cheek.

"*Mee-gway-chee-wahn-dum*, thank you," Mariah said, then began running softly in the direction where she had heard the gunfire, which had now ceased, troubling her. She feared that she had dallied too long and that he had ceased with his practicing, already moving back toward the village.

Breathlessly she continued onward, then stopped with a start. Up ahead, through a clearing in the trees, she caught her first sight of Echohawk. The reason she had not heard any more gunfire was that he was now practicing with a bow and arrows.

She crept closer and hid behind a tree only a few yards away, watching with an anxious heart as he shot one arrow after another at the remains of a weathered buffalo skull positioned in the fork of a tree.

She ached for him when he missed the skull altogether each time he shot at it, but was proud of him when this did not dissuade him from trying again. A determined man, he kept notching his arrows onto the string of his bow, continuously shooting.

Mariah moved closer, her moccasins silent on the thick grass, until she stood within only footsteps of Echohawk. She was afraid that with his weakened eyes, his sense of hearing might be better and that he might realize that she was there.

But so intent was he on practicing, he still did not know that she was there.

Mariah stood her ground and continued to admire Echohawk more and more by the minute for his determination and endurance.

Ah, but wasn't he handsome! she marveled to herself, as though this were the first time she had set eyes on him. He wore a breechclout and moccasins, revealing all his muscles and the sleekness of his copper chest and broad shoulders. Held by a beaded headband, his raven-black hair framed his face and was worn loosely to his shoulders, occasionally lifting from his shoulders to flutter in the gentle breeze. His jaw and sculptured lips were tight. His midnight-black eyes were mystically beautiful, which made Mariah even more regretful over his sight having been impaired.

Realizing that she was getting too caught up in the wonders of this man, Mariah wrenched her eyes away from him, swallowing hard. She knew that if she allowed herself the feelings of a woman, which had for so long been denied her by her ruthless father, she could love this handsome Chippewa with all her heart.

Being swept up too much in feelings that were all but forbidden to her, Mariah turned to leave, but was stunned at what she found approaching, its narrow gray eyes on Echohawk.

A wolf!

And she could see by the slaver of its jaws that it was not just any wolf.

This animal was rabid!

She glanced from the wolf to Echohawk, then back at the wolf, realizing that Echohawk was not aware of the wolf's presence, no more than he had been of her scrutiny. And even if Echohawk had been aware of the wolf stalking him, he surely would not be able to see well enough to kill it before it leapt on him!

Without further thought, knowing what she must do, Mariah made a mad dash for Echohawk's rifle, lunged for it, and aimed it at the wolf, shooting it between the eyes just as it was getting ready to make its final approach on Echohawk. She watched wild-eyed as the impact of the bullet caused the wolf's body to lurch wildly in the air, then fall dead to the ground.

Startled by the rifle fire, Echohawk whirled around, and when he saw the hazy shadow of Mariah standing there, he dropped his bow and arrow to the ground and lunged for her, tackling her by the ankles. As she fell to the ground, the rifle fell out of her hands, and she soon found herself pinned to the ground, Echo-hawk atop her.

"Your aim was bad," he growled, leaning his face down into hers. "Why did you fire upon me? What enemy of mine are you?"

"I am not your enemy, Echohawk!" Mariah cried, her heart pounding, her wrists paining her where he so unmercifully gripped them. "It is I, No-din, Echo-hawk. I . . . I . . . was not shooting at you. I shot and killed a wolf that was stalking you. It was rabid, Echohawk! Rabid!"

"No-din?" Echohawk gasped, releasing her wrists. "You fired the weapon? You say that you fired upon a wolf?"

"*Ay-uh*, yes," Mariah said, her voice drawn. "I came to . . . to watch you practice. You did not know that I was here." She paused, her pulse racing at the nearness of him. That she was with him at all made her heart hammer almost out of control. Never had his lips been so close! She could even feel the heat of his breath upon her face, warming her insides into something deliciously magical.

"Nor did you know that the wolf was there," she quickly added. "Had I not been here, Echohawk, you would even now be the victim of the wolf's rabid bites."

Echohawk could not find the words to explain his feelings at this moment. He was torn between anger at her for not honoring his wish to be alone in his disgrace, not being able to fire a weapon at a target accurately, and gratefulness that she had cared enough to defend him, even though, had she missed the wolf, it could have turned on her and torn her to shreds.

And he was stunned at her ability to kill the wolf in the face of danger. He was used to men rescuing women—not women rescuing men. Although his wife had been a woman of gentleness and sweetness, he had always admired a woman who possessed grit. A woman of fire!

No matter, perhaps, if her skin was white. . . .

"No-din, I am forever in your debt," Echohawk said softly, yet not venturing to rise away from her. His heart was pounding as though someone was within his chest beating a drum. This woman with the sweet voice, and gentle, caring heart, and skin that was as soft as all snows in the winter, had been slowly capturing his heart as she had sat at his bedside. And the feeling was no less now that she was here, her body captured beneath his, at his mercy.

He became annoyed and frustrated, so wanting to see the face of this woman, and knowing that he could not.

Would he ever be able to? he agonized to himself.

Was he blinded for life?

Yet wasn't it best that he couldn't see her face?

He reminded himself that No-din was white, born into this world of those who were the Chippewa's natural enemies.

"You owe me nothing, Echohawk, for what I have just done for you," she murmured, guilt plaguing her again, for if he only knew the truth, he would see that it was she who was forever in *his* debt. Oh, but she did owe him so much!

"No-din," Echohawk said, sliding away from her and helping her to her feet. "Woman of the wind. Such a beautiful name." He reached a hand to her face, sending waves of desire crashing through Mariah. His fingers moved gently over her features. "You feel as though you are as beautiful as your name. Your features are delicate. Your lips are as soft as a rose petal . . ."

Echohawk could not deny to himself that he was intoxicated by Mariah. She had proved that she was indeed a friend, perhaps even more. He drew her into his arms and with trembling lips kissed her heatedly.

Mariah was taken off-guard by the suddenness of the kiss, momentarily stealing her breath away. But having wanted this for so long, and soon overcome by a sweet, unbearable desire, she twined her arms around his neck and returned the kiss with a passion that she had never known was locked inside her.

And when his hand crept between them and moved down to curve over her breast through her buckskin dress, she was shocked at the intensity of her feelings. It was as though something was melting at the pit of her stomach—such a wonderful, blissful melting that was spreading . . . spreading . . .

And then he was gone from her arms, his back to her, leaving Mariah shaken and staring at him.

"Let us return to my wigwam," Echohawk said thickly. "There we will share a night of talk and pleasure." He turned and faced her, reaching out to cup her chin in the palm of his hand. "Until today I have been cold to you. No matter that you had sat vigil at my side, I still saw you as no better than an enemy. But today that has all changed. You will see. We shall share much that I have been denying myself as well as you."

Mariah started to reply, but her words were stolen from her when he kissed her again, making the world spin around, frightening and thrilling her in the same breath and heartbeat. She so badly wanted to be free to love him, but she did not see how that ever could be possible. Not while the threat of unspoken truths lay heavy on her heart.

Echohawk reluctantly released her, a desire gnawing at him that he had denied himself since his wife's burial. Perhaps it was time to place the past in the past, yet something kept nagging at him not to be hasty in this thing that he was feeling for a woman—a white woman who, in truth, should be his enemy.

"No-din, for now you can be my eyes if you wish," Echohawk said, on his knees, trying to find his weapons. "Please help me gather my rifle, bow, and as many arrows as you can find."

Mariah was glad to be able to busy her hands and mind, yet could hardly take her eyes off this man—the man she would never be able to forget, much less deny herself loving.

She began gathering up arrows, feeling his presence behind her before she felt his hand on her wrist. Her body turned to liquid as he drew her up next to him again.

She moved into his embrace and snuggled next to him, glad that this time he was just wanting to hold her. She knew that if he kissed her again, while she was still recovering from the last kiss, she would be lost to him.

"You feel right in my arms," Echohawk said, stroking her back. "And how do I feel in yours, No-din?"

"Wonderful," Mariah sighed, closing her eyes, relishing the rapture she was feeling. "Oh, so wonderful."

"Then you do care?" Echohawk whispered, turning her face up to his. "You sat by my bed, tending to me, because you truly cared?"

"*Ay-uh*, because I truly cared," Mariah said softly, his eyes, though sightless, mesmerizing her.

"And why is this?" Echohawk asked, puzzling over it. "Why would you?"

"The moment I first saw you I knew that I must do whatever I could to make you get well again," she said.

"Then am I, a Chippewa brave, the first?" he asked. "How can that be? When I touch the features of your face, my fingers tell me that you are beautiful."

"I have never thought of myself as beautiful," Mariah murmured, casting her eyes downward, knowing that her father had tried to make her feel anything but pretty.

"Not only do my fingers tell me that you are," Echohawk said, again moving his fingers over her face, memorizing her every feature, "but also my heart."

Delicious shivers of desire enveloped Mariah, her body screaming for something further, yet not quite understanding what. She was breathlessly glad when he moved away from her.

"Gather up the weapons," he said huskily. "We can share more talk when we return to my wigwam."

Mariah smiled weakly at him, wondering where else their feelings would take them tonight. She was anxious to experience more of these sensations that had been awakened today, to fulfill this need that seemed to be torching her insides into a heated inferno.

11

So sweet the blush of bashfulness,
Even pity scarce can wish it less.

—BYRON

Feeling almost bashful now in Echohawk's presence,
her lips still tasting his kiss, Mariah munched away
at an apple, while Echohawk sat beside her eating
cranberries sweetened with maple sugar.

Since their arrival at his wigwam, there had been a
strained silence between them. Mariah's nervousness
stemmed from having never experienced feelings of
desire before.

Echohawk sucked the tart juices from the cranberries as he swirled them around inside his mouth, his
thoughts troubled. He had never wanted to have feelings for a white woman, had even thought it might be
impossible, until now.

No-din! He could not get her off his mind. She had
proved her loyalty to him in more ways than one.

And she had responded to his kiss as one does who
is in love.

Yet he kept reminding himself that *ay-uh*, yes, she
was white. He did not see how it could be wise to
reveal to her his true feelings for her.

"Tell me something about your family," Mariah
blurted out, surprised herself by the suddeness of her
decision to break the silence between them.

And to ask about his family, when she already knew
the fate of his father!

How could she?

But she did not know about a wife.

A mother.

Perhaps even children?

Echohawk turned to face Mariah, again regretting not being able to see her face—a face that he knew must be beautiful and alluring. He so badly wanted to run his fingers along her delicate features again, but thought better of it, remembering how touching her had affected him.

Until he could resolve within his heart and consciousness this fear of allowing himself to love a white woman, he must keep his feelings to himself.

"My family?" he said, scooting his birchbark dish aside. He stared into the fire, frustrated anew when he was able to make out only the color and shadows of the dancing flames. "I am the last. There was only one son born to my *gee-bah-bah* and *gee-mah-mah*. And there were no daughters."

"I, too, was an only child," Mariah said, dropping her apple core into the fire. "Throughout my childhood I was very lonely. There were no neighboring children for me to play with. My mother spent time with me until . . . until she died. But after that I was so very much alone."

"You had your father," Echohawk said, turning his eyes to her. "You seem to have spent much time with him. You shot the firearm today with the skills of a man."

"Yes, my father made sure I knew how to shoot weapons so that I could always defend myself in the Minnesota wilderness," Mariah said, realizing that she was sounding bitter, and unable not to. Whenever she thought of her father and how little love he had given her through the years, she could not help but be filled with a strange, painful longing. "He also taught me how to ride a horse. But that was the only sort of companionship I ever had with him. Other than that, I had to fend for myself."

"And that is why you fled from him?" Echohawk asked, forking an eyebrow. "Because you were *nah-szhee-kay-wee-zee*, lonely? Because you needed more than what he had given you?"

Mariah's eyes wavered as she looked slowly over at him. She swallowed hard, afraid that this conversation was leading to too much that was dangerous to reveal. "Yes," she murmured. "I had hoped to begin a new life. I had hoped that Colonel Snelling and his wife, Abigail, might help me in deciding how this could be done."

Echohawk wanted to tell Mariah that she did not need to ask Colonel Snelling and his wife for guidance. What she needed was a man—a man who would treat her like a princess.

And *he* was that man!

But still he could not find within himself the courage to tell her anything of the kind, especially since he still had so much to sort out within his own mind and life.

"And when will you travel on to Fort Snelling?" he said instead.

Mariah tensed at this question she did not have an answer to. In truth, she never wanted to go to Fort Snelling at all. She wanted to find a way to resolve all her differences with Echohawk and stay with him. Forever! She had found in him everything that she could ever desire in a man.

"I have asked Chief Silver Wing if I can stay awhile longer in his village," she said softly. "And since I have no one expecting me at Fort Snelling, I would like to stay even longer than first anticipated. Nee-kah has become a special friend, something that I have never had. And . . . and . . ."

"And in me you see a special friendship also?" Echohawk said, having to force himself not to reach out to touch her.

"*Ay-uh*, yes," she murmured, having to force herself not to reach out and touch him. She even had to fight back the urge to scoot over next to him, to snuggle. Within his arms she had found such a wonderful, blissful peace. They were so strong, so comforting. This was something quite new to her, since her father had never afforded her a single hug.

"You speak the Chippewa word 'yes' quite excellently," Echohawk said, chuckling. "Nee-kah has told me that you are an astute student."

"My father taught me many words of your people. I have enjoyed being taught more of your language and also your customs," Mariah said, picking up a stick, idly stirring the cold ashes at the sides of the fire. She glanced over at him. "Echohawk, I truly love everything about your people."

Echohawk's heart soared with this knowledge. If things could work out between them, she had already taken her first steps to becoming Chippewa!

And she had done this willingly.

"That is good," he said, trying to hold back any excitement that he feared might be there, evident in his voice.

"Echohawk, you did not tell me much about your family," Mariah said, her voice filled with caution, yet needing to know about his love life.

"There is no more to tell," he said, his jaw tightening. "There is no wife. There are no children. My mother died many winters ago after wasting away with some strange coughing disease. My father and I—we were quite alone in the world, except for the love and devotion of our people."

Mariah smiled sweetly over at him, her heart filled with delight to know that, indeed, there was no wife, yet finding the fact hard to understand, since he was so handsome, so virile.

But perhaps he had chosen to center his life around his people. And if so, would he truly ever find room for her inside his heart?

His kiss had revealed that he wanted her, yet since they had returned to his wigwam he had not made any more overtures toward her. There seemed to be something there, stopping him, just as there were her own doubts there, plaguing her and keeping her from boldly going to him.

Echohawk rose to his full height and went to the back of the wigwam, searching inside a buckskin bag. He circled his fingers around the flute that he had asked Nee-kah to lend him, then went back and sat down beside Mariah.

"I shall play some tunes for you in a way to repay you for your continued kindnesses to me," he said, positioning his fingers on two of the three holes of the flute.

"How lovely," Mariah said, drawing her legs up before her, circling her arms around them. As he played on the flute, she became mesmerized by the sweetness of the tunes. They were soft and lilting, reminding her of the birds in the trees outside her upstairs bedroom window that she had heard at daybreak in the early spring every year. She had lain there marveling at the sweet melodies, the same as she now marveled at the sounds that Echohawk was creating with the flute.

She sighed as she watched him, wondering how her father could have ever wanted to see him dead. Here was a man who was gentle and tenderhearted. Here was a man who stirred her into feelings that made her heart soar . . .

A commotion outside the wigwam drew Mariah's eyes to the entrance flap, then back to Echohawk as he laid the flute aside and rose to see what was causing the interference.

Mariah rose quickly to her feet and followed him from the wigwam, her eyes widening when she discovered a beautiful horse that had apparently wandered into the village, now standing there as though it belonged.

Echohawk walked over to the horse, his heart pounding, and began running his hands over its withers. He then offered the palm of his hand to the horse for nuzzling.

When the horse did as Echohawk bade, lovingly nuzzling his hand, neighing gently, Echohawk's lips lifted into a quavering, thankful smile. "It *is* Ish-sko-day, Blaze, my horse," he said, placing an arm around the horse's neck, hugging it. "He is not dead and he has found his way back to me. No-din, do you see? Blaze has searched until he found me!"

"I would say that is a miracle," Mariah said, smiling at the man and horse. "I didn't know that animals could be this devoted."

She watched the reunion of "friends," silently recalling how the horses had become so frightened by the gunfire during the raid on Echohawk's people. She could see even now, in her mind's eye, how they had feverishly broken through their protective fence and scattered in all directions. That his horse had found him again, under these circumstances, *could* be no less than a miracle.

"A man is nothing without a devoted horse," Echohawk said, now smoothing his hand across Blaze's rust-colored mane. "Now that I have mine back again, the burdens of that fateful day are lessened inside my heart."

Mariah stepped up next to Echohawk and ran her hands over Blaze's left flank, the fleshy part of the side between the ribs and the hip. She had never seen such an elegant horse. And he was so very, very muscled!

And strangely enough, the horse still wore a saddle—a cushion of leather stuffed with buffalo hair and ornamented with porcupine quills.

A rope around the underjaw seemed to be there to take the place of a bit.

"He is a magnificent horse, Echohawk," she murmured. "No wonder you are proud. I'm so glad that he found you."

"Blaze is of the wild breed of Mexican horses," he explained. "Long ago, during a raid on the Sioux to reclaim things stolen from my people, I stole this horse. The Sioux had stolen it themselves from some other tribe on lands far from the Minnesota wilderness."

"I would love to ride the horse," Mariah said, thrilling at the thought. "Perhaps one day soon . . . ?"

"Ay-uh," Echohawk said, taking Blaze's rope, leading him to the corral. "And it will be an interesting experience for you. I do not even need reins while on Blaze. He requires no guidance. He knows my every mood. He is even so accustomed to my silent commands that he could lead me into battle without any prompting from me. His skills are honed to such a degree that I can depend on him at all times, for anything."

"That he has found his way to you today is proof of that, it seems," Mariah said, opening the gate to the corral and stepping aside as Echohawk led Blaze in with the other grazing horses. She gazed warmly up at Echohawk, wishing that this closeness to him would never end. She could not deny that she felt as though she were becoming entwined within a golden web of magic, and she would not—*could* not—give this up. She would have to find a way to make him understand and forgive her role in the attack against his people.

Yet, while doing so, she had to find a way to protect her father. Although she had grown to loathe him, she did not want to see him harmed.

She did not want to see him die!

Yes, she concluded to herself, she had to find a way to resolve all of these differences, first in her heart, then with Echohawk.

She helped Echohawk feed and water Blaze, and then went back to Echohawk's wigwam with him, going only as far as the entrance flap. When he didn't invite her inside, Mariah felt awkward and a little embarrassed that she had actually wanted him to.

"I guess I'd best go," she said softly. "I don't want to wear out my welcome."

Her breath escaped her in a slight gasp when he placed a hand at the nape of her neck and drew her close to him. Scarcely breathing, she gazed with a building passion into his dark eyes. His lips so close, his hands so gentle—her insides tingled and her heart cried out to be kissed.

Disappointing her, he then turned away from her, his brow furrowed with a frown. "It is time to retire for the evening," he said smoothly. "Tomorrow there will be more shooting practice, but this time for live prey. I must rest for this outing."

Mariah placed a hand on his arm. "May I go with you this time?" she asked, her voice a soft pleading. "As I said before, Echohawk, I am quite skilled with firearms. I would enjoy the hunt. Please allow it?"

Echohawk turned back to her, his eyes squinting as once again he tried to see her features, dying a slow death inside when again he could not. "It is not a usual thing, a woman hunting with a man, but *ay-uh*, you can join me," he said, nodding. "It is good— these times with you."

"I am so glad you feel that way," Mariah said, her knees weakening as he ran his fingers along the curve of her chin and over her cheeks. "I so enjoy being with you also, Echohawk."

He drew away from her, his jaw tight. "You go now," he said softly. "You rest also. It has been a long day, has it not?"

"It has been a glorious day," Mariah said, daring to lean up and brush a quick kiss across his lips. Not giving him time to respond, she turned and ran from him toward her own wigwam, almost overwhelmed by her erratic heartbeats.

She looked to the darkened sky. "Lord, I love him," she cried to herself. "What am I to do? I love him!"

Putting his full weight on his cane, Victor Temple limped slowly up the stairs to the second story of his house, defeat slouching his shoulders even more than usual.

Weary from the long ride, during which he had not found Mariah, he felt empty, clean through to the core. Until now, when he was forced to believe that he might never see her again, he had not realized just how much he loved her.

And recalling how brusquely he had treated her at times, he did not expect her to have even an inkling of how he truly felt about her. The purpose first and foremost on his mind had been to protect her from becoming like her mother.

But now he felt that he had been wrong. He should have put more trust in her.

Yet hadn't he trusted his wife? When he had discovered her infidelities, all of his trust in mankind had been stolen away, it seemed.

Stopping at the head of the staircase, he turned solemn eyes to Mariah's bedroom. Tears filled his eyes, in regret at what he had forced on her before leaving for the Indian attack. He had given her just cause to hate him, that was for sure!

Limping to her bedroom, his fingers clasped hard to the handle of the cane, he stepped just inside the room and saw her long strands of hair lying across the foot of the bed in the dimming light of evening.

A sob grabbed at his chest as he went to the bed and picked up some of her hair and held it to his cheek. "Soft," he whispered. "So thick and soft. Why did I cut it? Why?"

Sitting down on the edge of the bed, he gathered up the rest of her hair and held it to his chest and slowly rocked back and forth, immersed in thoughts of the daughter that he had loved, perhaps too much. If he had not loved her so much, he would have been more generous with her. He would have given her more freedom.

"And now I will never be given the chance to make it up to her," he said, almost choking on another sob. "I'm sorry, Mariah. So damn sorry."

He stretched out on the bed and closed his eyes. "Mariah, Mariah . . ." he whispered until he fell asleep.

12

Thou waitest late, and com'st alone,
When woods are bare and birds are flown—
                                    —BRYANT

The day was brilliant with sunlight, the air sporting only a slight chilling breeze. It was a fun and carefree day for Mariah as she stood beside Echohawk in a meadow spotted with autumn wildflowers, amazed at his quickly improving skills with a rifle, though he was still half-blinded.

She watched breathlessly as he reloaded his rifle, then aimed and shot at the blue-winged teal, the most delicious of feathered creation, as the flock flew past. When one fluttered to the ground lifeless, the others changed directions in unison, yet did not immediately fly away from the danger of more gunfire. They continued to soar overhead, seemingly oblivious of the continuing threat.

Echohawk went to the fallen bird and picked it up by its legs and carried it to his horse, securing it with a rope behind the saddle. "As you see, though my eyesight has been impaired by the white man's blow to my head, I shall master again my weapons," he said as Mariah stepped up beside him. He gazed into the sky, seeing only smears where there were birds— the teals still enjoying sweeping high, then low across the wide stretches of the meadow.

"I am so proud for you," Mariah said, smiling at him, trying not to think about the man responsible for his dilemma.

Her father!

She knew that she would never wholly relax until somehow she settled things with Echohawk about her true identity.

"You see how the birds fly high, then low?" Echohawk said, resting the barrel of his rifle in the crook of his left arm. "It is best not to fire upon the blue-winged teal if they are flying high in the autumn of the year, for they are fattened on the wild rice of the river and would burst open upon falling."

"I went on hunts with my father often, but mostly for animals, not birds," Mariah said, feeling sad when she gazed at the beautiful thing hanging lifeless on Blaze. "It seems such a pity to kill something so . . . so . . . beautiful."

"When you live solely off the land and animals, as the Chippewa have for generation after generation, you close your eyes to the beauty of those birds and animals that you kill," Echohawk said softly. "You look at them as food for your people, for their survival."

He frowned down at Mariah. "Until the white people came to our land, there was not such a struggle each day to find food," he said, his words edged with bitterness. "Each day there are fewer animals, for the white trappers have used steel teeth in which to trap the innocent animals, and not only a few daily. They trap many each day. Soon, even, some of the animals that roam the lands today will become extinct. Then what of the red man?"

Mariah's lips parted, and she blanched, knowing exactly what he was referring to. Her father and his men moved through the forest daily, taking from it what they could, not stopping to think about the harm in killing in numbers.

They wanted the pelts, at any cost.

"Let us travel onward," Echohawk said, offering

Mariah a hand. "There is some place I would like to take you."

Mariah sighed shakily as she let him help her into the saddle, then relished the solid strength of his arm as he placed it around her waist and settled into the saddle behind her.

Echohawk took the reins and wheeled his steed around, soon galloping across the sun-drenched meadow. They rode for some time; then he drew rein at the foot of a butte.

"We must go the rest of the way on foot," Echohawk said, dismounting, then assisting Mariah from the saddle. "Up there," he said, pointing at the high butte overhead. "What I want to share with you is on the butte, a place of peace, where land and sky become as one."

"What is it you wish to show me?" Mariah asked, falling into step beside him as they started walking up a narrow path.

Echohawk did not respond. He moved determinedly upward. A strange sort of haunting in his eyes caused Mariah to become apprehensive. What had he so adamantly chosen to show her?

She quickly reminded herself that she had thus far placed much trust in him, as well as the rest of the Chippewa, and hoped that such trust was warranted.

Yet now, with their adventurous day marred by his indifferent, cold attitude, she was not sure if she had trusted too quickly!

What if he had discovered who she was and planned to shove her off the butte as payment for her treachery. It would be so simple for him to lead her into a trap!

But her worries were cast into the wind, so it seemed, when they reached the top of the butte. Where the land leveled off, her breath was stolen away when she saw the site of many graves lying side by side.

"My fallen people's resting places," Echohawk said, looking glumly down at the mounds of earth.

He walked to a grave marked with a cedar post and knelt beside it, placing a hand on the mound of earth. "This is my father's," he said, his voice breaking.

"If only it were I lying there instead of my beloved father!" Echohawk said, his voice filled with anguish. "My heart cries out for him both night and day. Never were a son and father so close! So devoted!"

As Mariah watched Echohawk despairing so deeply over the loss of his father, she covered her mouth with a hand, stifling a sob behind it, regret and guilt fusing within her. She wanted to shout to Echohawk that she was sorry for his distress. She had never had such a shared love with a father, and now that she knew such things could exist, she ached inside for having participated in destroying that special bonding.

Echohawk turned to Mariah and offered her a hand. "Come," he said. "Kneel beside me. Let my father feel your presence at my side. Because of you, his son is still alive."

His words, his trust in her, made Mariah's heart feel as though it were tearing in shreds. But she had to put on a good front, for even though he could not see the pained expression on her face, he would be able to hear it in her voice. This was not the time to reveal truths to him. Not while he was at his father's grave, where only peaceful thoughts should be shared.

But the fact that he was presenting her as someone special—as someone who had saved him—made her feel ashamed. His father was dead because of *her* father. What a travesty she was acting out! What a sham!

Having no choice but to do as he asked, no matter how torn she was inside over being there in the presence of so many that had died because of her dreadful father, Mariah knelt beside Echohawk, her eyes wavering, her heart pounding.

"I cannot see, but on my father's grave marker should be emblazoned his ranks and achievements," he said, reaching to run his fingers across the engraved letterings. "Also there should be three black emblems posted there, representing the three scalps that he had taken from evil white men."

He doubled his hand into a fist and his jaw tightened angrily. "Soon I will present my father with, not one more scalp, but four. The scalp of the evil white man who led the recent raid, that of the young lad who rode with the raiding party, the renegade Sioux White Wolf's scalp, and that of the man with yellow eyes who also took much from me, even my heart! Someday, somehow, these scalps will sway in the wind from my father's grave post!"

Mariah grabbed at her stomach, suddenly ill, Echohawk's warnings reaching clean to her soul, for although he did not know it, her scalp was one of those he sought!

"Please take me back to your village," she said, stumbling quickly to her feet. She grabbed at Echohawk as he rose quickly beside her. "I . . . I . . . feel ill, Echohawk. I . . . need to lie down."

Echohawk placed his hands to her shoulders and steadied her. "Speaking of scalps was unpleasant to you, and unwise of me for being so thoughtless," he said gently. "I am sorry, No-din. It was not my intention to upset you."

"Echohawk, it's not so much that," Mariah said, sighing deeply. "I . . . I just never thought *you* could be capable of . . . of scalping. That is a savage act. You are anything but savage!"

"Killing innocent Chippewa is savage!" he defended hotly.

He spun away from her and began working his way down the side of the hill. When Mariah saw his feet slip, endangering him, she ran to him and placed her hand at his elbow, which he just as quickly wrenched away from her.

"I did not mean to use the word 'savage,' " she tried to explain. "And I did not use it to describe you, Echohawk. Only the act of scalping."

"Many white people have referred to the Indians as savages," Echohawk grumbled, walking steadily downward. "They should look in mirrors more often! They then would see who is the true savage!"

Not to be dissuaded, and not wanting him to stay angry at her, Mariah grabbed his hand and would not give up her hold when he tried to jerk it free. She forced him to stop and turn to her. "I'm sorry, Echohawk," she murmured. "Please forgive me? I would never do anything to hurt you, nor your feelings. I . . . I think too much of you *and* your people. Have I not proved this to you by staying instead of going on to Fort Snelling?"

"I have wondered about this decision of yours," Echohawk said, his voice wary. "But of course you know that. I have voiced this aloud to you more than once."

"Then why question it again?" she murmured, her pulse racing as she moved closer to him. "Echohawk, we have found something special between us. Please, let's not do anything to jeopardize it."

Echohawk reached his free hand out to her, placing it on her cheek. "*Ay-uh*, there is something special between us," he said hoarsely. "But before it grows any stronger, there is much I must resolve inside my heart. Also, yourself. Do you not have much troubling you, that you have not spoken aloud to me? I have felt it in the hesitation of your voice at times."

Mariah's face paled at the thought that he might be astute enough to catch her moods, which she had tried to keep hidden from him.

"But of course I have been torn about many things of late," she murmured. "I am eighteen and I have just left home. Would you not feel somewhat unsettled were it you having made such a decision about family? I have separated myself from all of my life as I have known it. I have found a different way of life with your people—and am dismayed that I am able to accept it so easily, even enjoy it. So do you see why you felt my moods? Echohawk, I have not learned how to master them. Perhaps I never shall."

"Nor have I, mine," he said, in his mind's eye recalling so many things of his past that were gone from him forever. A wife. An unborn child. A mother. And now a father. "I, too, have things to resolve within my mind and heart. And I plan to resolve some of them today."

He stepped closer to Mariah and framed her face between his hands, drawing her lips to his. "You are so much what I desire in a woman," he whispered against her lips. "This is a part of what I must find answers to today. I will return you to my village and then I shall leave again, to go and commune, alone, with the Great Spirit. He will guide me. He knows everything about everything. He rules over all."

His mouth covered Mariah's lips with a gentle kiss that left her weak. She drew a ragged breath when he drew away from her, her eyes filled with a soft wonder.

Mariah sat in Nee-kah's wigwam, trying to be an alert student as Nee-kah explained about the storage of food, but her mind kept wandering to Echohawk. He had been gone into the depths of the forest for several hours. The sky had just darkened into night, wolves baying at the full moon an eerie sound in the distance.

"No-din, the meat from the deer should be sliced up thin and hung up to dry in the sun," Nee-kah said, quite aware that Mariah's mind was elsewhere. Her thoughts were clearly with Echohawk, who had left the village to commune with the Great Spirit. And from past experiences Nee-kah knew that Echohawk could be gone for days. As troubled as he was, he would not return until he had answers that would guide him into right decisions about his future, about his people, and about No-din.

"No-din, you break up the bones of the buffalo and boil them to get the grease out," she explained softly, trying to reclaim Mariah's attention. "You take the large intestine and stuff it with a long piece of meat, raw. This whole thing is then boiled and eaten . . . No-din!" Nee-kah said, moving to her knees in front of Mariah, blocking her view of the fire that she had been so intensely staring at. "Our teachings are over for the night. Let us join our people outside by the fire. They are singing. Do you not hear them? They are singing in an effort to lift the spirits of those who have recently lost so much." She took Mariah by the hand. "Come, No-din. Let us join them. You need some uplifting yourself."

Mariah jumped with a start, having been shaken from her reverie by Nee-kah's determination. "What did you say?" she said, her voice lilting, her eyes wide.

"Let us join those outside by the fire," Nee-kah urged, yanking on Mariah's hand as she rose to her feet. "We will sing. We will be happy!"

Mariah forced a smile and went outside with Nee-kah and sat down beside the fire with the rest of the people. Yet she could not help but glance toward the forest, wondering when Echohawk would be back, and what decisions he might have reached. She prayed to herself that the Great Spirit did not give him too many answers—those that could condemn her in his eyes.

In a place of serenity, where the stars and moon reached down through the umbrella of trees overhead,

Echohawk placed tobacco on a rock as a tribute to the Great Spirit, begging the Great Spirit for guidance.

"O Great Spirit, what am I to do?" Echohawk said in a troubled whisper, lifting his eyes to the heavens, yet seeing with his impaired eyesight only the blur of the moon smeared across the sky in strange, quivering whites. "Am I selfish for thinking of a woman now, at a time when my thoughts should only be on my people's sorrows? I cannot get her off my mind! She is there. Day and night. I have not wanted a woman as much since my beloved wife departed from this earth."

He swallowed hard, then continued voicing his concerns in agonizing whispers. "I do not want to love a white woman!" he despaired. "In my mind and heart I despise the white race for the cruelty inflicted on my people. Yet No-din is separate from those evil ones! She is not responsible for any of my hurts. Yet somehow I cannot erase from my mind that she is an enemy because her skin is the color of those who are!"

Not getting any signs from the heavens which could give him answers and direction, he spoke awhile longer, telling his sorrows to the rock and stars, then stretched out on the ground, fatigued.

"*Wah-bungh*, tomorrow," he whispered to himself. "I shall receive answers tomorrow. I shall stay and wait for those answers!"

A noise behind him drew him to his feet. He whirled around, wary. "Who is there?" he asked guardedly.

"It is I, Proud Thunder," one of his most valiant braves said. "Echohawk, it is with a sad heart that upon our return from the hunt we braves found our ravaged village. We have searched for you and our people. We have finally found you. Tell us, Echohawk. What of your father, my chief? Echohawk, the Great Spirit has led us to you. We are all here to listen."

Echohawk reached a hand out and found Proud Thunder's shoulder and clasped his hand to it. "*Ay-uh*, the Great Spirit led you to me tonight," he said softly, marveling over this miracle and feeling guilty that his thoughts only moments ago had been only on No-din!

Not of his people. His braves.

So often of late his thoughts strayed, and always to No-din!

"Proud Thunder," he said firmly, "let me tell you the extent of our people's sorrows."

13

My lips pressed themselves involuntarily to hers—a long, long kiss, burning intense—concentrating emotion, heart, soul, all the rays of life's light, into a single focus.

—BULWER-LYTTON

The wind pushed dark clouds across the autumn sky—a deer paused on a ridge close by. The river was like a clear mirror, the surface only slightly ruffled by the waves made by many canoes slicing through the water, all crewed by women.

Mariah was only half-aware of moving the paddle in and out of the water, Nee-kah sitting beside her in the canoe, doing the same, a woman kneeling at the stern, both paddling and steering the vessel. Mariah's thoughts were not on the chore at hand—the *manomin*, wild rice, that she would soon be helping the Chippewa women to harvest.

Mariah had spent a sleepless night, *still* worrying about Echohawk. And when she had discovered that he had not returned home at all through the night, her worries had increased twofold. She would never forget how defenseless he had been against the rabid wolf that she killed before it got close enough to attack him. Last night the wolves were howling in the distance incessantly. What if they had sniffed out Echohawk while he was absorbed in his meditating?

"Is it not beautiful here in the river, with the autumn foliage reflecting like bursts of sunshine in the water?" Nee-kah said, smiling over at Mariah. "Are you not glad that you came with me? Has it helped get your mind off Echohawk?''

Mariah smiled weakly at Nee-kah, pausing momentarily in her paddling. "It is beautiful here," she murmured. "But, no, it has not gotten my mind off Echohawk. I doubt if anything would." She then added quickly, "I do appreciate you asking me. You are ever so kind, always, to me. I'm not sure if I deserve such a friendship as yours."

"Your friendship is cherished by me, No-din," Nee-kah said, reaching over to place a hand on Mariah's shoulder. "Mine to you is enduring, *ah-pah-nay*, forever."

Mariah's eyes wavered and she looked away from Nee-kah, worrying again about Nee-kah's reaction when she would one day discover exactly who this "friend" was.

Then she looked slowly back over at Nee-kah. "Mine, also, to you is as enduring," she said, wishing their promises to each other could be true, as everlasting as they both wished.

But too soon so many things could change—especially such friendships.

Her paddle dipped smoothly into the water as they continued traveling upstream between tree-lined banks. The canoes were made with a birchbark box in the middle and used only for the wild-rice harvests, the flails lying in the bottom of the box.

A blue-gray kingfisher that lived along the river, nesting in the banks, swept from a high bank to Mariah's right and hovered above the river. Then he dived into the water, appearing a moment later with a fish struggling in his long black bill.

And then the wild rice came into view, the canoes moving steadily toward it.

"*Ee-nah-bin*, look!" Nee-kah said, her eyes beaming. "Have you ever seen such a sight, No-din? See how the wild rice grows so abundantly in the shallow waters of the river? The plants are so heavy with rice this year! And they are the tallest I have ever seen. They must stand twelve feet above the water."

"Rice is an important food of the Chippewa?" Mariah asked as they finally reached the rice, and along with the other canoes, began poling their vessel among the plants.

"*Ay-uh*, it is a staple food of the Chippewa," Nee-kah said. "It is eaten in a great variety of soups and broths, as a vegetable with fish or meat, boiled on its own, or mixed with maple sugar, or parched. It is a most delicious and versatile food."

Mariah was amazed at how simply the rice was harvested. The stalks of rice had been tied in bundles during the previous moon. The women had only to bend the rice-laden stalks inboard with their hooked flails, the curved ricing sticks pulling down the stalks so that the heads of the plants hung over the birchbark box in the center of the rice canoe. With a flat flail, Mariah followed Nee-kah's lead and beat the heads until the long needlelike grains spilled into the box.

Mariah was glad to have something productive to do, which, for the moment, did lighten the burden of her worries about Echohawk. She became absorbed in the process of the harvest, now paddling their rice-heavy canoe toward shore.

Once there, the women transferred the rice from their canoes with wooden buckets, then poured the rice into a deerskin-lined hole in the ground, six inches deep and two feet across. The rice was then flailed with curved sticks to loosen the husks. Winnowing was then done by pouring it from a bark tray in a breeze.

The rice was then placed on mats to dry in the sun. After drying for three days, it would be put into a large kettle to parch so that the tough hulls would split open. The women would then take turns tending the fire and stirring the grain so that it would parch evenly.

And again they rowed back to the stalks of rice, and the process was repeated. Even though there was a lot of work involved in collecting and preparing the rice, Mariah was enjoying her day, and for the moment was able to place Echohawk from her mind if not her heart.

In another part of the forest, Mariah was the center of Echohawk's thoughts. He had directed Proud Thunder and his other braves to Chief Silver Wing's village to rejoin their relatives. A blessed thing, Echohawk had thought upon seeing Proud Thunder, that the Great Spirit would send him in his time of meditation.

During his long vigil in the forest the previous night, he had recalled many things, yet resolved nothing within his troubled heart and mind. He was haunted by his father's words spoken to him over and over again this past year—that it was time for him to take a wife so that a son might be born to him to help ensure the future of his people.

Deep inside himself, where his desires were formed, he knew that he had chosen a woman for a wife—Nodin. She was the only woman who stirred his passion since the passing of his lovely wife.

"But why must she be white!" he whispered remorsefully through his clenched teeth, his hands circled into tight fists at his sides.

Then he rose slowly from his prostrate position and took a small buckskin pouch from the waist of his fringed breeches. Again he sprinkled tobacco from it onto a rock, an offering to the Great Spirit. He moved to a kneeling position and raised his eyes to the heavens, his heart pounding. The sighing of pines came to him as the rustle of eagle wings, to help carry his cries to loftier heights. The whispering winds told his tale to the clouds. He then uttered the cry of his soul to the Great Spirit.

"Great Spirit, you who guide my every thought and action, hear my pleas!" he cried. "My heart is heavy! Give me strength and courage to guide my people in this, their time of sorrow. Give me a sign that will free me of my bitterness and allow me to love the white woman without resentment." He bowed his head humbly. "O Great Spirit, I thank you for sending Proud Thunder and my braves to me, but I have waited all night long for another sign. Is there not to be one? Must I return to my dwelling without your blessing? Do I not deserve such a blessing? Am I wrong to ask for so many things?"

A close-by noise, coming from the direction of the river, drew Echohawk's head up. His pulse raced and hope rose within him that the Great Spirit had heard, and had finally sent him a vision.

Suddenly, through the haze of his impaired eyesight, he could see movement ahead. Trembling, he was awe-struck by what was now within the sphere of his vision. He watched breathlessly as his eyes suddenly cleared to see a snow-white doe followed by a fawn of the same color.

Surely it was a vision, for he could not believe that this was truly happening. One moment he was alone, and the next moment he was in the presence of a mystical phenomenon. The creatures were there so suddenly, it seemed that they had come out of the water!

Echohawk slowly pushed himself up to a standing position and stood rooted to the ground, never taking his eyes off the beautiful animals. And he, who had never feared the face of man, was trembling like an aspen with terror!

The animals, seemingly unaware of Echohawk's presence, advanced slowly toward him, and passed so near that he might have touched them with his hand. But transfixed by wonder, he did not attempt it.

Slowly he turned and watched them as they ascended the bank, soon losing sight of them.

When he recovered from the shock, he stretched out his arms after them. "Do not leave me!" he cried. "Come back. Let me see you again!"

Having regained the use of his limbs, he rushed up the bank, but did not see them.

Humbled by the experience, he fell to his knees and smiled as he looked to the heavens. "O Great Spirit, thank you!" he cried, appreciating the meaning of what he had just witnessed. The white doe was No-din and the fawn must represent their future child. He was suddenly feeling great rushes of happiness throughout him. He was free to love—to love No-din!

And freed, also, was he of the other burdens of his heart. He knew now that he had the power—the courage—required of him to guide his people.

And he also knew that in time his eyesight would be restored. Had not the Great Spirit allowed him his eyesight long enough to witness the vision? In due time, when the Great Spirit deemed it necessary, his eyesight would return—to be his forever!

An anxiousness suddenly seized him. "No-din," he whispered, his heart soaring. "I must go to No-din. There is so much to say to her that I was not free to say before."

His chin held high, feeling blessed and guided by the Great Spirit's power, Echohawk began running in the direction of the village. "No-din will be mine!" he shouted, so that everything would share in his happiness.

He shouted to the wind . . .

the sky . . .

the trees . . .

the forest animals!

*   *   *

Her arms and back aching from her long day of rice harvesting, Mariah slipped a clean buckskin dress over her head. It fell below her calves, belted at the waist with a beaded thong, a fringe at each end. She pulled on fringed knee-high moccasins resplendent with colorful beads. Her skin smelled clean, like the river, after her bath. Her hair was dripping and fragrant from Nee-kah's precious soap.

After getting dressed, she began running the comb that Nee-kah had lent her through her hair, wincing when again she was reminded of its dreaded length.

Laying the comb aside and picking up a mirror, Mariah began practicing with bloodroot juice, dabbing it onto her cheeks to redden them. She needed to do something to keep her worries about Echohawk from worsening. It was now midday, and still he had not returned. She did not want to envision him lying injured or dead in the midst of the forest. She would not allow herself to conjure up any more fears. He was a man of the forest. He was in tune with all nature, and he knew how to survive within it.

A noise at the entrance flap drew Mariah's eyes away from her reflection in the mirror. An anxious blush, even more red than the juice of the bloodroot that she had dotted onto her cheeks, rose from her neck upward when she found Echohawk standing in the doorway smiling down at her.

"You have returned," Mariah said, moving shakily to her feet. She so badly wanted to go to him and lunge into his arms. She wanted to cling to him and never let him go again. Never had she been as relieved as now. He was alive! He was well! And he was smiling at her as though all of the burdens that had been troubling him had been lifted!

"*Mah-bee-szhon*, come," Echohawk said, going to her to take her hands. "Come with me to my lodge. There I will say many things to you. There you will have decisions to make and answers to give."

Caught up in an ecstasy that just being with him evoked, and speechless, Mariah nodded and went with him to his wigwam. There she found the air scented sweetly with the perfume of sweet grasses that burned in the embers of his lodge fire. There she found many beautiful pelts strewn around the fire. There she found platters piled high with all sorts of delicacies.

There she found herself being held within Echohawk's arms as he led her down beside the fire, seeing a blissful peace within his eyes and in the soft smile that he gave her.

"We shall eat, and then, No-din, there is so much I wish to say to you," Echohawk said, releasing her from his embrace.

They sat down side by side and ate in silence. Mariah's heart raced excitedly, so happy that Echohawk had reached some sort of peace with his Great Spirit, and within himself. She only wished that she could come to the same sort of peace within her own self!

Her God seemed to be taking longer to answer her prayers than Echohawk's.

After they had eaten their fill, Echohawk lifted Mariah onto his lap, facing him, his hands holding her there at her waist. "No-din, the Great Spirit gave me a vision while in the forest," he said eagerly. "This vision gave me hope—and courage. No-din, I have come away from that vision with a happy heart, one that I wish to share with you for a lifetime."

Mariah's pulse raced and her head was reeling with the wonder of the moment, anxious to hear what else he had to say, yet also fearing it. Because of who she truly was, she had many things to fear in Echohawk's presence.

"No-din, woman of the wind, be the 'flower of my wigwam,' " he said softly.

Mariah was taken aback, not having expected this. She was stunned speechless. Marriage? That was what he meant?

She knew that marriage to him was an impossible dream. She had lied to him about her true identity.

For so many reasons she could not accept a proposal that her very soul cried out for!

"No-din, I love you," Echohawk said, easing her down onto the pelts, moving over her. "My heart has been so lonely. No-din, fill it and my life with your sweetness!"

Before she could refuse Echohawk's proposal, Mariah felt the press of his lips against hers, so warm and soft, yet demanding, for a moment frightening her.

She welcomed the lethargic feeling of floating and swooning, glad to forget everything but Echohawk and the way he made her realize that she was very much a woman.

How fiercely Echohawk wanted Mariah, yet he fought against going too quickly with her. She was inexperienced, hardly more than a girl in her innocence. It was easy to tell that she had not yet been with a man intimately, and he wanted the experience to be something that she looked back on with pleasure. He wanted her to desire such a union as badly as he. Their future would be filled with such moments, for he would not take no for an answer when he again asked her to marry him!

As he continued to kiss her, he slowly snaked his hand up inside her dress and cupped her at the juncture of her thighs, where he could feel the pulsing at the center of her passion. As he began to caress her there, he felt her body tremble, her gasp of alarm against his lips.

But he did not pull his hand away. He continued to gently stroke her, smiling to himself when he felt her relaxing, and now emitting soft sighs against his lips.

Mariah was becoming weak, her senses dazzled by his skills of awakening her to passion. His hand was where no other man's hands had been before, and his other hand—it was lifting her dress slowly up away from her.

She knew that she should stop this madness that had begun between them.

But she was too full of strange, wondrous desire to turn her back on whatever else lay ahead these next wondrous moments with the man that she loved with all of her heart.

Echohawk leaned slightly away from Mariah in order that he could remove her dress. Then, once it was tossed aside and his hands were smoothing over her body, feeling her slim, graceful loveliness with his fingers, excitement leapt inside him. His hands moved to her breasts and cupped them, his lips lowering to a nipple, nipping it with his teeth.

Mariah's heart raced, her breathing almost out of control. She was acutely aware of Echohawk's body as he now knelt beside her and discarded all his clothes. Mariah's face heated with a blush as she gazed down at his manhood, the first time she'd ever seen this part of a man's anatomy.

Something strange happened at the pit of her stomach, as though someone had set a fire within her, when he began to move his hand in slow strokes over his hardness. It was such a seductive sight, and Mariah realized by the way his jaw tightened and the muscles of his legs corded that what he was doing must be intensely pleasurable.

Boldly, as though he silently beckoned her to, Mariah crept to her knees and replaced his hand with hers, her heart leaping when she felt the heat of his velvety shaft, and how it seemed to jump with a life of its own as she began moving her hand on him.

She watched his expression as his eyes closed and his teeth gritted together, wondering how anything could feel that wonderful, to cause such a reaction.

Suddenly Echohawk placed his hands to her shoulders. "*Mee-eewh*, enough," he said huskily. "It is time to share our pleasure. It is time to fit our bodies together as one."

Little stabs of warmth ran through Mariah and she felt a strange new sensation rise in her as his hands slid down her back, cupping her buttocks. Slowly Echohawk laid her down on the soft pelts, then moved over her.

Trembling, she let him part her thighs and caress the damp valley, unleashing waves of weakness in her lower limbs. She was acutely aware of his pulsating hardness, now pressed against her thigh.

And when he parted her legs with a knee and she felt the first burning touch of his hardness at the center of her passion, she melted into him.

As he slowly entered her, coaxing sweetness from her, Echohawk kissed her again, his mouth forcing her lips apart, his tongue hungrily surging between her teeth.

She felt herself surrendering to him, thrilling to every nuance of his lovemaking. She did not even cry out with the shock of his first plunge inside her. A sharp pain only momentarily robbed her senses of pleasure, before she once again abandoned herself to a wild ecstasy.

Sculpturing himself to her moist body, Echohawk anchored Mariah fiercely still as he pressed endlessly deeper inside her. She knew that the passion he offered her would overshadow any pain that she had felt.

His hands moved down her body and cupped her buttocks, relishing their softness, then urged her hips into his, glad when she strained toward him on her own. Their naked bodies sucked at each other, flesh against flesh in a gentle rhythm.

A surge of ecstasy welled within Mariah, filling her, spilling over and drenching her with a sweet warmth. She twined her arms around Echohawk's neck and clung to him as she felt a great shudder in his loins and then experienced an incredible splash of bliss, crying out at her fulfillment as his body subsided exhaustedly into hers.

Stunned by the intensity of the feelings that had overwhelmed her, like white heat traveling through her veins, she lay within Echohawk's arms, breathing raggedly. She was afraid that if either of them moved, she would discover that all of this had been of her imagination, caused by her longing to be free to love this handsome Chippewa.

But when he stirred and slid away from her, yet only as far as to lie at her side, one of his hands still on one of her breasts as though it belonged there, she realized that, yes, all of this had been real enough.

"My *ee-quay*, woman," Echohawk said, his voice deep and husky. He drew Mariah next to him, her breasts pressed into his hard chest. He ran his fingers along her delicate facial features. "I cannot see you clearly with my eyes, but you are quite real in my arms and in my heart, and that is enough. Stay with me. Warm my bed every night until we are old and gray. Say that you will gladly be my wife."

Mariah was glad that he could not see her at this moment. He would see the tears of regret in her eyes—regret for loving him so much and knowing that he should despise her!

Echohawk saw her hesitation in agreeing to be his wife. He was troubled by this, yet thought that perhaps she was carrying some pain in her heart at leaving her people forever. He would no longer press her for answers. He smiled to himself, knowing there was truly no need. Yet he would give her time to go and release her own sorrows within the peaceful confines of the forest and then reveal to her that she had already become his wife, through their own private ceremony tonight.

They lay within each other's arms, for the moment blissfully content. For Mariah it had been proved tonight that no matter to what lengths her father had gone to turn her into a man, she was every inch a woman. And she owed it all to Echohawk. He had brought out the true woman in her.

And, oh, how she adored him!

14

Sweet were his kisses on my balmy lips. As are the breezes breath'd among the groves of ripening spices in the height of day.

—BEHN

Feeling herself to be part of a magical dream when she awoke in Echohawk's arms at daybreak, Mariah now rode beside him away from his village. She liked the feel of the horse beneath her again. There was something about being on a horse, the feeling of freedom that it evoked, as though for that time, at least, she was the master of her own destiny.

Her gaze went to Echohawk, who rode tall in his saddle, the fringes of his buckskin shirt and breeches lifting gently in the breeze. He had said that their plans for today were special, but had yet to tell her exactly what these plans were.

But she had noticed that he had taken a much different weapon with him today. A spear. It seemed their hunt today would be for much larger prey than birds.

She turned her eyes away from Echohawk, just enjoying the moment, knowing that he would tell her in good time what their destination was. It was just enough for her that she was with him today, and at his very own request. He had told her that he trusted her and her skills with a horse and a gun, even though he was still amazed and puzzled by her prowess.

His confidence in her made her proud. Without knowing it, her father had taught her skills that had saved the very Indian he had wanted dead!

Mariah smiled to herself, feeling anything but manly today. In her mind's eye she replayed last night's love scene, thrilling inside as though she were experiencing it again at this very moment.

And the dress she wore today was so utterly feminine—fashioned from snow-white doeskin, designed intricately with many-colored beads, and fitting her snugly, like a glove. She knew that Echohawk would be quite taken by her appearance if he could see clearly.

She glanced at him again, saddened by his impaired eyesight.

Not wanting to get into feelings again that could ruin this special time with Echohawk, though, she wrenched her eyes away from him and blocked out sad thoughts by observing the wonders of this land that lay on all sides of her. The sunrise mist was hanging above the river and somber hills. Small cottonwood trees of sleepy sparrows swayed in the morning wind. Two pheasants stood in a forest of sunflowers. And broad, jagged leaves of wild grape vines rustled in the wind.

Mariah's lips parted with a gasp when not so far in the distance she saw what looked like hundreds of antelope and buffalo grazing amidst patches of red, brown, and gold wildflowers called *gaillardias*, or Indian blankets.

She was not at all surprised when Echohawk reached a hand toward her as he drew his horse to a shuddering halt.

"Do my eyes see correctly?" he said, squinting as he peered ahead. "Is that not many buffalo grazing in that valley?"

"Buffalo *and* antelope," Mariah said, still marveling at the sight. "Echohawk, I have never seen so many!"

"That is good," Echohawk said, smiling confidently. He motioned with a hand. "*Mah-bee-szhon*, come. We shall settle ourselves close by until one strays from the others. Then I will show you the worth of my spear!"

"It is the buffalo you are hunting today?" Mariah said, paling. "Now I understand why you didn't tell me earlier. You were afraid that I would try to talk you out of coming."

"And was I right to think that?" Echohawk said, his lips tugging into a smile. "Would you have tried to convince me not to come?"

"You know that I would have," Mariah said, sighing heavily. "And it is not too late to turn back. Echohawk, I have never killed a buffalo before. And what if your eyes aren't as accurate as when hunting birds? When missed, birds do not attack. Buffalo do! Certainly I am not the right person to back you up, should you miss."

"But the size of the prey counts for something valuable," Echohawk tried to convince her. "Do you not recall my accuracy at shooting the blue-winged teal? It was small, Mariah, and we carried one home for a hearty meal, did we not? The buffalo is a large beast, making a wide target. When I aim, I will not miss. I am very practiced, so much so that even if I closed my eyes, I would still find the animal with my spear. I have brought home many buffalo for my people in my lifetime. They find many uses of the buffalo, not only for food but also for household utensils."

"But, Echohawk, still—"

Echohawk interrupted. "Now, follow me. We shall position ourselves down by the river. When a buffalo strays and comes to the river for a drink of water, we shall be there, ready."

Knowing that it was no use to try to argue further with him, Mariah followed his lead and led her horse to a narrow steep-sided ravine and dismounted. She and Echohawk secured their horses behind a boulder and thick stands of forsythia bushes, then hurried away from them and crouched down in the ravine, scarcely visible.

In the ravine, the river only footsteps away behind her, Mariah thought the air seemed colder, sending chills across her flesh. She hugged herself, her teeth chattering, then was warmed clear through when Echohawk placed his arm around her and drew her next to him. In his other hand he held the spear.

"*Wi-yee-bah*, soon," he whispered. "We will have company soon. There is always a curious one that strays from the others. If not for a drink of water, just to see if the grass is greener. The mild weather has kept the buffalo close by, and made hunting easier."

"How will you know it is near if we cannot see it?" Mariah worried aloud. "I . . . I do not feel at all comfortable about this, Echohawk."

"No-din, have faith in your man," Echohawk said, placing a finger beneath her chin, drawing her face around. He squinted in concentration, again so wishing that he could see her features! In his mind's eye he had already seen her—but that was not enough.

Mariah searched his face, then looked intensely into his dark eyes, seeing their blankness as he peered down at her. "I'm sorry," she murmured. "I don't mean to make you feel less a man by my complaining. Forgive me, Echohawk."

His mouth covering her lips in a passionately hot kiss was his response. His kiss was all-consuming, setting fires within her that threatened to rob her of her senses. She was relieved when he drew away from her, her heart having almost gone out of control with its erratic beatings.

"No more talk now," he said, smoothing a hand across her cheek. "We must be quiet or the buffalo will go elsewhere."

Mariah nodded and knelt beside him, quietly admiring Echohawk, both for his determination to prove his worth even with half his eyesight, and because he was so magnificent to look at, especially now, as he moved not a muscle, only the wind lifting a lock of his hair, then laying it back along his neck. His jaw was tight with determination, his eyes two points of fire.

Oh, how she loved him . . . how she admired him!

Echohawk scarcely breathed, taut with the excitement of the hunt. He felt as though he were the lord of the universe. For him the universe was this landscape today, the vast Minnesota wilderness. For him there was no possibility of existence elsewhere.

Suddenly there was a blowing—a rumble of breath deeper than the wind.

Wide-eyed, her heart racing, Mariah looked quickly over at Echohawk, then looked up when overhead some of the hard clay of the bank broke off and some clods rolled down, scarcely missing hers and Echohawk's heads.

"It is here," Echohawk said in a whisper that resembled a hiss. "Do not move, No-din. Just watch."

Then there appeared on the skyline just to the left of where Mariah and Echohawk crouched, watching . . . waiting, the massive head of a long-horned buffalo, then the hump, then the whole beast, huge and black against the sky, standing to a height of seven feet at the hump, with horns that extended six feet across the shaggy crown. For a moment it was poised there; then it lumbered obliquely down the bank to the river.

Still Echohawk and Mariah did not move, though the huge beast was now only a few steps upwind. There was no sign of what was about to happen.

The buffalo meandered.

Mariah and Echohawk were frozen in anticipation.

Then, as Mariah watched in awe, the scene exploded.

In one and the same instant Echohawk sprang to his feet and bolted forward, his arm cocked, the spear held high.

The huge animal lunged in panic, bellowing. Its

whole weight was thrown violently into the bank, its hooves churning and chipping earth into the air. Its eyes were wide, wild, and white.

Its awful frenzy caused it to become mired and helpless in its fear.

Echohawk hurled the spear with his whole strength, and the point was driven into the deep, vital flesh of the buffalo. The animal, in its agony, staggered, crashed down, and was dead.

Mariah was stunned silent by the performance, her eyes glued to the animal. Then her awe of Echohawk was so intense, she moved her gaze to him and her insides quavered with a giddy warmth as he stood over the animal, his chest swelled with pride.

Scrambling to her feet, Mariah went to Echohawk and lunged into his arms. "You did it," she murmured. "Oh, Echohawk, you did it!"

Then she leaned away from him. "I knew that you could," she said, smiling sheepishly up at him.

Echohawk chuckled, knowing that her pretense was too obvious, but understanding why. He drew her close and gave her a soft kiss. "Before taking the largest portion of the beast back to my people, we shall have a private feast ourselves," he said. "But we must wait until the other buffalo wander onward."

Mariah gazed down at the buffalo, then back up at Echohawk. "My, but he is huge," she murmured.

"A beast his size feeds many mouths on a cold winter's day in our village," he said reverently. "But these animals are dwindling in number because of the arrival of the white man. It is impossible to understand how they can kill without reason."

Mariah sighed heavily, again reminded of her father's slaughters. Then she forced such thoughts aside. She was no longer a part of that life. She gazed up at Echohawk, wishing that she had half his courage. If she did, she would confess so many things to him.

*   *   *

Mariah sat comfortably on thick pelts beneath the lean-to that Echohawk had fashioned from a blanket, having attached it to the side of a cliff that he and Mariah had found close to the ravine. He had collected a dozen large stones and laid them across the spot chosen for a fire. The fire had been quickly kindled, and over it cooked a steak cut from the yet-warm flank of the animal he had slain. While the steak was cooking, Echohawk cuddled Mariah close to his side and sang to her.

Enraptured, warmed not only by the campfire but also by Echohawk's strong arms around her, Mariah listened as he sang of the bluebells and wild heliotrope; of clematis, called "ghost's lariat"; of the horned lark, called "little black breast"; and of the chinook winds that he called "good old man." It was a time of wondrous peace and love, undisturbed by thoughts that could destroy the moment.

And when his last song had faded into the wind, Echohawk eased Mariah downward, her back pressing into the soft pelts spread beneath her. "My woman, let us stay here forever," Echohawk said huskily, smoothing Mariah's dress down from her shoulders, freeing her breasts. "Let us pretend there are no worries, no sorrows, no tomorrows filled with bitternesses. There is only us, only today. . . ."

Mariah sucked in a breath of wild ecstasy and closed her eyes when he leaned over her and covered the nipple of one of her breasts with his mouth. He teased its taut peak, his hands roaming her body.

Her head spinning, she was hardly aware of how they became fully unclothed, or that the day was dimming, a heavy chill slicing the air. All she knew was that Echohawk had moved his body over hers, molding himself perfectly to the curved hollow of her hips.

She stifled a sob against his muscled shoulder as he pressed gently into her, then began moving within her in a steady rhythm. She lifted her hips to him, taking him even more deeply, and rocked and swayed with him.

She locked her arms around his neck and drew his mouth to her lips. She trembled with passion as he kissed her long and hard, his hands at her breasts, softly kneading them.

Caught in passion's embrace, she felt her entire body responding to his loving her, all of her senses yearning for the promise he offered.

Gasps echoed like thunder throughout her when again his lips moved to her breast, sucking on her nipple until it throbbed. She thrust her pelvis toward him, now only half-aware of making whimpering sounds, and then a surge of ecstasy raged and washed over her, and she again reached the ultimate experience a man and a woman can share.

Echohawk had been holding his own pleasure back, wanting it to linger until he was near the bursting point. He smiled to himself when he sensed her intense pleasure, glad that again he had been able to pull her into that realm of sheer bliss.

Breathing hard, his loins on fire, Echohawk withdrew from inside Mariah and moved into another position that she was not familiar with, yet she knew that she had much to learn—and Echohawk seemed to be the most masterful teacher!

Echohawk stretched out on his back and very gently moved Mariah so that her face was only a heartbeat away from his throbbing hardness. Placing his hands on each side of her face, he urged her lips to him.

Mariah recoiled at the thought of what he seemed to want her to do, yet, loving him so much, and wanting to please, she thrust her tongue out and briefly touched his satin hardness. When she heard his groan of pleasure and watched his expression become passion consumed, she resumed with what she knew had to be perhaps the keenest pleasure of all.

She loved him in that fashion, the strange ritual

even firing her own desires again. When he placed his hands at her waist and lifted her atop him in a sitting position, so that his hardness was soon inside her, again she was introduced to a new way of loving him.

Riding him, moving with him as he drove himself up into her, she held her head back and closed her eyes, feeling a strange soft melting energy warming her insides. The air became heavy with the inevitability of release, each stroke within her promising more.

And then they both seemed unable to hold the energy back any longer, and in unison trembled and shook against the other.

When the bliss slowly ebbed away, Mariah crept from atop Echohawk and snuggled next to him, feeling so wonderfully at peace, deliciously in tune with the man she loved.

When her fears of his discovering who she was began edging back inside her consciousness, she quickly cast them aside.

For now she must forget the doom that awaited her when she revealed all truths to the man she loved. For now there was a pure and beautiful understanding between them.

She glanced over at the meat cooking over the fire, ravenous, yet not wanting to give up whatever time she had with Echohawk to eat. Food meant absolutely nothing to her in his presence.

Echohawk was all that she desired.

Only him.

15

We both can speak of one love,
Which time can never change.

—JEFFERYS

Sunrise splashed a golden sheen through the smoke-hole overhead. After a breakfast of pemmican cakes made of meat, dried and pounded to a pulp, and wild honey, Mariah was filled with joy as she left the wigwam with Echohawk to again accompany him to target practice. Just as they reached their tethered horses, a familiar voice behind them drew them around.

"There is something I would like to show you," Chief Silver Wing said, a mischievous sparkle in his dark eyes. He beckoned with a hand. "Come with me to my dwelling."

Having grown comfortable even with this noble, powerful chief, Mariah walked in a casual gait beside Echohawk as they went with Chief Silver Wing to his wigwam.

"*Nah-mah-dah-bee-yen*, sit," Silver Wing said, gesturing toward mats that lay thickly cushioned beside the lodge fire. Snug in a finely dressed buffalo robe that befitted his high position, he sat down opposite them, reaching for something inside a small buckskin pouch that hung from the waistband of his fringed breeches. "I may have something of interest for you, Echohawk."

Mariah eased down onto a mat beside Echohawk. Then her whole world as she had come to know it these last wonderful days was threatened as she saw what Chief Silver Wing took from the pouch. She paled and stifled a gasp as she looked warily at a gold-framed pair of eyeglasses that he was handing toward Echohawk.

Eyeglasses! she fretted to herself.

Her whole body became enveloped in cold shivers as she guardedly watched Echohawk take the eye-glasses, seemingly puzzled by them as his fingers fa-miliarized themselves with their shape and with the glass that lay within the frames.

"What is this?" he asked, still fingering the object. "It feels like what I have seen white people wear. I believe they are called eyeglasses?"

"*Ay-uh*, I offer you eyeglasses that I took from a white pony soldier many, many snows ago while de-fending my village against their attack, long before the time of our mutual friend Colonel Snelling," Chief Silver Wing said, nodding. "I have heard that eye-glasses are supposed to better one's vision. You have a problem with your eyesight. Perhaps they will bene-fit you somehow—make you see. Wear them. See if there is magic in them."

Mariah felt light-headed in her fear as Echohawk continued feeling the glasses, his fingers smoothing slowly over the lenses.

This was the moment she had dreaded most.

His discovery of who she truly was!

If the eyeglasses should work for Echohawk, he would soon see to whom he had given his heart and his total trust.

With that thought, an ill feeling swept through Ma-riah. One moment she had been so happy her heart had sung, and the next, her whole world was tumbling around her.

Mariah's heart pounded and she held her breath as she watched Echohawk slowly slip the eyeglasses onto the bridge of his nose.

Echohawk squinted as he looked through the lenses;

then the blood pumped maddeningly through his veins in his excitement over discovering that, *ay-uh*, he *could* see! The eyeglasses *were* made of some sort of white-man magic! He could make out everything distinctly!

A slow smile tugged at his lips as he turned to Mariah, having so badly wanted to see the woman of his heart.

But what he discovered made everything within him turn cold. The person he was seeing—the woman he had poured out his feelings to—had a face familiar to him before his eyesight had been impaired.

Then his gaze moved jerkily to her hair, seeing its length.

His gaze went to her dress as he now recalled that on that dreadful day of many deaths she had not been dressed as a woman, but as a lad!

Ay-uh, that had been the difference the day of the attack. She had been disguised as a boy, to fool him and his people. It had been the dark ash spread on her face to strengthen her disguise that day that had kept him from seeing the truth!

Mariah went limp with fear, having seen within his eyes the horror of recognizing who she truly was. She was frozen to the spot, afraid to move, then flinched when he suddenly leaned close to the lodge fire and gathered up a handful of ashes.

A scream froze in her throat when he turned suddenly to her, roughly spreading the ash all over her face. She wanted to die when he let out a ear-splitting wail when he fell back away from her and gazed at her knowingly.

"It was you!" he cried, rising shakily to his feet. "Without the ash on your face, I . . . I . . . was not sure. But now I am! You are not at all who you pretend! You betrayed me! You betrayed all Chippewa! You are an enemy!"

"What is this?" Chief Silver Wing asked, dismayed

at Echohawk's performance. "Why did you color her face with ash? Why do you call her an enemy? She has proved her loyalty to our people! She cannot be an enemy!"

Mariah finally found the courage to scramble to her feet. She reached a hand out to Echohawk, tears streaming from her eyes. "Please listen," she cried. "Oh, Echohawk, that day . . . it was not of my doing!"

But she could not find it within herself to go further with her confession. She could not openly blame her father. Thus far, Echohawk did not know his identity. She would not be the one to point an accusing finger at him. If she did, she would never be able to live with herself.

So she stopped short of what she knew had to be said to make Echohawk believe her. She could not involve her father, even though he did not warrant such protection from her. But to convince Echohawk that she had been forced to join the raid, a full explanation was needed.

"Echohawk, I love you," she murmured, still reaching a hand out to him. "I love your people. And Neekah! I feel toward her as though she were my sister— a sister that I never had! Please don't turn me away! Please . . . ?"

Her words did not seem to reach him at all. He stood solemnly still, coldly staring at her, his arms folded across his chest. She took a shaky step away from him; the hatred in his eyes appalled her very soul.

Sobbing, her heart breaking, having lost everything now because of her evil, marauding father, Mariah turned and fled from the lodge.

Blinded with tears, she ignored Nee-kah as she cried out for her to stop. She ignored the Chippewa people as they stopped and stared at her in her frenzied flight toward her horse. She was only vaguely aware of mounting the horse and grabbing the reins, for everything within her seemed dead and empty.

She had lost Echohawk!

Not only that, she had lost her very reason for living.

Wheeling the horse around, Mariah sank her heels into his flanks and sharply snapped the reins. Tears splashed into the wind as she rode through the village, dogs yapping at her heels, children shouting at her in dismay.

She was glad when she reached the outskirts of the village, able then to send her steed into a hard gallop across the flower-dotted meadow. She was no longer numb inside. With the realization of what had truly been lost to her came the hurt. She could hardly bear these feelings ravaging her insides, racking her body with torture. Everything within her now ached, especially her heart.

When she heard a horse fast approaching from behind, she did not take the time to glance over her shoulder to see who it was. She feared many things. Now that her true identity had been revealed, Echohawk could have sent a brave to stop her escape. Soon she could be tied to a stake in the center of the village, a victim of their vengeance—of intense hatred.

But she would not save herself if it meant seeing her father take her place at the stake—or at the end of a hangman's noose—for his crimes against the Chippewa. He deserved punishment, certainly, but she would not be the one to cause it.

Never!

Terror leapt through her when out of the corner of her eye she discovered the horse pulling alongside of her. Her eyes widened and she screamed when an arm reached out and grabbed her, dragging her onto the other horse. She was held firmly on the lap of her pursuer as he drew his reins tautly, stopping his horse.

Her pulse racing, weak with fear, Mariah turned

and gazed frantically up at the man whose muscled arm held her prisoner. Her heart bled when she saw that it was Echohawk, the hate in his eyes no less as he looked down at her through the eyeglasses.

She swallowed hard, then tried to squirm free of her bondage, surprised when he let go of her and she tumbled away from him and the horse to the ground. Dazed, she lay there for a moment; then, when a shadow fell over her, her eyes turned slowly upward, and she recoiled against the ground when she found Echohawk staring flatly down at her, his arms folded stiffly across his chest.

"Echohawk, I didn't mean you any harm," she cried. "I did not purposely betray you. What I did, caring for you and learning your ways, was done from the goodness of my heart. The day of the raid, I—"

Her words were stolen from her when he leaned over and grabbed her by the arms and jerked her to her feet. Echohawk now seemed to be a giant as he towered over her in his anger. When he began shaking her, her senses seemed to scramble, yet she heard what he shouted at her, understanding well the word he spoke in his Chippewa tongue.

"*Gay-gay-nah-wi-shkee*, liar," Echohawk gritted out between clenched teeth, his eyes two points of fire as he continued shaking her. "Liar! You . . . are . . . a . . . liar!"

He released her so suddenly she again fell to the ground.

Devastated by his accusation and tormented by his final good-bye, she watched him mount Blaze and ride away, tears flowing fiercely from her eyes.

And when he was gone from her eyesight, she buried her face in her hands, her crying having turned to low sobs.

She had lost everything.

Everything!

And all because of a father who did not deserve

such loyalty as she had afforded him, she thought bitterly to herself.

Slowly regaining her feet, Fort Snelling again her destination, she went to her horse and pulled herself into the saddle. As she urged him to a gallop, a sudden pain gripped her insides. There would be no more moments in Echohawk's arms, ever again.

The day had been grueling, Mariah having stopped only to get an occasional drink and to wash from her face the dreaded ash that had condemned her in Echohawk's eyes.

It was now growing dusk and she thankfully saw Fort Snelling in the distance, relieved to finally be there after her long and arduous ride.

The fort, an outpost of western civilization in a vast wilderness, was the northernmost fort in the Mississippi Valley, having been established to prevent the British from carrying on the fur trade in America, as well as to keep peace between the Sioux and Chippewa Indians.

Mariah had studied Fort Snelling's history extensively in newspaper articles and from fliers and brochures that were passed around to the settlements to entice everyone to go to Fort Snelling for supplies. She knew that the fort was manned by up to two dozen officers, most of whom were graduates of West Point—and as many as three hundred enlisted men.

A four-story commissary carved into the perpendicular riverbank stored four years of provisions and supplies.

The fort's strategic position and stone construction made it virtually impregnable. It had never been attacked by Indians, Colonel Snelling being a friend to them, one and all. Fort Snelling, built to Snelling's personal specifications, was *the* finest fort in the American West.

As Mariah drew closer, she admired the fort once

again, as she had in the past. Walled and turreted, it might just have been a castle on the Rhine! There was a small settlement along the river, protected by the fort set on the cliff above it. Even now, although it was nearly dark, merchants crowded in to supply the fort and the needs of the heavy flow of river travelers. The air was humming with the sound of saws and hammers. On the outskirts of the cleared ground men and women were returning in their carts from the forest, where they had been cutting wood.

Mariah caught sight of several canoes traveling the river, manned by copper Indian braves, passing silently on their way to the fort. Waves of melancholia swept through her, she missed Echohawk so much. She then looked toward the banks of the river, where many braves were unloading the hides they had brought along to trade.

Not wanting to be swallowed by grief again over her loss of Echohawk, Mariah sent her horse into a faster gallop, soon entering the wide gate that led into the courtyard of the fort. Colonel Snelling had served as both architect and construction superintendent during the building of the fort. Mariah gazed around her, familiarizing herself with the setting again. The buildings and a diamond-shaped parade ground were enclosed within the twelve-foot stone wall. A round tower had been erected to command the western approach to the post from the prairies. Cannon had been placed on platforms atop the roof, and muskets could be fired from loopholes placed strategically in the lower walls.

The hexagonal tower had five of its six sides extending beyond the wall. A powder magazine and guardhouse flanked the round towers, and wooden pickets bristled atop the wall adjacent to the round tower.

In one sweep of her eyes she saw well houses, sutler's store, two barracks, several shops, and many other buildings. Then she became aware of something else—many eyes following her as she rode on toward Colonel Snelling's house, set at the east end of the parade ground.

Mariah held her chin high, ignoring the gaping soldiers on all sides of her, eyeing her, surely confused by her Indian attire.

As she had previously done, she silently admired the colonel's house, thinking that he lived like a country squire in a house whose every inch resembled a European manor house. The square cut-stone house, Georgian in spirit, but with a flamboyant Flemish gable, was known to be a jewel of the frontier.

When she drew rein in front of the house, she had to reach deeply within herself for the courage to go and knock on the door, begging assistance from those who clearly disliked her father for one reason or another. Although they had treated her with much kindness in the past, she feared that when faced with her request for assistance, they would surely see her as a nuisance in their lives.

But they were her only hope, now that she had lost Echohawk's trust and love.

Dispirited, she slowly dismounted her horse.

16

Tell me not in mournful numbers,
Life is but an empty dream!

—LONGFELLOW

Mariah's knees trembled as she stood at the massive
front door of the Snelling residence, awaiting a response after having knocked. A new fear suddenly
grabbed her. What if Colonel Snelling had found out
about her father's raid, and her part in it? What if her
father was even now imprisoned at the fort?

She would be walking right into a trap!

Not understanding why she hadn't thought of this
possibility before, Mariah turned and began to leave,
thinking that she would have to pick up the pieces of
her life elsewhere, but stopped dead in her tracks
when the door opened and a voice as soft as a summer
breeze spoke behind her.

"Yes? What can I do for you?" Abigail Snelling
said, stepping out onto the narrow porch.

Her heart pounding, Mariah turned slowly around
and faced Abigail, her eyes wavering, fearing a quick
tongue-lashing once Mrs. Snelling recognized her.

She squared her shoulders and straightened her
back, awaiting Abigail's reaction to seeing her there,
herself admiring the colonel's wife, as she had so often
in the past.

A woman with the reputation of performing grandly
as the commandant's lady, Abigail was beautiful, with
raven-haired tresses that nearly reached the ground.
She was slender, with an oval face and dancing green

eyes with thick lashes shadowing them. She was surely
the most lovely of all the women today at the fort, in
her highly gathered pale blue velveteen dress with lace
at the high collar and at the cuffs of its long sleeves.

Mariah knew firsthand that Abigail was full of compassion, for not long ago, upon discovering that Mariah was a girl instead of a boy, dressed in boy's garb
because of a paranoid father, she had scolded Mariah's father almost unmercifully.

"Mariah?" Abigail gasped, paling as she took in
Mariah's cropped hair. Her hands crept slowly to it,
her lips parted in horror. "Your beautiful hair! Lord,
Mariah, did your father . . . ?"

Mariah sighed heavily, relieved that her hair appeared to be the only cause for Abigail's alarm—not
that Mariah was a fugitive at her door, asking for
asylum!

"Yes, my father cut my hair," she said softly. "I
begged him not to. But . . . but . . . he wouldn't listen." Her bottom lip stiffened angrily. "Mrs. Snelling,
nothing anyone said or did could dissuade my father
from wanting to turn me into a man! My being a
woman threatened him, somehow." She lowered her
eyes. "He . . . he even burned all of mine and mother's dresses. All that was left of my wardrobe were
the horrid men's breeches and shirts."

Abigail smoothed her fingers over Mariah's hair,
tsk-tsking, then placed a gentle hand to Mariah's
cheek as she roved her eyes over her attire. "You are
not wearing men's clothing today," she murmured,
then gazed into Mariah's sad eyes. "Mariah, you are
wearing a buckskin dress—one quite beautifully decorated with beads. Did your father approve of the dress?
Perhaps he got it in a trade with the Chippewa?"

Then Abigail placed a hand to her mouth, gasping
behind it, her eyes wide with remembrance. "Mariah,
I am just now recalling a visit from your father!" she

cried. "Seeing your hair cropped short momentarily stole my memory from me."

"My father was here?" Mariah asked, panic filling her. "When? What did he say?"

"Mariah, he was here at Fort Snelling searching for you," Abigail said, cocking an eyebrow quizzically. "He did not give any details as to why. After he found out that no one had seen you at the fort, he rode away without any further explanation."

Tears filled Mariah's eyes; she understood her father's desperation to find her, since he had ruled her life for so long. Upon discovering her gone, he had lost control. Victor Temple was not a man who ever let anyone dictate to him about anything. His alarm was surely not caused by having possibly lost her, but because she had openly defied him by leaving!

Down deep inside himself, he had to know that she had not been abducted . . . that she had left on her own initiative.

"Oh, my dear, you are about to cry," Abigail said softly, placing an arm around Mariah's waist. "Do come inside my home. Let me get you a lemonade to make you feel better. And then we will talk this out."

"Thank you," Mariah said, wiping a tear from her cheek as she was whisked into the parlor.

"I shall return shortly," Abigail said, guiding Mariah to an upholstered chair that sat before a roaring fire in the massive stone fireplace. "Sit yourself down, dear. You do look in need of my special refreshment."

For a moment, while awaiting Abigail's return, Mariah was catapulted into another world as she gazed with awe around her at the handsomely furnished sitting parlor. The room, furnished in the best European traditions, bespoke the Snellings' polished tastes. Lemon-colored satin draperies hung at the windows, a thick Brussels carpet covered the floor, and cherrywood tables with marble tops were positioned around the room. A tall clock ticked away time close by; a Latin dictionary stood open on a stand beside a massive oak desk.

Something quite grand grabbed Mariah's full attention.

A piano, she marveled to herself as her eyes locked on the ebony-wood upright that sat against the far wall, a candelabrum, its half-dozen candles burning, gracing its top.

She had only seen pictures of pianos in books, and heard them described by her mother, but never had they seemed as beautiful as the one in the Snelling parlor.

She was tempted to go to it and run her fingers across the keys, but thought better of it when Abigail entered the room carrying a tray which held a pitcher of lemonade and two glasses.

"You *will* feel much better after drinking my lemonade," Abigail said, setting the tray on a table beside Mariah. She enthusiastically poured two glasses of lemonade, handing one to Mariah. She then sat down opposite Mariah, sipping from her own glass.

Although she was hungrier than she was thirsty, both Mariah's tongue and her lips seemed parched from the grueling ride.

And she had never tasted lemonade before!

As the sweet liquid rolled down her throat, her eyes widened. Never in her life had she experienced anything to compare with this delicious drink!

She drank it in fast gulps, then blushed with embarrassment as she took the glass from her lips and noticed Abigail watching her with a soft smile.

"Let me pour you another," Abigail said, her eyes dancing. She gazed over at her box of imported chocolates, then picked it up and handed it toward Mariah. "And please have a chocolate."

Mariah's lips parted in another slight gasp as she peered into the box of cream-filled chocolates. She had never seen any such delicacy, much less eaten one.

Her fingers trembled as she reached for the one closest to her. "Why, thank you," she said, plucking the chocolate from the others.

When she placed it between her lips, her taste buds danced wildly, the chocolate even more wonderfully delicious than the lemonade! She chewed it slowly, savoring the taste as long as possible.

"And now more lemonade?" Abigail asked, setting aside the chocolates and again lifting the pitcher.

"Yes, please," Mariah said, smiling bashfully at Abigail. "It is a most delicious refreshment."

Not wanting to make a complete fool of herself, Mariah sipped the second glass for a moment, then set it aside. She wanted to get the preliminaries behind her. Rarely had she asked for anything from anyone. Most times she had been forced to just take what had been handed her, which, in truth, had been the bare essentials of everyday life.

"Now, tell me, Mariah, why are you here?" Abigail said, reaching over to pat Mariah's arm. "I will do anything I can to help you."

Apprehensive, not wanting to reveal any truths to Abigail that might jeopardize her father's welfare, Mariah paused for a moment, then looked wide-eyed at her hostess. "You know how forceful and determined my father is," she blurted out. "Mrs. Snelling, I . . ."

Abigail reached a hand to Mariah's cheek, within her eyes a deep compassion. "Please call me Abigail," she murmured. "Being called Mrs. Snelling makes me feel like a stodgy old maid." She laughed softly. "And, my dear, you know that I am anything but an old maid. I have seven beautiful children."

Mariah laughed nervously, yet felt wonderfully breezy inside to know that Abigail Snelling would do anything to make a troubled person more comfortable in her presence.

"That is very sweet of you," Mariah said softly. "I would love to call you by your first name."

Abigail sat back more comfortably in her chair. "Now, continue with your story," she said, relaxing her hands on her lap. "I am a very good listener." She leaned forward and smiled at Mariah. "And I have instructed my servants to keep the children out of the parlor. I feel you do not need their noise while confiding in me."

Mariah smiled back at her, amazed at the woman's consideration. She then sighed deeply and scooted back in the chair, feeling strangely at home. "I just could not stay with my father any longer," she said, gazing into the fire, for an instant reflecting on the shared moments beside the fires in Echohawk's wigwam.

"You made this decision after your father cut your hair?" Abigail said, wrenching Mariah's thoughts back to the present.

Mariah looked quickly over at Abigail, troubled that she could get lost in thoughts of Echohawk so easily, when, in truth, she knew that she had to forget him.

"Yes, I left after father cut my hair," Mariah said in a half-truth. She could never tell Abigail that what had really made her flee her father's wrath was the attack on the innocent Chippewa. At that point she had lost all respect for her father.

"Where did you go?" Abigail asked, her gaze settling on the buckskin dress. She looked back into Mariah's eyes again. "Just before your father left the fort, after discovering you weren't here, he said something about going to check the Indian villages for you." She paused, then added, "Mariah, have you been with a band of Chippewa? Is that where you got the dress?"

"Yes, I've been with the Chippewa," Mariah said, lowering her eyes, troubled as to how much more she could reveal to Abigail. Not only was telling too much dangerous, it would also be painful to talk about

Echohawk, Chief Silver Wing, and Nee-kah's kindnesses to her.

At this very moment, back at their village, she was looked on as a traitor!

"How did you happen to be there?" Abigail persisted softly. "You . . . you weren't forced, were you? The Chippewa in these parts are known for their civility."

"And what is said about them is true," Mariah said, tears burning at the corners of her eyes as, in her mind's eye, she reenacted that fateful day when so many Chippewa had died.

She blinked nervously to erase the painful thoughts, then continued to explain.

"Upon my flight from my father, my horse threw me," she said. "Nee-kah, the wife of Chief Silver Wing, found me. She took me to their village, where I was treated graciously."

A sudden thought seized Mariah, making her heart skip a beat. Echohawk could come to Fort Snelling and inform Colonel Snelling of her role in the raid. Abigail could soon lose all belief in her!

Even by now Echohawk could have put two and two together and realized that it was her father who had led the raid. Even now he could be at her father's trading post. Her father could even now be dead!

"Mariah?" Abigail said, reaching to take one of Mariah's hands in hers. "Dear, you have suddenly grown so pale. Is there something more you wish to tell me? I am here to listen. Pour it all out to me. You will feel much better for it."

"There is nothing more," Mariah said softly. "I left the Chippewa village to come to you to see if you might assist me in some way, to help me decide what I must do with the rest of my life."

She swallowed hard, knowing that she would have to live from day to day, praying that Echohawk would not hate her so much that he would come for her and demand that she be handed over to him to be taken back to his people and punished for being a traitor.

Her only hope was that Echohawk would search deeply within his heart and realize that she could never have done anything purposely against his people. Time was her ally, it seemed, for if Echohawk would weigh it all inside his heart, he would know that she was sincere in all of her thoughts and deeds.

"Perhaps I could work here at Fort Snelling in some capacity," Mariah suddenly stated. "I can ride a horse and handle firearms as well as any man . . ."

Abigail gasped with horror at Mariah's suggestion. "My dear, I want to hear no more talk of you mingling with the men, behaving as one of them," she scolded. "You cannot be serious in wanting to continue living the life your father forced upon you—a life that you have rightly fled from."

She rose from her chair and took Mariah's hands and drew her up before her. She gently embraced Mariah, then held her at arm's length. "My dear, it would delight me to help you," she murmured. "But in a much different way than you have suggested. You have suffered enough since your mother's death. I demand that you stay with me and Josiah. It would delight us both to have you in our home."

She reached to Mariah's cheeks and smiled into her eyes. "I will take you to my wardrobe and let you choose the laciest dress that you can find," she said softly. "Now, do you understand that you are to forget that foolishness about shooting firearms and riding horses? There are better things to do with one's time!"

Mariah gasped and her eyes widened. "You would do that for me? You would take me in? You . . . you would even give me dresses to wear?" she said, her cheeks coloring with an anxious blush. "I can't expect you to be that generous, Abigail. How would I ever repay you?"

"My dear, I must confess I am guilty of being a

trifle selfish in my offerings to you," Abigail said, smiling mischievously at Mariah. "You see, I am always searching for excuses to give parties or hold a grand ball. The fort is a most boring place for married women of breeding! My dear, your entrance into our lives is the perfect reason to give a ball. It will be in your honor. I will show you off to all of the other women at the fort!"

Mariah was stunned at first by this confession, then recognized that Abigail was teasing, and she laughed softly along with her. "But, Abigail, I shall shock all of the women with the length of my hair," she teased back, finding this sudden lighthearted mood so refreshing.

Then again she was catapulted back to the real world when she thought of her father. "My father," she said warily. "He will find out. He will come for me."

"Don't fret, dear," Abigail said, firming her chin. "My Josiah will handle him."

"Did I hear my name being spoken in a conversation between two lovely ladies?" Colonel Snelling said, making a grand entrance into the parlor.

Mariah turned with a start, then smiled at Colonel Snelling as he walked stoutly into the room, resplendent in his blue uniform. He was a red-haired man, slightly balding, and she had never considered him handsome, but he had a smile that could melt one's heart.

Yet she knew his reputation of being a tough-minded disciplinarian with the men under his command. A veteran of the War of 1812, he was a practical man who valued highly his soldiers' capacity for work, but neglected the drills and smart appearances usually associated with army life. The rank and file of his garrison were kept busy maintaining or constructing buildings and roads.

Colonel Snelling promptly recognized Mariah, and

his steps faltered; his smile faded when he caught sight of her hair. He went and stood tall over her, running his long lean fingers through her hair.

"And whom do we blame for this?" he grumbled, his brow furrowed with a deep frown. "But of course, I need not ask. It was your father. He went this far to make you take on the appearance of a man. Damn him. He ought to be horsewhipped!"

"Darling, Mariah has left home," Abigail said, going to Josiah's side, locking an arm through his. "I have asked her to stay with us. Of course I knew that you would approve."

Josiah smiled again, and placed a hand to Mariah's cheek. "Our home is yours for as long as you like," he said softly.

So grateful was she, tears pooled in Mariah's eyes. Yet she did not know how long even this happiness would last.

Always there were truths that would condemn her! Always!

"Thank you so much," she murmured. "Thank you both."

Josiah slipped a silver snuffbox from his inner jacket pocket and opened it. Pinching out a quantity of the brown powder, he dusted it onto the back of his left wrist and drew it up with two quick sniffs.

"Let Abigail take you to the guest room," he said, slipping the snuffbox back into his pocket. "We'll talk more at length later."

Abigail took Mariah by the hand and ushered her from the room, down a corridor, up a short flight of stairs, down another corridor, and into a room that took her breath away at first sight. She stepped delicately across the threshold, eyeing the great Tudor oak four-poster bed hung with crewelwork curtains; bamboo-backed chairs that had surely come from China; and hand-painted Chinese wallpaper which lent a gay touch to the room. The lone window was draped with a sheer lacy curtain, drawing Mariah to it, to touch its softness.

"It is all so beautiful," she said, sighing deeply, yet her thoughts were quickly drawn elsewhere when she looked through the window upon a half-moon shining in the sky, encircled by a great hazy ring. She could not help but wonder if Echohawk was looking at the same moon, perhaps thinking of her.

She looked away from the moon, and then at the sky, which was unsullied by a single cloud. She gazed at the stars, wishing upon them that Echohawk could find it in his heart to recall their moments together. The sincerity of her feelings for him, if he would only let himself believe it, would prove that she was not capable of anything but love for him and for his people.

She felt an arm circle her waist and was drawn back to the present. "My dear, in time you will forget all the ugliness of your past," Abigail assured her. "I will see to it, Mariah. I promise."

Sobbing, Mariah turned to Abigail and eased into her embrace, allowing herself to pretend, at least at that moment, that it was her mother who was comforting her.

17

Who is the happy warrior?
Who is he that every man in arms should wish
to be?

—WORDSWORTH

Two Weeks Later

The air was crisp and cool. The autumn leaves had
fluttered from the trees to the ground, making a bed
of color beneath them. Kneeling beside his father's
grave, Echohawk bowed his face into his hands. "*Gee-bah-bah*," he whispered mournfully. "It has now been
fourteen Chippewa sunrises and still I have not been
able to place No-din from my mind. How can I continue to love a woman who is my enemy? How?"

Except for the wind whispering in the soft breeze
of late afternoon, there was a keen silence.

And then the silence was broken by a sound behind
Echohawk. He turned with a start and found himself
looking up at Chief Silver Wing.

"My son, I have come to urge you to join the other
braves around the council fire in my lodge," Chief
Silver Wing said, placing a solid hand on Echohawk's
shoulder. "We have much to discuss and you have an
integral role in the discussions. Place all sadnesses
from your heart and mingle with your people again.
You cannot forget that you are now the leader of your
band of Chippewa. They await your guidance. Come.
Show them that you are now ready to be their leader
again."

Echohawk moved slowly to his feet and faced Chief
Silver Wing with a humility never known to him be-

fore. In the elder chief's presence, more and more, Echohawk felt as though he were once again with his father. This chief's heart and thoughts were so much in tune with his father's, it seemed—even including his paternal love of Echohawk.

"It is *because* of my people that I come to commune with my father," Echohawk finally said. "In life he guided me. Even though he is dead, I still await a vision that he might send to me from the Land of the Hereafter."

He swallowed hard, then clasped a hand onto Chief Silver Wing's shoulder. "But I now see that it was not necessary to escape here each day, when it was you I could share my thoughts and sorrows with," he said humbly. "And my *gee-bah-bah* would want that."

"*Ay-uh*, my son, he would want that," Chief Silver Wing said thickly. He stepped closer to Echohawk, then quickly embraced him. "Soon you will see the good in life again, if you will just allow it to happen. The woman. You will soon forget the woman."

Echohawk relished the embrace, closing his eyes, pretending it was his father, then stiffened at the mention of "the woman," knowing to whom Chief Silver Wing was referring.

No-din.

She was on everyone's mind, it seemed.

He eased from the elder chief's embrace and peered at him through the eyeglasses, finding that each day his eyes were improving, if only slightly. "You have asked me more than once why I called her an enemy," he said, his voice drawn. "Until now I could not tell you. The anger within my heart was too intense to allow me to discuss her."

"But now?" Chief Silver Wing said, folding his arms casually across his chest. "You wish to speak of her now?"

"*Ay-uh*, perhaps it is best," Echohawk said, turning to view the darkening meadow below him, aching inside when he recalled having ridden across that meadow beside No-din, a happiness so keen within him he had feared it would not be everlasting.

And he had been right.

Nothing seemed everlasting for the Chippewa.

Nothing!

"Then I will listen," Chief Silver Wing said, taking a noble stance beside Echohawk.

"I trusted No-din," Echohawk gritted out through clenched teeth. "I even gave her my total love!" He turned to Chief Silver Wing. "Though she is not aware of it, I took her as my wife after she shared a feast with me and then my bed. And all along, this woman that I poured out my heart and soul to was guilty of having been a part of the raid that took my father from me!"

Chief Silver Wing's eyes wavered. "She was a part of the raid?" he gasped.

"You saw how I spread ash on her face?" Echohawk said, his voice softening. "It was to see if her face then matched that of the young lad who rode with those who ravaged our village."

"And it did?" Chief Silver Wing said, his voice showing the strain of the discovery. He kneaded his chin and looked down at the meadow, nodding. "It makes sense now—the way she was dressed when she arrived at our village. And the short hair . . ."

"The way she was dressed when she arrived?" Echohawk said, turning questioning eyes to the chief. "How was she dressed?"

"No one told you?" Chief Silver Wing asked, dropping his hands to his sides.

"I am sure that no one saw the need," Echohawk said, his eyes narrowing. "Tell me. How was she dressed?"

"In clothes worn by white men," Chief Silver Wing said solemnly, now recalling Nee-kah's dismay when she discovered that No-din was a girl, not a boy. For a moment he could see the humor in it again and chuckled low. "When Nee-kah saw her undressed and saw her breasts, it gave her quite a fright. She thought it was a boy with breasts."

Then his brow furrowed into a deep frown. "You say she was among those who raided your village?" he grumbled.

"*Ay-uh*," Echohawk grumbled back.

"Let us talk more before returning to the council meeting," Chief Silver Wing said, needing to sort out within his mind the reasoning behind all of No-din's actions. He had seen her as something special—a woman with pride and spirit—but never a woman of deceit!

"Come with me to lower ground," Chief Silver Wing encouraged him. "Let me get my pipe from my horse. We will share a smoke while we discuss the 'Woman of the Wind.'"

Echohawk nodded and left the butte with Chief Silver Wing. When they reached their grazing horses, Echohawk took a blanket from his saddlebag and spread it on the ground, then watched Chief Silver Wing's slow, dignified gait as he went to his horse and removed his long-stemmed pipe from a buckskin bag. It was evident to Echohawk that Silver Wing had planned this meeting of minds between just the two of them, for he had brought not only a pipe but also a pouch of tobacco and a case fashioned from stone that carried within its confines a heated coal with which to light the pipe.

When Chief Silver Wing returned, they sat down in a cross-legged fashion on the blanket. Echohawk sat stiffly, his hands resting on his knees, watching the elder chief prepare the pipe for smoking. In the red stone bowl he sprinkled tobacco from its pouch—a mixture of tobacco and the dried and pulverized inner bark of the red willow, known to the Indians as *kinikinik*, which was like incense, pleasing to the spirits, a vehicle of prayer. The peace pipe was the tribe's "secret to Happiness," its "good heart maker."

Echohawk silently admired the chief's pipe. Its stem was three feet long, ornamented with eagle feathers, porcupine quills, and human hair that had been dyed red, which had been taken from the scalp of the enemy of the Chippewa—the Sioux.

Echohawk's thoughts would stay away from Mariah for only a short time, and then, as now, his mind would drift back to her and he would be torn with remorse and anger all over again for having loved a woman who proved to be his enemy. He did not see how talking about her to the elder chief was going to change any of his feelings. For fourteen Chippewa sunrises he had awakened with thoughts of her, torn between loving and hating her. How could it be any different today, tomorrow, and many moons to come?

No-din had stolen his heart, and almost his sanity!

Chief Silver Wing could see how Echohawk drifted between being troubled and being angry, then back again to being troubled. He plucked a twig from the ground and leaned it against the hot coal, soon setting it aflame.

Straightening his back, he placed the flame to his tobacco and puffed eagerly on the stem until the smell of burning tobacco filled the evening air with a pleasant sweetness.

He puffed from the pipe for many more breaths, staring at the night shadows thickening in the forest beyond, then pointed the stem north, east, south, and west, and finally toward the sky and the earth, and blew smoke in these six directions.

Silver Wing then passed the pipe on to Echohawk, and he in turn puffed, then pointed it in the same six directions Chief Silver Wing had, before passing it back to the elder chief.

Silver Wing rested the bowl of his pipe on his knee and remained silent a moment longer, not giving way to something so undignified as a smile, but breathing easily.

He then turned to Echohawk, his eyes reflecting his kindness, his warmth for the young chief. "Echohawk, this woman who to the Chippewa is called No-din should not be looked upon with hate or anger," he said softly. "Remember always that she is the victim of a cruel father. But she is a courageous woman. She fled the life forced on her by a father whose heart is dark. I welcomed her in our village with open arms because I saw much gentleness in her eyes, a reflection of her inner being." He paused and frowned, contemplating his next words. "Yet you say that she rode with those who ravaged your village. There has to be an explanation which will reveal that her role in the raid was an innocent one."

"Would you call her innocent if you knew that she fired upon one of my braves?" Echohawk said, seeing it in his mind's eye as though it were happening now.

Chief Silver Wing leaned forward and placed a hand on Echohawk's knee. "Sometimes a gun is fired against another because the life of the one who fires the weapon is threatened," he said reassuringly. He wanted so badly to find the truth behind No-din's actions, not only to make peace within his own heart about this woman who had become a heroine in his people's eyes but also to soothe Echohawk. He wanted to end Echohawk's torment.

Echohawk gazed into the forest, which was now cloaked in darkness, again reliving that day that would forever haunt him. He recalled the hate he had felt for the young lad who had fired upon his brave, yet he now also recalled that his brave had taken aim on a white man—the man that No-din had defended by shooting the brave.

"That was her father!" Echohawk said, his voice shallow.

He turned quick, wide eyes to Chief Silver Wing.

"It had to be her father!" he said anxiously. "She shot the brave to . . . to save her father!"

"So you do see, Echohawk," Chief Silver Wing said, nodding. "She is a woman of much courage and loyalty. Although she held much resentment against her father, she could not let him die. She shot your brave only because her father's life was in jeopardy."

Echohawk was alert to Chief Silver Wing's words, himself beginning to see why No-din had been with the raiders. "Her father forced many things upon No-din," he hissed. "He cut her hair. He made her wear men's clothes."

He again looked quickly at Silver Wing. "She was also forced to ride with her father to witness the spilling of Chippewa blood."

Silver Wing nodded, his eyes locked with Echohawk's. "*Ay-uh*," he said softly. "That is how I also see it."

"And she fled from her father soon after," Echohawk said, his heart thundering within his chest at the thought of being freed of all resentments toward No-din.

"It seems so," Silver Wing said, again nodding. "And so you see, Echohawk, you have been wrong to condemn No-din within your heart. *Her* heart has always been in the right place. With *us*."

"*Ay-uh*," Echohawk said, nodding slowly. "I am seeing it all very clearly now." His eyes widened as another thought grabbed him. "Her father! *He* is the one responsible for my people's sorrow. Do you know him, Silver Wing? Do you know where he makes his residence?"

A warning shot through Silver Wing, who realized that Echohawk was still plotting vengeance whenever he thought about the day of the raid. Silver Wing also felt a deep, burning resentment toward certain white men, yet he had his people's welfare to consider. Once an open war broke out between the Chippewa and *any* white man, no matter that the white man might deserve to die, in the end it would be the red man who would suffer.

"I know of him, and where he resides;" Silver Wing said solemnly. "But I think it best if you do not know. Think peaceful thoughts, my son. Too much Chippewa blood has already been spilled on Mother Earth. Do not let your life be guided by hate and the need of revenge. Put your people first, your hunger for vengeance last."

"The *ee-szhee-nee-kah-so-win*, name," Echohawk said flatly. "The location of his dwelling."

"I will give you what you ask only because I feel honor-bound to share it with you," Silver Wing said, reaching a hand to Echohawk's shoulder, clasping his fingers gently to it. "His name is Victor Temple. He runs a trading post not far from Fort Snelling. I have never dealt with him because he is a *wah-yah-szhim*, a cheat and a liar. If you insist, I will instruct one of my braves to point out his residence to you. But before I do, promise me that you will only look, not attack."

"I can promise nothing," Echohawk said, his voice hard.

Silver Wing's eyes filled with sadness. "You will be shown the location," he said, sighing heavily.

"That is good," Echohawk said, nodding.

"No-din," Silver Wing said. "Have you thought of her? Will you kill her father—a man she defended with such courage?"

"I cannot say," Echohawk said.

"Will you seek her out?" Silver Wing further questioned. "Will you ask her to return with you to our village as your wife?"

"I cannot say," Echohawk repeated.

"She will be at Fort Snelling," Silver Wing offered. "That was her destination before her horse threw her, leaving her helpless in the forest. I am sure that is where she went when fleeing from your anger and accusations."

"Fort Snelling . . ." Echohawk said contemplatively. "Fort Snelling."

"*Ay-uh*," Silver Wing said. "And the mention of Fort Snelling brings me back to why the braves wait in council for us even now, Echohawk."

"The great powwow at Fort Snelling is soon," Echohawk said, nodding. "The yearly powwow between the neighboring tribes, even the Sioux. I have heard of this powwow that Colonel Snelling has every year at his fort, hoping to draw the Chippewa and Sioux into a lasting friendship." He laughed sarcastically. "How can that ever be? The snakelike Sioux will be the enemy of the Chippewa *ah-pah-nay*, forever! I shall carry within my heart much hate for that renegade Sioux White Wolf! Always!"

"I dislike White Wolf no less than you, and I do not expect he will be among the peace seekers at Fort Snelling," Chief Silver Wing said solemnly. "It is for Colonel Snelling that I urge you to go to the powwow. He makes an attempt to bring peace among the Chippewa and Sioux, whereas no other white man before him even cared. In fact, I'm sure they were glad to see us kill each other off."

Echohawk turned his eyes to Silver Wing. "You are going?" he questioned.

"*Gah-ween*, no," Chief Silver Wing said, shaking his head slowly back and forth. "I think it is wise to let others who are younger go and experience this time of camaraderie and bring back the news of it to their chief."

Echohawk rose quickly to his feet, his eyes and heart alive again. "I will go," he said, smiling at Silver Wing as he rose before him. "I am eager to go to the fort. My chosen braves and I will proudly ride with the representatives of your band of Chippewa. We will listen to words of peace with open hearts and minds."

"That is good," Chief Silver Wing said, wrapping Echohawk within his arms, giving him a warm hug. "And remember, my son, keep peaceful thoughts about those who have wronged you. Somehow they will pay for their evil ways. But for now, your thoughts must remain pure to ensure the safety and future of both your people and mine."

Echohawk could not help but be attentive to Chief Silver Wing's warnings. Like Echohawk's beloved father, Silver Wing was a man of wisdom. Echohawk wanted so badly to respect his wishes, yet hate was eating away at his heart for this man who he now knew beyond a shadow of a doubt was No-din's father.

"Still I can make no promises to you," Echohawk said, easing from Chief Silver Wing's embrace. "But hear me when I say this to you. I respect you and your reasons for asking me to have a peaceful heart. In you I see my father. With you I feel as though I am *with* my father. I hope somehow to repay you one day for your kindnesses to me."

Chief Silver Wing placed a hand to Echohawk's shoulder. "Echohawk, from this day forth, you *are* my son, in every respect," he said sincerely. "Now, let us go and sit together in council with our respective braves. It is best that they share these good feelings between two chiefs."

"*Ay-uh*," Echohawk said, warmed through and through by Silver Wing's gifts of love and guidance.

18

Beauty is truth, truth beauty—that is all
Ye know on earth, and all ye need to know.
—KEATS

A Few Weeks Later

The aroma of smoke awakened Victor Temple with a
start. He bolted from his bed when he heard men
shouting outside, and quickly saw the reflection of fire
on the ceiling of his bedroom.

"Damn!" he gasped, scurrying into his breeches.

Shirtless, he left his room, but just as he stepped
out into the corridor, he cried out with pain as something came down hard on his head. Blacking out from
the blow, he crumpled to the floor, unaware of rough
hands picking him up, carrying him down the stairs,
and outside, tying him to a horse.

When he finally came to, his head throbbing with
pain, he squinted into the darkness, soon realizing that
he had been shackled to a wall, nude.

"Lord have mercy," he cried, the room darker than
a moonless night. He winced and tried to pull his feet
up from the floor when he heard rats scurrying
around, squeaking, but his legs were tied too securely
to the wall for him to move his feet.

"Help!" he shouted. "Someone, please help me!"

He became quiet, listening. Fear gripped his insides
and sweat pearled up on his brow when he still heard
no sounds but the rats.

"Who are you? *Where* are you?" he cried. "Why
have you done this to me?"

But still no response.

It was as though he was in a deep dark tunnel, alone except for—

A rat's sharp teeth sank into the flesh of one of his bare feet. He let out a bloodcurdling scream, then fainted. . . .

Excitement welled up inside Mariah as she stood before the mirror. She stared in amazement at her reflection, thinking that by some miracle Abigail had fussed enough with her hair to make it actually look pretty with all of its waves and curls.

Mariah gazed down at the satin gown Abigail had let her choose for the ball. It had transformed her into someone that even she thought might be called beautiful! Pale green, it was trimmed in delicate white lace, its bodice low, revealing a cleavage that made her blush. So captivated was she by the vision in the mirror, she didn't hear soft footsteps coming up behind her.

"My dear, you are absolutely ravishing," Abigail said, stepping to Mariah's side, a picture of loveliness herself in her off-the-shoulder black velveteen dress, her hair coiled at the top of her head with long, lustrous ringlets hanging down at the back. The top curves of her breasts were just barely exposed, and above them lay a sparkling diamond necklace.

Abigail clasped her hands before her. "Mariah, you are going to turn every man's head at the ball tonight," she said, sighing dreamily. "And my but aren't you going to be busy dancing the night away! I will have to assign Josiah to stand guard, just to fight the men off you."

Mariah paled and turned quickly to Abigail. "Abigail, I don't know what I was thinking of, getting so dressed up for the ball, or why I was so excited to attend it," she said, her eyes wide. "I don't know the first thing about dancing! I . . . I will make an absolute fool of myself should I even attempt to!"

"There will be many anxious to teach you," Abigail said, gently patting Mariah on the cheek. She glanced toward the window, hearing a commotion outside in the courtyard. Some Indians had already started arriving for the powwow.

She glanced again at Mariah, having succeeded thus far this evening in getting her mind off the gathering of the Indians. In time, Mariah had felt more comfortable in taking Abigail into her confidence, and had spoken of her love for Echohawk, yet had not given her reason for having left him. But it was quite evident to Abigail that Mariah still loved him. It was always in her eyes and voice when even the mention of the Chippewa came into the conversation at the dinner table.

Mariah grew tense, having noticed Abigail's sudden apprehension. Mariah herself was acutely aware of the noise coming from the Indian camps in and around the walls of Fort Snelling. She had been told of the powwow that Colonel Snelling had planned to create a peaceful union between two warring factions of Indians.

Last night she had been unable to sleep while listening to the low thumping of the drums, and the songs and chants of the Indians. She had watched all day for signs of Echohawk—yet had not seen him. She had to wonder if he would eventually come. And if so, would she see him? Would she speak to him?

Unable to stay away, and having only a faint evening light left to study the gathering Indians, Mariah brushed past Abigail and went to the window and slowly eased the sheer curtain aside. Her gaze roamed slowly around below her, watching for a tall, handsome Indian who would be set apart from all of the others by an incongruous pair of spectacles.

Those damn eyeglasses! she fussed to herself. If not for them, she would still be a part of Echohawk's life!

But she knew that it was foolish to blame eyeglasses, for even without them, he in time would have discovered her deceit.

"He could be among those encamped outside the walls of the fort," Abigail said, moving to Mariah's side, slipping an arm around her tiny waist. She gazed down at those who were inside the fort, sitting and smoking around a great outdoor fire. Some were Chippewa. Some were Sioux. She hoped with all her heart that they would feast and fraternize in perfect accord.

"I know," Mariah said softly. "And I am foolish for even caring." She caught herself, having come close to telling Abigail truths that would condemn not only herself in the commandant's wife's eyes but also her father.

"Yes, it is a bit foolish, my dear," Abigail said, brushing her fingers across Mariah's brow, smoothing some red curls into place that had fallen from the rest. "His culture and yours differ so much. You were wise to leave when you did and not allow your feelings to grow stronger. Although it has been done, it is unwise for a white woman to marry into a family of Indians. The life is hard, Mariah. So very hard."

"I am sure it is," Mariah said, sighing. Then her heart fluttered wildly in her chest when she caught sight of many more Indians approaching the courtyard, Echohawk in the lead.

"He's here," she whispered just loud enough for Abigail to hear. She clasped her hands tightly together before her. "Echohawk has come." Then her eyes wavered. She was not sure if he even knew she was at Fort Snelling. Of course he had come only for the powwow. By now she would be completely banished from his mind and heart!

"How odd," Abigail said, gasping. She moved away from Mariah and leaned closer to the window. "Mariah, Echohawk is wearing eyeglasses. I have never seen an Indian wear eyeglasses. And where would he have gotten them? Had he traded for them at the fort, everyone would have been talking about it, for an Indian, no matter how handsome he is, looks rather odd in eyeglasses."

Guilt spread through Mariah like wildfire, since she knew all of the answers yet was unable to tell Abigail.

Her father!

He alone was responsible for Echohawk's injured eyesight!

"Yes, it does seem odd," Mariah said, her voice drawn, taking her eyes off Echohawk just long enough to see others in the courtyard stopping to stare at him.

Then she turned her attention back to him, thinking that nothing could diminish his handsomeness. Everything within her seemed to melt as she watched him ride further into the courtyard, so proud and tall in his saddle. He wore fringed white doeskin breeches and a shirt embellished with colorful beads and porcupine quills, his raven-dark hair held back with a colorfully beaded headband.

There was just enough light left to see his chiseled bronze face with its bold nose and strong chin and night-black eyes behind the absurdly out-of-place eyeglasses.

Tears burned at the corners of Mariah's eyes as she envisioned him nude, seeing even now in her mind's eye the expanse of sleekly muscled chest, the wide shoulders tapering to narrow hips, and the hard, flat stomach.

She could even now feel his hands on her face, framing her lips before kissing her.

She could even now feel his hard strong arms pressing her willing body against his. . . .

"Mariah?" Abigail said, interrupting Mariah's thoughts. "Dear? Let us go down to the ballroom. The string quartet is even now starting the waltzes."

Abigail placed a hand to Mariah's elbow as Mariah looked gloomily at her. "Come, dear," she persisted.

"We must give you a reason to erase that frown from your lovely face. It will be better for you to mingle with other people and get your mind off Echohawk."

"Yes, I'm sure you are right," Mariah said, swallowing hard. She wanted to take a last glance at Echohawk, but she turned away from the window.

"We will have such a wonderful time tonight," Abigail said, sweeping Mariah from the room and hurriedly down the corridor and then the narrow staircase.

Mariah's heart pounded as they moved down another corridor, the sound of music and laughter drawing closer. She sucked in a nervous breath, then went into the ballroom at Abigail's side. She stopped and took a quick step back, struck almost numb with fear when she saw the throng of people. Some were milling about, sipping either punch or wine from long-stemmed glasses, while others were whirling across the polished parquet, crinolines and silken ruffles billowing, the string quartet on a platform at the far end of the room.

Abigail laughed softly and took Mariah's hand, leading her into the room. Mariah's heart fluttered and her face became flushed with a building excitement, and she was glad for the moment to be able to put Echohawk at least partly from her mind. She allowed Abigail to usher her around the room, introducing her to the other guests.

Soon Mariah found herself spinning around the room with one handsome gentleman after another, her dress billowing prettily about her, the ruffle of her petticoat seeming to foam around her delicate ankles.

She excused herself each time she stepped clumsily on the feet of the men, trying to hide her embarrassment behind winning smiles.

But too soon her merriment became strained, and even more awkward, when Tanner McCloud was suddenly there, his strange yellow eyes gleaming into hers. She did not have time to protest when he grabbed her roughly by the hand and took her among the dancers and began whirling her around the room, all the while smiling in his leering way.

Everything about him made her uncomfortable. She saw him as a repulsive, vile old man. And he always seemed to have the stench of death on him after working with dead animals all day, removing their pelts.

"Tanner McCloud, this one dance is all you will get from me," she said icily. She glared up at him. "Must I remind you that my father sent you away when you brought the bride price to pay for me?"

"That was then," Tanner said, chuckling. "This is now."

"Nothing has changed," Mariah fumed. "Nothing!"

"I'd say everything has changed," Tanner said, leaning down into her face, the stench of alcohol on his breath causing Mariah to turn her face away, gagging. "It's apparent you've run away from your pa. As I see it, because you ain't with him and his bossin' ways any longer, you can make your own decisions." His yellow eyes gleamed into hers. "It's all up to you, Mariah. Marry me. I'll give you the world."

"Marry you?" Mariah said, staring disbelievingly up at him. Then she threw her head back and laughed. "Not if you were the last man on earth!"

Then she grew sober and looked up at him with narrowing eyes, trying to jerk herself free when the string quartet stopped playing and all of the dancers paused between songs.

"Let me go," she said, her voice a low hiss. She tried to jerk herself free again, but to no avail. Tanner continued to stand there, his hold on her wrist solid, his lips twisted into an ugly smile.

"I'd let her go if I were you," a man said suddenly behind Mariah.

She turned her head with a start, finding herself looking at a young man with ruddy yet handsome features and hair the same color as hers—as red as autumn sunsets. He was taller than Tanner, and when he bowed civilly and cut in to rescue her, she smiled up into dark and dancing friendly eyes.

"Thank you, sir," she said as Tanner released his hold on her and quickly lost himself in the crowd, moving away from her and the stranger.

Abigail came in a rustle of petticoats to Mariah's side. "My son, William Joseph, is your hero for tonight," she said, laughing softly as she placed a gentle hand to her son's cheek, patting it. "And, son, this is the young lady I told you about. This is Mariah Temple."

Mariah blushed and her hand went to her hair when she found William Joseph gazing bemusedly at it, then sighed with relief when his attention moved from her hair, to smile warmly down at her again.

"And she is everything that you said she would be," William Joseph said, lifting Mariah's hand to his lips, kissing it. "Lovely. Enchantingly lovely."

Mariah lowered her eyes, blushing; then, before she could say a word to William Joseph, he had whisked her into the midst of the whirling dancers and begun guiding her masterfully around the floor.

"Mother told me about your father," he said frowning. "I think it was very courageous of you to leave home on your own to seek a new way of life without Victor. You have come to the right people for assistance. My mother and father are most kindhearted. They will do right by you."

"I am ever so grateful," Mariah murmured, gasping with embarrassment when she half-stumbled over one of William Joseph's feet as they made another wide turn on the dance floor.

"Pardon me," she said, laughing softly as she looked up at him, so glad that she did not find mockery in his eyes. "I . . . I have never danced before tonight. It is such an awkward thing to do!"

"You dance like an angel," William Joseph said, firming his grip on her waist. He leaned his face closer to hers. "And may I say, my dear Mariah, you *look* like an angel."

Not used to a man flirting with her, and wanting never to become enamored of a man again, she changed the direction of their conversation.

"Tell me about yourself, William Joseph," she said, smiling up at him. "Your mother said that you are a restless soul, seeking adventure wherever you can find it. If I were a man, I would want to live the same sort of life."

"My wild life has taken me too often from my family," William Joseph said, glancing over at Abigail, who was busy chatting with several women as she stood at the refreshment table dipping punch into cups and glasses. "But of course my father is too busy to notice, and my mother has other children to take her mind off a wandering son."

"Tell me about your adventures," Mariah said, her heart crying out for Echohawk. Above the string quartet's music she could hear the singing and the thumping of the drums outside, where the Indians had gathered.

Oh, how she wanted to be there!

She wanted to be by Echohawk's side, sharing the powwow with him.

She forced herself to be attentive to William Joseph's tales about his adventures with the different Indian tribes while serving as an interpreter.

But when William Joseph spoke sadly of his marriage to a lovely Indian maiden, and how circumstances had torn them apart, that was all it took to break Mariah's composure.

Sobbing suddenly, she broke away from William Joseph and fled from the ballroom, out onto the terrace, then down several steps which led to a small flower garden behind the stately mansion.

She buried her face in her hands and cried a moment; then, when she heard anxious footsteps approaching, she dried her eyes with the backs of her hands and squared her shoulders, just as William Joseph appeared, his eyes troubled.

"Why did you run away?" he asked, peering down at her through the darkness. "Was it something I said?"

"It was my clumsiness," Mariah said, forcing the lie across her lips. "I . . . I just couldn't stay there and continue making a fool of myself while all of the other women were dancing so smoothly. I am sure you understand."

"The air is damp," William Joseph said, reaching a hand toward her. "Come back inside with me. I promise I won't ask you to dance. I will get you some refreshment."

Finding it impossible to return to the ballroom when her heart ached for Echohawk, Mariah shook her head. "No," she murmured. "Please go back without me. I . . . I need a breath of fresh air."

William Joseph removed his green velveteen coat and slipped it around her shoulders. "At least wear this so that you won't get a chill," he said softly. "Stay awhile, then come back inside. I will serve you punch and cake."

"That would be delightful," Mariah said, snuggling into the coat. "I shall return shortly."

William Joseph smiled warmly down at her, then began to walk away. As Mariah turned longingly toward the powwow grounds, she pulled up with a start and almost fainted when Echohawk was suddenly there blocking her path.

She composed herself and looked up at him, and thrilled through and through when she could tell by the way he looked at her that he still cared for her, regardless of what she'd done.

"You knew that I was here?" she said, her voice trembling with emotion.

"*Ay-uh*," Echohawk said, his gaze taking in the gentleman's coat on her shoulders. He had watched William Joseph place it there, and jealousy plagued him. "I know this and much more."

"What else?" Mariah dared to ask, her heart pounding.

"Your reason for having been among those who raided my village," Echohawk said stiffly. "It was one more thing your evil father forced upon you. Chief Silver Wing told me your father's name and where he resides. He also told me that your father not only abuses his daughter but also is a liar and a cheat!"

Realizing that the secret was out—who her father was, and where he lived, and his part in the raid— Mariah paled. Although she no longer loved or respected her father, she did not want him to be killed.

And she did not want the man that she loved to be responsible for his death.

But she also knew that she had no control whatsoever over her father's destiny, nor over Echohawk's role in it.

"No-din," Echohawk said, taking her hands in his, "I forgive you your part in the raid. I forgive you everything! I want you back. My heart has been lonely without you. Return with me to my dwelling. Be the 'flower of my wigwam' again! You filled my heart with love and happiness. It can be that way again, if you will allow it."

Hearing the sadness and pain in Echohawk's voice, and feeling so deeply for him, and feeling free to show her emotions to him, Mariah moved into his arms and hugged him tightly. "Echohawk, I'm so sorry about so many things," she cried. "Oh, Echohawk, I love you so much. Let me show you how happy we can be!"

Echohawk's heart thundered wildly. "You will be

mine again?" he asked, placing a finger to her chin, tilting her eyes up to his.

"*Ay-uh*," she murmured. She smoothed her fingers over the lenses of his eyeglasses. "How is your eyesight? Has it improved at all?"

"Somewhat," he said, then very intently brushed William Joseph's coat from her shoulders.

But as he leaned down to kiss her, footsteps approaching made him draw away from her and move quickly into the bushes to hide.

Mariah reached a hand out to him, to tell him that it was not necessary to hide from anyone. She was going to shout their love to the world! She was proud of him—proud to be his woman!

William Joseph rushed to Mariah and placed gentle hands on her bare shoulders. "Mariah, I've got some bad news to tell you," he said, his voice drawn.

"What?" Mariah asked, a sudden fear grabbing at her insides. "What is it, William Joseph?"

"Your father's trading post has been burned and your father is missing," he said in a rush of words.

Mariah stared up at William Joseph, stunned numb by the news. Then her gaze went to the bushes where Echohawk hid, her eyes locking with his before he turned and ran soundlessly from her, hidden from William Joseph by the black cloak of night.

Echohawk, she whispered to herself. *Oh, God, no. Surely not Echohawk. . . .*

But she would never forget how he had vowed revenge against those responsible for his people's sorrow.

All he had lacked was a name.

19

The good are better made by ill,
As odors crush'd are sweeter still.

—ROGERS

"Mariah?" William Joseph said, clasping his fingers more tightly to her shoulders.

Her name being spoken wrenched Mariah out of her sad reverie, her grief over having perhaps lost with one blow both her father *and* the man that she loved. If Echohawk was responsible for this latest tragedy in her life, then what they had said only moments ago to one another meant nothing at all.

"I must go and see for myself what happened at my father's trading post," Mariah said, wrenching herself free from William Joseph.

She gathered the skirt of her gown into her arms as she rushed away from him, determined not to think about Echohawk's likely role in what had happened. Her father had to be her prime interest now.

She had to find out if he was alive—or dead!

"Perhaps I might find tracks that could lead me to him," she said over her shoulder as William Joseph came after her. "I won't let myself believe that he . . . that he is dead. I just won't."

"You can't do that, Mariah," William Joseph fused. "I'll go. I'll take care of things."

"William Joseph, he is my father and I insist that I ride with you to see if there is anything that can be done to find him," Mariah said, taking the steps up to the veranda two at a time.

"It won't be safe," William Joseph said, hurrying ahead of her, opening the door for her.

She breezed into the ballroom, past gawking party-goers, and into the corridor, very aware now that Abigail had joined William Joseph, one on each side of her. "Abigail, tell your son that I am capable of riding with him to search for my father," she said, giving William Joseph an annoyed glance. "I can ride a horse as well as you, William Joseph. And I can also handle a firearm just as well."

"But, Mariah," Abigail fussed, walking on into Mariah's bedroom with her as William Joseph paused and waited in the corridor, "you are so beautiful tonight in that gown. You can't seriously want to . . . to play the role of a man again. Let William Joseph take care of things. I assure you he is a most capable man. He can do anything he sets his mind to."

Mariah turned and gave Abigail a stern stare. "So can I, Abigail," she said flatly. "And so shall I tonight!"

"Oh, Mariah," Abigail said, nervously clasping and unclasping her hands. "Please don't do this."

Mariah was already out of her dress, petticoats, and fancy slippers. She went to the chifferobe, grabbed her buckskin dress from a hook, and hurried into it. Again her thoughts returned to Echohawk, the dress a reminder of the many hours spent with him.

She did not want to believe that Echohawk could come to her, professing his love for her, even forgiving her for her role in the raid, right after having taken vengeance against her very own father.

She could not see how he could be gentle and caring one moment, a vicious savage the next.

Even though Echohawk had many reasons to hate her father, she just couldn't envision him burning and killing at the very same moment he was planning to come to her to ask her to be his woman.

No.

It did not make sense.

But she had to be sure.

The buckskin dress turning her back into the woman that Echohawk had fallen in love with, Mariah slipped hurriedly into knee-high moccasins, ignoring heavy footsteps that entered the room.

"What is this that William Joseph told me?" Colonel Snelling said in a threatening growl.

Mariah turned with a start. Her eyes widened and her back stiffened when she saw the anger in Josiah's eyes. "I must go to my father's trading post and see for myself what has happened," she murmured, feeling dwarfed as the colonel towered over her, a sternness in his flashing dark eyes that she had never seen before.

"I have assigned a unit of men to ride to the trading post," Josiah said, his hand clasped to a saber at his side. "William Joseph will lead them. You will only be in their way, Mariah." His gaze raked over her, seeing her change of clothes; then he glared at her again. "Change back into your gown. Return with Abigail to the ball. Let men do men's work."

Firming her chin, insulted that Josiah would think that she could dismiss the welfare of her father so frivolously from her mind, Mariah placed her hands on her hips and glared up at him.

"I do not need reminders that I am not a man," she said stubbornly. "And caring about what has happened to my father does not make me any less a lady. I am going to accompany your men, Colonel Snelling. If you still say that you will not allow it, I shall ride alone."

Josiah kneaded his chin, slowly shaking his head back and forth, then placed his hand on her shoulder. "I can't have you riding anywhere alone beyond the walls of the fort," he said glumly. "Not while those who are going around killing and burning are running loose close by. I'll tell William Joseph that you are riding with him and his men." He leaned closer to Mariah's face. "But I'll also tell him to keep an eye on you. I don't care if you can ride and shoot like a man, I am not going to let anyone hurt you!"

Tears welled up in Mariah's eyes and she felt ashamed for having been so harsh with this man who was only looking out for her welfare. She crept into his arms, so wishing that her own father could have been as compassionate—as caring.

When his strong arms swung around her waist, holding her to him, she relished the moment, pretending he was her father—wishing it were so.

And then, realizing that time was passing quickly and that her father's life might be ebbing away as the clock ticked away each second, she eased from Josiah's arms and walked toward the door. When she found William Joseph outside waiting, having changed into buckskin riding attire, she walked proudly with him outside and mounted her horse beside his.

When Colonel Snelling and Abigail came to look at her, she was touched deeply when Josiah handed her a rifle.

"Ride with care," he said as she took the rifle.

"Please be careful," Abigail said, blowing Mariah a kiss as Mariah nodded and wheeled her horse around, riding beside William Joseph at the head of the group of soldiers.

"Please be careful!" Abigail said again, waving frantically at Mariah and William Joseph until they rode on through the opened gate that led out into the forest.

Abigail sobbed and turned to her husband. "I wish they had waited until morning," she said, shivering as she looked into the dark depths of the forest, hearing the howl of a wolf and the hoot of an owl somewhere in the distance. "The killers could be just waiting outside the fort walls. It would be so easy . . . to . . . to ambush our loved ones."

"Now, now," Josiah comforted her, placing an arm around his wife's waist. "Let's not let our imagination run away with us."

"So many tragedies have happened of late, Josiah," Abigail said sullenly. "The attack on Echohawk's village. And now on Mariah's father's trading post. Her father is missing. What can happen next, Josiah? As long as those who are responsible are running around loose, how can I not be afraid for our son and for Mariah?"

"We must have faith in God that we will find those responsible soon," Colonel Snelling said, sighing heavily. "Until then, darling, you must keep your faith."

Abigail nodded, but found it hard at this moment to feel secure about anything.

Riding his horse hard through the night, Echohawk desperately needed to get back to Chief Silver Wing's village. Those white men who might point an accusing finger at Echohawk for the tragedy that had befallen No-din's father tonight would come searching for him, and once they were at Chief Silver Wing's village, might decide to punish all of the Indians there for good measure.

He could not allow that to happen. He had to warn Chief Silver Wing. He and his people, and Echohawk's must disband and take their village elsewhere.

Having won and lost Mariah again almost in the same breath tonight made a bitterness soar through him. It did not seem that he was meant ever to have a peaceful heart. If not one thing, it was another! And that his losses included Mariah over and over again made it almost too hard for him to bear.

It was up to him to clear his name before ever approaching No-din again. Even if she was with him, she would not be safe. If tragedy befell the Chippewa again, and if she were with him, performing in the capacity of wife, transformed, herself, into Chippewa, she could be counted among the dead. . . .

The reflection of orange in the sky from outdoor fires made Echohawk realize that he was almost at Chief Silver Wing's village. His heart ached over having to tell the noble chief that he would no longer be safe in the village that he had established many moons ago—a village where corn grew in abundance and where wild rice was always there in the autumn, thriving, just for the Chippewa, it seemed.

When he advised Chief Silver Wing that he, Echohawk, had brought possible doom to Silver Wing's people, he did not want to think of the emotions the chief would be feeling. To survive an attack, they must move elsewhere, or stand and fight a fight that was not theirs and risk losing a whole generation of Chippewa children.

Had it not been for his own troubles, he despaired, Chief Silver Wing's people would continue to be safe—would continue to be content.

Echohawk rode into the village, his chin held high, yet his heart aching with an utter sadness and remorse for what lay ahead of him. After he helped uproot Chief Silver Wing's village, and also his own people, and saw them to safety, Echohawk and several braves would disband and travel alone, to search for the *real* culprits.

Lightning, a strange phenomenon for the month of November, was flashing in the sky overhead, illuminating everything around Mariah for seconds at a time, making her discoveries worse, even eerie, at what was left of her father's trading post—and what had been her childhood home.

Torn with how she should feel, Mariah stood beside the charred remains, recalling so many things, both happy and sad. Her happiest times had been when her mother had still been alive.

Her mother had been everything to her.

But since her mother's death Mariah had found it a hard struggle to live in the company of a father whose heart had seemingly turned to stone.

Except for her memories of her mother, there was no sorrow at viewing what was left of the trading post.

"There are no signs of your father anywhere," William Joseph said, stepping gingerly to Mariah's side. "And there are no clear tracks leading anywhere. Whoever abducted your father was clever. They erased all tracks leading to and from the trading post."

"Then you are certain that my father is not . . . is not among those ashes?" Mariah said, gesturing toward the smoking rubble.

"One of his men who survived the fire told of seeing your father being dragged toward a horse," William Joseph said somberly.

Mariah turned quickly to him. "If there was a man alive to tell that, surely he saw who was to blame for everything else that happened here tonight," she said, looking anxiously up into his dark eyes. "Or someone else. Surely there were others to ask."

"They were apparently all slain while running from their bunkhouse," William Joseph said, gesturing toward that burned-out structure. "Only one lived long enough to talk to those who discovered the massacre."

"And? What else did he say?" Mariah asked, her voice rising in pitch. But she felt close to being able to know the truth about Echohawk.

Whether he was innocent or guilty.

"Before he had a chance to say who did it, he died," William Joseph said, sighing heavily. "And so now we must return to Father and ask his advice. I'd say a search party must be formed. And soon."

Disappointed that she had not been able to get a clear answer about Echohawk, Mariah nodded weakly, then walked limply to her horse and swung herself into the saddle.

Disconsolately she rode beside William Joseph back in the direction of the fort. Although she was concerned over her father's welfare, her thoughts kept wandering to Echohawk. Just prior to William Joseph's appearance in the garden to tell her the disturbing news about her father, she had made promises to Echohawk—promises that now meant nothing, it seemed. Echohawk had fled from her like a man guilty of a fiendish crime, and she had immediately accused him within her heart, as though she had no faith in him whatsoever.

How can one base a future on such weaknesses as that? she wondered sadly to herself.

The fact that she could think Echohawk guilty of the vicious deed lay heavy on her heart.

Dispirited, she rode with the others, yet felt no better even when they reached the fort and were once again in the company of Colonel Snelling, reporting their findings. Soon they would depart again and search for not only her father but also those responsible for his abduction or death.

The rain was splashing hard against the study window as Colonel Snelling paced his study, his hands clasped behind him. William Joseph and Mariah stood quietly by, watching him. Just as he turned and faced them again, they were interrupted.

"What is it?" Josiah said in a snarl, gazing without affection at Tanner McCloud as he stepped into the room, soaked to the skin, sending off an aroma similar to wet dog's fur. "I hope you have good reason for entering my study without first being announced."

Tanner swallowed hard and shifted his feet nervously on the carpet as he came to a sudden stop beside Mariah. "I heard about Mariah's father," he said, glancing guardedly at her, then back at Josiah.

"I think I may have some valuable information you should be interested in hearing."

"It had better be valuable enough to warrant you being here in my office, when I can hardly stand to look at you, much less be in the same room as your stench," Josiah said, his eyes filled with warning. He went to Tanner and leaned into his face. "When you had the gall to mix with my acquaintances at the ball tonight without a formal invitation, I had a good notion to shoot you on the spot. If not for my beloved wife's prohibition on blood spilling in her home, I'd have done it. Now, say your piece and get the hell out of here."

Tanner gasped and took a step back from Josiah. "I've heard rumors that an Injun wearing eyeglasses was seen leading a raiding party tonight close to Victor Temple's trading post," he said in a rush of words. "The ones who saw this were just passing through or I'd have brought them here to tell you what they saw, eye to eye."

Mariah had stood by listening to Tanner's tale, then blanched and felt suddenly dizzy when he was through. She reached for the back of a chair and steadied herself, finding it hard to think clearly, much less speak in Echohawk's behalf.

And how could she? Hadn't she already been doubting Echohawk, even before Tanner had brought the news to Colonel Snelling? The knowing made her feel desperately ill to her stomach.

"An Indian wearing eyeglasses?" William Joseph said, kneading his chin. His eyes widened. "Why, Echohawk was wearing eyeglasses tonight. Everyone saw him. It was such a strange sight on an Indian brave that surely no one missed it."

"Perhaps you saw Echohawk wearing eyeglasses tonight, but that doesn't mean that he is the guilty party," Colonel Snelling said in Echohawk's defense. "I have never known Echohawk to be anything but wise and reasonable. I won't believe that he is guilty of this crime tonight."

"Now, just how many Injuns do you see wearin' eyeglasses?" Tanner scoffed, his lips twisting into a smug smile. "None, I tell you. None. Only Echohawk, Josiah. Only Echohawk! I say he's guilty as sin!" He turned to Mariah. "He's the one, Mariah. He's got your pa hid away somewhere. Don't let Colonel Snelling tell you otherwise."

"How can anyone ever believe anything you say?" Mariah said, finally finding her ability to speak. "My father despised you, Tanner. I know you didn't care beans about him. So why would you even care what's happened to him?"

"I don't want to see anyone at the mercy of Injuns," Tanner quickly explained. "I wouldn't wish that on my worst enemy."

"And you are so sure it was Echohawk?" Mariah said, her voice trembling.

"Positively certain," Tanner said, squaring his shoulders.

"Well, I'm not," Colonel Snelling said, slouching down in his chair behind his desk. He looked up at William Joseph. "Go out to the powwow and find Echohawk. Bring him back inside so that he can have his say in the matter. Echohawk must be given a chance to convince me that he *is* the son of his father—a man of peace."

"I don't believe that Echohawk will be found at the powwow," Mariah said, firming her chin defiantly at their surprised expressions. "He'll be at Chief Silver Wing's village. I assure you of that. He is innocent. And thank you for letting him prove it to you."

"Mariah, how is it that you know where Echohawk has gone?" William Joseph asked, looking down at her with concern in his eyes.

"It's . . . it's not important now," Mariah said, giving him a set stare, "but if he's left the powwow, he will have returned to his people."

"It's a waste of time," Tanner said, shrugging. "He won't be there either. He'll be runnin' scared."

Mariah turned and glared at Tanner, suddenly feeling strangely suspicious of how adamant he was to get everyone to believe that Echohawk was the guilty party, when, in truth, Tanner had as much reason as Echohawk to kill her father.

The vile man was capable of all sorts of evil deeds!

All along, she hadn't wanted to believe that Echohawk was guilty, and she didn't now that Tanner had pointed an accusing finger at him. She especially wanted to prove Tanner wrong, not only for her own and Echohawk's sakes but also to possibly turn the accusing finger back at Tanner.

"I don't think I need any more advice, Tanner," Colonel Snelling said, rising from his chair. He went to Tanner and took him by the elbow and ushered him to the door. "Now, go and find someone else to pester, will you?"

William Joseph chuckled; then his smile faded when he gazed down at Mariah, seeing so much seething hate for Tanner McCloud in the depths of her eyes. "Mariah?" he said, gently taking her hand. "Are you all right?"

"Yes, I'm fine," Mariah said, then swung away from him. "William Joseph, we're wasting time standing here talking. Let's go to Chief Silver Wing's village. Let's prove Tanner wrong!"

William Joseph fell into step beside her, Colonel Snelling giving them a salute as they walked past him.

The rain had stopped. Daylight was just breaking along the horizon, and birds were chattering in the trees overhead when the search party arrived at Chief Silver Wing's village—what was left of it.

An eerie feeling gripped Mariah at the pit of her

stomach and she grew numb as she looked slowly around her. There were now only the remains of wig-wams where they had once stood stately beside the river. Stripped clean of their rush mats and bark cov-erings, they gave the appearance of skeletons standing across the land.

William Joseph edged his horse close to Mariah's. "Seems that Tanner may have been right about Echo-hawk," he said, his voice drawn. "I hate it like hell, Mariah. Like hell."

"I still don't believe it," Mariah murmured. "There has to be an explanation. There just has to be."

A soldier rode up next to them. "All signs of depar-ture have been erased from the land," he said. "We'll have one hell of a time trackin' them."

"We'll do our best," William Joseph said, resting his hand on a holstered pistol at his right hip.

Mariah's eyes lowered; then she nudged her horse with her knees and rode along with William Joseph. She dreaded finding the answers—which would surely condemn Echohawk. Not only had he fled the fort upon the discovery of what had happened to her fa-ther, but apparently he had also encouraged Chief Sil-ver Wing to pull up roots and run.

"We need to rest before moving on," William Jo-seph said, dismounting. "Let's make camp for a while. We'll sleep, then leave again around noon."

Mariah did not like this decision of William Jo-seph's—to make camp where the Indian village had just been vacated. It did not seem right, as though they were trespassing on hallowed ground.

But having no heart to argue, she dismounted and helped make camp while some of the men went in search of food.

After they had eaten and she was finally alone snug in her bedroll, she found that sleep would not come for her. Although it had been a full day and night since she had slept, her mind kept wandering to Echo-hawk, and where he might be.

Loving him so much, she felt guilty for being a part of the search for him, but if it would lead her to her father, and if it would clear her beloved's name . . .

Mariah tossed and turned in her bedroll for a while longer, then decided that no matter how hard she tried, she wasn't going to be able to go to sleep.

She rose on an elbow and looked into the distance, recalling the burial grounds where Echohawk's father lay. Something compelled her to slip out of the bed-roll, draw a blanket snugly around her shoulders, and sneak from camp. She led her horse a short distance from the campsite, then mounted it and rode away. She was not sure why, but she had to go to the burial grounds.

20

Kiss the tears from her eyes, you'll find the rose
the sweeter for the dew.

—WEBSTER

Fog pressed in on Mariah as she rode beside the river,
the early-morning sun peering through in shadowy orange sprays. She turned her horse in another direction
and rode briskly across a wide stretch of meadow,
the dew on the knee-high grass sparkling like tiny
diamonds.

Mariah's heart began to race when she saw ahead
the butte to which she had gone with Echohawk not
long ago to visit his father's gravesite.

As the day grew brighter with sunlight and she came
closer to the butte, something else made her almost
go limp with joy.

Blaze!

Blaze at the foot of the butte!

Her gaze darted upward, now able to make out a
man standing at the edge of the butte, watching her
approach.

"Echohawk!" Mariah marveled, not understanding
how she had been drawn there, yet clearly for this
purpose!

She took one long lingering look, seeing that today
he was dressed in only a brief breechclout, the wind
fluttering it against his muscled thighs. She swallowed
hard, lost in desire, admiring his stance of a noble
leader.

And his leadership was being threatened.

She looked to the heavens and silently mouthed a prayer: Oh, God, let me help him. Please prove to me that I have been wrong to doubt him! Please let him be innocent!

A soft breeze brushed against her face, a caress, and she shivered, believing that somehow she had just been given an answer from the Almighty.

And at that moment she suddenly felt a gentle peace wash over her.

Smiling, sending a silent thank-you to the heavens, she nudged her heels more deeply into the flanks of her horse and rode hurriedly on, soon losing sight of Echohawk as she drew rein beside Blaze in the shadows of the butte.

Her pulse racing, she quickly dismounted. As she turned to climb the steep terrain, she found that it was not necessary.

Echohawk was there.

He had come to her. . . .

"No-din," he said, momentarily standing before her, his eyes heavy with doubt.

But when she moved into his arms and hugged him, all doubts were erased and he embraced her long and hard.

"Echohawk," Mariah said, clinging, her cheek against his powerful bare chest. "Oh, Echohawk, I've been so worried about you. Thank God you are all right."

Echohawk embraced her for a moment longer, then eased her away from him, holding her at arm's length. "You came," he said thickly. "All night long I summoned you here. It was with the Great Spirit's blessing that you came."

"It was you?" Mariah said, gasping softly. "You are the reason that I felt compelled to come to the place of your father's burial?"

"That is so," Echohawk said, nodding.

"But what if I were followed?" Mariah asked, taking a quick glance over her shoulder, having not once thought of that possibility while forging onward through the night.

"I did not beckon anyone else," Echohawk said dryly. "Only you. So no one followed. When William Joseph awakens and finds you gone, only then will you be missed."

"They will come looking for me," Mariah worried, looking quickly up at Echohawk.

"But they will not find you," he said, smiling smugly. "You are going with me and my braves to learn the truth. William Joseph and his men will be looking elsewhere."

"How did you know that I was with William Joseph?" Mariah asked, her eyes wide.

"My scouts watch. They see many things," Echohawk said, dropping his hands from Mariah. "Come. We must go. My men wait in the forest."

"Where are you taking me?" Mariah asked, not hesitating to mount her horse as Echohawk helped her into the saddle.

"Where you will see my innocence," Echohawk said, going to Blaze, quickly mounting. "And then, my *ee-quay*, woman, we will prove to Colonel Snelling that he has been right to put faith in me."

"You are being accused of burning my father's trading post and of his abduction," Mariah said, easing her horse closer to Echohawk's.

"And did you also accuse me of such crimes?" he asked, examining her through his eyeglasses. His eyesight was improving more quickly each day, yet not enough to cast aside the white man's magic.

Mariah lowered her eyes so that he would not see the guilt in their depths. Then, knowing that she must, she looked slowly back up at him and locked her eyes with his. "I could not help but doubt you," she murmured. "You had spoken of vengeance more than once to me. And when you fled after hearing William

Joseph tell me of my father's tragedy, what was I to believe? You could have stood your ground and defended yourself. But you fled, Echohawk! You ran away. And not only you, but Chief Silver Wing's entire village."

"And do you think that had I stayed and professed my innocence I would have been exonerated by the white man's law?" he said in a growl. "No, No-din. It would have not been that way. Not even Colonel Snelling has the power to keep the white men from hanging an Indian who in their eyes is guilty. Once white people are enticed to kill an Indian, no one can stop it."

"You think someone purposely spread the word that you did this to my father?" Mariah asked, thinking of Tanner McCloud and how he had so adamantly spoken against Echohawk to Colonel Snelling.

"*Ay-uh*," Echohawk said, frowning at Mariah. "One man alone has done this. My scouts probed and found out who. It is the man I call Yellow Eyes. It is he who has caused much sadness in my life. It is because of him that my people's number has been reduced, my beloved Fawn among those who were killed during the massacre led by Yellow Eyes and his renegade Sioux companions led by White Wolf. It is time for Yellow Eyes and White Wolf to die!"

"Yellow Eyes?" Mariah said, her heart skipping a beat. She was picturing Tanner McCloud's eyes, having always wondered why the whites were so yellow. Echohawk must be referring to Tanner!

"*Ay-uh*," Echohawk grumbled. "Finally I have found him. It is good to know that the evil white man with the eyes of a coward is near. I am going to make him pay for his deeds."

"This man you call Yellow Eyes," Mariah said guardedly. "Do you know his true name? Could it be Tanner McCloud?"

"*Ay-uh*, that is what he is called by the white men," Echohawk said.

Anger suddenly raged through Mariah. Her eyes narrowed. "Then I was right," she said, circling her hands into tight fists. "He is the one who did this to my father."

Then she looked anxiously over at Echohawk. "You said that you would take me with you to find Tanner," she said, grabbing up her reins. "What of my father? Once we get to Tanner's hideout, we will surely find my father there. Echohawk, now that you know my father's role in the most recent raid against your people, is it in your plans to kill him?"

"And what would you have me do?" Echohawk asked, his jaw tight.

Mariah swallowed hard, not knowing how she could answer him, not wanting to be forced to choose between the man she loved with all of her heart and her father, whom she despised. It would be far too easy for her to make the choice. Oh, but how torn she felt at this moment!

"So you see?" Echohawk said, leaning a gentle hand to her cheek. "The answers are not always so easy to sort out within one's heart."

With that he grabbed his reins, wheeled his horse around, and rode away.

Mariah stared after him for a moment, then rode in pursuit, soon pulling up beside him. "Where are we going?" she asked, the warmth of the autumn sun welcome on her face. "Where is my father?"

"Nothing is known about your father," Echohawk returned, glancing at her. "Yellow Eyes is the only one I truly seek at this time. And my scouts discovered that he hides from the world across the river from the Falls of St. Anthony. This is my destination."

Soon they met and joined with several other braves, and rode on together through the forest. Mariah had

heard of the beautiful Falls of St. Anthony but had
not seen them.

She had also heard of the river's treacherous waters
at the foot of the falls, which she would soon be
crossing.

It was late afternoon when they arrived at the Falls
of St. Anthony. Mariah was stunned by the grandeur
of the falls, the river there no more than half a mile
wide, breaking into sheets of foam and rushing to the
pitch over a steeply inclined plane.

The falls themselves, she noticed, were not high—
the rock face broken and irregular. Huge slabs of rock
lay scattered below, in wild disorder. Some stood on
their edges, leaning against the ledge from which they
had broken. Some lay piled upon each other in the
water, in random confusion.

A long, narrow island divided the falls nearly in the
middle. The eastern fall was not perpendicular, but
broken into three distinct leaps, below which the twisting and swirling eddies threatened destruction to any
living thing that entered them.

On the western side, in the boiling rapids below, a
few rods from the fall, lay an island—rising steeply
from the waters and covered with forest trees. Tanner
McCloud was on this island, somewhere deep within
the forest.

And, perhaps, her father. . . .

They made camp, planning to attack Tanner
McCloud's encampment early the next morning. Hungry and bone-tired, Mariah welcomed this pause, and
now, having eaten a delicious meal of cooked rabbit,
she sat with Echohawk in a cozy lean-to beside the
simmering logs of the campfire. Echohawk's braves
had fanned out from the camp to stragetic spots, keeping watch for any sudden intruders in the night.

It was nearing dusk, the air filled with a damp chill.
Echohawk placed a blanket around Mariah's shoulders

and drew her next to him. He gazed down at her without his eyeglasses, seeing her clearly and wonderfully as his. Nothing would separate them again.

He knew that he would have to think through this question of her father, should he be found at Tanner McCloud's hideout. No-din came first. If that meant having to let her father go, to keep from causing her further pain and guilt, then that was how it must be.

And perhaps because No-din was with Echohawk and his people, her father would not cause any more problems for the Chippewa. He would surely think twice before doing anything that would endanger his daughter.

"The falls are lovely yet frightening," Mariah murmured, snuggling closer to Echohawk. "This wild and picturesque beauty is surely unequaled."

"Many spirits abide here," Echohawk said, looking into the distance as the tremulous laughter of a loon came wafting over the water. "Do you hear the loon? The great northern diver is restless tonight. He does not like sharing his habitat with strangers."

"I have been told that ghosts haunt this spot," Mariah said, trembling. "There have been many deaths in the crashing waters of the falls. I . . . I even fear having to cross them myself."

Even now she could hear the crashing of large tree trunks as they drifted over the falls, plunging down into the chasms of the rocks, tumbling then into the foaming and roaring rapids, never to be seen again.

"*Ay-uh*, there have been many deaths here," Echohawk said solemnly. "The Chippewa tell of a warrior who, in the darkness of night, was deceived by the false beacons lighted by the ancestors of his enemies and paddled his canoe into the rapids. He never came out alive. And that is only one tale. There are many more."

"How awful," Mariah said, gazing around her when the loon's cries seemed closer.

"There was a song written about this warrior's death in the rapids," Echohawk said, turning to her. "Shall I sing it for you?"

"Please do," Mariah said, smiling at him.

" 'The Great Spirit calls,' " he sang softly. " 'I hear his voice in the warring waters. Soon, soon, shall they close over my head, and my song shall be heard no more. . . .' "

Echohawk took Mariah's waist in his hands and eased her onto her back on a thick pallet of furs. "My heart has been so lonely without you," he whispered. "Stay with me forever, No-din. Forever."

Mariah twined her arms around his neck, oblivious of the night's chill, aware only of Echohawk's mouth closing over hers in a fierce kiss, and of the warmth of his hand easing beneath her dress. She raised her hips, making it easier for him to remove her undergarment. After that was tossed aside and Echohawk closed his hand over her throbbing center, she sucked in a wild breath of ecstasy. When he thrust a finger within her, and his tongue began probing between her lips, the pleasure was so intensely beautiful, the world seemed to be melting away beneath her.

Moving over her with his body, his breechclout now cast aside, Echohawk smoothed her dress up past her hips and moved gently into her, then pressed endlessly deeper as she raised her hips and strained to meet him.

Mariah sucked at his lips and tongue, her hands traveling over his muscled back and then around to where she could get occasional touches of his satin shaft as he moved generously in and out of her.

She closed her eyes, a spinning heat seizing her, rising and flooding her whole body, pushing at the boundaries of her senses. That she was with Echohawk again, sharing the wonder of his embrace, was all that mattered. Their bodies and souls fused, becoming one entity.

When he moved slightly away from her, she reached out for him and drew him back. Placing her hands at the nape of his neck, she brought his lips to hers and kissed him passionately, as once again he entered her. Her gasps of pleasure became soft whimpers as she felt the pleasure mounting, then sweeping through her as his body reached a matching passion, finally subsiding exhaustedly into hers.

They lay there for a long while, Mariah gently stroking his back. "I'm sorry for having doubted you," she whispered. "You do forgive me, don't you?"

"It is easy to doubt the red man," Echohawk said, turning on his side toward her, tracing the outline of her face with his forefinger. "I am not sure that will ever change."

"It must," Mariah said, moving into his embrace, hugging him to her. "It's not fair."

"Not much in life is fair," Echohawk said. He eased away from her and drew on his breechclout and eyeglasses.

Mariah pulled her dress over her head, slipped her undergarment on, and placed a blanket around her shoulders as she moved closer to the fire. She began to speak more apologies to Echohawk, but something else drew her attention. Wide-eyed, her heart skipping several beats, she saw a loon in the fading light of evening, surely the one that they had been hearing. It was caught in the rapids.

Horrified, Mariah watched the bird as it struggled with fate for a while, but finding escape impossible, it faced downward and went under, screaming hideously, soon lost in the foaming, roaring rapids below.

"How awful!" Mariah cried, paling.

Echohawk moved to her side and sat down, his face solemn. "The red man is like the loon," he said somberly. "We struggle with fate, but to no avail. Like the river to the loon, the white man is the victor, always."

An intense chill encompassed Mariah, his words like ice water splashing through her consciousness.

"And yet you love me?" she murmured. "A woman whose skin is white?"

Echohawk turned her to face him. He lifted her onto his lap and cradled her close. "My woman, you too were a victim of a man with white skin, a man whose heart was black," he murmured. "It is I, a red man, who will make the wrongs right for you."

Mariah's eyes filled with tears. She moved her mouth to his lips and kissed him softly, sweetly. "*Mee-gway-chee-wahn-dum*, thank you, my love," she whispered against his lips. "Thank you."

21

'Tis not the richest plant that holds the sweetest
fragrance.

—DAWES

The shore was low and wet where Echohawk's braves
dragged several macinac boats into the water. They
had brought them there ahead of Echohawk's arrival,
for the purpose of crossing this treacherous river. Mariah hugged a blanket around her arms. The chill of
morning was more biting each day as autumn turned
into winter.

Seeing these larger boats, instead of canoes, gave
Mariah more confidence in their ability to make it
across the wide river. They were large and strongly
built, flat-bottomed, and pointed at both ends to as-
cend and descend dangerous rapids.

Mariah stifled a scream and took several shaky steps
backward when out of the corner of her eye she saw
a huge king snake basking on an exposed part of the
riverbank. It lay in the warmth of the morning sun,
its entire length ringed with narrow bands of brilliant
red, black, and light yellow.

"Do not fear the snake," Echohawk said, moving
to Mariah's side. "It has been slowed down by the
coldness of the night. By the time it is warmed clear
through, we will be on the other side of the river."

"Thank goodness for that," Mariah said, laughing
nervously.

"*Mah-bee-szhon*, come," Echohawk said, placing a

hand to Mariah's elbow. "The boats are loaded into the water. They are ready for travel."

The pit of Mariah's stomach felt somewhat woozy, and her throat was dry at the thought of attempting such a dangerous expedition with Echohawk and his braves. Yet, so much good could come as a result of the river crossing.

She needed to find her father, and to clear Echohawk's name.

These things alone made her step determined as she walked with Echohawk toward the boats.

The water lapping at her moccasined feet, Mariah stood in awe of Echohawk all over again when he broke into a sad, lamenting song, gazing with arms outstretched to the heavens. She listened to the words, knowing that they were meant for Echohawk's Great Spirit.

" 'Master of Life!' " Echohawk sang. " 'Look down on my braves, who have suffered wrong at the hand of the white man, and are now about to avenge it.

" 'Master of Life! Let our enterprise prosper. Let us not be seen by the enemy, and defend us from evil spirits.

" 'Master of Fate! Return us safely to our people.' "

When the song was over, Echohawk stood quietly and with great dignity in the midst of his men. Then, as he motioned to them with the gesture of a hand, his braves dispersed to their respective boats, while Echohawk helped Mariah into the one that he would command.

Once on board, sitting among many soft pelts, Echohawk and several other braves manning the oars, Mariah clung to the sides and shivered as the damp river wind dashed against her face.

Her eyes kept alert, watching the fevered changes in the water's currents. When the water slammed against the sides of the boat, it shuddered dangerously. The pit of her stomach stirred strangely when the boat would dip low, then quickly rise again as the white water tossed it about.

But, she noticed, not a sound could be heard over the roar of the falls as the boat moved steadily toward the opposite bank. As the oars dipped rhythmically in and out, it was with a silent cadence that they flowed soundlessly through the water.

Mariah inhaled a shaky breath, so relieved that the opposite shore had finally been reached. Her nose and cheeks were so cold they felt as though they might snap in two at a mere touch.

Echohawk and his men beached their boats, then Echohawk came and helped her from the boat, carrying her to land that was not damp with mud.

Once higher grasses were reached, Echohawk placed Mariah to her feet. A brave came to them. He gave Echohawk a rifle, then placed a rifle in Mariah's hand.

Echohawk smiled down at Mariah, gave her a light kiss, then nodded for her to follow him to where they soon found a faint footpath that led into the forest.

The pines were tall and straight and clean-trunked . . . worthy pillars of the forest temple. There was a light undergrowth of saplings, and many fallen tree trunks, upturned roots, and a tangle of dead branches. Quiet reigned, and sunlight flickered down through the treetops, dappling the cool greens in light and shadow.

They continued following the path for a time, then stopped sharply when through a break in the trees a short distance away they caught sight of two sentries asleep beneath a tree. Echohawk gave a signal to his braves to go on ahead and do what was necessary while he stayed behind with Mariah.

Mariah's eyes were wide as she witnessed the silent approach of the braves, creeping as silently as the padded footsteps of the panther. They grabbed the men and had them gagged and tied to the tree without even a small outcry.

Echohawk nodded for her to follow again as he began moving through the forest, the path more distinct now.

Soon voices could be heard up ahead. Mariah's eyebrows quirked when she realized that she was hearing a noisy, gleeful group of children at play.

And when she and Echohawk came close enough to see them, she watched as the children played with their dogs. She could tell that the dogs were more than likely beasts of burden and instruments of torture, for their fur was hopelessly matted, and where there was no fur, there were signs of deep lacerations across their backs. And most limped as they tried to romp with the children.

Echohawk gripped Mariah by an arm and held her close to his side as he peered at the children through a cover of bushes, and then at the women who were bent upon their tasks close to several run-down log cabins that stood in a circle of the clearing. Some were carrying great loads of wood into the camp on their backs. Some were washing clothes in a wooden tub.

But it was not so much the labor of the women or the play of the children that caught Echohawk's eye. It was that the women were a mixture—both white and Indian. The children were either half-breeds or white. This confirmed his belief that Yellow Eyes consorted with the Sioux. The proof was there for him to see.

"What of the children and women?" Mariah whispered, leaning closer to Echohawk.

He inhaled a deep breath, then set his jaw as he nodded toward the braves awaiting his commands.

Mariah watched as one by one the women and children were seized. Some of the braves took them to the boats to guard them until they could be taken to a place of safety once the confrontation with Tanner and his men was over.

Echohawk and his braves raised the war whoop and poured a shower of bullets and arrows into the cabins. The true fight began as men scurried from their cabins, some only half-dressed, surprise etched on their bearded faces.

But to Echohawk's confusion, none of these men were Sioux!

Every last one was white-skinned!

The battle raged for only a short time, the ambush having been successful. All of the men were slain. Even Tanner McCloud lay on the ground with a mortal wound.

Echohawk and Mariah went to Tanner. Mariah glared down at him as Echohawk began grilling him.

"Yellow Eyes, where are the renegade Sioux who so often accompany you on your raids?" he asked, his eyes filled with fire. "Where is White Wolf?"

Mariah knelt beside Tanner. She did not pity him the wound in his abdomen, blood pouring from it. "Where is my father?" she demanded, then paled when she saw him clutch feverishly at his chest, emitting a loud scream of pain. If he died before she discovered where her father was, she might never find him! Her eyes swept around her. The cabins seemed deserted now. Her father was surely not there.

A thought came to her which made her feel ill. If her father was not here, then he was probably dead.

Reaching a hand to Tanner's shirt collar, grasping it frantically, Mariah leaned closer to his face. "My father!" she cried. "Where is he? I know you are the one who burned his trading post. You are the one who abducted him. Where did you take him? *Where?!*"

Tanner's breathing was shallow, yet he managed a sly smile as he gazed up at Echohawk, then glared at Mariah. "You are accusing the wrong man, Mariah," he said, wheezing. "I'm not responsible for what happened to your father."

Mariah's lips parted in a gasp and her hand dropped

away from Tanner. She paled when Tanner looked slowly over at Echohawk and raised a shaky finger and pointed it at him.

"He . . . did . . . it," he whispered. "Echohawk did it. Dammit, Mariah, why don't you believe me?"

Rage lit Echohawk's eyes. He grabbed Tanner by the throat and yanked his head up from the ground. "You lie!" he hissed. "Even taking your last breath, you lie, white coward. Do you know that you cannot enter paradise with a lie on your lips?"

Tanner tried to laugh, but gurgled instead. "The Sioux? White Wolf?" he said, his voice only a thread now. "Not long ago they were defeated in a skirmish with other Sioux." His eyesight was getting hazy, but his mind was still clear. He knew that White Wolf and his renegade companions were at Fort Snelling, mingling with the other Indians at the powwow. Tanner knew that once they heard of his demise, they would retaliate, to avenge their friend's death. Tanner naturally wanted this to come as a total surprise to Echohawk.

"How can I believe that this is true when you have lied so easily about No-din's father?" Echohawk said in a snarl. "Surely honor in death is not as important to the white man as it is to the Chippewa!"

"No-din?" Tanner said, coughing up blood. "Who is this No-din you speak of?"

Mariah leaned down into his face. "*I* am No-din," she said, proud of her Chippewa name.

Tanner looked from Mariah to Echohawk. "You are with the Chippewa, dressed in Chippewa garb," he said, blood now curling from his nose. "And you now have a Chippewa name?" He grabbed at his chest and groaned, yet his eyes were still locked with Mariah's. "You choose a savage over me?"

"You are the savage," Mariah said flatly. "And you have always turned my stomach, Tanner. As for Echohawk, I adore him. I proudly warm his bed at night!"

Panic seized Mariah when she saw the wildness in Tanner's eyes and heard the shortness of his breath. She realized now how foolish it had been to speak of anything to him but her father. She still did not know where he was, and she was absolutely positive that Tanner did.

She leaned closer to his ear when his eyes closed. "Please," she begged, "tell me where I can find my father. Before you die, Tanner, please do one decent thing. For me, Tanner? Please?"

When Tanner's eyes opened and looked up at her, a strange sort of peacefulness in their depths, she felt hope rise within her, thinking that somehow she had reached a corner of his heart that hadn't hardened.

But with a shock she discovered that she was wrong. The reason for the restfulness in his eyes was that he was dead!

"*No!*" she screamed. She grabbed his shoulders and began shaking him. "You can't die! Not before you tell me where my father is!"

A gentle hand on her shoulder drew Mariah's head around. Through her tears she saw Echohawk. "He's dead," she cried. "And he didn't tell me where Father is! Echohawk, now what will I do? I shall never be at peace until I know of his welfare!"

"Perhaps it is best," Echohawk said quietly. "Yellow Eyes had no compassion. How your father died may not be a pleasant thing to know."

Mariah rose slowly to her feet, wiping tears from her face with the back of a hand. "Echohawk, it is the same for the white people as it is the red man when a beloved person has died," she said, choking back a sob. "The loved one is given a proper burial." She lowered her eyes. "Although I did not approve of my father's ways, it is only appropriate that I, his only child, see him laid to rest."

She gazed quickly up at Echohawk again. "He

would want to be buried beside my mother," she murmured. "So that they can rest in peace together."

"We shall try to find him," Echohawk reassured,
drawing her against him, giving her a warm hug. He
looked around him at his braves, who were awaiting
his orders. "Search the cabins, remove what is valuable, then burn them."

Mariah eased from Echohawk's arms and watched
guardedly as the braves went from cabin to cabin.
When one came out of Tanner's cabin carrying five
raven-black scalps, war whoops filled the air as they
went and stood beside Tanner's body, waving the
scalps over him.

"Those are scalps of my people," Echohawk said
angrily. "I know this to be true, for Yellow Eyes
would not take from his friends, the Sioux."

Some cabins were already burning, with one left to
enter. The door was bolt-locked and had to be forced
open by several braves crashing their shoulders against
it. A ray of hope sparked inside Mariah's heart when
she heard the braves shouting that they had found
another white man.

"Could it be . . . ?" Mariah said, looking questioningly up at Echohawk.

"We shall see," he answered, taking her by the
elbow, walking her to the cabin.

Mariah approached to step inside, but jumped with
a start when a rat scampered past her, desperate to
get outside.

Collecting herself, Mariah went into the cabin, and
grew instantly numb when through the dim light of
the room she viewed her father shackled to the wall,
nude and emaciated, his eye sockets like two holes in
his face, one foot partially gnawed away.

"Papa!" she gasped, fighting back a strong urge to
faint.

"Release him!" Echohawk ordered his braves.
"Take him outside!"

Her knees trembling and weak, Mariah could not help but cover her nose with a hand to ward off the stench as her father was carried past her.

Pale and nauseated, Mariah ran after him and knelt beside him as he was placed on the ground.

Echohawk came quickly to Mariah's side and placed a blanket over her father's body, up to his chin.

"Papa," Mariah cried, reaching out to touch him, but drawing her hand back as though she had been shot when he began wheezing and trembling violently with a chill.

"Mariah? How can it be? How . . . can . . . you be . . . here?" Victor Temple said, turning his weakened bloodshot eyes up to her, making out only a hazy shadow. "Thank God. You . . . are . . . all right. God, Mariah, I looked high and low for you. Where have you been? I . . . I thought you were dead."

"I was with Echohawk and his people for a while, and then I went and stayed with Colonel and Mrs. Snelling," she said, trying to keep her composure even as she saw that her father was near death. She could tell by the rattles in his chest. And she could tell by looking that he had not eaten for days. "I am here now because Echohawk brought me. Papa, I—"

"Echohawk?" Victor said, interrupting Mariah. He squinted as he tried to make out Echohawk beside Mariah. He slowly rolled his head back and forth. "No, Mariah. Not Echohawk. You can't be consorting with Indians. And especially not Echohawk. His father . . . he and your mother . . ."

"His father and my mother . . . ?" Mariah said, leaning closer to his face. "What about them, Papa?"

Victor turned his head away from her, not knowing how to tell her the truths that would hurt her. He would talk of something else. He licked his parched lips, and felt the warmth of tears flooding from his eyes and across his cheeks. "Damn that Tanner," he said, only barely audible. "He abducted me. He hated me. But with reason. I . . . I . . . I've cheated Tanner on a regular basis, and because I refused him your hand in marriage, he did this to me, Mariah."

Wonderfully happy to know that Echohawk had just had his name totally cleared of any crime, Mariah flashed him a warm smile. Her father continued to ramble on, as though seeking a way to repent for all the wrongs done to her. She listened attentively, growing more numb by the minute.

"Before I die I've many things I've got to tell you. And now," Victor said, looking pleadingly up at her. "I've protected you from so many things in your lifetime—among them the truth that could have hurt and confused you as a child. But it is only fair to you that you know everything. You are now an adult and can stand up against such knowledge better than you could have as a child."

He paused and coughed, blood spewing from between his lips.

Mariah winced and bit her lower lip, still caring too much for her father not to feel remorse for him as he lay dying before her eyes.

"Long ago, Mariah," Victor continued, knowing that he could not delay telling her any longer. "When me and Colonel Snelling were stationed with General Hull's army in Detroit, your mother had an affair with Colonel Snelling. Mariah, you are the offspring of that affair, but even I didn't know of this deception until your mother confessed the truth on her deathbed."

He coughed again and stopped to take a long shaky breath, then continued, oblivious of Mariah's bloodless complexion and wide eyes, her hands at her cheeks, stunned speechless by this revelation.

"Mariah," Victor said, lifting a bony hand to her cheek, patting it, "I knew of your mother's affair with Josiah Snelling, but I had not been aware that you were his. She was very clever in her deceptions! She had more than one affair while married to me. She had an affair with Chief Gray Elk. She killed herself over that Indian who put his people's welfare before hers, a white woman."

Echohawk grew stiff and his jaw went slack, to hear such a thing about his beloved father. Even while a dutiful father to Echohawk, Gray Elk had been in love with a white woman!

He turned his eyes away, ashamed, yet now understanding why Mariah's father had hated Chief Gray Elk with such a vengeance—and why he had long ago come to the village of Chippewa and killed and maimed so many.

He looked down at the dying white man, knowing that if it had been he whose wife had wronged him with another man, he would have hated as much. He would have become as hard-hearted.

Ay-uh, it was easy now to see the reasoning behind this man who had pretended to be Mariah's father for her sake.

In truth, he was a man of good heart!

Mariah was finding it hard to comprehend what was being said to her, yet knew that it must be the truth. It would make no sense at all for her father to lie to her now.

Yes, she concluded sadly, it was all true. Her dear sweet mother had been guilty of many infidelities. It was hard to accept—harder still to know that this was not her true father who lay at her feet dying.

But she did understand so much now—why Victor Temple had grown to hate all women and why he had forced Mariah to dress and behave like a man. She understood why he had become a cold and embittered man.

And the fact that he was not her true father? How could he have loved her at all, except that he had already raised her as his for six full years before knowing the truth. By then, in his heart, she *was* his daughter.

Mariah now saw many more pieces fall into place. Her father's coolness toward Colonel and Mrs. Snelling. And the way he tried to keep her from becoming their friend, when she accompanied her father to the fort for supplies. And the true reason for Victor Temple attacking Chief Gray Elk again after all those years. It was not so much for his lame leg as because of a grudge that he had carried with him over a woman!

Mariah stared down at the man she had always called Papa and watched him reach out to her, pleas for forgiveness on his parched lips. Knowing what he had been forced to endure because of his faithless wife, and now understanding this man whose heart had turned bitter, yet still had done his best to raise a child that was not his, Mariah leaned over and hugged him, her tears wetting his clammy cheeks.

"Papa," she sobbed. "I'm so sorry about everything. If I had only known. I would have made life much simpler for you. I . . . I would have been nothing but good to you."

"Mariah," he whispered harshly, coughing. "My dear sweet Mariah!"

She winced when his body tightened, then went limp, and his breathing ceased.

"No," she whispered, still clinging. "Please, Papa, let me make it all up to you!"

"Mariah, he is gone," Echohawk said gently, placing a hand on her arm, drawing her reluctantly to her feet. He drew her into his embrace. "We were both wrong about him. Deep within his heart, there was much good."

"I know," Mariah murmured. Yet as much as she pitied Victor, she could not help but be relieved to know who her true father was.

Colonel Snelling was a man of honor.

Colonel Snelling was a man of morals.

He was a father who could be revered, trusted, and relied upon.

This man at Mariah's feet had long ago lost all of those virtues.

Filled with sadness and regret, Mariah turned to Echohawk. "We must travel to Fort Snelling soon to clear your name," she said. "And I want to face my father with the truth. Surely he will be as happy as I to know this. There has been a bond between us from the very beginning. Now I know why. Somehow we surely sensed our blood ties."

"It may be best to keep this truth hidden within your heart," Echohawk suggested.

"I doubt that I can," Mariah said, thinking of William Joseph, and that he was her half-brother. How grand to know that she actually had a brother. And Colonel Snelling had fathered seven children by Abigail! That meant that Mariah had seven brothers and sisters, if even only half kin to her.

"Let us leave this sorrowful place," Echohawk said softly.

Mariah glanced back down at Victor Temple. "After I see to his burial," she murmured. "It can't be as I had at first wanted it. He would not want to be buried beside my mother's grave, after all."

A deep sadness came into her eyes as she thought about her mother and how she had always worshiped her in her memories.

She did not know how she should feel now.

22

A merry heart goes all the day,
A sad tires in a mile.

—SHAKESPEARE

The sound of singing and throbbing drums marked a victory celebration at Chief Silver Wing's newly established village—a village bordering a serene lake, very pretty with its encircling of majestic pine and maple trees.

Mariah was taking comfort in Echohawk's arms as she sat beside him before a roaring fire in the dance lodge, venison steaks simmering and dripping tantalizing juices into the flames.

As the drumbeats quickened, Mariah tried to enjoy the merriment. But she was unable to shake her sadness over Victor Temple's death and his last confessions. She snuggled closer to Echohawk and concentrated her thoughts on the celebration. Several men and women in colorful attire formed an immense circle inside which sat seven drummers around a huge drum. As the drummers beat a continuous rhythm, lusty voices shouted and wailed the songs which belonged to each dance. The sound was a strange mixture of a raucous coyote chorus and the minor music of a storm-brewing wind.

A young girl dressed in white doeskin stepped away from the others, shaking a *she-she-qua*, rattle, and started a rhythmic chant that seemed to be all timing and no tune. Soon other young girls joined in her chant and began to dance.

"Is it not a beautiful performance by the young Chippewa maidens?" Echohawk said, taking Mariah's hand, clasping it. "They would welcome you if you wish to join them."

Recalling her clumsiness at Abigail's ball, Mariah gazed over at Echohawk, smiling. "I don't believe I would be welcome for long," she said. "I am not a skilled dancer, Echohawk, I seem to have four feet instead of two when I try to dance."

He laughed heartily, then turned and nodded a hello to Nee-kah as she came and sat down beside Mariah. "And how are you faring, Nee-kah?" he asked, eyeing her abdomen, which was developing rapidly with child. His eyes softened with affection as he reached around Mariah and placed a gentle hand on Nee-kah. "Soon you will have a child to join the dancing and singing. Of course the child will be a son."

"*Ay-uh*, a son," Nee-kah said, in her heart praying that it would be so. For her husband she must bear a son! And for herself—for she did not want to be cast away so that he could take another wife who might have more luck at birthing sons than she.

Echohawk's gaze returned to Mariah. "No-din and I will have many sons and daughters," he said, his eyes twinkling into Mariah's. "Is not that so, No-din?"

Mariah's face reddened with a blush; then she looked at Nee-kah. "*Ay-uh*, many," she murmured. "Just like Josiah and Abigail Snelling. It is not fair to a child to be raised without brothers and sisters." She smiled radiantly at Echohawk. "For so long I was without brothers and sisters. But now I have many!"

The sound of horses arriving outside the dance lodge caused all merriment to cease. Everything became so quiet, only harsh, frightened breaths could be heard.

A brave, one who had been guarding the approach of the village, entered the lodge and went to stand before Chief Silver Wing, who sat opposite the fire from Echohawk.

Chief Silver Wing rose slowly to his feet, frowning. He tried to hide the alarm in his eyes that had sprung there upon hearing so many horses, when he knew that almost all the braves were in the dance lodge attending the celebration. Only a few had been outside in strategic places to keep watch for intruders.

"What is it?" Chief Silver Wing grunted as Echohawk came to his side, as stern and as quiet as the elder chief. "Whom have you escorted into the village of Chippewa?"

"William Joseph Snelling and soldiers from Fort Snelling," the brave said, his gaze moving from Chief Silver Wing to Chief Echohawk. "He comes in peace. He wishes council with the two chiefs of this village. Do I escort him to the council house? Should I say that you will be there soon to smoke the pipe of peace with him?"

Mariah's heart was thundering wildly, torn over how to feel. She was anxious to see William Joseph, now knowing that he was her blood kin. Yet she was apprehensive of him being here, for Chief Silver Wing had moved his village far from Fort Snelling and all white people because he felt safer in isolation.

Also, she feared for Echohawk. Although his innocence had been proved, they had not yet gone to Fort Snelling to clear his name.

"Tell him we will share a smoke with him," Chief Silver Wing said after getting a nod of consent from Echohawk. "Take him there. We will soon follow."

As quickly as the people had gathered for the celebration, they were gone, leaving the dance lodge eerily quiet.

Mariah went to Echohawk and placed a hand on his arm. "Take me with you," she said. "Let me sit in council with you. Echohawk, I may be needed to convince William Joseph of your innocence. Neither my father nor Tanner McCloud is alive to explain it. Let me sit beside you to speak for you, if necessary."

Nee-kah went to Chief Silver Wing and clung to his hand. "I, too, wish to sit in council," she said softly. "My chieftain husband, I am saddened greatly that the white pony soldiers have found our village again."

Chief Silver Wing and Echohawk exchanged troubled glances, then nodded. Mariah warmed clear through when Echohawk placed a blanket around her shoulders. Chief Silver Wing placed a blanket around Nee-kah's, and together they left the lodge and stepped out into the frosty night air.

Mariah shivered as the cold pressed against her face. The first snows were near. Every morning and evening now the little streams which led away from the rivers were puckered with ice.

Tonight the moon was high in a velvety clear sky, and the stars shone so brightly, it was as though hundreds of thousands of candles were burning in the heavens.

In the distance the silence was broken by a lone coyote howling at the shadow of the moon. A shiver not related to the cold fled down Mariah's spine as she caught sight of several soldiers standing beside their horses close to the large council house.

Her gaze swept over them. William Joseph was among them. When their eyes locked, Mariah's pulse raced, for now that she knew that he was her brother, she could see so many resemblances in their features!

But her attention was quickly drawn from her brother. With Echohawk she entered the council house, where a fire was already burning brightly. Solemnly, and with a humble heart, Mariah went with Echohawk and sat down beside him on a platform cushioned with many animal pelts, while Chief Silver Wing and Nee-kah sat down beside them on the same platform.

A young lad entered, carrying a large pipe with

many colorful feathers attached at its bowl. He took
the pipe to Chief Silver Wing, which he accepted and
rested on his lap, while the young lad knelt on his
haunches on the floor beside him.

"Tell William Joseph that he can now enter," Chief
Silver Wing said, nodding at a brave, who quickly
responded to the command and soon returned with
William Joseph at his side.

Remaining seated, Chief Silver Wing gestured with
a hand to William Joseph. "*Nah-mah-dah-bee-yen*,
sit," he said without expression. "Let us share in a
smoke. Then tell us why you have come with many
pony soldiers to my village."

As William Joseph settled down on a rush mat beside the fire, his gaze stopped at Mariah. He looked
at her quizzically. It looked as though she belonged
beside Chief Echohawk, but why?

The young lad rose and brought a flaming twig to
Chief Silver Wing and placed the flame to the tobacco.
Chief Silver Wing drew on the stem, the sweet aroma
of tobacco soon rising into the air.

Chief Silver Wing then straightened his back, waved
the lad away, and puffed on the pipe for a moment,
passing it then to Echohawk, who also smoked from
it and in turn handed it to William Joseph.

After all three had shared in the ritual, Chief Silver
Wing rested the bowl of the pipe on his knee. "Now,
William Joseph, tell us why you are here," he said,
his expression guarded. "It was not my intent that any
pony soldiers ever ride into my new village. I meant
to lead my people to a place of peace. Your presence
threatens this peace."

William Joseph's gaze moved from chief to chief,
then momentarily locked on Mariah again, still confused by her presence here. But of course she was
here on her own initiative. Neither Echohawk nor Silver Wing abducted white women! His mind was swirl-

ing with questions, yet he straightened his back as once again he focused his full attention on the chiefs.

"For several days I have been in pursuit of Chief Echohawk," William Joseph said. "One of my trusted scouts came to me with the news of this location. I had hoped to find Chief Echohawk with you."

"And what do you want with Echohawk?" Chief Silver Wing asked, his shoulders stiffening.

"Answers to questions about the disappearance of Victor Temple," William Joseph said, his gaze once more moving to Mariah. "And also the disappearance of Mariah from my camp. I see that she is safe. That is good."

"And what questions do you have concerning me?" Echohawk interjected, seeing William Joseph's intenseness as he stared at Mariah, yet no longer jealous of such attention. William Joseph did not know they were related, but it was enough that Mariah knew.

"We at Fort Snelling received word that an Indian identified by his eyeglasses was involved in raids close to Victor Temple's trading post," William Joseph said, clearing his throat nervously as he felt everyone's eyes heatedly looking at him, even Mariah's. "Of course I had to follow such leads and question Echohawk. That is why I am here. To get answers and take them back to my father, who has sent me on this mission."

"And does your father see me as guilty of such crimes?" Echohawk said, his voice a low growl. "He has always known me to be a peace-loving man. Would gossip mean more to him than how he has always perceived me?"

"My father did not believe the gossip," William Joseph said, placing his hands on his knees, leaning forward. "That is why he has sent me to ask you to return to Fort Snelling. All he needs from you is your word that you had no part in what happened to Victor Temple." He glanced over at Mariah. "I need no further explanation myself. Mariah wouldn't be sitting at your side if you had had anything to do with her father's disappearance."

William Joseph paused, then added, "Mariah, I don't understand. Why are you with Echohawk? You sit at his side as though you are his—"

"Wife?" Mariah said, interrupting. She lifted her chin proudly. "William Joseph, I am not his wife yet. But I will be soon. I plan to make my future with Echohawk."

"But you went to Mother and Father, asking for their assistance," William Joseph said, his confusion and dismay apparent.

"That was only because I did not think Echohawk wanted me," she said in defense. She slipped a hand over one of Echohawk's. "But I was wrong. He wants me very much."

Mariah wanted to reach out to William Joseph and tell him that he was her brother, but she did not think this was the appropriate time. It would be best, she thought to herself, first to tell William Joseph's father—and then the rest of the family.

She suddenly realized that the truth might be hard for all concerned to accept, except for herself. She, of course, was jubilant with the knowledge.

"And how is it that you *are* with Echohawk?" William Joseph asked.

"Because I could not sleep that morning in your camp, I took a ride," she softly explained. "And I came across Echohawk at that time. I went with him then to—"

"She accompanied me and my braves to find out the truth," Echohawk said, taking over. "The truth about her father's disappearance—and many more things. Tonight when you arrived my people and Chief Silver Wing's people were celebrating a victory over the truths that were uncovered."

"Truths?" William Joseph asked, arching an eyebrow. "What do you mean?"

"Yellow Eyes," Echohawk said blandly. "The truth about Yellow Eyes."

William Joseph leaned forward. "Who is this Yellow Eyes?" he asked, looking from Echohawk to Mariah.

"That is Echohawk's nickname for Tanner McCloud," Mariah quickly explained.

"Tanner McCloud?" William Joseph said, again arching an eyebrow. "What about him? What does he have to do with any of this?"

"Tanner McCloud is the one who spread the lie about Echohawk," Mariah said before Echohawk could speak for himself. "Tanner was the one who burned my father's trading post. He's the one who abducted my father." She swallowed hard, then added, "He's the one responsible for my father's death."

"Your father is dead?" William Joseph said in a low gasp.

"After abducting my father, Tanner locked him up in a cabin without food and water," Mariah said, lowering her eyes, the thought of her father's dying breaths almost too painful to bear. "He died because of this mistreatment."

"And Tanner?" William Joseph dared to ask. "What of him?"

"He is no longer among the living," Echohawk said without hesitation. "And that is good. For years he has abused my people *and* yours. He was a worthless cheat and liar. He was greedy. His spirit hovers now, somewhere between darkness and light, never to be at peace."

William Joseph wiped a hand across his face, shaking his head slowly back and forth, then peered at Echohawk with a warm smile. "I'm glad that your name has been cleared," he said softly. He gazed with compassion at Mariah. "But I'm sorry about your father."

Mariah's lips parted, and she came close to telling William Joseph that he wasn't her father—that *his* father and hers were one and the same.

William Joseph rose to his feet. "I will return to Fort Snelling and tell my father everything," he said, smiling down at everyone. "And when you have the time, Echohawk, *and* Silver Wing, come and speak peace with my father. It will look better in the white community for those who will still carry doubts about your innocence in their hearts."

Mariah rose along with Echohawk and Silver Wing and Nee-kah and went to William Joseph. One by one William Joseph embraced them, and when he came to Mariah, she looked adoringly into his eyes, seeing a reflection of herself in their depths. She was so very happy that he was her kin!

"Thank you for everything," she whispered, clinging to him as he pulled her into a hearty hug. "Tell Abigail and your father that I appreciate what they did for me, and that I'm sorry if I gave them one moment of concern. I should have sent word to them that I was all right."

"That you are is all that is important," William Joseph said, easing her from him and holding her at arm's length. He winked down at her. "Whenever you like, Mariah, I'll give you a few dancing lessons."

Mariah covered her mouth, stifling a giggle. "I have dancing lessons to learn here," she finally said. "And the Indian dances are even more complicated than those I encountered at the fort."

"No-din is an apt student," Nee-kah said, smiling at Mariah. "She will learn everything of the Chippewa culture very quickly."

"No-din?" William Joseph said, stroking his chin as his eyes smiled at Mariah.

"She is 'Woman of the Wind' to the Chippewa," Echohawk said, placing a possessive arm around her waist, drawing her close to him. "No-din. Woman of the Wind."

As they all stepped from the council house, the first snowfall of winter was upon them. Mariah looked up at the snow as it fell from the sky, the flakes so big it was as though petals from wild plum trees were settling on her upturned face.

She looked at the wigwams, the snow on them making them look like huddled ghosts on the open plain.

"Come soon to Fort Snelling," William Joseph said, swinging himself up into his saddle. He gave a vigorous wave, then barked the command that sent the soldiers away in a hard gallop.

Chief Silver Wing turned to Echohawk. "It is good that that is behind us," he said, heaving a long sigh. "Now, Echohawk, before the snows become heavier and more frequent, you must concentrate on establishing for yourself a new village. If you so desire, build it side by side with mine. We will be as one, yet led by separate chiefs."

Echohawk contemplated this suggestion for a moment, then placed a gentle hand on Chief Silver Wing's shoulder. "Thank you," he said, smiling broadly. "My people will accept your offer with a glad heart!"

"That is good," Chief Silver Wing said, clasping Echohawk's arm in brotherhood and good faith.

"I am cold," Nee-kah said, clinging to the blanket around her shoudlers.

"The woman with child must be seen to," Chief Silver Wing said. He whisked Nee-kah to his side and walked her away to their wigwam.

Echohawk and Mariah went to their own wigwam and embraced with a long, sweet kiss.

"Lie down beside the fire and cover yourself with the warm buffalo robes," Echohawk said softly.

Perfectly content, Mariah did as he suggested, then

watched as he busied himself heating several smooth round stones in the fire.

After these were thoroughly heated, Echohawk wrapped the rocks in strips of warm blankets, then knelt beside Mariah and placed them at her feet. "You will be warmed clear through soon," he said, crawling beneath the piles of heavy robes beside her. He embraced her and drew her against him. "When will you say that you are ready to be my wife? How much longer do I have to wait for you to voice this aloud to me, the man who loves you?"

"Do you doubt at all that I will be your wife?" Mariah asked, smoothing her hand along the sculptured lines of his face. "I am here, am I not?"

"*Ay-uh*, and I will never let you go," Echohawk said, brushing a kiss across her lips.

"Echohawk, before we speak vows of marriage, I first want to make things right in my life," she murmured. "I want to reveal myself to my true father."

"I understand," Echohawk said, nodding. "As soon as the new wigwams are built and my people have a sense of belonging again, we will travel to Fort Snelling. We will both meet with Colonel Snelling, but for separate reasons."

"*Ay-uh*," Mariah sighed. "And then, my love, I will go through whatever ceremony is required to be your wife."

Echohawk smiled to himself, knowing that she would be greatly surprised when he told her that a private ceremony had already been conducted that had made them man and wife.

When the time was right, *ay-uh*, he would tell her!

He looked through the smoke hole overhead and to the sky. It was no longer snowing, the clouds having drifted away. Tonight the stars seemed to be the eyes of the gods, shining down at him and his beloved . . .

23

Of all the tyrants the world affords,
Our own affections are the fiercest lords.
                              —EARL OF STERLING

Several Weeks Later

The wind swept across the snow-silent slopes. Mariah and Echohawk's horses loped along the crusty white trail, obscured by a blizzard of spinning snowflakes. Even though Mariah was wearing a snug bearskin coat, its hood framing her face, and winter moccasins lined with rabbit fur, she still trembled, her teeth chattering, as the bitter chill of the early evening stung her cheeks and nose. When she and Echohawk had set out for Fort Snelling earlier in the day, the sun had been brilliant overhead, and the snow that had fallen the previous day had begun to melt from the limbs of the trees.

And then an unexpected snowstorm had blown in over the land. In the forest that fringed the river, powdery snow smoked into the wind from the limbs of the great cottonwoods, and grass spiked upward through the icy crusts that stretched across the meadows.

Mariah and Echohawk had been too far from their village to turn back. They had decided that it was best to travel on to Fort Snelling, since they had postponed the trip already too many times. Their newfound love, free of all doubts and suspicions, absorbed them completely. And the unusually harsh weather had made it hard to gather the appropriate materials for the new village's wigwams.

But in time, when the dwellings were finally built, Echohawk's people were able to settle in for the winter. Chief Silver Wing's generosity extended even to helping supply Echohawk's people with enough staples to get them through the winter.

And now Echohawk felt free to leave his village and people to take care of his affairs at Fort Snelling—to talk peace with Colonel Snelling and to see that his name was completely cleared.

Mariah glanced over at Echohawk, seeing how wonderfully handsome he was, even though mostly covered by a bearskin coat which matched hers. He rode tall in the saddle, as though he were an extension of his prized Blaze.

And he no longer had to wear the eyeglasses, although he still found them useful for hunting and target shooting. Mariah didn't mind them at all, in fact she secretly loved the quirky addition to his rugged features.

But she knew that *he* detested the eyeglasses and was awaiting the day he could cast them aside entirely, for he felt that they took away from his nobility—his prowess as a great hunter and invincible leader.

Her mittened hands clutching onto the reins, her eyes now directed straight ahead, she tried to ignore how the wind continued to hurl stinging pellets of snow at her. Her thoughts turned to her own reason for going to Fort Snelling, besides traveling with the man she loved for moral support. She was finally going to come face-to-face with her true father. She was determined that he know she was his daughter. And surely he would be as happy about it as she. He had always treated her as though she were someone special.

But perhaps that was because he had always felt sorry for her, never having approved of the way she had been forced to live with Victor Temple—as though she were a boy, instead of a girl with a girl's desires and dreams.

She wanted more than pity.

She wanted the love of a true father.

Her thoughts went to Abigail. What would she think of this revelation? It was not Mariah's wish to hurt her feelings, yet Abigail did not seem the sort whose feelings could be injured all that easily. She was a strong breed of woman who had experienced many misfortunes in life while accompanying a husband whose ambitions took him in the way of opportunity and temptations. But of course Mariah would tell Josiah privately and let it be his decision whether or not to break it to his wife.

And then there was William Joseph. Mariah was proud to be able to call him her brother. He was such a dear sweet man, kindhearted through and through. She had even felt a strange sort of bonding with him upon their first acquaintance.

Now she knew why.

And she had to wonder how *he* would feel!

Evening shadows were beginning to lie long and dark on the snow as Fort Snelling came into view through the break in the trees ahead. Mariah was barraged by assorted emotions as she anticipated the moments ahead with her true father. She had waited a lifetime, it seemed, to tell him her secret.

She looked guardedly at Echohawk. He had not offered much conversation this entire journey, and she understood why. Even though William Joseph had assured them that Echohawk's name would be cleared, she and Echohawk knew that it was hard for the white community to cast aside suspicions where an Indian was concerned. So many could still insist that Echohawk was guilty in spite of the evidence to the contrary. It was those people that she feared.

Echohawk turned to Mariah. He reached out to her, smoothing the cold flesh of his fingers across her cheeks, rosy with color from the freezing air. "Your face is too cold," he grumbled. "This journey would have been best delayed again."

"No, I don't believe so," Mariah said, extending a mittened hand, covering his. "I am fine. Just a little bit chilled, but fine. But what of you? You don't have as much on as I."

When they had first set out on the journey, she worried about him withstanding the cold, for he said that a chief did not wear hand coverings, nor did he hide beneath a hood. His peripheral vision must not be impeded by anything worn around his face, having to be alert for any unsuspecting traveler on the trail, and his hands must not be encumbered, having to be free to use a weapon quickly should the need arise.

"Since childhood I have learned to endure many things," Echohawk said, frowning. "Among them the cold months of winter. It is the Chippewa brave who must learn early how to withstand the cold, for it is the brave who must see that food is on the table. The hunt does not end just because the snows come."

As the wide-open gate of the fort was upon them, Mariah and Echohawk became silent as they rode into the courtyard.

Mariah sighed with relief when she found the courtyard all but deserted, seeing only a few straggling soldiers trudging through the snow, their heads bent to the wind. Only a few looked up and stared at Mariah and Echohawk.

Other than that, only the sentries posted at each side of the gate had taken full notice of them.

But the sentries, knowing Echohawk so well, had waved him and Mariah on without questioning them.

Mariah's attention was now on the house that sat at the far end of the courtyard. Her heart began to pound at the prospect of knocking on the door, her father perhaps the one to open it. Even though the Snelling household was well staffed, she had noticed in the short time that she had lived there that if Josiah was at home and not busy with his ledgers in the study, he would go to the door instead of the butler.

Riding onward in a slow lope, Mariah looked over at Echohawk. "Soon, Echohawk, things will be cleared up and we can return to a peaceful life with your people," she said, anxious for that also. Through all of the difficulties these past weeks, they had not yet taken the time for the marriage ceremony. Mariah did not like to feel as though she were living in sin by not being married. She only hoped that as the good Lord looked down from his place in the heavens, he would have seen her recent difficulties and understood.

"I owe so much to Chief Silver Wing," Echohawk said. "It was with a sad heart that he did not accompany us on this journey of peace. But I saw his reasoning as wise. Our villages should never be left without a chief. Our people need the reassurance a chief's presence affords them."

"I believe that he again was thinking of your welfare by deciding not to accompany us," Mariah said softly. "He wanted this moment to be yours alone. It is your vindication sought here, Echohawk. Not so much Silver Wing's."

Echohawk nodded. "*Ay-uh*, that is so," he said, then grew silent as the shadow of the great Snelling mansion loomed over them.

Together Echohawk and Mariah dismounted and secured their reins to a hitching rail. With an anxious step and heart, Mariah walked beside Echohawk up the stairs to the porch, inhaling a nervous breath before knocking.

She waited with wide eyes for the door to open. When it did, she took a step back, not recognizing the man who answered it. While living with the Snellings, she had become acquainted with all of their servants, and this man's face was not familiar to her.

There was something unnerving about the man, a

cold aloofness to his stance that made a chill ride Mariah's spine. He was tall and thin, his clothes black except for a stiff white collar that framed a long, narrow face with tight, drawn features—and eyes that appeared empty in their opaque grayness.

"Yes?" the man said, looking suspiciously from Mariah to Echohawk. "What can I do for you?"

"We have come to meet with Colonel Snelling," Mariah said, firming her chin. "Please tell him that Mariah and Echohawk are here."

"That would be impossible," the man said stiffly. "Colonel Snelling no longer resides here. So if you will excuse me, I must see to my other duties."

Mariah was stunned speechless by the man's words. She stared up at him for a moment, her lips parted, then placed a hand to the door, stopping him from closing it. "You must be mistaken," she said, her voice quavering. "This is Colonel and Mrs. Snelling's house. They must be here."

"Mariah? Echohawk?"

Mariah and Echohawk turned around in unison when the familiar voice spoke behind them.

"William Joseph!" Mariah said, rushing down the steps, grabbing one of his gloved hands. "Your parents. Where are they?" She gave the servant a quick glance over her shoulder, then turned questioning eyes back to William Joseph. "Tell me that he is wrong. They aren't gone, are they?" Her gaze lowered, and she swallowed hard, then looked up at William Joseph again, panic rising within her. "They have to be here. Tell me they are!"

Echohawk came to Mariah's side. He swept an arm around her waist and drew her next to him. "We have come to have council with your father," he said. "If he is no longer living in this house, take us to his new residence. We have traveled a long way, through much cold weather, to speak peace with your father. We wish to do it now, William Joseph."

"My father has been transferred to Jefferson Barracks in Saint Louis," William Joseph said, looking apologetically from Mariah to Echohawk. "I've neglected getting a message to you. I now see that I should have, but the weather has been bad. I was waiting for it to break, and this happened so suddenly."

Mariah paled. "Your father has been transferred?" she gasped, her hopes of ever being able to reveal her special secret to her true father waning. "Why? When?"

"He received his orders from Washington only last week," William Joseph said solemnly. "My parents departed for Saint Louis on a riverboat as quickly as they could get things settled here."

"But what about Echohawk?" Mariah blurted, for the moment forgetting her own reasons for having come to Fort Snelling. "Your father was to assure him that his name has been cleared. Now what is Echohawk to expect? Will the white community still condemn him? Will he never be able to ride free of worry, in danger of someone ready to shoot him in the back for . . . for crimes he didn't commit?"

"I assure you both that Echohawk's name has been cleared," William Joseph said, placing a hand of friendship on Echohawk's shoulder. "Before my father left, he sent out a decree wide and far, stating your innocence. You have nothing to fear, Echohawk. Nothing."

Echohawk smiled warmly at William Joseph. "That is good," he said. "When you see your father again, thank him for me."

"I will not be seeing him soon," William Joseph said, his eyes wavering as he glanced down at Mariah. "I'm returning to Boston. I am through with my adventuresome days of being an interpreter. I am going to pursue a career in politics in Boston."

Mariah's heart skipped a beat with this news, now

realizing that she was going to lose William Joseph from her life almost as quickly as she had discovered that he was her brother.

It wasn't fair.

None of it!

A part of her wanted to cry out to William Joseph that she was his sister, yet another part warned her that this was not the best thing to do, since she might never be able to tell her father the truth.

This saddened her—this silence that she felt compelled to maintain.

"No-din, we must return to the village," Echohawk said, turning to her. "The weather. It could worsen. It is best that I get you home, warm between blankets beside our fire."

William Joseph gave Echohawk and Mariah an anxious look, then said, "You are surely tired from your travels. Why not stay the night in my cabin, then leave tomorrow? You will travel much more safely if you are rested."

Mariah was bone weary, and her disappointment seemed to have worsened her fatigue. And she felt strangely empty, having so looked forward to seeing her true father, and now he was gone.

Echohawk considered William Joseph's offer for a moment. He looked at Mariah, knowing of her disappointment and sadness, and feeling that was enough to cope with tonight without forcing her to ride the entire night in the freezing cold.

He turned grateful eyes to William Joseph. "*Mee-gway-chee-wahn-dum*, thank you. Your offer is accepted," he said. "Your warm fire will be welcomed tonight."

"You can leave your horses here," William Joseph said, stepping between Echohawk and Mariah. "I'll send my groom to take good care of them." He placed an arm around each of their waists and led them on across the snow-covered courtyard. "And you can have my cabin all to yourselves. This is my last night at Fort Snelling. I've a few things to settle with some of the men." He chuckled when he saw Mariah's anxious look, knowing she'd misinterpreted what he had said. "A poker game, Mariah. I plan to get into a hot game of poker tonight."

Mariah laughed loosely, sighing with relief. She gladly walked with Echohawk and her brother to William Joseph's cabin. Once inside, she went to the fireplace and let the warmth soak into her flesh, then removed her coat and gloves. Echohawk followed her lead, removing his.

"You two make yourselves at home," William Joseph said, his gaze sweeping around the sparsely furnished room, where he had stayed only since his parents' departure for Saint Louis. "It's not much, but there is plenty of food. Eat what you like. I'll see you two in the morning."

William Joseph turned to leave, but stopped, having just remembered something. He went to a cabinet and opened a drawer, taking a small buckskin pouch from inside it. He took it to Mariah and placed it in her hand.

"My father left this with me to give to you when I next saw you," he murmured, closing her fingers around the pouch. "He said that he'd owed your father a debt for some time—something about gambling while they were stationed with General Hull's army in Detroit a long time ago. Somehow they both forgot about the debt. Father just happened to remember it the other day. He said that since your father is no longer alive to collect on it, then it should be yours."

Mariah's lips parted in a surprising gasp. From the heaviness of the pouch, she knew there must be considerable money there. "Why, I don't know what to say," she said, her face coloring with an excited blush. She had never had anything she could call her own.

The money she had spent at Fort Snelling had always been her father's, used only for supplies.

Oh, how often she had eyed the lacy bonnets in the mercantile!

And the satin ribbons!

Now she could buy what she chose, yet it felt strange to be taking money that was not really hers.

"Thank you, but I can't accept this," she murmured. "Please, William Joseph, take it back. It was my father's. Not mine."

"Mariah, it is now rightfully yours," William Joseph said, moving toward the door. "And you deserve it. From what Mother and Father told me, you were hardly more than a slave to your father." He smiled at her over his shoulder. "Take this as fair payment."

Mariah stared at the pouch, then looked up at William Joseph. "Yes, I shall," she said, smiling.

As William Joseph placed his hand on the door latch, she rushed to him and flung herself into his arms. "Thank you," she murmured. "I shall miss you."

"We shall never truly be apart," William Joseph said, relishing having her in his arms, at least just this once. "You will always be in my thoughts."

He gave her one last hug, then swung away from her and left, Mariah feeling strangely empty in his absence. But she understood why. She had only recently discovered that she had a brother, and she'd expected to develop a close relationship.

It tore at her heart, thinking of this loss.

Seeing Mariah's sadness, Echohawk drew her into his embrace. He ran his fingers through her hair, comforting her. "I am sorry about your father," he said softly. "That you did not see him is unfortunate. And I am sorry about your brother—that you did not feel free to tell him that you are blood kin."

Mariah sniffled, fighting back tears. "I wish there was a way . . ." she whispered, clinging to Echohawk.

"Being able to see my true father and telling him my discovery meant so much to me."

Her eyes widened and she leapt from Echohawk's embrace, the pouch of coins still heavy in her hand. "Echohawk, there *is* a way!" she said in a rush of words. "I am sure that I have enough money to take us to Saint Louis by riverboat! And there would surely be enough for our lodging once we arrive there. What a wonderful idea! We can go to Saint Louis and surprise my father with the news!"

Echohawk's jaw tightened and his eyes narrowed. "It is not a thing a Chippewa does—ride in a white man's great wheeled vessel, the 'walk in the water.' It is a strange canoe, even larger than the voyageurs' big transport canoes," he said uneasily. "The Chippewa's place is with his people. Not on a giant canoe among whites."

"Echohawk, this is something new for me also," Mariah pleaded. "Let us share this new experience together."

When he did not answer her, she knew that she had no choice but to defy him, for she had made up her mind to go to Saint Louis. She would never be totally content until she came face-to-face with her true father.

"Echohawk," she quickly added, "I *must* go to Saint Louis. *Please* understand. And if you do not go with me, I will be forced to travel alone."

Echohawk's eyes blazed with fire. "You would do this even if I forbid it?" he said, his voice drawn.

" 'Forbid' is a strong word," Mariah said, taking a step back from him. "My father forbade me so much. Am I now to expect such behavior from the man I love? I cannot live like that, Echohawk. My judgment—my decisions—must be considered important or I . . . I cannot live with you."

Stunned by Mariah's stubbornness, Echohawk stared at her for a moment, then went and jerked a blanket from the bed and placed in on the floor close to the fireplace. Stretching out on it, he ignored Mariah as she gaped at him in disbelief. It was not a time to speak further words. He had much to sort out within his heart.

Seeing that Echohawk was settled in for the night, his back to her, Mariah stifled a sob of agony, then went to the bed and threw herself across it. Silent tears flowed from her eyes. She had never thought that her need to see her father would come to this. Echohawk was actually making her choose between him and her father, a father she had only recently discovered.

24

Laugh if my cheek too is misty and drips—
Wetness is tender—laugh on my lips.
—EASTMAN

The pit of her stomach feeling hollow, seeming always to lose more than she gained, Mariah wiped a fresh flow of tears from her cheeks, yet did not allow herself to cry out loud. She did not want Echohawk to know that he had hurt her so deeply.

Yet he had, and she was not sure if she could ever forgive him.

His mood—his anger—had stung her heart, her total being!

So caught up was she in her hurtful feelings that Mariah did not hear Echohawk's approach to the bed. When he was suddenly there, stretched out behind her, his body pressing into hers from behind, her breath was momentarily stolen away.

Then she closed her eyes in ecstasy as he turned her around to face him, his mouth soon covering her lips in a tender, loving kiss. She was fighting her feelings, appalled that she could so quickly forgive him his anger. Even that he had made demands of her seemed to be dimming in her consciousness.

She loved him so much, so very, very much. . . .

Echohawk drew his mouth from her lips. His hands framed her face gently. "No-din, I was wrong," he said, drawing her eyes flutteringly open. "I should never have made demands on you. While with me, my woman, I want you to feel free to make your own

decisions. I understand how it was for you while living
with the man you thought was your father. I never
again want to be compared to that tyrant. If you have
the need to seek out your true father, I will not object.
It is not my right to. Although you have promised
yourself to me, that does not mean that you have
handed over to me your freedom. Perhaps that is so
between many men and women. But with us it will
not be so. I love you too much to stifle you."

"But moments ago you . . . you behaved so differently," Mariah murmured, unable to completely relax
with Echohawk's change in moods. She wanted to,
oh, how she wanted to! "Echohawk, you made demands on me. Are you saying that you will no longer
do this? Ever? Once I speak wedding vows with you,
it is to be *ah-pah-nay*, forever. I want to live with you
with a peaceful heart."

"My woman," Echohawk said, brushing a soft kiss
across her lips. "Did you not listen well to what I
said? I have seen the wrong in my demands. Never
will I do this again. While with me, you will have the
freedoms you desire, to make you feel a complete
woman. No-din, your pride is as important to me as
my own. Never will I give you cause to ride with lowered, humble eyes. While riding at my side on your
steed, always you will have a lifted chin and proud,
bright eyes!"

Tears filled Mariah's eyes again, but this time they
were of pure joy. She crept into Echohawk's arms.
"My darling, handsome Chippewa chief," she said,
her heart soaring. "Oh, how I adore you."

They kissed. They embraced feverishly. And then
Echohawk drew his lips away only a fraction. "One
thing," he said thickly. "You cannot go alone to Saint
Louis on the white man's large canoe. My people are
at peace and safe with Chief Silver Wing. I will send
him a message that my return will be delayed. *Our*
return will be delayed. Together, you and I, we will

go in search of Colonel Snelling. You will have that opportunity to speak words of love to your true father."

"You would do that for me?" Mariah said, breathless at the thought of traveling on the riverboat, the thrill now doubled at the thought of being with Echohawk on such an adventure.

"For you, anything," Echohawk said, smoothing his hands through her hair. "My woman, you have been without a happy heart for too long. It is my duty to see that your heart has cause to sing all the days of the rest of your life."

"Only moments ago I was filled with such despair," Mariah said, gazing into his fathomless dark eyes. "But now? I feel as though I am floating. And all because of you, Echohawk. You are so understanding. So kind."

"And I am sorry for having caused you despair," Echohawk said, gazing lovingly at her. "You have forgiven me my moment of stubbornness?"

"*Ay-uh*," Mariah said, smiling softly up at him. "How could I not forgive, when you are giving me the world? And how could I not, when I love you so much? You are my life, Echohawk. When I thought that I had lost you because of a misunderstanding, I could hardly bear it. I . . . I felt completely hollow. Thank you for giving me back my reason for living, darling."

She frowned as a sudden thought came to her. "You say that you will send word to Chief Silver Wing about your decision to travel with me to Saint Louis," she said. "Darling, whom would you trust to do this? You do not want the location of your village known to anyone but the Chippewa."

"It is no longer a secret," Echohawk said, his voice strained. "Do you forget the pony soldiers who accompanied William Joseph there?"

"How could I have forgotten?" Mariah said, paling slightly at the thought.

"I will question William Joseph about those who rode with him," Echohawk said, his fingers busy working Mariah's dress over her shoulders. "I will ask him to assign his most trusted scout to go to my people—to speak with Silver Wing. He will do this for us, No-din. William Joseph is a man who cares, not only for his own welfare but also for yours—and mine—for everyone who deserves his kindnesses."

"Yes, he is a most special man," Mariah said, again filled with sadness over not being able to share her secret with William Joseph. "My brother is a very, very special man."

"Enough talk," Echohawk said, smoothing Mariah's dress on down her body, revealing her silken pink flesh to his feasting eyes. "We are alone. We are in love. Let us *make* love."

Mariah sucked in a wild breath of ecstasy as he moved his lips to one of her taut nipples, taking it in his mouth, his tongue swirling slowly around it. Her heart pounding, she busied her fingers disrobing him.

When he was also nude, she ran her fingers down the smoothness of his copper skin, stopping one of her hands where his velvety shaft lay against her thigh, hard and heavy. As though having done this thousands of times before, in truth having only recently learned such skills, Mariah curled her fingers around his hardness and began moving her hand on him. When he threw his head back in a throaty groan, she knew that she was giving him pleasure—the same as he then gave her as his hands cupped her breasts, kneading them.

And then he urged her hand away from him and moved over her with his body. Gently nudging her knees apart, he pressed himself into her and began his rhythmic strokes.

Her body quivered with the wondrous rapture his movements created inside her. She locked her legs around his hips and rode him, her hips moving with him. She closed her eyes and moaned against his lips as he kissed her, the feelings awash throughout her a mixture of agony and bliss.

When he paused in his loving her, drawing his body away from her, she beckoned for him with outstretched arms, her heart on fire with need.

Echohawk smiled down at her as he moved to kneel beside her, his lips moving close to her again. Her blood quickened when his lips burned a trail down her neck, teasingly brushing them against her breast in only a slight touch, and lower still, across her abdomen.

When he moved his body again, this time positioning himself between her outstretched legs, she felt as though she was soaring above herself when he began loving her gently with his mouth and tongue where she so unmercifully throbbed.

She felt uneasy about this way of loving, yet she abandoned herself to the torrent of feelings that overwhelmed her, her excitement rising with this different, exquisite fashion of loving.

When Echohawk began to bring her to that ultimate of sensations, she gripped his shoulders lightly and urged him up and over her again.

His eyes dark and knowing, Echohawk twined his fingers through her hair and brought her lips to his. He kissed her long and hard, darting his tongue into her mouth, causing new sensations to awaken within her.

When he entered her again with his pulsating hardness, she shuddered and lifted her hips to meet his every thrust. His mouth moved from her lips, brushing the glossy skin of her breasts. Her head rolled and she bit her lower lip to stifle a cry of sweet agony when he began sucking her nipple. His mouth was hot and demanding on her breast. His movements within her were becoming more intense. She opened herself more widely to him, absorbing each of his bold thrusts.

And then she could feel his body stiffen and could hear his breath coming in short raspy sounds. He paused loving her for a moment, stopping to gaze at her with hot passion in his eyes. Then he brought his mouth to her lips with a savage kiss as once again he plunged into her, over and over again.

The euphoric moment they had been seeking suddenly claimed them. Their bodies jolted and quaked into each other, their moans of pleasure mingling as their lips met in an even more heated kiss.

Then at last they lay clinging, sweat glistening on their bodies like small pearls shining beneath the sunshine. Mariah ran her fingers through Echohawk's thick hair and kissed his wet brow. "Will we truly have a lifetime of such moments as these together?" she whispered, her body still slightly trembling from the intensity of the lovemaking. "It is like a dream, Echohawk—being able to share such wondrous bliss with you."

A sob rose from deep within her and she hugged him tightly. "I adore you so," she whispered. "Please always, always love me as much as you do now."

"Our lives are now intertwined, as one entity," Echohawk whispered back, softly kneading her buttocks with his hands. "Your heartbeat is mine. Mine is yours. Our souls are the same. *Ah-pah-nay*, forever, No-din. Until the Great Spirit decides to take us from this earth." He leaned away from her, smiling. "Even then we will be together. We shall walk hand in hand, always, in the Land of the Hereafter."

"How wonderful it is," Mariah said, smoothing her forefinger across his full sculptured lips. "That you are mine forever is a miracle."

He rolled away from her and rose from the bed. Drawing a blanket around his shoulders, he went to the table and eyed the fruit that lay on a platter. He glanced over his shoulder at Mariah.

"Making love makes you hungry, does it not?" he asked, laughing softly as he heard her stomach growling even from this distance. He picked up an apple and took it to Mariah. "We shall share the fruit, like we have shared our bodies."

He placed the apple to her lips. Leaning up on an elbow, Mariah smiled at him with dancing eyes as she sank her teeth into the apple, taking from it a large hunk. She began to chew, and watched as Echohawk took a bite, chewing also as he gazed at her with his deep black eyes.

Mariah rose suddenly to a sitting position and ran the fingers of a hand over his brow. "Darling, I'm so glad you can see more clearly now," she said, looking into the depths of his dark eyes.

Echohawk sat down on the bed beside her and looked around the room, having to squint to be able to see the objects in the far, shadowed corners. "*Ay-uh*, I can see perfectly," he said, "but when I look into the distance, there is still a slight blur."

Mariah hopped from the bed, excitement filling her. "That means, Echohawk, that you will surely be able to see one hundred percent soon!" she cried, clasping her hands together before her. "Isn't that wonderful?"

Seeing her standing there, silkenly, exquisitely nude— the fullness of her breasts, her slimness, the supple broadening into the hips with their central muff of hair, and her long, smooth thighs—made his hunger increase, but not for food. He wanted his No-din again. This was evident in how his manhood had risen into a tight hardness again, the ache the kind that only being with No-din could quell.

Mariah saw the sudden passion filling his eyes, and as he tossed the apple and the bear pelt aside, she felt the heat of desire flood her through and through when she saw his readiness for her.

With a feverish need, she went to him and quivered with ecstasy as he gathered her into his arms and led her back down onto the bed. The sensations were searing within her as his fingers and lips moved purposely slowly over her body, teasingly stroking her flesh.

Her hands sought and found his pulsing hardness and caressed him, making him shiver and groan with the ecstasy. When he leaned away from her and brushed her hand aside, she molded her body up against his as he knelt over her and filled her with his length. She absorbed the bold thrusts with rhythmic upward movements of her hips, his mouth crushing her lips with a fiery kiss, drugging her.

Their bodies strained together hungrily, and then once again their passion was sought and found.

Afterward Mariah nestled close to Echohawk, breathing hard, her loneliness banished forever. When he leaned away from her and looked down at her with adoring love in his eyes, she pulled his head down and kissed him.

She melted into him when once again he entered her with his revived hardness. She shuddered and gripped his buttocks lightly. Her mouth clung to his in a long, blistering kiss. The delicious pleasure filled her again, and her body rocked and swayed in her passion.

She moaned throatily as once again she found that wondrous ecstasy within her lover's arms. . . .

"How can it be?" she whispered against Echohawk's perspiration-dampened face afterward. "We have made love three times so quickly. My darling, not long ago I did not even know the *ways* of making love!"

"In time I shall show you many ways of taking and giving pleasure," Echohawk said, smoothing dampened strands of hair back from her brow. "Nee-kah was right when she said that you were an astute student. My woman, you have learned already many ways of loving."

"Only because it was you teaching me," Mariah said. She sucked in a wild breath as he lowered his head to her nipple and circled it with his tongue, then trailed his lips wetly downward, stopping at the juncture of her thighs. As he thrust his tongue against that part of her that still throbbed from his lovemaking, she closed her eyes and let herself enjoy it all over again.

This man, she marveled to herself. *Ah, this delicious, heavenly, wonderful man.*

Because of Echohawk, she had been transformed into a woman, and felt blessed that it had not been too late for her.

25

A girl with eager eyes . . . waits me there . . .
Oh heart . . . ! . . .

—BROWNING

Several Days Later

For the first several days the riverboat had moved calmly through the waters of the Mississippi. But on the seventh day, the day planned for the arrival to Saint Louis, snow had begun to fall, the wind blowing with tremendous violence.

Mariah and Echohawk were in their cabin waiting out the storm, uneasy as they could feel the boat pitching to and fro in the water. They could hear the pounding of the waves, beating like thunder against the sides of the boat. The splash of the great paddle wheel seemed puny as it struggled through the fevered water. Oh, how the noise grated against Mariah's nerves!

"Perhaps we shouldn't have boarded this . . . this monstrosity," Mariah said, gladly accepting Echohawk's arms around her. "At first I thought the boat was beautiful with its lacy latticework trim and fancy spindles, but now I feel as though it is nothing more than a toy." She clung more strongly to him. "I'm afraid, Echohawk. What if the boat suddenly gets swallowed whole by the angry river?"

"Without people manning the paddles, I do not see how the boat is maneuvered anywhere," Echohawk grumbled. "It is not at all like the canoes of my people."

Mariah clung a moment longer, then eased out of

his embrace when she became aware of a lessening of the howling winds and the steadying position of the boat as it moved more smoothly through the water.

She went to the small window and gazed outside through the muck and mire of the glass. She felt much relieved when she saw that the snow was no longer whirling about, so obscuring the atmosphere that objects could not be distinguished at a distance of one hundred yards. It had been one of those tremendous storms called *poudries*, in which neither the Indians nor white people normally dared to stir abroad and when even the wolves flew to the woods for shelter.

"It's finally stopped snowing," she sighed heavily. She turned and gazed eagerly at Echohawk. "We haven't left the cabin much since we've been aboard. I would like to now, before arriving at Saint Louis. Would you go with me, Echohawk, to take one last look?"

"If you can stand the cold," he said, going to her, taking her hands. "No-din, living with the Chippewa, you will *have* to learn to accept the cold temperatures of winter better than you did living the life of a white woman. There are always duties for both men and women outside the wigwam. After the lakes are frozen, it is required that all men and women be strong enough to ward off such temperatures, to be able to get wood for warmth and water for drinking. The winter months require more stamina than the summer months."

"And I won't disappoint you," Mariah said, smiling. She eyed the door, then looked up at him again. "Let's go. Let's explore."

She had not encouraged much exploring after boarding the boat. She could not help but see an uneasiness creep into Echohawk's eyes, even though only moments ago he was trying to convince her of so many things. Earlier, as they had boarded the boat, and the few times they had mingled with the others, she had seen how the other travelers gaped openly at him, then had looked at her with disgust when they recognized that she was with him, a woman whose skin was white.

She understood quite well that to most people it was a forbidden thing—the union of an Indian man and a white woman. She herself had feared ugly comments while traveling the full week to Saint Louis. But she had prepared herself for any and all snide remarks. She would defend her right to be with Echohawk to the end, if necessary.

She would defend Echohawk with her life, if need be!

Echohawk helped Mariah into her bearskin coat and then slipped into his own. Together they stepped out onto the deck. The temperature was not much below the freezing point, but the wind pierced their garments like a knife. The snow had finally stopped, and Mariah went to the rail and peered over the side, seeing that the riverboat was following close to the banks, partially sheltering it from the blast of the wind.

At times during the journey the boat had struggled, grating upon snags, and hanging for two or three hours at a time on sandbars. The weather had now cleared, showing distinctly the broad and turbulent river with its eddies, sandbars, ragged islands, and forest-covered shores.

Mariah had read in her studies that the Mississippi River was constantly changing its course, wearing away its banks on one side while it formed new ones on the other. At present the river was low, and it was almost frightful to see dead and broken trees firmly embedded in the sand, all pointing upstream, ready to impale any riverboat that at high water should pass over them.

Shivering, Mariah looked up at Echohawk. "I've seen enough," she said, laughing softly. "Let us return to our cabin. I plan to place much more wood in the small stove. I am ready to be toasty warm again."

Echohawk swept an arm around Mariah and led her across the deck past several cabins before reaching their own, the passengers consisting of traders, gamblers, soldiers and their wives from Fort Snelling, and Oregon emigrants and "mountain men."

Just as they reached their cabin, Mariah and Echohawk were stopped when suddenly a man in a black cape blocked their way as he quickly exited the cabin on their left side. Mariah stiffened when his dark eyes shone with mockery as he glanced from her to Echohawk. He looked like the villains that she had read about in books, his mustache as black as the hair that was partially exposed at the edges of the top hat he was clutching with one hand, a cigar between the fingers of his other.

"What do we have here?" the man said in a snarl, his eyes still roaming over Mariah and then Echohawk. "I've seen you once or twice these past several days. A white woman and an Injun. Now, ain't that an interesting combination?"

Echohawk's eyes lit with fire, yet he willed himself not to show the anger he was feeling. "Step aside, white man," he said, his voice smooth and even. "Nodin is cold."

The man's dark eyes widened and his mustache quivered as he smiled wryly down at Mariah. "Nodin?" he said mockingly. "It wasn't enough that you chose a damn savage as a travelin' companion, but you let the Injun give you the name of a squaw?" He reached a hand out for Mariah. "Come on. Let me show you the real world."

Before Echohawk could stop him, the man had jerked Mariah into a cabin filled with laughing, raucous men sitting around a table, cards scattered across the top, along with many coins, and bottles of whiskey.

Frightened, not only for her own safety, but also for Echohawk's should he do anything to antagonize these men, Mariah did not attempt jerking herself free. She scarcely breathed when Echohawk moved stealthily into the room, illuminated by one lantern, smoke hanging low over the table like billows of fog.

"Men, look what I've brought you. A little plaything," the man said, shoving Mariah further into the room, close to the table. "We have us a little squaw here." He jerked Mariah's coat off, revealing her buckskin dress. "She ain't only travelin' with an Injun, she has an Injun name and she's dressed like one."

The men cocked their eyes up at the man and gave him annoyed stares. "Blackie, goddammit," one of the gamblers said exasperatedly, "what do you think you're doin'? Let her go. Do you hear? We don't want no trouble. We just want to sit here peaceful-like, playin' poker. The last thing we need is Injun trouble."

"It's only one Injun," Blackie said, turning glaring eyes at Echohawk. He took a step toward Echohawk and stared up at the eyeglasses. "And I can't figure this one out. He's wearin' spectacles." He laughed throatily as he grabbed the eyeglasses from Echohawk's nose and dropped them to the floor, crushing them with the heel of his boot. "Now. Should you decide to defend your little whore, I can fight you fair and square, since you don't have spectacles on to hide behind."

Goaded beyond human endurance, Echohawk could not hold back his rage any longer. He reached a hand out to Blackie and locked it behind his neck, forcing him quickly to the floor, on his stomach. Echohawk straddled him, and leaned his mouth close to his ear. "Hear me now, white man," he warned, his voice a low hiss. "You push me too far and you will regret it."

"All right, all right," Blackie said, his eyes wild,

one cheek pressed hard against the floor. "I apologize. Just let me up. I won't bother you no more."

Believing him, Echohawk let his hold on the man grow slack. And just as Echohawk started to rise away from Blackie, Echohawk found himself at the disadvantage and on the floor. A knife was quickly drawn from a sheath at Blackie's waist and held close to Echohawk's throat.

"Now who is threatening who?" Blackie said, laughing boisterously.

Her heart pounding, and seeing that the other men were not going to intervene, even though they apparently did not approve of Blackie's tactics, Mariah knew that she must be the one to make the next move. Eyeing a whiskey bottle on the poker table, she inched her hand toward it. She was surprised that the men allowed even this, for when she picked the bottle up by its slender neck, they did not shout out a warning to Blackie.

Her knees weak with fear that she might cause Blackie to plunge the knife into Echohawk's flesh, she crept closer to the man, then stopped and said his name—sweetly and seductively.

"Blackie? Why bother with him when you can have me?" Mariah said tauntingly.

Seemingly stunned by her flirting, Blackie forgot his concentration and eased the knife aside as he turned to look up at Mariah. She grabbed this opportunity to bring the whiskey bottle down on his head, the knife in his hand no longer a threat to Echohawk.

Glass shattered and Blackie's body lurched from the blow, his eyes wild as they locked with Mariah's, and then he tumbled over sideways onto the floor, unconscious, the knife at his side.

One of the gamblers scrambled to his feet. Mariah was expecting to be assaulted for what she had done, but instead found kind arms propelling her away from the unconscious man, allowing Echohawk to rise from the floor.

"We apologize, ma'am," the gambler said, his blue eyes soft and kind as he gazed down at Mariah from his six-foot-four height. "Blackie ain't nothin' but a troublemaker. And rest assured we'll keep him away from you and your friend until you are safely off the boat."

"That is kind of you," Mariah said. "Thank you ever so much."

Echohawk came to her, brushing his hair back from his eyes. He grabbed up Mariah's coat, took her by the hand, and whisked her out of the cabin, embarrassed that it was she, a woman, who had defended him, the man, again!

Yet by doing so she had demonstrated her intense love for him, and that made his heart swell with pride.

"Your eyeglassess," Mariah said, going into their cabin beside Echohawk, closing the door behind them. "Echohawk, that evil man broke your eyeglasses. Now what are you doing to do?"

"I will do well without the white man's magic," Echohawk grumbled. "I can see nearly as well as I did before."

Relieved to be back in the privacy of their cabin, Mariah held her hands over the stove and rubbed them together, warming them. "You don't have to be inconvenienced for long," she said, glancing at him over her shoulder. "While we are in Saint Louis we can use some of my money to fit you with new eyeglasses."

"The man did me a favor," Echohawk said, tossing his coat aside. "I am glad the eyeglasses are gone."

When someone knocked on the door, Mariah turned with a start and her face paled, wondering if Blackie had come to finish what he had started. She stifled a gasp behind her hand when Echohawk went to his belongings and grabbed a rifle in his large hand.

He turned to Mariah. "You step out of the way," he whispered harshly. "I don't want you taking a bullet that was meant for me."

"Oh, Echohawk, I hope we're wrong," Mariah said, moving around to stand beside the bunk. "I hope that man doesn't ever wake up!"

"You hit him hard enough," Echohawk said, moving stealthily toward the door when someone continued to knock. "But it always seems that an evil man's head is harder than that of one born with kindness in his heart."

Aiming the rifle with his right hand, Echohawk moved his left slowly to the door latch. He opened the door quickly and found himself aiming the barrel of his firearm directly into the eyes of the riverboat captain, whose color drained instantly from his face.

"Please . . . ?" Captain Johns muttered, his eyes frozen wide. "I've only come to apologize for the inconvenience you encountered at the hands of . . . of that damnable gambler Blackie. I've forbidden him on my ship in the past. So shall I now, in the future!"

Echohawk turned the barrel of the rifle away from the captain, holding the firearm at his side. "Your apologies are accepted," he said, feeling Mariah's presence at his side as she came quickly to him.

"Also, I have come to tell you that Saint Louis is within range should you wish to view it," Captain Johns said, lifting his hat, wiping beads of perspiration from his pale brow.

"Let's go and watch as the boat is moored, can we, Echohawk?" Mariah said, looking anxiously up at him.

Echohawk inhaled a nervous breath, then stood the rifle against the wall and stepped outside with Mariah and the captain.

Mariah's breath was taken away when she saw the size of the city set back from the waterfront. The buildings were quite impressive, some even four stories high! And the roads! They were filled with many horses and buggies and fancy carriages!

But what she was most anxious to see was Jefferson Barracks. Even though she wanted to go into some of the fancier shops to see the ribbons and laces, and perhaps even purchase herself a fancy bonnet and dress before presenting herself to her father, it was Colonel Snelling himself who was most prominent on her mind now.

"Sir, where might I find Jefferson Barracks?" she blurted as Captain Johns moved beside her at the rail.

"Ma'am, Jefferson Barracks is up the river a ways," he said, pointing beyond Saint Louis proper. "You can hire a carriage to take you there."

Mariah beamed up at Echohawk as he gazed down at her. "Echohawk, I shall see my father soon!" she said, thrilling to the thought. "Can you imagine? We are finally here and I . . . I will be able to see my father."

"Your father?" Captain Johns asked, forking an eyebrow. "Does he make his residence at Jefferson Barracks?"

"Yes," Mariah said, clasping her hands excitedly together before her.

"What is his name?" the captain asked, smiling. "Perhaps I know him."

Mariah's smile faded, not feeling comfortable about revealing her father's name before he knew himself that he *was* her father.

But somehow it just came out.

"Colonel Josiah Snelling," she blurted. "He's my father."

She frowned and cocked her head when she saw a sudden sour look come across the captain's face. He turned and walked away without another word.

"Why did he behave so strangely?" she asked, looking confusedly at Echohawk. "Perhaps he doesn't like my father."

"Do not let one man's attitude take away your excitement today," Echohawk said, placing an arm around her waist. "It is *your* day. Yours and your father's."

Mariah inhaled a shaky breath, Echohawk's comforting words already causing her to forget the strange behavior of the riverboat captain. She was looking dreamily into the distance, ready to count out the moments until she could embrace her true father, until she could proudly present herself as his daughter.

26

She is most fair, and thereunto,
Her life doth rightly harmonize.

—LOWELL

After leaving the riverboat, Echohawk held on to Mariah's elbow as they climbed the steep incline that would take them into the major part of the frontier town of Saint Louis. In 1825 it was a mere village on the western bank of the great Mississippi, on the edge of a vast unexplored land.

The sun warmed the snow, melting it, making their footing more sure as they finally reached the cobblestone street that reached out on both sides along the river. The town extended in both directions on either side, clusters of stone houses standing on the western bluffs.

Mariah was absorbing everything as she and Echohawk crossed the thoroughfare and stepped up onto a wooden sidewalk, soon mingling with an assortment of passersby—white-, red-, and black-skinned alike.

A scattering of teams and saddled horses were hitched to the wayside posts. And mingled amidst the buildings were picturesque whitewashed houses which stood close to the street behind high picket fences. Most of them were built of logs set upright on the ground, but some were puncheon walls and shingle roofs, with piazzas running all four sides. All were clean and white, surrounded by fruit trees, long gardens stretching behind them.

In one sweep of the eye Mariah saw several saloons,

a millinery shop, two hotels, and various merchant shops. Her nose took her to stand at the window of a bake shop, emanating from it a rich aroma of cinnamon, apples, molasses, yeast, and the smoke of hickory and oak.

She looked anxiously up at Echohawk, who was tense and quiet beside her. Although she had never been to such a large town herself, she knew that it had to be an even stranger experience for Echohawk. She had seen how he had looked so warily at the men who sported large firearms at their hips, those men having stared just as warily back at him as he held his rifle tightly within one of his powerful hands.

She saw how Echohawk looked with wondering eyes at the dark-skinned men and women hustling by, apparently having never seen black people before. She had tried to explain that most were more than likely slaves, perhaps in town gathering up supplies for their masters, but he could not fathom the idea of one man owning another.

She saw how Echohawk flinched as he walked in the shadows of the taller buildings, having never seen anything as high, except for the walls at Fort Snelling and the high bluffs in the Minnesota wilderness.

"Echohawk, I have enough coins not only for lodging and a new dress and bonnet but also for a sweet bread," Mariah said, trying to draw him into conversation. He had been so subdued, so quiet, since their arrival in Saint Louis. She wanted him to relax and enjoy it, the same as she. Before the end of the day she would even have cause to celebrate. She was going to claim her birthright!

"Sweet bread?" Echohawk said, forking an eyebrow. "What is a sweet bread?"

Mariah took his hand and began leading him toward the door of the bake shop. "It is something quite wonderful and delicious," she said, giggling. "Come on. Share with me."

Echohawk was hesitant, then went inside with her, his nostrils flaring with the pleasant aromas wafting through the air. He watched silently as Mariah transacted the business of acquiring what she called sweet bread. He saw her shake several coins from her buckskin pouch and hand them to the proprietor, dressed in white, then watched as she smiled broadly as she was handed something in a small sack.

"It smells and looks delicious," Mariah said, leaving the bake shop with Echohawk. "Afer we settle down in a hotel, we shall have ourselves a private feast. I have had a sweet bread only once, and that was at the Snellings' residence. The icing! It just melts in one's mouth!"

They walked on, once again in silence, taking in everything. Men in colorful frock coats, narrow trousers, and high boots, and women in their silken finery, fur capes, and fancy bonnets brushed past them, ignoring them as though they weren't there. A boy was sweeping out a stableyard. A man strolled by, slouched, his aged shoulders seeming heavy beneath his ragged coat, a basket on his arm, apparently carrying his eggs and butter to the market for selling. An occasional pig rambled by, scavenging. They were lean, lanky creatures and had noses long and slender enough to drink out of a jug. A few pigeons also strutted along the thoroughfare, scattering in all directions when threatened by an approaching, thundering carriage.

But something else drew Mariah's keen attention, making her wonder how she could have forgotten this special season of the year.

Christmas!

With all of the recent traumatic experiences, she had forgotten about Christmas!

They were now walking in the part of the frontier town that displayed only the finest of boutiques and art galleries, where the shopping was enhanced by a town-wide effort at seasonal decorating. Beribboned greens wreathed and outlined the shops and buildings. Trees with shining ornaments graced each window.

The powerful perfume of the pine boughs reminded Mariah of the Christmases that she had shared with her mother before she had passed away. Without the aid of her father, Mariah and her mother had gone into the forest and had chosen the largest tree they could drag back to the house. They decorated it together, giggling and singing.

Once done, its boughs were heavy with myriad precious things. Amid many tapered candles had been hung intricate paper cutouts, cookies, pieces of taffy, tiny toys, gilded ornaments, strings of popcorn and cranberries, ribbon bows, and dried flowers.

At the tree's peak had floated a delicate angel. . . .

Tears burned at the corners of Mariah's eyes, her vision of her mother clouded with the truths she now knew about her. She glanced over at Echohawk, knowing now that her mother had been immoral not only once, but many times. And Mariah was the result of one such affair!

Deep within her heart, Mariah knew that she could never forgive her mother for these infidelities.

This, again, reminded her of her mission today. Her true father! She did not want to delay seeing him much longer. She must hurry and buy herself a beautiful dress and bonnet. She then must find a hotel that would accept her and Echohawk as guests in the same room.

Mariah smiled up at Echohawk as they stopped in front of a shop that displayed velveteen dresses and matching bonnets. "Do you understand my need to dress differently today?" she asked softly. "I so want to look as pretty as I can for my father. And, Echohawk, I have wanted a velveteen dress and bonnet for so long! Just this once, darling. Then I shall never again wear anything but buckskin."

She paused, then added, "And I want to buy a gift for Nee-kah . . . something that she will treasure."

Echohawk placed a gentle hand to her cheek. "Today is your day," he said softly. "You do what you must."

Mariah hugged him, then grabbed his hand and led him into the shop with her.

When the woman in charge caught sight of Echohawk, she inhaled a quick startled breath and paled. She covered the diamond necklace that lay against the velvet of her dress, her thin lips pursing angrily as she glared at Mariah.

"I wish to see your most lovely velveteen dress," Mariah said, ignoring the frustrated sales clerk, whose beady eyes annoyed more than angered her. "The color I prefer is pale green."

"There are no dresses here for you," the woman said, her narrow face pinched into a deep frown. "Now, be on your way."

Echohawk took a bold step toward the woman. He towered over her and his eyes narrowed. "My wife sees many dresses," he said, his voice drawn. "One of them will be hers." He nodded to Mariah. "Find the one you wish to buy. Choose a bonnet. I have no doubt the lady here will take your gold in payment."

The lady took a step back from Echohawk, fear in the depths of her eyes. "Yes, my dear," she said thinly. "I will be . . . be happy to help you choose, if you wish."

"No, that's not necessary," Mariah said, hurriedly finding her size, the correct color, and then the bonnet that she felt was the loveliest of the many, with lace in abundance on it. She chose her special gift for Nee-kah, Echohawk's warm smile showing his approval, then quickly paid the clerk and waited for her purchases to be wrapped. She was glad to leave the shop, having hated putting Echohawk in such an awkward position.

Prejudices, it seemed, ran rampant everywhere, even in this frontier town of Saint Louis. She was saddened that it was hard for anyone to believe that there was such a thing as a peaceful Indian.

She dreaded the next chore, feared entering the hotel with Echohawk, and what the desk clerk's attitude might be when she paid for only one room—and only one bed.

But of course the clerk would not know that they were not married, so that did not concern her as much as what his attitude might be over an Indian staying in his hotel.

Again there were difficulties to be faced—and conquered!

Under any other circumstances Mariah would have been thrilled at the prospect of staying a full night in a fancy hotel room. Many times she had passed her lonely nights reading books that her father had acquired for her at various trading posts. She had read of the hotels where plush carpets covered the hardwood floors and satin draperies hung at the windows. She could not even conjure up thoughts of how soft the beds must be in such elegant rooms.

She silently said a prayer of thanks to Josiah Snelling for having remembered owing her father a gambling debt. She was taking much delight in spending the money!

The shadow of a four-story hotel fell across Mariah and Echohawk as they stepped up to the door. She looked at Echohawk, his arms filled with her purchases, his rifle resting in the crook of his left arm.

Then she walked on into the hotel, her chin held proudly high. Without hesitation, ignoring the murmurs and glances as people broke away on both sides, making room for her and Echohawk, Mariah went to the desk clerk and shook many coins from her buckskin pouch.

"I would like whatever room my money can pay

for," she said, looking square into the desk clerk's nervous eyes.

His eyes shifting to Echohawk, the clerk reached for a key behind him and grabbed one without seeing even which one he had chosen, then slapped it down on the desk. "And how will you be signing the register?" he asked, running a thin finger around the stiff white collar of his shirt.

"Mariah Temple," Mariah said matter-of-factly. She took up the pen and scratched her name on the register, then grabbed up the key and held it out for Echohawk to see.

"And how about . . . about the Indian?" the clerk asked, now running his fingers nervously through his thinning gray hair.

"He is to share my room, of course," Mariah said over her shoulder, prancing toward the steep staircase.

She again ignored those curious eyes in the lobby as Echohawk walked beside her to the stairs. But when he stopped and gazed slowly around, at the grandeur of the lobby, and then up the staircase, his eyes filled with wonder, Mariah understood.

"It's as new and as awesome to me," Mariah said, leaning close to Echohawk so that only he heard her. "I've never seen anything as grand. Nor have I ever been on the fourth floor of a building. My, but we shall see perhaps clean down the river to Jefferson Barracks!"

They went up the stairs, stopping at each landing take a look from the window at the end of the corridor, then proceeded until they reached the fourth floor and found their room. When they stepped inside, Mariah's heart leapt with delight. It was as she had always dreamed a hotel room would be—grand and spacious.

She rushed into the room and jumped onto the bed, sinking deeply into the feather mattress. Her eyes took in the satin draperies . . . the plush cream-colored carpet . . . the heavy oak furniture.

Then she went to the window and grew solemn, anxious. From this vantage point she *could* see Jefferson Barracks on the edge of the river in the distance. It was not as grand as Fort Snelling, but that did not matter. It housed her father!

Echohawk laid the packages aside, and also his rifle. He walked lithely across the soft carpet, comparing it to thick beds of moss in the forest. Very gingerly he bent low over the bed and pressed his fingers into the mattress, jumping back, startled, when it gave way to his touch.

And then he crept over to stand beside Mariah, his heart thundering wildly when he took a look from the window and saw how high he was off the ground, and how the river looked like a large snake winding along the ground not far from the hotel.

Mariah leaned into his embrace. "Isn't it beautiful?" she marveled; then her smile waned when she looked into his eyes. His expression had taken on a wistful, somber quality that did not match her giddy joy.

He peered into the distance, at the forest that stretched out far onto the horizon on the opposite side of the river. He could see many tepees, and wondered which Indians made residence so close to this frontier town of Saint Louis. It would be good to smoke with them, yet this was not the time for powwows between two factions of Indians. The powwow today was to be between Mariah and her father.

He drew her around and framed her face between his hands. "Let us wait no longer to go to your father," he said earnestly. "Your heart is anxious. I can see it in the pulsebeat at the hollow of your throat."

"*Ay-uh*, I am very anxious," Mariah murmured, her face beaming with anticipation.

Echohawk lowered his mouth to her lips and kissed

her gently, then went and stared curiously at an upholstered chair. He eased himself into it, and watched
comfortably as his woman changed clothes and became transformed into a vision of loveliness.

Mariah and Echohawk arrived by carriage at Jefferson Barracks. Once inside the massive stone walls,
Mariah saw a neat row of buildings. She noticed that
Jefferson Barracks was a hubbub of activity, soldiers
and civilians coming and going, mingling in the courtyard on foot, and on the roads, on horseback and in
carriages.

Mariah's gaze stopped at the stone headquarters
building as the carriage stopped before it. Soldiers
soon appeared at the carriage, one on each side.

As the door was opened beside her, Mariah quickly
explained why she and Echohawk were there, and the
hesitation of the soldiers seemed to be because Echohawk was with her.

Mariah and Echohawk were not invited from the
carriage. One of the soldiers went inside the building,
and soon a stout man dressed neatly in a blue uniform,
with brass buttons picking up the shine of the sun,
came to Mariah and reached a hand out to her, helping her from the carriage.

"Young lady, what is this about you having come
to see Colonel Snelling?" the soldier asked, casting
troubled glances at Echohawk as he kept his seat in
the shadows of the carriage.

"I have made a long journey to see the colonel,"
Mariah said, her voice edged with irritation. "He is
the commandant here. Please take me and my companion to him."

Again the stout man gave Echohawk a questioning
stare, then focused his attention on Mariah again.
"My dear, your travels were in vain," he said blandly.
"Colonel Snelling is no longer here." He cleared his

throat nervously and kneaded his chin as one of his thick gray eyebrows arched.

Then he spoke further without hesitation. "You see, Colonel Snelling has been ordered to Washington," he said, clasping his hands together behind him. "He is being charged with mishandling government funds. The gossip is that Colonel Snelling has been plagued with a peculiar ailment for many years and has become addicted to opium, the standard treatment for the disease. The treatment is expensive. Snelling used some of the government's money to purchase it."

Having admired Colonel Snelling for as far back as she could remember, Mariah was stunned speechless by the news. Her stomach suddenly felt hollow. She had now been disillusioned by two fathers!

Without saying another word to the stout man, who was perhaps her father's replacement at Jefferson Barracks, Mariah climbed back inside the carriage and ordered the driver to return her and Echohawk to the hotel.

"Echohawk, how could he have done this to me?" Mariah said, staring blankly into space. "How?"

"He did not do it to you," Echohawk said, taking her hand, squeezing it reassuringly. "He did it to himself. His loss is greater than yours. He will never know the wonders of a love such as yours."

"No, he shan't ever know me," Mariah said, stifling a sob of regret. "For my search is over. My secret is best left unspoken."

She turned tear-filled eyes to Echohawk. "Take me home, darling," she murmured. "I . . . I feel so foolish to have even asked you to bring me on such a . . . such a fruitless mission."

She flung herself into his arms, her bonnet slipping from her head. "Take me home to your people so that I may become your wife soon," she softly pleaded. "*You* are my life. I will forget my foolish notion of ever calling Colonel Snelling father to his face."

"The boat we will travel on back to our people does not depart until morning," Echohawk said, gazing down into her eyes. "Forget your disappointments. Being together is all that matters."

"I *have* looked forward to staying in the hotel room this one night," Mariah said, struggling to be grateful for what she did have in life. She had never truly had Josiah Snelling to call her father, so it should not be so hard to accept that she could not call him father even now.

Yes, she stubbornly decided. She *could* accept the loss, for it was a loss that she had lived with all of her life.

Mariah cuddled close to Echohawk, and when they arrived at the hotel, dusk had fallen. When they went inside the hotel lobby, the only candles that were lit were those on the branches of a ceiling-high Christmas tree. A fire crackled in the large stone fireplace at the far end of the room, casting a romantic glow around the room.

"Come and join in the merriment," a kind voice said to Mariah and Echohawk from among those sitting around the fireplace and tree. "It is a time dearer than any other part of the year, a time to open hearts to one and all alike. Tomorrow is Christmas!"

Mariah questioned Echohawk with her eyes, and when he nodded yes to her, she went with him and sat down on the floor beside the tree, removing their coats, placing them on the floor beside them. They were each given a stout mug filled with a sweet convivial brew of hot hard cider made of crabapples and spices.

A tall lean man stood among those enjoying this peaceful moment, and raised his potion in a spirited toast. *"Waes hael,"* he cheered in an Anglo-Saxon tongue. "Be thou hale!"

They all put their mugs to their lips and drank, Mariah slipping a hand over to Echohawk, taking hold of his hand, needing it for reassurance. She could not quit thinking about Colonel Snelling. He had been disgraced! He had always been a proud, kind man. Now his reputation was a ruin of what it had once been.

Echohawk set his mug aside and placed a finger to Mariah's chin. "You still worry about Josiah?" he said softly.

"Ay-uh," she whispered back. "How can I stop? I had so counted on today—seeing him again."

"My people lost an ally when he left the land of lakes," Echohawk said solemnly. "But always remember the good that he did. Keep that thought, and you will not be as disappointed in the man you now know is your father."

Mariah gazed raptly up at him, always in awe of how wise he was. He seemed to be able to reason things out so that one could see what was unpleasant in a different light. And he was right about her father. She should not condemn him for his faults, because his kindnesses outweighed his faults ten to one.

"Thank you for reminding me," she murmured.

Then her eyes were drawn quickly away from Echohawk, when across Echohawk's shoulder, behind him, in the dark shadows of the room, stood someone she would never forget. Blackie! The gambler from the riverboat!

She turned her eyes back to Echohawk and yanked on his hand, urging him up from the floor. She did not want him to see the gambler. She wanted their night in the hotel to be one of sheer pleasure. Even though she would wonder the night through what Blackie had on his mind, at least Echohawk would not be bothered with the threat.

"You are ready to leave?" Echohawk asked, leaning down to retrieve their coats.

"I am bone-weary," Mariah said, making sure that Echohawk did not turn and make eye contact with Blackie, glad that Blackie was standing in the darker shadows of the room.

"Then you will have your rest," Echohawk said, ushering her up the stairs to their room.

Once inside, the door closed and bolt-locked, both of them soon forgot that anyone had spoken of being weary. They quickly undressed and found incomparable pleasure in lying on the feather bed, making long, enduring love filled with promises.

27

Contentment, rosy, dimpled maid,
Thou brightest daughter of the sky.
                              —LADY MANNERS

Several Days Later: New Year's Eve

On the return trip to Fort Snelling, Mariah stood beside Echohawk on the main deck of the riverboat, keeping watch on the clouds building overhead. The weather had become threatening again; the sun, low in the west, was gradually effaced in a gloom of thickening clouds. A rough wind had just risen, and there was a spitting of snow from the sky.

"We should be arriving at Fort Snelling soon," Mariah said, watching the activity of the river, fearing it. It was always tearing away at the banks, an aggressive, implacable monster, it seemed.

Yet she knew that there were some positive benefits in the raw energy of the river. As the water washed off land on one side, a sandbar would start opposite, and soon willows would begin to grow, at length building up so that it could be cleared and cultivated. The stream progressed by many loops, so that the valley was full of abandoned channels.

Captain Johns stepped up to the rail. "Since we will be arriving at Fort Snelling before midnight, our crew are celebrating the new year now," he said, puffing on a fat cigar. "Join us in my cabin. Share a glass of wine with us." He nervously cleared his throat. "I regret what happened on the other voyage. Let me make up for your inconvenience." He paused, clasping his hands behind him as he gazed intensely into

Echohawk's dark eyes. "I understand about prejudices. My grandmother was a full-blooded Cherokee.
My mother had many of her mother's features. She
was shunned by many because of that." He eased his
hand onto Echohawk's shoulder. "Chief Echohawk, it
is my sincere pleasure to have met you."

"I welcome you as my friend," Echohawk said,
placing a fist over his heart. "My heart welcomes
you."

Mariah was moved almost to tears by what she was
witnessing, Echohawk so noble, so handsome as he
accepted the captain's friendship. She almost melted
into Echohawk as he swung away from the captain
and placed an arm around her waist, ushering her to
the captain's master cabin.

Shedding her coat, Mariah smiled at each crew
member as they passed by her, introducing themselves
to her and then to Echohawk, creating a relaxed atmosphere that turned into a time of laughter and camaraderie. Mariah accepted a tall-stemmed glass of wine
and looked over at Echohawk as he refused the one
offered to him.

"I do not put firewater in my body," he said, folding his arms across his chest. He gazed down at Mariah and started to tell her that it was not wise for her
to drink the firewater either, that he had seen it dis-
color too many red men's logic.

But he quickly reconsidered. He had promised Mariah freedom of choice. The firewater was no different
from anything else. He did not want to interfere with
his woman's free spirit.

Captain Johns placed an arm around Echohawk's
shoulder. "It is a wise man who refuses to put alcohol
into his system," he said, nodding away one for himself when it was offered. "For a spell I depended on
alcohol too much to get me through the day. But after
a tragedy aboard my riverboat, for which I was responsible, I have never touched another drop of whis-

key, nor any sort of alcohol. Normally my crew doesn't drink while on the job either. But this is New Year's Eve. I did not think a glass or two of wine could do them harm."

"What sort of tragedy?" Mariah asked, setting her half-empty glass aside on a table.

"It didn't occur on this boat," Captain Johns said, stepping away from Echohawk, taking a long stare from the small window. "It was another one, in fact the first riverboat I ever commanded." He turned slowly and looked at Mariah and Echohawk. "It was a beautiful boat, but it burned quickly, and along with it several . . . several passengers."

Mariah paled and placed a hand at her throat. "How horrible," she gasped.

Captain Johns looked down at his cigar, and just as quickly mashed it out in an ashtray, a sudden involuntary shiver visibly gripping him. "It was a mixture of whiskey and cigars that did it," he said, his voice strained. "I drank too much and fell asleep with the cigar in my hand. The fire and smoke awakened me, but I was too drunk to save anyone but myself."

He looked admiringly at his crew. "Most of these men you see here today were part of the crew on that fateful journey. They are responsible for saving those that were saved. If not for them . . ."

He shook his head, swallowed hard, then looked again at Mariah and Echohawk with wavering eyes. "It took many years of building up my courage to invest in another riverboat," he said thickly. "But when I finally did, most of my crew came back to me. And here we are today, one big happy family."

"It is good that you have resumed life again as you knew it before your tragedy," Echohawk said, placing a gentle hand on Captain Johns's shoulder. "You are a man to be admired. Not every man would have the courage that you have shown." His eyes darkened with remembrances of his own recent tragedies. He looked at Mariah. She accounted for so much of his own regained confidence. If not for her . . .

A loud commotion surfacing from the adjoining cabin made a startled silence grip the room.

"It seems as though someone's New Year's celebration has gotten out of hand," Captain Johns said, rushing from the cabin, his crew following him.

Echohawk and Mariah were left alone, but for only a moment. Soon Blackie slunk into the room, a drawn pistol in his right hand, a sinister smile on his lips. "I'm pretty good at sneakin' on a boat and causin' distractions, wouldn't you say?" he said, smirking. "I chided one of the suckers into accusin' one of the gamblers of cheatin'. In no time flat a fistfight broke out, and I slipped past them without no one noticin'. I hid in the shadows until after the captain and his men left you alone. Now, Injun, I'm at the advantage, wouldn't you say?"

Mariah's pulse raced. She had forgotten about Blackie when he hadn't made any attempts to bother Echohawk at the hotel. Now she understood why. His plans were for later, while in the middle of the river, away from lawmen.

Fearing for Echohawk, she gave him a quick glance. With a firearm aimed at him, he was powerless.

Then she looked toward the window. The storm had worsened, causing the waves to thrash wildly at the boat's hull. She had to grab for a chair for support when the boat lurched sideways, and at the same time she saw that the advantage was now Echohawk's, for Blackie had lost his balance, his feet sliding from beneath him as the boat quickly righted itself again.

In a blur, it seemed to Mariah, Echohawk was on Blackie, knocking his firearm from his hand and wrestling him to the floor, straddling him. Mariah scrambled to grab the pistol, then stood back and watched wide-eyed as Echohawk suddenly jerked Blackie to his feet and yanked his arm behind him, forcing him to the door.

"Open the door, No-din," Echohawk said, looking at Mariah over his shoulder. "There is only one solution I can think of to rid ourselves of this man, without killing him."

Mariah rushed to the door and opened it. "What are you planning to do?" she said, following Echohawk as he forced Blackie ahead of him.

The wind was wild and cold, the snow stinging her cheeks as Mariah followed the two men to the rail. Still clutching the pistol, she sucked in a shallow breath when she realized what Echohawk's intentions were for the gambler. She cringed when Blackie began shouting for help as he looked over the side of the boat into the swirling muddy water.

"You can't do this to me!" Blackie cried, struggling to get free as Echohawk began lifting him over the rail. "No! Don't! I'll freeze to death!"

Echohawk looked at Mariah. "Aim the firearm at the gambler!" he shouted, then looked with an amused smile down at Blackie. "If you prefer a bullet to the water, she can very easily pull the trigger." He paused, laughing beneath his breath when he saw the wild pleading in the gambler's eyes. "What is it to be, white man? A bullet? Or the muddy, cold Mississippi?"

"Neither!" Blackie cried. "I beg of you. Let me go. I won't bother you again. Ever!"

Echohawk held him even lower over the rail for a while longer, then brought him back to the deck and let him go, the suddenness of his release causing Blackie to tumble to the floor, cowering. "I think the boat's captain can think of a place to put you until we reach Fort Snelling," Echohawk said, wiping his hands on his buckskin breeches, as though to remove the stench of the gambler from his flesh.

"There you will be seen to by the white pony soldiers. They will not like to hear that you threatened Chief Echohawk and his woman's life—not once, but twice. They are friends of No-din and the Chippewa. They will see to your punishment. I believe you would prefer their choice of punishment over that of the Chippewa!"

"Yes, yes, I would," Blackie said, nodding anxiously as he scooted back from Echohawk on the deck.

A loud round of applause broke out. Mariah looked quickly around, having been so absorbed in Echohawk's performance that she had not seen Captain Johns and his crew arrive, also to observe.

"Well done!" Johns said, coming to lock an arm around Echohawk's shoulders.

He gave his crew a stern look. "Take that scoundrel Blackie below!" he ordered. "Secure him well!"

Then he turned back to Echohawk. "Now, if it had been up to me, I'd have tossed the sonofabitch overboard. I'd have loved seeing him choke on the muddy river water," he said, laughing heartily. "But since you are an honorable man, of course you have spared him the humiliation."

"This time, *ay-uh*," Echohawk grumbled, taking the pistol from Mariah's hand, quickly ushering her away, toward their cabin. "But next time? *Gah-ween*, no. My patience is running thin for this man whose heart is bad toward me and my woman."

"I must see to my duties," Captain Johns said, since they were nearing land, the fort's walls now in sight. His brow knit into a worried frown. "I hope the blizzard doesn't impede our landing."

Mariah looked over her shoulder at the snow tumbling from the sky in a sheet of white, then was glad to reach the warmth of her cabin. Once inside, she stepped close to the small stove, trembling.

"We are near to Fort Snelling," Echohawk said,

placing a blanket around Mariah's shoulders. "Soon we will be with our people again."

"We are lucky to be anywhere," Mariah said, sighing deeply. "This journey was fraught with danger and disappointment."

"But we survived it all, didn't we?" Echohawk said, smiling down at her, his finger at her chin, tipping her face up to his. "My woman, my No-din, you worry too much."

Echohawk was worrying, wondering if the riverboat could get to shore during the ravaging storm that was upon them. "I will be back soon," he reassured Mariah, slipping into his coat. "I wish to see if it is too hazardous to take the white man's large canoe to shore."

Mariah smiled weakly at him, and after he left, turned her eyes back to the window, seeing the ever-swirling snow floating past. She was not fearing the landing of the riverboat as much as the journey back to Echohawk's village. This weather was not favorable to traveling on horseback!

Echohawk hurried across the top deck to the rail, and held on as the boat slowly pushed its way up into the willows skirting the bank close to Fort Snelling, the gangplank succeeding in reaching out to the shore.

His gaze went further, into the far stretches of the forest. He knew the dangers of traveling during such a storm, but he had had enough of the white man's world! Nothing would delay his travels back to his people! Nothing!

Eight moons heavy with child, Nee-kah panted hard as she trudged through the snow from the river, carrying a jug of water. Chief Silver Wing had warned her against not only traipsing out alone in the danger-ous weather but also carrying their water. He had told her to assign another, younger woman to do the chores.

And she had, for a while, but boredom had set in.

And she had felt useless watching someone else do what she had always been able to do for herself and her husband.

A thick hooded fur cloak secured around her shoulders, Nee-kah blinked snow from her heavy lashes as it began to fall more furiously from the sky. Her snowshoes were awkward as the snow deepened, and a quick panic rose inside her when she could no longer see the village through the raging snowstorm.

But she kept trudging onward, holding faithfully to the jug of water, stopping in shock only when someone stepped out of the snowy shadows directly in her path.

Nee-kah stifled a scream behind her mittened hand, knowing that the Indian standing threateningly before her, his knife drawn from his sheath, was not a Chippewa. All Chippewa were friends! Not snakes who threatened helpless pregnant women! It could only be a Sioux!

She dropped the jug of water and felt her knees weaken when several other Indians, attired in thick fur coats, stepped into view, their dark eyes narrowing as they gazed down at her.

"Nee-kah?" White Wolf said in very simple Chippewa language. "Wife of Chief Silver Wing? And friend of Echohawk and his white woman who is called No-din?"

"I could lie and say that I am someone else," Nee-kah said, stubbornly lifting her chin. "But I am too proud to behave in such a weak, cowardly manner. I declare to you that, *ay-uh*, I am Nee-kah. And now that you know, what are your plans for me?"

She was grabbed suddenly from behind and half-dragged to a waiting horse. She did not fight back as she was placed into the saddle, for she feared for her child more than for herself. Finally her husband had found a wife to bear him children . . . and now this wife was being stolen from him—perhaps never to be seen again!

She still held her head high, but could not stop the flow of tears that sprang from her eyes. She had let her husband down by disobeying him.

Now he might lose not only his wife but also his unborn child!

She looked to the heavens and prayed to the Great Spirit not to let this happen, and promised never to be so bullheadedly, stubbornly willful again.

Then her gaze was drawn to her abductors and her eyes narrowed when she heard the lead Indian being addressed by a name. White Wolf. It was the renegade Sioux who was guilty of this cowardly act today!

It would be with much rage and hate that Chief Silver Wing would avenge what White Wolf did today!

The council meeting over, Chief Silver Wing leaned into the wind and blowing snow and hurried to his wigwam. Once inside, and after shedding his fur wrap, he looked around the room for Nee-kah, a sudden foreboding lurking at the pit of his stomach.

She was not there.

And the weather was too bitter for her to have gone out into it.

His gaze went to the water jugs that sat at the side of the wigwam, and mentally he counted them. One was missing.

"She has gone to the river!" he said, his teeth clenched. "She still persists in believing she is capable of fending for herself, even . . . even in this blizzard!"

Throwing his fur cloak around his shoulders, he went from the wigwam shouting orders to his braves. He told several to go and search for Nee-kah down by the river. He told others to go in all directions close to the village, checking to see if she had lost her way in the blinding snow.

He mounted his horse and rode ahead of those on their way to the river, his heart pounding out the fear of not finding her before she froze to death.

He did not get far. He saw the water jug lying partially hidden in the snow. Quickly dismounting, he fell to one knee and grabbed up the jug; then his heart sank when he looked in all directions and could not find any footprints.

Fresh snowfall had covered them.

He looked to the heavens and let out a loud wail of despair, then bowed his head in a silent meditation with the Great Spirit.

When he arose back to his full height, he found himself circled by his braves on horseback.

"She is nowhere near," one said, this pronouncement agreed on by the others.

"Then we must search until we find her," Chief Silver Wing said, his jaw tight with determination.

"The blizzard . . . ?" Wise Owl said, gazing up into the swirling snow.

"We will ride until we cannot see to ride any farther." Chief Silver Wing wheeled his horse around, urging it through the thick, heavy snow. Doubts of ever finding his woman were pressing in on his heart, yet he could not believe that she could have gotten far, unless . . .

His eyes narrowed with hate. "Unless she was abducted!" he cried aloud, alarming the men who rode beside him.

"The Sioux!" he whispered to himself. "If they came on my land and took my woman, they will pay!"

He shook the snow from his shoulder-length hair and snapped his reins, regretting that he could not go faster on his steed.

Time.

Time was his enemy in this weather of life-threatening temperatures.

His Nee-kah.

She could even now be lying beneath a covering of snow.

Or, he thought bitterly, she could be lying beneath her enemy!

28

Oh! Who would inhabit
This bleak world alone?

—MOORE

The sky was lightening along the horizon. The storm clouds had diffused into something tranquil—into white puffs of clouds floating gently across the sky. Mariah's fingers were cold and stiff as she clung to the horse's reins. Her cheeks felt tight from the stinging cold wind.

The ride on horseback from Fort Snelling through the snow and cold, frosty air had been hard, but she had weathered it all and could only grieve to herself that her main complaint was that of being sleepy. Even food did not sound all that good to her. In fact, the thought of it made her feel ill to her stomach. Her main desire now was to stretch out on her pallet of furs beside the fire in Echohawk's wigwam.

Her eyes were burning with the need of sleep.

She was finding it hard to keep her eyes open. . . .

The aroma of smoke wafting through the air caused Mariah's eyes to widen and her heart to sing.

Finally!

Finally, after almost a full night of riding through the snow, and fighting occasional drifts piled high against the trees, they were near their village.

"No-din, soon you can be warmed by a fire," Echohawk said, giving her a worried look. "I fear my decision to ride directly to our village was wrong. The night has been long and cold." He smiled at her. "Yet you did not complain once. My woman, tonight, as so many times before, you proved to me that you can withstand anything. You are a woman of grit—of strength. I am proud of you, No-din. Very proud."

"Echohawk, you have given me so much strength, by just loving me," Mariah murmured. "I never want to disappoint you. I want you to be proud of me always."

Echohawk did not have the chance to reply. Two of his braves were suddenly there on horseback, approaching them, rifles clutched in their hands, their faces painted with red streaks—the color of warring.

Echohawk jerked his horse to a shuddering halt and awaited their arrival. He eyed them warily as they stopped before him. "What has happened?" he asked. "You do not greet me with a friendly hello. You wear war paint. Why is that, Proud Thunder?"

Mariah drew her horse to a stop beside Echohawk's, shivering at the sight of the braves, who seemed hellbent on vengeance.

"Nee-kah!" Proud Thunder said, his eyes narrowing with rage. He thrust his rifle into the air. "She is gone. It is believed to have been the Sioux who are responsible for her abduction. We help Chief Silver Wing search for her. We cannot find her, nor the Sioux camp."

Echohawk's face paled. So Yellow Eyes had lied! White Wolf, the renegade Sioux who was responsible for so many of Echohawk's sadnesses, was alive, and again creating havoc.

But this time White Wolf was taking his vengeance out on Echohawk's friend Chief Silver Wing. Could White Wolf have done this thing against Chief Silver Wing only because it would draw Echohawk into a confrontation with them?

The terrible news about Nee-kah made Mariah feel faint, and then her shock registered even more sharply when she remembered Nee-kah's delicate condition.

The baby!

It was due in only a month.

The trauma that Nee-kah was going through, if she were still alive, could cause her to deliver early.

"And where is Chief Silver Wing?" Echohawk said, his voice drawn.

"He and many braves are still searching," Proud Thunder said, gazing into the distance, through the snow-laden trees of the forest. Then he looked at Echohawk, an apology in his eyes. "Brown Fox and I searched the whole night through. We returned hesitantly, but we feel that further searching is in vain." He paused, then added, "And we fear the villages being left so unprotected." He looked guardly at Mariah, then back at Echohawk. "We can never forget raids of the white people. We cannot relax our guard, ever."

Echohawk nodded. "This is so," he said, reaching a heavy hand to Proud Thunder's shoulder. "But I must go and find Silver Wing. Together we will search a while longer for Nee-kah, and if she cannot be found, I must encourage the elder chief to return to his village. He is no longer a young man with the endurance of a bear. But of course I will be delicate in saying so."

Echohawk then reached his hand to Mariah and placed it gently to her cheek. "No-din, go ahead to the village," he said. "Brown Fox will take you. You get your rest. When you awaken, hopefully I will be there at your side to give you good news that not only is Chief Silver Wing back in his village, but also Nee-kah."

"I so badly want to go with you," Mariah said, sighing deeply. "I love Nee-kah as though she were my own sister."

"You have been in the cold long enough," Echohawk said firmly. "It is time for you to be warmed and to get some rest."

Mariah felt dispirited about having to agree with him, but she *did* know that she could not go another mile on the horse. She was exhausted. And she would only delay Echohawk's search.

"*Ay-uh*, you are right," she said, again sighing deeply. "I would only get in the way." She turned and smiled at Brown Fox. "You do not need to travel with me to the village. Go on with Echohawk. He needs you more than I."

Echohawk edged his horse closer to Mariah's. He placed a finger to her chin and brought her eyes back around, to meet and hold with his. "There has been one abduction, there is not to be another," he growled. He nodded at Brown Fox. "Go. See to my woman. Stand guard outside her wigwam. Watch over her for me, for she is my life, Brown Fox."

Mariah was touched deeply by how Echohawk so openly spoke of his feelings for her to his braves. She would have thought that a powerful Indian chief would not want to express such feelings to his braves—perchance looking weak in their eyes.

Over and over again Echohawk proved his intense love for her, she marveled to herself, and she suspected very strongly today that she just might have a way to repay him. She had missed her monthly weeps. She was feeling nauseated. Just perhaps . . . she was with child! What a gift to give her husband!

"*Mah-bee-szhon*, come," Brown Fox said, nodding to Mariah. "Do not fear. I will see to your safety."

Mariah's eyes wavered as she gave Echohawk one last look, hoping it would not be the last time she was allowed to. She wanted to believe that he would return to her. Their lives would soon be tranquil. They would wed, and together they would watch her body grow with child.

Sinking her heels into the flanks of her horse, she rode away from Echohawk, a feeling of foreboding hanging over her, as though she were engulfed within a dark cloud. She swallowed back a fast-growing lump in her throat, knowing that this was not the time to lose faith and waver in her courage.

Echohawk gave Mariah a lingering look, concerned for her as she rode away, her shoulders slumped. It seemed the burdens he kept placing on her shoulders were many.

And now?

What of sweet Nee-kah?

Would there ever be cause to celebrate a lasting peace among the Chippewa tribes?

Always there was cause for delay in the laughter and smiles!

He had begun to think that it never would change.

If not—he had drawn his No-din into a life of continued miseries.

Wheeling his horse around, he rode off beside Proud Thunder. They rode and searched with their eyes for what seemed hours; then suddenly before them were many horsemen riding toward them across a vast snow-covered meadow.

"Silver Wing!" Echohawk said beneath his breath, recognizing the elder chief from the others by the slight slouch of his shoulders—a chief who had once ridden so tall and straight in the saddle, now bent with age and years of disappointment and sadness.

He urged his horse into a strong gallop, then came to a halt beside Silver Wing's steed.

"I have heard!" Echohawk said, placing a hand on Silver Wing's shoulder. "I am saddened."

Silver Wing's eyes lowered and he shook his head slowly back and forth. "It is with much regret that I have to return to my village without my Nee-kah," he said glumly. "But we have searched, it seems, to the ends of the earth, and she is nowhere to be found. I fear she is dead, somewhere in the snow, the snow her grave."

"Chief Silver Wing, you are weary from the search,"

Echohawk said, his voice thin. "Return to your village. I shall search awhile longer. When you go to your bed alone tonight, you will then know that everything has been done to find Nee-kah."

"She is *gee-mah-gah*, gone," Silver Wing said, lifting weeping eyes to the heaven. "My wife! My unborn child! They are gone! Why, Great Spirit, why? What have I done to deserve such sadness as this?"

"Silver Wing? My husband?"

Echohawk and Silver Wing gave each other a sudden quizzical look.

"Did you hear a voice?" Echohawk said, his eyes wide as he stared over at Silver Wing.

"Did you hear the voice also?" Silver Wing said, his jaw tightening, having thought that wanting it to be so, so badly, he had imagined hearing Nee-kah's voice calling his name.

Suddenly in view, only a few yards ahead, where they now could distinguish the small figure of a woman from the brightness of the snow, Echohawk and Silver Wing saw Nee-kah stumbling through the snow, one hand clutching a blanket around her shoulders, her other hand outstretched toward them.

"My husband, it is I, Nee-kah!" she cried, suddenly clutching her hand to her abdomen, sharp pains gripping her there. "Silver Wing, come to me. Silver Wing!"

Silver Wing sank his moccasined heels into the flanks of his horse and rode off in a hard gallop toward Nee-kah, and when he reached her, dismounted in one leap. He grabbed her into his arms and hugged her tightly.

"My wife. My sweet Nee-kah. You are safe!" he whispered, his heart pounding with joy. He held her away from him and looked her up and down. "And are you all right? The baby?"

"Nee-kah is fine," she said, then grabbed at her abdomen when the pains assaulted her again. She did not want to tell him that she was concerned about the child—that perhaps she was going to have the child early. She knew her husband well enough to know that he would want to go and settle things with the Sioux himself, instead of sending warriors to battle them for him. She would have to pretend that she and the child were fine.

Later, she decided. Much later she would tell him of her concerns.

Perhaps by then he would already be a father!

Silver Wing clasped his fingers to Nee-kah's shoulders. "I looked everywhere," he said softly. "How is it that I did not find you?"

"The Sioux camp is not far," Nee-kah said, giving Echohawk a soft smile as he rode up and dismounted. "Beyond the meadow, just inside the forest, there is a cave. The horses and the Sioux are well hidden there. I . . . I escaped when they slept. Being heavy with child, they did not think I would chance escape." She laughed softly. "But they do not know Nee-kah, do they?"

"You are a different sort of woman, that is true," Silver Wing said, his shoulders relaxing in a heavy sigh.

"Nee-kah is so sorry to cause you such worry," she said, moving into Silver Wing's arms. "I did not listen to you. I went to the river for water. Because of that, because of my stubbornness, I was abducted."

"That you are here now, safe, is all that is important," Silver Wing said, easing her out of his arms. "You go now. Rest beside a warm fire until my return. We go and take many scalps today!"

"The Sioux who is responsible for Nee-kah's abduction is called White Wolf," she murmured.

Echohawk and Silver Wing exchanged knowing glances, fire quickly lighting their eyes.

Then Silver Wing looked down at Nee-kah. "Your

abduction will be avenged," he growled. "White Wolf's scalp will decorate my scalp pole tonight!"

Nee-kah bit her lower lip with worry, then let Proud Thunder help her onto another brave's horse, and smiled weakly at Silver Wing as she clung to the brave as he rode gently away.

Echohawk and Silver Wing nodded, then swung themselves into their saddles and rode hard across the meadow. They entered the forest, but were stopped when a volley of arrows came at them seemingly from out of nowhere. The bowstrings twanged a death song, arrows humming like angry hornets at the Chippewa.

Suddenly many Sioux braves appeared on horseback, riding toward the Chippewa, White Wolf in the lead. Guns bellowed. Gunfire filled the air. More arrows screamed from their bows.

Echohawk threw back his head and uttered a war whoop almost in unison with Silver Wing's throaty cry. Kicking his horse into a run, Echohawk soon lost sight of Silver Wing as the Sioux and Chippewa mingled, all whooping and charging. They met in a head-on clash, clubs striking deadly blows, horses floundering and slamming onto their sides in the snow when they received the bullets meant for their riders.

The air soon thick with black powder smoke, Echohawk fought hard for his life, unable to look around him, to see how anyone else fared.

But soon the firing ceased and all that could be heard were the groans of the wounded.

Echohawk sat stiffly in his saddle as his gaze moved around him, seeing the death that lay strewn around him, the blood like roses in the snow.

And then his heart plummeted with despair when he spied a familiar face among the fallen. He quickly dismounted and ran to Chief Silver Wing, easing his head up from the snow onto his lap.

"Take the scalps of our enemy to our people," Silver Wing said between deep, quavering breaths. He grabbed at his chest, where his fur cloak had been ripped open from the explosion of a bullet, blood freezing in shreds along the matted fur.

"There is no time for scalps," Echohawk said, his voice drawn. "That time will be spent in taking you to your people. To your wife. Your Mide priest will perform magic over you. Your wounds will soon be healed!"

"Gah-ween," Chief Silver Wing said, blood now trickling in a stream from the corner of his mouth. "The Mide's magic will not be strong enough for this elder chief this time. The wound is a mortal one." He struggled to get up. "Take me to Nee-kah. I will not let myself take that last breath until I can hold her in my arms again."

"If only it were I lying there wounded," Echohawk said, his voice filled with regret.

"You are young. You have a lifetime ahead of you. I have had a full, rich life." Silver Wing paused, closed his eyes for a moment while taking some quick breaths, then looked up into Echohawk's eyes again. "And soon, Echohawk, a child will be born to Nee-kah. *My* child. And . . ." He managed a peaceful smile. "And it *will* be a son, Echohawk. I know that to be so."

"Ay-uh," Echohawk said, filled with remorse. It was as though he was holding his father in his arms, watching *his* life ebb away, all over again. In so short a time, two men of his heart had been robbed of him! What in life *was* fair?

He looked slowly around him, seeing that not one Sioux had lived through the fight, and his heart swelled with pride. Never again would this band of renegade Sioux be able to take loved ones from him!

His heart skipped a beat, a thought springing to his consciousness, making him groan with a frustrated anger. In the confusion and concern over Silver Wing's welfare, he had forgotten about White Wolf!

"He is not among the dead!" he whispered between gritted teeth. "He escaped. Even now I do not get my full vengeance!"

Turning his attention back to Silver Wing, Echohawk placed his arm gently beneath him and lifted him from the snow and carried him to his horse. Tears filled his eyes when he saw how Silver Wing found that last ounce of strength to hold himself upright in the saddle. He would enter his village one last time as the great proud chief of his people. They would see him as the noble man that he was.

Echohawk eased onto the horse behind Chief Silver Wing and placed an arm around him and held him in place before him. Leaving behind enough braves to tend to the wounded, the others followed humbly behind their two chiefs.

29

There is nothing held so dear as love, if only it
be hard to win.

—INGELOW

Mariah was cozy warm beside the fire, many pelts
drawn up to her chin, but yet she could not sleep. She
was feeling guilty for being safe and warm while Nee-
kah was out there somewhere, perhaps dying in the
snow, or at the hands of unmerciful abductors.

And Echohawk and Silver Wing!

Both were riding into the face of danger, perhaps
instant death, should they find Nee-kah's captors.

Unable to bear just lying there, so troubled by her
fears for those she loved, Mariah smoothed the blankets and pelts aside and moved to her knees before
the fire, wishing that she were with Echohawk, riding
as boldly as his braves at his side.

Then she placed a hand to her abdomen, knowing
that now, as never before, it was best to behave re-
sponsibly. If she *were* with child, she had to protect it
at all cost. And she tended to think of the child as a
boy—Echohawk's son, the future leader of his people.

Her thoughts were catapulted back to the present
when she heard the sound of an arriving horse outside,
sounding as though it were nearer to Silver Wing's
wigwam then Echohawk's. She grew tense when she
heard people shouting Nee-kah's name.

"Nee-kah?" Mariah said, rising quickly to her feet.
"Have they found her? Has Echohawk returned
safely?"

Having not taken off her dress before lying down, Mariah scrambled into her knee-high moccasins and snatched up her fur cloak, then rushed toward the entrance flap. Once she was outside, she fled over the short distance dividing Echohawk's and Silver Wing's villages, and was soon torn with feelings. She was joyous over seeing Nee-kah just being helped from a horse by a brave, yet troubled over not seeing Echohawk with her.

So many worries flashed through her consciousness.

Had only one brave and Nee-kah survived an attack on the Sioux?

Was Echohawk even now lying in the snow, dead?

A sob lodged in her throat. Afraid to hear the answers, yet knowing that she must, Mariah tore from the wigwam and ran through the ankle-deep snow until she reached Nee-kah, who was being helped to her wigwam.

"Nee-kah, oh, thank God, Nee-kah," Mariah said, clutching Nee-kah into her arms, giving her a fierce hug. "I was so worried about you."

"I am fine," Nee-kah said, smiling up at Mariah as she stepped away from her. "I am like you. Strong-willed and able to fend quite well for myself."

"Echohawk?" Mariah asked, her pulse racing. "Where is Echohawk? Where is Silver Wing?"

Nee-kah's eyes wavered. "When I last saw them, they were well," she said, then grabbed at her abdomen when another pain assaulted her. "But they now will be fighting the Sioux," she breathed out between clenched teeth, her eyes closed. "I so fear for our Chippewa braves!"

Mariah was quickly alarmed when she recognized the pain that Nee-kah was in, and how sweat was pearling on her lovely copper brow, even though the temperature was way below freezing.

Though her every heartbeat belonged to Echohawk, Mariah was thrown into worries about her friend, knowing that even though Nee-kah had another full month before the time of her child's delivery, it had been as Mariah had earlier feared: the trauma forced upon Nee-kah could cause an early labor.

"Let me help you into your dwelling," Mariah said, taking Nee-kah by an arm, slowly walking her to the entrance flap. "I can tell you're in pain. Nee-kah, it's the baby, isn't it?"

"*Ay-uh,*" Nee-kah said, brushing the entrance flap aside, gingerly stepping inside, every footstep seemingly causing the pains to increase in intensity. "It is the baby." She turned wild eyes to Mariah. "It is too early, No-din. Do you know any white-people secrets that can make the pains of childbirthing stop? I . . . I fear birthing my child early. If anything should happen to the child . . ."

Mariah helped Nee-kah to her sleeping platform beside the fire. She was aware of much commotion behind her, and out of the corners of her eyes saw many women coming into the wigwam, each carrying assorted items to be used during the birthing procedure.

She turned her full attention back to Nee-kah when Nee-kah grabbed at her stomach again and screamed, her color paling. "Let's get your cloak off, and then your dress," Mariah said, trying to keep herself calm, though her heart was pounding with fear. She had never even seen a small baby before, much less helped bring one into the world.

But of course she saw that she was not needed at all. Nee-kah was soon surrounded by many women looking down at her adoringly. They had come to help. They had all the knowledge necessary to help Nee-kah deliver the baby.

After Mariah had Nee-kah undressed and a blanket drawn over her up to her armpits, she stepped aside and watched as the women began their ritual of assisting Nee-kah as her labor pains came more frequently, now scarcely seconds apart.

"Silver Wing," Nee-kah cried, her eyes wild as one of the women slipped her hand up the birthing canal, trying to help the baby move through it. "My husband! Oh, Silver Wing! If you were only here!"

Nee-kah turned frightened eyes to the circle of women. "No-din!" she said, her voice quavering. "Where . . . is No-din?"

Two of the women stepped aside and made a space for Mariah at Nee-kah's side. Mariah smoothed her hand over Nee-kah's perspiration-laced brow. "What can I do?" she murmured. "I . . . I feel so helpless."

"Just hold my hand," Nee-kah said, circling her fingers around Mariah's hand. "Just . . . hold . . . my hand, sweet friend."

"I wish I could do more," Mariah said, holding tightly to Nee-kah's hand as Nee-kah squeezed her fingers into Mariah's, once again crying out with pain as she bore down.

"Surely it won't be long," Mariah said, yet greatly fearing the early birth. "And, Nee-kah, just you wait and see. Your child will be healthy, like its mother and father."

"It . . . is . . . coming!" Nee-kah cried, grunting as she bore down again, harder . . . harder. . . .

And soon the child was lying in the hands of one of the Chippewa maidens, proving its lungs were of adequate capacity with wails that reached far from the wigwam to the outside, into the early-morning air.

"It is a son!" Mariah said as the child was held high for all to see. She leaned down into Nee-kah's face, Nee-kah having momentarily fainted from the trauma of the delivery. "Nee-kah," she whispered, brushing a kiss across Nee-kah's cheek. "You and Chief Silver Wing have a son!"

Mariah's joy was short-lived when Nee-kah did not awaken abruptly, but still lay in what seemed some sort of comatose state.

Her fingers trembling, Mariah placed them at the

vein of Nee-kah's neck. Tears of relief flooded her eyes when she felt a very steady pulsebeat there. Nee-kah's eyes fluttered open and she looked around her, still stunned and confused.

When her gaze fell on the small bundle being held by one of the Chippewa women, her son now wrapped in a blanket, Nee-kah swallowed back a choking sob and held her arms out to the child.

"Let me see my baby," she murmured, her voice weak.

Knowing the bond that had formed between Mariah and Nee-kah, the woman laid the child within Mariah's arms, then nodded toward Nee-kah.

Mariah felt a strange sort of melting at the pit of her stomach when she peered down at the tiny copper face, dark eyes shaded by thick black lashes blinking back at her. "So lovely," she whispered, then laid the child in Nee-kah's arms. "Nee-kah, your son. He is so very, *very* lovely. And healthy. You have nothing to fear. He will grow up to be a great man."

Nee-kah looked through tears at her son, then with one hand unfolded the blanket from around him. She gasped with delight. She smiled up at Mariah, then looked slowly around her at those who had ministered to her in her time of need.

"My son will be called Strong Branch until he has his special vision," she said proudly. She looked adoringly back down at her child again, sighing. "Is he not a long, slim baby, as straight as a northern pine?"

"He is wonderful," Mariah said, very gently touching the baby's tiny arm, then smoothing her fingers over his even tinier fingers. "And soon he will have a friend to play with. As soon as I—"

"You are with child?" Nee-kah asked, wonder in her eyes and voice.

"Perhaps," Mariah said, blushing bashfully. "I hope so."

Their moment of joyous beginnings was drawn

abruptly to a halt at the sound of many horses stopping outside the wigwam. All eyes were locked on the entrance flap when it suddenly was drawn back and Echohawk came in, carrying Silver Wing.

Mariah rose quickly to her feet, her knees weakening when she caught sight of the blood on Silver Wing's clothes and the paleness of his face. And she also recognized the sound of death, for she would never forget hearing the death rattles only moments before her mother had died, and also Victor Temple's.

An instant dizziness gripped Nee-kah when she caught sight of her beloved husband as Echohawk carried Silver Wing toward her.

"No!" Nee-kah cried, fighting to stay alert as the trauma of seeing her wounded husband sent her heart into a tailspin of despair. She clung to her baby and tried to rise to a sitting position, but her weakness would not allow it. "My husband!" she cried, reaching a hand out to Silver Wing. "No! Tell me you are not injured badly!"

"Nee-kah?" Silver Wing said, his voice barely audible.

Echohawk took Silver Wing to Nee-kah and placed him beside her on the sleeping platform, then stepped back and stood beside Mariah, circling a comforting arm around her waist.

"My wife, I have come back to you to say a final good-bye," Silver Wing said, his failing eyesight not having even seen the child, nor that Nee-kah was on the sleeping platform. "Take my hand. Let me feel the softness of your skin one last time."

Fighting back tears, Nee-kah turned to him as best she could, but it was not her hand that she placed in her husband's hand.

It was the small hand of their son.

When Silver Wing became aware of the size of the hand, reaching his other hand to cover it, to feel the tiny fingers, tears began flooding his eyes. "The child," he said, his voice breaking. "You . . . had . . . our child . . ."

"*Ay-uh,*" Nee-kah murmured, leaning to kiss her husband's cold cheek. "And, my darling, it is a son. I have already named him. He is to be called Strong Branch. Can you not see? He is as straight as a northern pine!"

Silver Wing's hand roamed over his son, a look of bliss entering his eyes as he felt all of his son's features and his tiny body. When he found that part of him which told him that, *ay-uh*, he was a son, a deep rush of emotion filled him. "A son," he said, smiling through tears at Nee-kah. "*Ay-uh*, a son. Strong Branch? That is a good name. It fits him well."

Silver Wing felt a tightening in his lungs. "Take our son," he said, fighting back the urge to cough. "And remember that I will always be with you, Nee-kah, even though I soon will enter the Land of the Hereafter."

Nee-kah took Strong Branch back into her arms and wrapped him securely in the blanket, feeling as though a part of her was tearing away when Silver Wing turned his head from her and began coughing hard, blood now spewing from his mouth.

She sought deeply within herself for the courage to live through the next moments of her life, knowing that she would be saying a final good-bye to her dear, wonderful husband.

Oh, it was hard!

When he took his last breath, a part of her would be forever gone!

But she had to fight for the courage to want to live. She would live for their child. For Silver Wing, she must see that their son was raised to be a great leader, in his father's footsteps.

Silver Wing turned to his people, who had come into the wigwam. "Elders of my village, come and stand around me and hear my farewell words—listen to my last ruling as chief," he said, his voice almost failing him. When they were positioned, somber and sad as they gazed down upon him, he continued:

"My infant son shall rule upon my death," Silver Wing said. "I took a young wife for the bearing of a son who would be chief. Strong Branch *is* to be chief. But until he is of age, you who are the elders of this village must see that both villages, Echohawk's and ours, work together as one under the leadership of Chief Echohawk. If Echohawk will agree, he will become Strong Branch's father, to teach him everything about life."

Satisfied, Silver Wing closed his eyes and coughed again, exhausted from the long speech.

Echohawk was touched almost speechless. He knelt beside Silver Wing and took one of his hands into his, squeezing it affectionately, yet cringing when he felt its cold limpness. "I am here to do whatever you ask of me," he said, his voice drawn. "You so humble me, Silver Wing."

"Take my child," Silver Wing said, wheezing, now unable even to open his eyes. "Hold him to your heart. Acquaint yourself with him. From today forth, Echohawk, he walks in *your* shadow, not mine. Your children will become his brothers and sisters. They will be as one family within their hearts and souls." He coughed, and exhaled a quavering breath. "The same as it has been for you and me."

Echohawk swept the baby up into his arms. He unfolded the blanket and looked down at the tiny face, quickly taken by the child, as though he were his own.

He held the child up high, for all to see, chanting, then relinquished the child back to his father, laying him across his chest so that Silver Wing could be with his son until his last breath.

Silver Wing reached out a hand. "Echohawk, lean close," he said, his voice growing weaker.

Echohawk bent to one knee beside Silver Wing. "I am here," he said softly.

"Echohawk, for so long I have labored diligently for peace between the red man and white," Silver Wing managed to say between bouts of wheezing. "Repeatedly . . . I have averted bloodshed by taking hot-blooded braves out of a projected raid." He paused, inhaled a shaky breath, then added, "Echohawk, argue against war of retaliation. Renew pleas for peace."

"But what of White Wolf?" Echohawk questioned, deep inside his heart wanting to seek out the renegade and kill him slowly. "He still lives. *You* die!"

"The Chippewa have a high sense of honor to defend," Silver Wing said, his breathing becoming more shallow. "Forget White Wolf. He flees even now the wrath of the Chippewa, like a dog whose tail is tucked between his legs." He closed his eyes and sighed. "Echohawk, I have . . . spoken . . . my mind. Heed what I have said. . . ."

Nee-kah managed to scoot over close to Silver Wing. Sobbing, she clung to him, then stifled a scream behind a hand when she realized he had taken his last breath.

Mariah clutched Echohawk's arm and looked away from Silver Wing, overtaken by grief. Echohawk leaned down and took the child from Silver Wing, and after Nee-kah composed herself, gently placed the child back into her arms.

Echohawk took Mariah's hand and urged her down on her knees beside Silver Wing. Echohawk began to chant quietly, while Mariah listened. Recognizing the torment in her husband's voice, she knew of only one thing that could fill his heart with gladness again. That she was with child, *their* child. . . .

30

She was swayed in her suppleness to and fro
By each gust of passion.

—DESPREZ

Several Days Later

Her cloak around her shoulders, Mariah went to the entrance flap and smoothed it aside, anxious to go and visit with Nee-kah and Strong Branch while Echohawk was hunting, not only to see her best friend and her godson but also to try to lift Nee-kah's spirits since the death of her husband. Nee-kah knew of Mariah's anxiousness to become Echohawk's wife. But she did not know that Mariah was most definitely with child. Mariah was going to share two secrets with her best friend today.

Everything wonderful would happen tonight, Mariah marveled to herself, feeling giddy. She would finally be Echohawk's wife, and she was going to reveal to him that their lives were going to be blessed with a child.

Just as she stepped out into the snow, Mariah found a large buckskin bag lying close to the entrance flap, bulging with something inside it.

She lifted an eyebrow as she looked questioningly down at the bag, wondering why it was there, and what was in it.

"Take it inside," Echohawk said, suddenly there on his horse. He swung himself out of his saddle and went to Mariah. "This is yours. Take it inside and see what the women of the village have given you."

Mariah's lips parted in a surprised gasp. "But why?" she then said, looking with wonder up at Echohawk.

A young brave came and got Echohawk's horse and led him away to the others inside the fence at the far end of the village. Echohawk lifted the heavy bag and placed his free hand on Mariah's elbow, ushering her back inside the wigwam as she lifted the flap for their entrance.

"Remove your cloak," Echohawk said, setting the bundle on the mat flooring. "Sit by the fire and see what gifts the women of our village have given you."

Mariah slipped her cloak off, still marveling over the surprise. After Echohawk had his cloak off, she went and sat beside him close to the buckskin bag. Her fingers trembled as she opened the bag, sucking in a breath of delight when she caught sight of the lovely beaded necklaces, moccasins, and dresses.

"I still don't understand," she murmured, taking the items from the bag one by one, loving them all.

"These are yours today because I have given the women permission now to give you wedding gifts," Echohawk said, lifting one of the beaded necklaces, running his fingers admiringly over its intricate design.

Mariah's heart thrilled not only over the loveliness of her gifts and the generosity of the women but also over knowing that finally the time had arrived for their marriage ceremony.

Until now so many things had gotten in the way.

Mariah laid aside the blanket with beautifully colorful designs sewn on it and lunged into Echohawk's arms, causing him to drop the necklace he had been admiring. "Darling," she whispered, brushing his lips with a kiss, "I am so happy. We soon will be married! I had begun to . . . to feel like a loose woman, perhaps my mother's true daughter. I don't want to be like her, Echohawk. Please tell me that I'm not."

Echohawk held her away from him and looked intensely into her eyes. "Your heart belongs to only one man, now and forevermore," he said, his voice low. "I am not like the man you thought was your father for so long. I am a man of compassion. A man whose love is infinitely deep for you. I am a man who wishes to share your deepest thoughts. Your deepest longings. I will never give you cause to look elsewhere for these things that your mother did not get from her husband."

"As I will never give you cause to go seek from another woman what you wish from me," Mariah said, reaching a hand to his face, running her fingers over his handsome features. "I will be here for you, Echohawk. Always."

Echohawk framed her face between his hands and drew her lips to his mouth. He kissed her softly, then slipped his hands down and cupped her breasts through her soft buckskin dress.

Surges of ecstasy began washing through Mariah, flooding her whole body, the spinning sensations delicious as Echohawk eased her down to the mats, quickly undressing her.

His clothes removed, he rose over her. She lifted her hips as she felt his satin hardness seeking entrance inside her. And when he filled her, pressing endlessly deeper, she gave herself over to the wild ecstasy.

Echohawk's lips slid down, across her neck, and locked on one of her breasts, flicking a tongue across the nipple. Mariah closed her eyes, and when soft whimpers filled the wigwam, she knew they were her own.

His senses dazzled by the fire licking at his loins, his hot pulse racing, Echohawk savored the sweet taste of Mariah's flesh. He moved his body rhythmically within her, the fires of his passion burning brightly.

Again his mouth closed hard upon hers, his hands clasping her buttocks, molding her sweet, slender body against his. How fiercely he always wanted her!

While with her, loving her, he was frantic with the need to have more of her.

And how he loved the way she clung and rocked with him, her hips responding in a rhythmic movement all their own.

His fingers moved from her buttocks, up to her hair, and twined through the red tresses, then moved downward again, making a slow, sensuous descent along her spine until again his fingers were locked against her buttocks, squeezing her flesh gently as he felt the heat nearly exploding within himself.

Mariah's body turned to liquid as she was carried deeper and deeper into that sweet delicious state. A tremor went through her as Echohawk bent his head to her lips and gave her a gentle, lingering kiss.

And then, just as she was feeling the euphoria spreading within her, and felt his body stiffen and pause as he buried a groan between her breasts, she knew that they were close to that moment of exquisite bliss.

Their bodies shook and quaked together, exploding in spasms of desire.

Breathing hard, they clung together. Mariah gasped in rapture when Echohawk's lips brushed her throat and reverently breathed her name.

And again he kissed her. One hungry kiss blended into another, and again he buried himself deeply inside her and their bodies tangled.

Mariah felt the drugged passion mounting again. She moaned throatily as once again the incredible sweetness swept through her, but this time leaving her limp and satiated in his arms.

Echohawk lingered awhile longer atop her, then rolled away, lying beside her. The flood of emotions that he always felt while with her, which were doubled after sharing in passionate lovemaking, was there, his whole body strangely at peace with the universe.

He closed his eyes for a moment, relishing the feeling, one which no one could take from him and his No-din.

This love they shared, it was a wondrous thing! No more did he think of the past—of his losses. His No-din swept away all of his regrets, doubts, and unhappiness.

With her, everything was possible.

Mariah moved into Echohawk's embrace, loving the feel of his powerful body pressed against hers. She sighed, so perfectly content. She had never felt so desired. So at peace.

Then she eased away from him, looking into his eyes as he opened them, smiling at her. "The wedding gifts are truly a surprise," she said, giggling.

"They are gifts from the heart," Echohawk said, brushing a loose lock of hair back from her eyes. "As is mine that I now give to you."

Her eyes wide, Mariah moved to her knees beside him. "A gift?" she said, clasping her hands on her bare lap. "You also have a wedding gift for No-din?"

Echohawk leaned on an elbow and reached a hand to her cheek. "No-din, for so long you have not mentioned marriage to Echohawk," he said seriously. "I did not mention it to you. Always there were interferences. But today, No-din, I speak of it to you. I now tell you that we have been married since our first sexual night together. It is the Chippewa custom that all that has to be done to seal the bonds of the hearts in marriage is for the woman to accept food offered her by the man she wishes to marry, and also the holding of hands while speaking words of love together."

Mariah was stunned speechless, torn by mixed feelings. She was glad that she had been married to him all along, let free of her guilt for having given herself to him so brazenly, yet puzzled by his not having told her.

"We are man and wife?" she finally said in a soft murmur. "For so long, we have been man and wife?"

"*Ay-uh,*" Echohawk said, moving to a sitting position beside her. He placed his hands to her waist and lifted her onto his lap.

Mariah held back from twining her arms about his neck, feeling hurt for his not having been open with her. Being married was sacred! Not something to be kept a secret from the one you loved.

"Why?" she blurted. "Why did you wait so long to tell me?"

"At first I did not look on it as a marriage," he said, his eyes wavering as he saw her hurt expression. "As you will recall, I was wrestling with many feelings within my heart. I had experienced many losses. I did not want to allow myself to love you. You were white. Those who had caused my heartaches were white. I feared loving you, a white woman."

"I understand all of that," Mariah said, her reserves melting, in truth ecstatic to know that without a formal ceremony she was already his wife! The mother of the children they planned to have! "But why did you take so long to tell me? After you realized that your fears were invalid, you could have told me everything. That would have lifted much guilt from my heart, Echohawk. In the white people's eyes, I would be considered a wanton whore for having shared a bed with you before vows were spoken. I fought against such feelings, knowing that you had more than a marriage to me to worry about. Always there were interferences."

"My woman, that is why I did not take the time to tell you," Echohawk said glumly. "So many things kept clouding my mind. Yet now I see that I was wrong to place other things before you." He drew her close, her legs straddling his waist. He kissed her, then embraced her sweetly. "You will never be second in my heart again. Forgiven, No-din?"

"Always, my love," Mariah said, easing from his arms so that she could brush his lips with a kiss. Then she held away from him and smiled mischievously into his dark eyes. "I, too, have kept a secret from you," she said.

"But not for as long as you," she quickly added.

His eyes gleamed into hers. "This secret," he said, cocking an eyebrow. "Is it the sort that will make my heart soar even more than it already has today?"

"I believe so," Mariah said, moving closer to him, twining her hands around his neck. "Echohawk, darling, you have spoken often of children. Of sons. Have you not?"

Echohawk's heart began to race, knowing that she would not bring up the subject of children between them unless . . .

"*Ay-uh,*" he said, "and you have spoken of having many children, like the Snellings."

Mariah nodded, her eyes twinkling into his. "*Ay-uh,*" she murmured. She pressed a soft kiss to his lips, then whispered against them, "My darling, handsome Chippewa chief, we are going to have a baby!"

A sudden joy leapt through Echohawk. He lifted Mariah into his arms and rose quickly to his feet. He swung her around as she clung to him, laughing. "A child!" he shouted. "A *child!*"

"*Ay-uh,*" Mariah giggled. "And, like Nee-kah, my firstborn will be a son."

Echohawk stopped and eased Mariah from his arms, then gazed at her abdomen. Almost reverently he placed a hand there. "A child grows there, yet it is too early to see the growth in your body," he said, nodding. Then his gaze moved to her breasts. He placed a hand under each, cupping them. A slow smile tugged at his lips.

"I should have known before you even told me that you held this secret," he said, smiling down at her. "My woman, your breasts lie much heavier within my hands than that first time I touched them. Already, No-din, they are filling with our child's milk."

Mariah relished his hands on her breasts, and his

admiration of them. "In time our child will be suckling from my breasts. Surely nothing can compare with that." She snuggled into his embrace. "Except, my love, for being with *you*."

Echohawk held her for a moment, and then she stepped away, looking up at him without a smile. "My breasts have already changed," she said warily. "Soon my whole body will look different. Will you still be able to look at me with favor, Echohawk?"

"*No-din*, you will look radiant while heavy with child," he said, flashes of his Fawn there before his mind's eye, unable to cast the thought away as quickly as he wanted. He was recalling how beautiful she had been while carrying their child. He was recalling how he had enjoyed placing his hand to her abdomen, feeling the child kicking against it from deep within her womb. It had been a miracle of miracles, until . . .

Deep shadows fell upon Echohawk's face, the memories so painful—memories that he thought he had left behind.

He turned from Mariah, the pain gripping his heart, as though he had only yesterday witnessed Fawn's death, having lost more than her on the day of the raid.

His child.

His unborn child!

Mariah grew numb inside when she saw the sudden change in Echohawk. It did not take much to realize what had come over him at the mention of children. He had come so close to having a child, until Tanner McCloud had devastated Echohawk's village.

Trying to understand Echohawk's grief at this moment, when he should be so happy, Mariah stepped around and looked up at him, his eyes soon locking with hers.

"Darling, I understand," she murmured, leaning up on tiptoe, giving him a soft kiss on the lips. "It is only natural that you would be taken back in time,

remembering another wife . . . another child. And I
do not resent this, Echohawk. It only proves how devoted a husband you were. And how devoted a father
you would have been to the child that was denied
you."

She eased into his arms and pressed her cheek
against his smooth broad chest. "Let me help you,
darling," she whispered. "I am always here to help
you."

Guilt swam through Echohawk's consciousness, guilt
for having brought this sadness to his No-din, when
she had only moments ago given him the world.

He placed his arms around her waist and drew her
closer, molding her naked body into his. "No-din, my
No-din," he whispered, then kissed her with a gentle
passion and laid her back on the mats beside the fire.

With skillful hands and lips, and a body aroused
anew, he showed her all over again how much he
loved her.

Only her.

31

Our lives would grow together
In sad or singing weather . . .
If love were what the rose is,
And I were like the leaf. . . .

—SWINBURNE

Two Years Later, Early Winter of 1828

Outside, the wind whistled around the wigwam, the first snowfall of winter upon the Chippewa village, the creeks choked with ice. Mariah settled herself down next to Nee-kah beside the warm and inviting cook fire in Mariah's wigwam.

"Are they not the most handsome and healthy sons?" Mariah commented, turning her eyes to Night Hawk, hers and Echohawk's one-year-old son, and Nee-kah's son, Strong Branch, as they played with their miniature bows and arrows close beside them.

Mariah had watched Echohawk make their son's bow and arrows with their flint heads, wood shafts, and hawk feathers at the tails. He had used deer sinew to string the bow, but had explained that the skin from a snapping turtle's neck was the best bowstring because it wouldn't stretch or shrink, no matter the weather.

"Silver Wing would have been proud of his son," Nee-kah said, busying her fingers making herself a new pair of moccasins with her prized metal sewing needle, the special gift that Mariah had brought to her from Saint Louis. "Strong Branch already walks with the stance of a chief, so tall and erect. He will one day make his people proud. He will lead them as nobly as his chieftain father."

Her flaming red hair lustrously long again, hanging loosely across her shoulders instead of in two braids, as Nee-kah wore her raven-black hair, Mariah resumed her task of painting a new cradleboard for her second child, which was due in five months. "Strong Branch will be assuming the duties of chief before you know it," Mariah said softly. "The years pass quickly."

Nee-kah nodded and rested her needle and buckskin on her lap as she silently admired the colorful rainbow that Mariah was painting above where her child's head would rest on the cottonwood cradleboard.

"You paint well the 'arch above the earth,' " Nee-kah then said. "You've learned well the beliefs of our people."

Mariah smiled at Nee-kah. "Echohawk taught me the meaning of this design," she said. "He explained to me that the Chippewa believe that if mothers decorate the cradleboards in this manner, their papooses will be watched over by the 'Powers of the West.' I think that is such a lovely thought."

A young maiden came into the wigwam, clutching a buckskin robe around her shoulders, the cheeks of her round face rosy from the bitter cold temperatures of the early afternoon. "A lone rider was seen on the horizon," she said in warning. "He is a white pony soldier. Several braves rode out to meet him, to see what his mission is here at our village."

Mariah's eyes widened as she laid her paintbrush aside. "He is white?" she said, rising to her feet, unsure how to feel about this bit of news. Since Colonel Snelling had left and a new commandant been assigned at Fort Snelling, communications between the soldiers and the Chippewa were rare.

Yet she could not help but feel anxious at the prospect of perhaps William Joseph or Colonel Snelling returning to the Minnesota wilderness to see her and Echohawk again.

They *had* been fast friends.

She regretted that she had given up her quest to see her true father, at least once before one of them died. Even if he was a cheat and a liar, she had decided long ago that she above all wanted to see him.

Mariah turned anxious eyes to Nee-kah, whose fear was evident in the way she sat so tense, looking guardedly back at Mariah. Mariah understood why. Not only did Nee-kah have the Sioux to blame for her losses, but also white men!

"In my husband's absence, while he has gone to check the traps in the forest, I shall go and see what business the soldier has at our village," Mariah said, grabbing up a buffalo robe and swinging it around her shoulders. She went to Night Hawk and kissed his soft copper cheek, then left the wigwam with the young maiden who had brought her the news.

Just as she stepped outside, the soldier, dressed in full uniform, rode into the village, flanked on each side by braves armed with rifles. Mariah met their approach, walking toward them, her chin held proudly high. When the horses came to a stop and the soldier dismounted, the two braves quickly at his side, he smiled with recognition at Mariah.

"Mariah, it's good to see you again," the young lieutenant said, snatching his hat from his head. "I hope you have been well?"

"I do not know your name," Mariah said, offering a hand of friendship.

"Osborne. Lieutenant Dan Osborne. I served under Colonel Snelling," Lieutenant Osborne said, shaking her hand eagerly. "I was in line to dance with you at the ball." He laughed heartily, casting his eyes bashfully down to his boots. "But it seems you disappeared before I had a chance to ask for that dance."

"Why are you here?" Mariah said, remembering the ball, her face coloring with a blush when recalling how clumsy she had been that night, trying to learn to dance.

Lieutenant Osborne clasped his hat behind him, his smile fading as he brought his eyes back up, meeting Mariah's. "Ma'am, we at Fort Snelling have received word that Colonel Snelling has passed away," he said gently. "Colonel Snelling died in Washington on August 20."

The news came as such a shock to Mariah, it was as though someone had thrown ice water on her face. She paled and her hand flew to her throat, stunned to the core by the news. "Colonel Snelling is dead?" she gasped. "How can that be? He was not an old man. And the last time I saw him, he . . . he was healthy."

"Ma'am he was forty-six years of age," Lieutenant Osborne said, his voice drawn. "His death was attributed to chronic diarrhea, and/or its remedy, opium."

"You . . . you are so kind to take the trouble of coming to break the news to me and my husband," Mariah murmured, her heart aching in her sadness.

"It was not I who made the decision to come," Lieutenant Osborne said sheepishly. "William Joseph Snelling asked me to. He thought that perhaps you and Echohawk would like to know of Colonel Snelling's passing."

Mariah's heart skipped a beat, her eyes widened. "William Joseph sent you?" she murmured. Her color began to return at the hope of perhaps seeing him again. "Is he at Fort Snelling now? Will he be there for long? Or will he be leaving, to return to Washington for his father's burial?"

"William Joseph isn't at Fort Snelling," Lieutenant Osborne said softly. "He wired us the news. Ma'am, he hasn't been back to Fort Snelling since he left for Boston to become involved in politics."

A keen disappointment swept through Mariah. She lowered her eyes. "I see," she said, her voice breaking. Then she squared her shoulders and firmed her jaw. "Lieutenant, I thank you so much for coming to us to tell us of Colonel Snelling's passing," she said, reaching out for a handshake again. "Perhaps you would like to stay the night? It's a long ride back to the fort. And the temperatures are just barely above freezing."

Lieutenant Osborne looked uncomfortably from one brave to the other at his side, and smiled shakily at Mariah. "I appreciate your offer . . . your kindness," he said, shaking her hand vigorously, then placing his hat back on his head. "But I think it's best if I get back to the fort to see to my duties."

"You might want to at least have a bite to eat before leaving," Mariah said, yet wanting to be left alone to her thoughts—to her own silent grieving. Her father never knew of this daughter who could have loved him oh, so much, had she been given the opportunity!

"I've brought along enough provisions for myself," Lieutenant Osborne said, turning to swing himself quickly into his saddle. He tipped his hat to Mariah. "Sorry to be the one to bring you such sad tidings. Perhaps the next time we meet, it will be under more favorable circumstances."

Mariah smiled weakly up at him. "Yes, perhaps," she murmured, then waved as he gave her a last look over his shoulder and rode away at a gallop.

Unable to hold back the tears, Mariah let herself shed those for what had not been—for a father's love that had been denied her—and then she wiped her eyes clear of tears over one sadness, to be troubled by something else. She peered into the forest at the snow-laden limbs of the trees.

Echohawk.

Where is he? she worried to herself.

He had left early in the morning to check the rabbit and bird snares in the forest, but she knew that he should have been back by now. Yesterday they had received their first snowstorm of the season, but dur-

ing the night the storm had ceased. At sunrise the
cold had been extreme. The smaller twigs had been
covered with a thick rime, and the atmosphere had
held only minute glittering particles of snow.

That was when Echohawk had gone out into the
forest, even though Mariah had feared for his safety.
It had been a fretful night of wolves howling eerily.
She had had nightmares of the rabid wolf that had
come close to attacking Echohawk so long ago.

And also there was always the renegade Sioux
White Wolf to worry about. Still no one had found
him to make him pay for his wrongful deeds. And
while he was still free, hating Echohawk as he did,
Echohawk was not safe.

Her heart pounding out her fear, Mariah rushed
back inside the wigwam, breathless with her need to
go and search for Echohawk. "Nee-kah, can you
watch Night Hawk for a while longer?" she asked,
bending over her son, smoothing her hands through
his coarse black hair, the child an exact replica of his
father.

"Where are you going?" Nee-kah asked, rising
slowly to her feet, panic filling her eyes. "You aren't
leaving with the white pony soldier, are you? I thought
I heard his horse leave already. And why was he here?
I did not hear all that well what was being said. The
children were laughing and carrying on so!"

"*Gah-ween,* no, I am not leaving with the pony soldier," Mariah said, drawing on heavy fur mittens and
strapping snowshoes on her feet. She stopped and
turned sad eyes to Nee-kah. "The soldier brought
word of Colonel Snelling's death. I am saddened terribly by the news, Nee-kah. But I am suddenly worried
about someone else far more dear to me. Echohawk.
I must go and find him. He has been gone for too
long. I fear . . . I fear . . . something is wrong."

"I did not know Colonel Snelling," Nee-kah said
softly. "But I hear he was a fine man." She went to

Mariah and placed a hand on her arm. "As for you leaving, No-din, I do not see it as wise. Echohawk will be home soon. Do not worry so!"

"I cannot sit here warmed by the fire, laughing and watching our children, while Echohawk might be out there somewhere alone and in danger," Mariah said, grabbing up a rifle and slipping extra bullets into the pocket of her dress. She turned and walked toward the entrance flap. "I must go, Nee-kah. I must."

After stepping outside, Mariah pulled her fur hood farther forward to protect her face from the bitter cold, then trudged through the snow to her toboggan, feeling that it might be needed, in case she found her husband injured and unable to ride on his horse. She placed the rifle in the toboggan, then with eager steps began dragging it through the snow.

Since very little fresh snow had fallen since Echohawk's departure, she found the tracks of his horse, leading farther and farther into the forest. The cold nipping at her nose, the forest quiet, Mariah moved steadily onward, the sled behind her. The longer she walked, the less she could find the tracks. The winds had become brisk, shaking snow from the trees onto the ground cover of snow beneath them, erasing the tracks.

Her heart pounding, her legs becoming weak in her weariness, Mariah began to think of how foolish this search might have been, after all. The ache of her back was a reminder of her pregnancy.

Should she lose this child . . .

She came to an instant halt when she heard gunfire echoing and ringing through the trees from a short distance away to her right.

Panic filled her when there was then a strange sort of charged silence.

She took her rifle from the toboggan. Then, leaving the toboggan behind, she began running through the forest, forgetting everything but her desperate need to see if Echohawk had been the one to fire the gun, and at what.

She paled and felt suddenly weak-kneed when a short distance away she saw Echohawk lying in the snow, a wolf stalking him, two lying dead close beside her husband.

Then she stifled a scream when she saw the blood on his arm, and his torn buffalo robe revealing a rip in his flesh. His wounds must have rendered him too helpless to reload and fire a third shot against the remaining wolf.

Mariah watched the wolf snarl and draw back when he turned his silver eyes to her. Trembling, she raised her rifle and fired one shot and downed the last surviving wolf. Dropping her rifle to the ground, she ran to Echohawk and lifted his head onto her lap, cradling him, as she rained kisses on his face.

"A healthy wolf does not stalk a human," Echohawk said, leaning away from Mariah as he looked at the slain animals. "The wolf is brother to the Indian."

He paused, then said, "It was not I the wolves hungered for, but the dead rabbit I had just taken from one of my snares."

Echohawk reached his good arm to Mariah and circled it around her neck, drawing her lips to his mouth, and kissed her softly, then whispered against her mouth, "My No-din, again I am in your debt."

Mariah looked down into his dark eyes. "*Ay-uh*, you are in my debt," she murmured. "And your debt to me is to stay alive!"

Echohawk chuckled, then groaned as he tried to lift his injured arm.

"Echohawk, I had thought that perhaps White Wolf had . . . had stalked and killed you," Mariah said softly.

"Do not fill your thoughts with that snake!" Echohawk grumbled. "Never will he be the cause of my death."

Mariah's eyes wavered; then she helped him from the ground. "I've brought the toboggan," she said softly. She spied his horse tethered close by to a low tree limb. "This time you will ride much more comfortably on the toboggan than on Blaze."

"But you can't pull the toboggan with my weight on it," Echohawk fussed, cringing again when a sharp pain shot through his injured arm. "No-din, you are with child."

"I am strong," Mariah argued. "So is the child that grows within my womb."

Echohawk struggled free from her grip and went to Blaze. He uncoiled the reins from the tree, then managed to get himself into the saddle. "Get the toboggan. Attach it to the horse. We will ride together on Blaze into the village."

"You are a very stubborn man," Mariah said, sighing. She shuddered when she stepped around the dead animals, then went to the toboggan and did as Echohawk asked. When she climbed into the saddle behind him, and clung to his waist, a sudden fear gripped her. In his eyes she could already see signs of a fever, surely caused by the wound.

32

Under the arch of life . . . I saw
Beauty enthroned; and tho her gaze struck awe,
I drew it in as simply as my breath. . . .
—ROSSETTI

This was so familiar to Mariah, as though it were only yesterday that she had sat beside Echohawk in his wigwam, he in a fevered state and she bathing his heated brow. She had managed to get a medicinal drink made of dogwood bark between his lips, a concoction used against fevers.

She had learned many more ways of healing since Nee-kah's earlier teachings—a sharp bone instrument was used for pricking medicine into the skin; sphagnum moss was used for wound healing because of its absorbency; and sumac leaves were used to stop bleeding.

The fire's glow the only light in the wigwam, Mariah gazed down at Echohawk, who lay beneath many blankets, asleep by the fire. Her eyes saddened as she bathed her husband's fevered brow again, as she had all through the long, weary night.

Before, when he had not known her identity, only that she had cared for him with compassion, he had recovered. And she kept praying to her Lord that this time would be no different. She had cleansed and wrapped his wounds. She had forced medicinal herbal liquids through his parched lips. She had allowed a Mide priest to come and speak over him. She had bathed him with cool compresses all night.

345

Now all that was left was the waiting, and her continued silent prayers. . . .

She looked beyond Echohawk at the crib where their young son lay sleeping. She was filled with pride and love as she listened to his steady breathing, recalling that first night after he had been born and how strange it had been to have another person breathing in their wigwam.

But, ah, how she had cherished the sound!

Their son!

Oh, how he filled their lives, even more than she had ever expected. For many months her life had been centered only around Echohawk. Now she had two people who relied on her, and this was wonderful, for while she had been growing up, it had been only herself, fending for herself.

She had been so very alone as a child and young woman.

She looked up at the smokehole, seeing shadows softening into a light orange glow. "It's morning," she whispered. "It's another Chippewa sunrise."

"No-din?"

Echohawk's whisper drew Mariah's eyes back to him. When she found him looking at her, a slow smile fluttering on his lips, she almost shouted with joy. She reached a hand to his brow, gasping with delight. His fever had broken! The crisis had passed. He was going to be well again.

"Echohawk, oh, darling," Mariah said, tossing her cloth aside. She twined her arms around his neck and kissed him softly on the lips, then drew only slightly away from him, gazing lovingly into his eyes. "You gave me a scare, you know."

"Did I not tell you that I always pay my debts, my darling No-din?" he said softly. "My debt to you, always, is to stay alive, is it not?"

"Always, my love," Mariah said, beaming. She

eased her lips to his mouth and kissed him sweetly, content, yet still fearing the day that White Wolf and Echohawk would come face-to-face, weapon-to-weapon. . . .

Dear Reader:
I hope that you have enjoyed reading *Wild Ecstasy*. This book is the beginning of a major Indian series that I will be writing for New American Library. The next book will be called *Wild Rapture*, the sequel to *Wild Ecstasy*, and will carry on the story of Echohawk, Mariah, and the adult life of their son Night Hawk, and Briana, Night Hawk's beloved. *Wild Rapture* promises more passion and adventure!

I would love to hear from you all. For my newsletter, please send a legal-size SASE to:

CASSIE EDWARDS
R.#3, Box 60
Mattoon, IL 61938

Warmly,

Cassie Edwards

Cassie Edwards

Tides of Passion

- [ ] RETURN TO YESTERDAY by June Lund Shiplett.   (121228—$4.99)
- [ ] JOURNEY TO YESTERDAY by June Lund Shiplett.   (159853—$4.50)
- [ ] WINDS OF BETRAYAL by June Lund Shiplett.   (150376—$4.99)
- [ ] THE RAGING WINDS OF HEAVEN by June Lund Shiplett.(154959—$4.50)
- [ ] REAP THE BITTER WINDS by June Lund Shiplett.   (150414—$4.50)
- [ ] THE WILD STORMS OF HEAVEN by June Lund Shiplett. (126440—$4.99)
- [ ] SWEET SURRENDER by Catherine Coulter.   (156943—$4.99)
- [ ] FIRE SONG by Catherine Coulter.   (402383—$4.99)
- [ ] DEVIL'S EMBRACE by Catherine Coulter.   (141989—$4.99)

Prices slightly higher in Canada

Buy them at your local bookstore or use this convenient coupon for ordering.

NEW AMERICAN LIBRARY
P.O. Box 999, Bergenfield, New Jersey 07621

Please send me the books I have checked above.
I am enclosing $_____ (please add $2.00 to cover postage and handling).
Send check or money order (no cash or C.O.D.'s) or charge by Mastercard or
VISA (with a $15.00 minimum). Prices and numbers are subject to change without
notice.

Card #_____ Exp. Date _____
Signature_____
Name_____
Address_____
City _____ State _____ Zip Code _____

For faster service when ordering by credit card call **1-800-253-6476**

Allow a minimum of 4-6 weeks for delivery. This offer is subject to change without notice.